Love is patient.
Love is kind.
It does not envy
or boast.
It is not proud,
rude, or self-seeking.
It is not easily angry
and keeps no record
of past mistakes.
It does not delight
in evil.
It rejoices in the tur
truth.

Bastiano
ROMANO

a five syndicates novel

parker s. huntington

Editing/Proofing/Betas/Alpha:
Janice Owen
Gemma Woolley
Heidi Popelka Jones
Brittany Webb
Amanda Söderlund

ISBN-13: 978-1-950209-00-2

ISBN-10: 1-950209-00-8

ALSO BY PARKER

THE FIVE SYNDICATES SERIES

ASHER BLACK
NICCOLAIO ANDRETTI
RANIERI ANDRETTI
BASTIANO ROMANO
RENATA VITALI
DAMIANO DE LUCA
Marco Camerino
Rafaello Rossi

ALPHA MALES.
STRONG WOMEN.
RIVAL FAMILIES.

BRAVERY. ANGER. DUTY. LOYALTY. HOPE.
THIS IS LIFE IN THE FIVE SYNDICATES...

...and so the cruel prince fell in love with the liar.

I love my boss.
I love a man some call a monster.
love a man more accustomed to cruelty than kindness.

But we both have our duties.
Our laws.
Our worlds.

Two worlds never meant to touch.
Two people never meant to fall in love.

A mafia prince.
And the undercover agent sent to ruin him.

PLAYLIST

Power Over Me - Dermot Kennedy
Sorry - Halsey
Swim Good - Dermot Kennedy
Raincoat - Timeflies & SHY Martin
lovely - Billie Eilish & Khalid
For Island Fires and Family - Dermot Kennedy
Safe - Nick Santos
I Don't Wanna Live Forever - ZAYN & T. Swift
A Closeness - Dermot Kennedy
The Other (Stripped) - Lauv
A Drop In the Ocean - Ron Pope
An Evening I Will Not Forget - Dermot Kennedy
Make Me Cry - Noah Cyrus & Labrinth
Last Dance - Kait Weston
Without Me - Halsey
Moments Passed - Dermot Kennedy
Fetish - Madilyn Bailey

Rossi
Romano
De Luca
Andretti
SYNDICATES

I kept the recapping pretty short to avoid spoilers from the other books, but those spoilers are still there. GAH. Sorry. Either way, this is a standalone, so you can go forth without confusion.

Second thing—if you're looking for your conventional love story, where the hero is the golden boy, sweet and worthy of love... this isn't that. The hero is flawed. The heroine is flawed. There's hate and anger and lust—a provocative slow burn.

Third—I usually add a lesson in my author's note. Something

I learned while writing the book. Usually, it has to do with lessons the characters themselves learn. With Asher Black, Lucy finds courage just as I find courage in pursuing writing instead of med school. With Niccolaio Andretti, it was seeing pain beneath other people's masks and learning to respect them for it.

With Bastian, the lesson wasn't necessarily within the characters but what I learned while writing them. I suffered a loss. A huge one. One that, nearly a year later, still cuts deep.

I fear it will always cut deeply; I fear it won't always cut deeply.

I started this book in 2017. It's 2019. So much time has passed, so much pain has elapsed, I ended up rewriting this book five times. Five. Each rewrite, Ariana and Bastian changed, twisting and morphing into who they were meant to be.

In the first draft, Ariana started as a hardened FBI agent. This wasn't her. It was a mask. Bastian started as a cocky, heartless mafia prince. This wasn't him either. Yes, Ariana is tough. Yes, Bastian is emotionally distant. But the reasoning behind their flaws isn't superficial. It delves into the same pain I felt over the past year.

It was scary to write this way. To take a part of myself that hurt and let it bleed onto my pages. To let Bastian and Ariana take pieces of my pain and heal it. Even now, I feel vulnerable and stripped bare as I type this author's note.

Here is my lesson—let yourself feel pain. You are allowed to lash out. You are allowed to seek escapes. You are allowed to be bold in your pain. You are allowed to learn from it.

You are also allowed to heal.

As you read Bastian and Ariana's story, I hope you connect with them the way I did. And maybe, you will find the same lessons I found while writing their love story.

As always, thank you for reading.

xoxo,
Parker

For Chloe.

You have always been and
will always be my sun-loving,
food-guzzling, early-morning-bed-jumping,
silly-kisses-giving, forever-happy-feeling,
eager-to-run, love-your-brother-snuggling,
freedom-craving, pretty, perfect,
sweet princess, Little Girl.

You've given me the best
three years of my life.

The sun will always rise
and set with you.

Until we're reunited, Chlo.

In loving memory of Chloe.
(02/06/2015 - 03/08/2018)

she wasn't waiting for a knight
she was waiting for a sword

atticus

I wonder how many people don't get the one they want, but end up with the one they're supposed to be with.

—Fannie Flagg

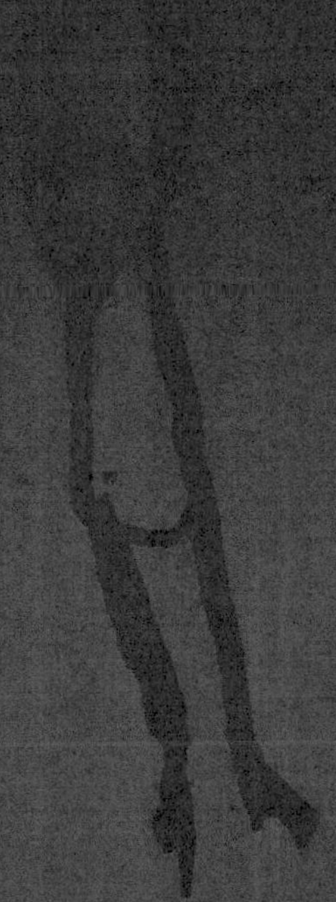

Graphic Expression and Figure Drawing
PLATE I
Free-Arm and Industrial Drawing
NATURAL AND COMMON OBJECTS
Description of the Plates

duty

Duty
/ˈd(y)o͞odē/
noun

1. a moral or legal obligation; a responsibility.
2. a task or action that someone is required to perform.

The word ***"duty"*** *can trace its roots to the Latin word for debt. To have a duty is to have a debt. The thing about debt, though, is it means nothing unless someone collects.*

Don't do something because you think you have to. Do it because you want to. No one on their deathbed has ever said, "Remember all the things I wanted to do but didn't? Those were the good times."

Take risks with love. Deal with the consequences later.

PROLOGUE

Yet it would be your duty to bear it…
it is weak and silly to say you cannot bear
what is your fate to be required to bear."

—Charlotte Brontë

DALIA RICCI
The Past

"Bless me, Father, for I have sinned." My pulse quickens, the fear simmering beneath my skin at what I know I have to do. *Run.* "It has been four years since my last confession."

The grating separating us smells musty, but I lean my cheek against it anyway. The walls of the confessional moan. Old, like everything else in Devils Ridge, Texas. The heart of the De Luca mafia syndicate. The heart of Hell.

"What ails you, my child?"

Everything.

I am helpless to men, to fate, the insignificant pawn housing a future queen in a game far greater than her. I don't say the things my heart feels. Instead, I cradle my stomach. I'm not showing. I still have some time. Not much but perhaps enough to figure out my options.

"I slept with a married man."

And I liked it.

Until I didn't.

And still, he wouldn't stop.

Father Luciano says nothing. I can picture him. The scattering of blond hair covering next to nothing on his receding hairline. His pudgy fingers pressed together like a steeple. His white clerical collar choking his thick neck. The all-black attire and stuffy booth running sweat down his hunched back.

Father Luciano. Two years my senior. The twenty-four year old who looks a day shy of forty. I'd pity him if I didn't need to reserve my pity for myself. My lips let loose a breathy sigh as I wait for his response, unsure why I bothered coming here. It felt right at the time.

The sigh is too seductive, but I can't help it. Half the men in this town tell me I am a goddess. The other half tells me I'm a curse. I know which half I believe. It is not the same half that visits me at the Landing Strip, leering at my body as I strip away my clothes and dignity to their praises.

I wonder, for a moment, what Father Luciano thinks as his breathing deepens, and the wooden bench on his half of the booth creaks with stilted movement. He knows who I am. He knows what I do for a living. I suspect he knows *who* I do, also.

He wants you, the Devil in me whispers.

I always listen to my Devil. She controls my future. Sometimes, I get antsy in this small town. One I stumbled upon after listening to her voice, following the pit stop of a groupie tour bus.

I'd call her Fate if it weren't for the series of bad decisions I've made. My Devil encouraged me to stay here. She wiped away my conscience and begged me to sleep with Angelo De Luca, a man unfit to run his own syndicate let alone lay his hands on me. I know I am my Devil, but I prefer distancing myself from the blame.

Because now, I live trapped in a world of four mafia syndicates pitted against one another.

Andretti versus Romano.

Camerino versus Rossi.

Two fractured coasts, warring within themselves.

And the fifth syndicate, cast to the side. The De Luca syndicate. Undeserving. A breeding ground for resentment. Ridiculed as inconsequential for centuries. Run by a mad man whose attention I have caught.

Father Luciano clears his throat and, perhaps, his lust. "Do you feel guilt, my child?"

"Yes."

Not to Angelo De Luca.

Not to his wife.

To my child.

A girl, my Devil predicts. If my Devil is right, she will die in this town like me. Insignificant. An illegitimate princess unable to claim her throne. Surely, there's a better way.

Run.

I stare at his hand before I take it. "Thank you."

"You don't sound happy."

"Says the man stranded on the side of the road."

"True." He shrugs as if every car that passed hadn't ignored him. They knew who he is. Just my luck.

Not luck but Fate, my Devil suggests as if she understands the word.

"I have a spare in my trunk."

He sends me a grateful smile that has my back relaxing. I can't pin point what this is. It's not lust. Nothing I'm used to encountering. It's human decency. Perhaps even familiarity. When the tire has been replaced, he shuts my truck and nods his head to the song on the stereo. It's an old one, where the Bhundu Boys sing about crazy things like Fate and Destiny.

He confirms my suspicions that he knows who I am when he says, "Dalia." His lips wrap around my name like a present, as if something pleasant hides within. "The goddess of Fate. Do you believe in Fate?"

I don't, but I answer, "Yes," because the way he asks makes me feel like he does.

He nods his head and considers something for a moment before his eyes cut through pretenses and narrow on my belly. "Would you like my help?"

I'd like help, yes, but I'm not sure from *him*. He and Angelo can be two sides of the same coin, but at least there's kindness in his eyes, and I'm not in the position to pick and choose which Devil to run from.

Mine or theirs.

"Why?" I finally ask.

"Fate," he answers, as if it exists.

1

Never mind your happiness. Do your duty.

—Peter Drucker

BASTIANO ROMANO

The Present

My cousin Asher tossed me the engagement ring like it didn't cost more than a brownstone on the Upper East Side.

"Jackass." I tucked it into the velvet case, slid it inside the inner pocket of my suit jacket, then threw him a clean shirt.

Blood clung to the fabric of his white tee, but it fazed

neither of us. The Romano syndicate possessed no shortage of enemies, and Asher's job as our fixer was to dispose of them when told. He swapped the soaked shirt for the clean button down, discarding the ruined material on my floor without a care for the stains on my hardwood.

"Ballsy," Asher remarked. Like a true fixer, his footsteps made no noise as he followed me down the stairs of my penthouse to the open-plan living room, sidestepping Elsa's lace panties by the piano with an arched brow. "Your dad won't like it."

Dad didn't like anything to do with Elsa, so expecting him to like this proposal would be like expecting a virgin to fake a convincing orgasm.

I picked the panties up and pocketed them for later, already imagining them stuffed in her mouth as I slide inside her after she accepts my proposal. "My dad won't know until it's too late."

"But Elsa's not royal." He shook his head. "Hell, she's not even mafia."

That was the point. Elsa was far from mafia with her Southern drawl, football obsession, and inability to eat any meal without a side of store-bought ketchup. She was also the smartest woman I'd ever met, fuck-hot, capable of script-worthy banter, and the first woman to make me fall in love. I had plans for tonight which included an engagement ring on her finger and my cock on her tongue.

Plucking my phone from my kitchen island, I shot a text to my assistant Lewis to confirm my plans. "Again. Dad won't know until it's too late."

As far as I was concerned, my dad had no say in this. I'd done everything right. The top boarding schools. The Ivy League education. Learning the Romano businesses—legal and less legal—inside and out. Any fucker—my dad included —who got in between me and Elsa could acquaint himself with my fist and, perhaps, the jagged blade of the knife Uncle Vince had gifted me when I'd turned nine.

I hadn't used it—that was what the enforcers were for—but I had the training and wouldn't hesitate to. People saw me as the privileged, over-educated spawn of Giovanni Romano. I did little to alter their perception, mostly because I gave no fucks, but also because I enjoyed being underestimated.

Asher tucked his socked feet into his Jordans, still staring at me with those eery too-blue eyes of his. "Okay, Golden Child."

He still didn't believe I'd defy the syndicate. Dad expected me to marry another mafia royal. Not quite as drastic as his arranged marriage with Ma, but the daughter of an upper-level mafia figure of my own choosing at the very least.

Never once had I gone against my family's wishes before Elsa. My Uncles Frankie and Eli didn't have children. So, I'd been groomed to run the Romano empire from the business side, leaving enforcement to Dad's twin Uncle Vince—and eventually Asher Black, Uncle Vince's son by pseudo-adoption.

Asher got his hands dirty; I filled mine with business textbooks from Wharton. I graduated with my masters at twenty-two and came back with Elsa in tow, her Southern-belle eyes starstruck by the size of my penthouse and a lifestyle she never knew existed.

I loved that about her—how untouched she was by all this wealth, which never seemed to stop growing. Dad, on the other hand, hated every second he spent in her presence, nearly painted the town red when she moved in with me, and will probably stab someone when he finds out about my proposal.

Not like I gave a fuck.

I grabbed my keys and turned to Asher, who stood with his arms crossed, a little lanky but looking way older than his seventeen years. A smirk lifted the corners of my lips, my good mood bleeding all over my face. "There's blood on your Jordans," I remarked.

Then, I left Asher and his disbelief at the door, descending the elevator into the parking garage and sliding into the back of my Bentley Mulsanne. The driver took off, always briefed on my itinerary beforehand by Lewis.

I skimmed a few business emails on my phone. One of many Romano-owned businesses in the syndicate included Launder, Inc., the largest chain of laundromats on the East Coast. It started as a single cash business to launder dirty money through and grew into a corporation which grossed over one hundred million dollars last year.

I'd taken over as CEO a few months ago. Elsa didn't like the hours, but she understood. We made time for dates twice a week, each time a different surprise to make up for all the time I spent working.

The car pulled up to the Empire State Building.

Lewis greeted me instantly, opening the door before the driver could. His weasel-like face pinched between the eyes. "Mr. Romano—" Frown lines covered his forehead, but I didn't have time for his constant worrying. There was always something with him.

I slid out of the car. "Is Elsa here?"

"Yes, but—"

Taking long strides to the entrance, I cut him off. I was

already late, thanks to Asher's impromptu wardrobe change. "The building has been closed off?"

Lewis heaved out a breath as he struggled to match my pace. "Yes. Mr. Romano, I have—"

We entered the elevator, and I jabbed the button for the top floor. "Are the chefs done preparing the food? Ryker is on time, yes?"

Ever since he'd won Top Chef, he'd been a perpetually late pain in the ass.

"Mr. Romano, I—"

"It's a yes or no question, Lewis." I checked my watch. I'd been late for one of my dates with Elsa before, and she'd looked gutted.

"Yes. But I really have to tell you something."

The doors to the elevator opened to the top floor, where a little outdoor patio had been set up for my proposal tonight. I pocketed my phone and stepped out, an apology for being late on my lips when I came face to face with Dad and Elsa.

The New York City backdrop lit up the night, along with a string of lights I'd had Lewis set up. Our dinner sat on the table behind Elsa, untouched and growing colder by the second. Dad looked unaffected as he saw me, but guilt dripped from Elsa's widened orbs to the shocked parting of her lips.

She wore the silver Herve Leger bandage dress I'd gotten for her last week, paired with teardrop earrings quadruple the size of the real tear sliding down her cheek. Her cherry-red hair whipped in the wind, but she did nothing to tame it as she stared at me with those fern-green eyes. Unable to speak.

Dad's face gave nothing away. He took a step toward me, reached out to pat my shoulder, thought better of it, and straightened the lapels of his suit. "You have a duty to this family."

My eyes narrowed at his words and the way he left without a better explanation. I eyed the guilt smothering Elsa's face and turned to Lewis. "Return Senator Erickson's call and let him know I will be attending his function tonight after all. Have the car pick me up in twenty-three minutes—after I finish my dinner."

He glanced between me and Elsa. "Are you sure?"

I leveled him with a glare. "Do it."

He left, and I stepped around Elsa, took a seat, and slid the cloth napkin over my lap. I didn't know what I'd walk in on. Elsa had no interest in my dad, and Dad had no interest in Elsa. But something had plastered that guilt on Elsa's face, and I'd wait for an explanation as I ate.

The ring burned a hole in my pocket as I took my first bite of lobster. If I were being introspective, I would have asked myself why I'd told Lewis to send the last-minute RSVP before learning what had happened. My gut instincts told me Elsa had betrayed me somehow, but every other part of me refused to believe it.

I knew this woman. We'd studied together. Snuck alcohol onto campus and drank it on the soccer fields at night. Fucked under the bleachers during home games. She'd agreed to move to New York with me when she realized I would have moved to Alabama to be with her.

That woman, the one who woke up early to make me breakfast and took notes for me when family called me away from school, wouldn't betray me. She just wouldn't.

"I'm sorry," she whispered, not bothering to take a seat.

I finished off the lobster, then cut into the filet mignon, taking painstaking care to steady my movements.

She wouldn't betray you, I assured myself.

Why else would she apologize? Dad's presence in me asked.

Elsa stopped my utensils with a palm on my left hand. "I love you."

My eyes cut to her hand, then shifted to her other one, where she clutched a strip of folded paper. I reached out and plucked it from her hand. Her unrelenting grip tightened, and the paper tore at the corners as I stole it from her.

She gasped at the sound, her other hand shooting out to take the paper back from me but failing. I opened it up. A check. Five million dollars. Signed by one Giovanni Romano. He'd paid her off. To what? Leave me?

Ice-cold frost trickled into my body as I stared at her with dead eyes. "Five million dollars? Really?"

I flicked the check onto my plate. The butter from my lobster wet the edges, and she grabbed it, her eyes screaming guilt, but her hands reeking of desperation. I watched as she dabbed the check with the table cloth, trying and failing to dry the butter.

I reached into my pocket, pulled out her panties I'd pocketed earlier, and tossed them at her face. She caught them before they hit the ground. Her eyes widened when she realized what they were, but she used them to dab the fucking check anyway.

I'd never seen anything more pathetic.

With the check dried, she met my eyes. "I'm sorry," she repeated, sounding so stupid, I couldn't believe she'd graduated top of our class at Wharton. Couldn't believe this was the woman who'd insisted she pay for her half of every meal. "I-I... You don't understand. It's a lot of money."

"You would have had so much more, so thank you for reminding me how pathetic you are."

She flinched at my words, and I let loose a dry laugh and reached into my pocket. Her eyes widened when I pulled out the velvet case. She had to reach out and steady herself on the table when I unleashed the sixteen-million-dollar ring inside.

"Bastian—"

I plucked the ring out of its case and tossed it over the side of the building like it meant nothing. Like *she* meant nothing. She whimpered, running to the railing with an outstretched hand as I stole a fry from her plate and dipped it in her fucking generic-brand ketchup. If I took the time to stop—to breathe in the betrayal from her and my dad—I would probably burn the Empire State Building with both of us in it.

It wasn't toxic rage filling my veins but bruising betrayal, inching its way to my throat until my breaths halved, and I had to cough to breath again. She returned to the table, the ring long gone, and the torn and buttered check clutched between her white-knuckled fingers, like she thought I would toss that off the building, too.

I was tempted.

I'd never loved anyone before. I saw past thinly-veiled advances and the mafia bunnies who wanted me for my money and status. But Elsa was different. The wholesome girl from the wholesome family who never knew a world of corrupt Senators, Made Men, celebrities, penthouses, and designer clothes existed. Untouched by the Romano syndicate I was heir to.

She'd inched her way beneath my skin, little by little, and I'd let her because she was supposed to be different.

How hadn't I seen the signs?

She opened her mouth again—probably to beg—but I cut

her off. "I never loved you, Elsa." The lie tore past my lips, unapologetic as I ignored the fact that I would have given up everything—my family, money, and the entire Romano lineage—for her. "We were good for a bit, but it was just entertainment." I stood, wiped the tear off her cheek with her butter-stained panties, and patted her head. "You're not capable of providing anything other than a warm cunt to fuck, and I'm not capable of love."

2

Duty is what one expects from others.

—Oscar Wilde

BASTIANO ROMANO

Eight Years Later

I have career day for summer school. Billy is bringing his dad. Can you come?

Instead of replying "no" to Everett's text, I took a pull of my drink. I'd missed his seventh birthday party, too.

"Hey, Bastiano." The mafia bunny's low voice rasped. She probably meant for it to be seductive, but she sounded like a pack-a-day smoker with double lung implants. "Wanna get out of here?" Her acrylic-tipped finger trailed across my back before she took a seat to my right.

A condom filled with Icy Hot.

The vise grip of a pissed-off orangutan.

Two things I'd rather have on my dick than her.

"Leave," I replied, not bothering to see who it was or what she wanted.

Wasn't it obvious, though?

People had a tendency to get distracted by exteriors. I had a nice one. One that, had I not already been born with a gold-coated spoon dangling from my lips, would have afforded me opportunities I hadn't earned.

A body layered with muscles. Intense dark eyes. Sharp jawline. Thick, coffee-colored hair. A gentleman's cut that could cover your car payment and then some. Look past that, and I was a thirty-year-old—almost thirty-one—who didn't know what he wanted in life.

If there were a female version of me, I sure as hell wouldn't date her. Still, women fawned over me like my cock was made of gold and they were looking to strike rich. Their mistake.

I downed the rest of my scotch as my dad sidled next to me at the bar. I knew it was him without looking. I could count on him to always carry around a god-awful scent of pussy and alcohol—two things a son should never have to smell on his father, but it wasn't like I was any better.

He rapped his knuckles on the bar table. "I didn't raise you to be an asshole."

I snorted and picked my brain for something that would provoke him. "I know five nannies that would argue you didn't raise me at all."

Not that I minded. As a kid, I'd seen him often, lived a cushy life, had everything I needed. We'd never had problems until he paid Elsa off.

My dad ignored me. I could count on him to do that, too.

I lifted a finger, signaling for the bartender to send another scotch my way. He didn't even glance in my direction. Fuck. When did the service get to be so bad at L'Oscurità? I made a mental note to handle it myself or tell Asher, who had opened the bar I managed when he'd left the mafia. I'd decide later when I wasn't two-thirds of the way to getting shit-faced.

My dad turned to face me, but I didn't bother returning the favor. "That was Benny's girl. Good kid."

"Benny know his daughter's whoring around, Gio?"

His eyes flared. He hated when I called him Gio, but he hadn't regained the right to be called Dad.

"Was that what she was doing? Offering herself up to you?"

"Do you really need to ask?" I reached over the bar top, selected an opened bottle, and poured myself my own goddamn drink.

"Hey! You can't—" The bartender finally turned to face me. His words caught in his throat when we made eye contact. He looked torn between averting his eyes and sending puppy dog eyes my way in the off chance I'd show him mercy.

Fat chance.

He took a step toward me. "S-sorry."

Too. Late.

It wasn't my job to teach others how unforgiving the world could be, but I liked the taste of chewing people up and spitting out their hope. Also, my tolerance for incompetence was a whopping zero when it came to my employees. I ran a business not a charity.

"Mr. Romano, sir..." He faltered for words like a husband caught with his pants down.

I stared at him for a moment, drawing out the tension, amused by the trail of sweat dripping from his forehead to his collar. This was his last shift here, and he knew it. Almost nine million people called New York City their home. I could find someone more competent to replace him within the week. At the very least, it would give me something to do while Asher played doting sap to his fiancée Lucy and Elsa continued to keep Everett away from me.

Gio grabbed the bottle from me after I finished pouring myself three fingers' worth. He took a long swig straight from the rim that would have made a frat boy proud. "What's wrong with Benny's girl? She's a good-looking gal. Sweet, too, if I remember correctly."

"*You* fuck her then." I paused, my glass inches from my lips. "Or have you already?"

"Don't be ridiculous, son. I love your mother." His jaw ticked at my obvious amusement. It tempted me to list the affairs I knew about, but I didn't for civility's sake.

I wasn't even sure if *I* loved my mother. I almost forgot what she looked like with how little we saw one another. Looking in the mirror wouldn't help. I didn't get any of my features from her.

I had my dad's high cheekbones. His strong jawline. The

full lips and fawn-brown eyes. All of his strong Italian features. Whereas Mom's stature veered on the short and slim side, my dad and I towered several inches over six feet, built like Navy SEALs moonlighting for the WWE.

I slid a glance to Gio. "Sure."

"I do," he insisted.

He and Mom shared an arranged marriage of sorts. A total farce, if I'd ever seen one. Back when none of the five American families had gotten along, both of my great-grandfathers thought it would be a good idea to start the first alliance between syndicates, beginning with an arranged marriage between my parents.

It didn't really work. The Rossi and Romano syndicates weren't any closer than they had been before the marriage. Not until I came along, bonding the families with something thicker than half-assed marital vows.

Still, it wasn't like a Rossi would come up here for a few drinks and a Knicks game, but say one did. He'd no longer find himself floating face down in the Hudson River for it. Progress, I'd say.

"She's my wife. I love her."

It would have been a convincing statement had Gio not downed two fingers of whiskey after saying it. And that sex scent in the air. Someone with anosmia could smell the pussy clinging to his skin.

I muttered a curse, finally turning to face my dad. "Stop sending mafia bunnies my way, Gio. I'd rather fuck a spiked Fleshlight."

Giovanni "Gio" Romano intimidated people. He had to. It came with the territory. No one talked to a Romano *caporegime* like this. Ever.

Apart from me, that was.

It wasn't like I didn't love my dad. We had issues—a past I wanted to forgive yet couldn't—but I did love him. If he kept trying to rope me into the underworld, that love would dry up. He thought that if, by some stroke of luck, I fell in love with a mafia bunny, I'd follow his footsteps in the family business.

Never going to happen.

Not anymore.

That would take nothing short of a miracle, and I wasn't exactly the type of man to inspire one of those.

Gio ran a hand along his jaw. "We're not the plague. We're your family."

I grabbed the bottle from his hands, forgoing my glass and drinking straight from the rim. "Family. Not co-workers. Not bosses. Family. Jesus Christ, Gio. It's not the end of the world if I don't work with you. I'm happy here."

Not really.

I didn't need money. My inheritance exceeded the GDP of some countries, and my MBA from Wharton gifted me with the know-how to multiply my investments. I'd fired Lewis and quit my job at Launder, Inc. eight years ago. Managing Asher's restaurant was something I did to get Gio off my back. It wasn't my passion. I wasn't sure I had any passions, except getting laid, but even that got old.

Working here afforded me a little distance from the Romano family business. Technically, this wasn't a mafia establishment, but despite him leaving the mafia, Asher was close enough to the family that Gio had left me alone for a while.

Until last month.

About the same time Asher had proposed to Lucy, Gio had started stirring this shit up again, pushing the daughters of powerful Romano men my way. It needed to stop like Tila Tequila needed a filter.

"Well, if you're planning on spending the rest of your life managing college kids at a bar"—Gio nodded in the direction of the bartender, though we both knew I actually ran the three-time Michelin star restaurant connected to the bar by the drywall to my left—"you can at least make yourself useful."

I didn't take the bait, instead focusing on the last half of his sentence. "What do you want?"

He inclined his head in the direction of my office and stood, not bothering to pay for his drink or tip the bartender, not that the little shit deserved it. We walked there, passing an employee break room shared by the bar and restaurant employees along the way.

My ex Dana winked at me from inside. I ignored her and flicked a piece of lint from my suit lapel. As soon as we entered my office, Gio locked the door. Never a good sign. Fuck me. I was too buzzed for a serious conversation right now.

I didn't normally turn to alcohol to chase my demons—not even after Gio had betrayed my trust eight years ago—but I wasn't scheduled for work today and Asher, who I would usually be hanging out with right now, had a fiancée who monopolized most of his time. Don't get me wrong. I love Lucy like a sister, but times like this reminded me of just how lonely I was.

Loneliness your dad is responsible for, the unforgiving part of my brain never let me forget. *Loneliness Everett probably feels, too.*

I swallowed and sat down at my desk, not bothering to offer a seat up to Gio. He'd take it if he wanted to. That was the type of men we were. Takers. We only gave when it came to the family, and even then, the number of people who shared the Romano name or—like Asher, Lucy, and our current fixer Niccolaio—had worked their way into the heart of this family was slim.

"We need to talk business."

"My business or *yours*?"

One of his cufflinks fell to the floor. He kicked it under my desk, removed the remaining one, and tossed it in the trash like it hadn't cost a month's worth of rent in Greenwich. "Ours."

Translation: Romano business.

Translation of translation: nothing I cared to delve into.

I bit back a curse. I went to L'Oscurità to get away from the mafia business, not to have Gio throw it in my face every chance he got. At any given moment, at least a dozen mafia contacts or members wined and dined inside the building, but the actual revenue L'Oscurità made was a hundred percent legitimate.

Gio ignored my irritation. "Your Uncle Frankie's caught wind of a rat in our midst."

I laughed away my disbelief. "No kidding? You see anyone suicidal lately?"

"This isn't a joke. Our man in the bureau confirmed this."

And our FBI informants never made mistakes.

"Shit." The curse hissed past my lips, and rightfully so. By nature, a delicate ecosystem tethered the family business together, and even the slightest tremors could disrupt it. "Why tell me this?"

Exterminating rats fell within the jurisdiction of the head of enforcement for the Romano family. Uncle Vince. My favorite uncle. The most compassionate Romano. Go figure he'd have my least favorite job.

"Vince has narrowed it down to a list of four possible people. We've got tails on three of the four, but we need you on the last."

I gestured around the bare room. No shelves. Just a desk and chairs. "I've got a business to run."

"He's here. Works for you, Bastian."

I knew Gio hadn't meant it as an insult, but I took it as one anyway. "Are you telling me I hired a rat?" Each and every employee here had undergone a careful vetting process. I held a grudge against Gio, but I'd never take it out on Asher and the rest of my family or risk their lives.

Then again, you hired that incompetent bartender, the asshole in me reminded.

You don't even remember his name, the rest of me agreed.

The judgment in Gio's eyes didn't escape my notice. They flicked to the security monitor in front of me. "I'm telling you to be damn sure your house is clean. Before it starts infesting mine."

I ran a tired hand down my face. Ever since he'd paid off Elsa, Gio had been looking for a way to reshape our relationship. He had never drawn a line between me and the family like this before. He was serious about this, which made me more alert than I wanted to be while tipsy.

A rat was good for no one. A rat at L'Oscurità was worse. It meant everyone I gave a shit about—Asher, Lucy, Niccolaio, Gio, Everett, and the rest of my family—were at risk. I would have taken care of the rat without being asked. When people fucked with what was mine, I left them without a dick to fuck with. Simple as that.

"Fine. I'll take care of it." I slid my phone out of my pocket and unlocked the screen, dismissing Gio.

He nodded. "See you around, son." His footsteps paused a few feet short of the door. "You see Old Man Tony's daughter lately? She's got tits out to here." He stretched his arms out a foot away from his chest.

I spared him no attention as I said, "Kindly fuck off, Gio."

He laughed all the way out the door, and when the handle clicked shut, I let out a long exhale. This—caring for my family—was how I always got roped into the mafia life. I had gotten away with just running L'Oscurità for a while, but all signs pointed to my reprieve coming to an unwilling end.

And I wasn't close to ready for it.

3

One painful duty fulfilled
makes the next plainer and easier.

—Helen Keller

ARIANA DE LUCA

"Deep breaths, Ari," I muttered to myself, much like the homeless woman who'd taken up residence outside my new apartment building two days ago. "You can do this. Everyone has their first big cover."

My affirmations fooled no one.

The likelihood of coming out of this cover dead

outweighed my probability of living. I might as well get used to pasty skin and the matching hand-me-down funeral dress Aunt Nadia had made me promise to wear to the grave.

I sent my handler Simmons a quick coded text message, letting him know my position, and then I pushed him out of my mind. I hated being partnered with him. Simmons had a recognizable face—a near replica of his dad's, who served as the secretary of state for the current administration.

Nine out of ten times, someone recognized him before he could even start his cover. The bureau still hadn't pulled him from fieldwork. Nepotism at its finest. Today was one of those nine times, and I'd gotten the message that I was on my own only an hour ago. We'd already planned for it—I would be stupid not to with a partner like Simmons—but it didn't make it any more palatable.

Neither did the difference in the way the FBI treated me compared to Simmons. My boss Wilks told me time and time again that he thought of me as a daughter, yet he'd given the order for me to go undercover with my real name.

Ariana De Luca.

Worse, he'd recruited me, so only he knew what my last name really meant.

That I was one of *those* De Lucas.

I pushed the betrayal aside and tried to focus on my goal. Armed with a killer little black dress, nude Louboutins, and my padded resume, I entered L'Oscurità to... Well, I actually didn't know. Most of being a legend required winging it, but I at least expected to flirt, seduce, or show off my way into a bartending job here—despite every instinct of mine screaming at me to turn and leave if I valued my life.

A buzz hummed in the atmosphere at L'Oscurità, sending a dark thrill down my spine. The midnight-black brick wall split the restaurant in two—a fancy high dining restaurant with a year-long waiting list in the front and a low-key, dimly-lit bar hidden in the back.

The walled-off restaurant gave no indication of its affiliation with the bar. In fact, no sign hung above the bar entrance. There didn't need to be. If you didn't know where it was, you probably wouldn't get in anyway.

"Can I help you?" A woman approached me and ran her eyes down my body, myriad emotions flying across her face before she settled with disdain.

Jealousy did fickle things to people. It also happened to be the reaction I usually elicited from women. *Just like your mom*, Aunt Nadia had never failed to remind me. *Like a siren, always drawing attention. Good and bad.* I swiped a hand at the mess of honey-brown waves that reached the curve of my waist—my natural hair color for once—and tucked a loose lock behind my ear.

I could barely breathe with a tight bandage dress wrapped around my curves. Her eyes dipped down to my long legs, traveled to the generous swells of my breasts, and settled on the pop of my blue-green eyes past the smoky eyeshadow. Very rarely did I look out of place unless I wanted to. Perks of being a legend.

It took her a few seconds too long to nod at the resume clutched in my hand and say, "There's no job available."

I slid the resume into my bag and studied the woman, my silence clearly making her uncomfortable. Though she didn't wear a name tag, I knew everything I needed to know about Dana Till from the files I'd been given.

She worked as a server on this side of L'Oscurità and dated Bastiano Romano a while back. He managed the restaurant and, as the nephew of Frankie Romano, the head of the Romano family, boasted deep ties to the Italian mafia.

Without a doubt, if Dana already didn't like me, she most definitely wouldn't like me when I got a job here. So, I matched her stare, the disdain coming readily to me, and brushed past her. She was harmless, a minnow in a room full of sharks, and I hadn't the time nor inclination to deal with pests.

Given her visceral reaction to me, her history with Bastiano "Bastian" Romano, and the fact that she saw me as a threat in the first place, I knew without a doubt that her ex held my ticket into this place.

I ignored Dana and skimmed the room, forcing a look of indifference onto my face at the humbling sight of Bastiano Romano. He nursed an empty glass between his mammoth palms while the bartender rushed to satisfy the crowd on the other end of the bar. The irritation lining Bastian's face told me all I needed to know. He was short-staffed at L'Oscurità, and I had a chance to weasel my way into the business.

A woman chattered beside him, the curves of her body angled toward him as she traced a suggestive finger down the swell of his bicep. Light caramel skin. Waist-length raven hair. Dark eyes. Slender body. An exotic Mediterranean beauty, through and through, yet Bastian paid no attention to her. Instead, his eyes glared holes into the back of the bartender's head.

If it were only for the look on his face, I would have thought he was an alcoholic, but I knew better. Memorized his file. Heard the bureau's advance team wax on and on about the Romano family. This man possessed pure dominance, and dominant men didn't have vices that weakened them.

The woman dipped her head forward and leaned her chin

on his shoulder. He used that same arm to pop an ice cube from his glass into his mouth without acknowledging her. She nearly fell when his shoulder moved and stumbled to right herself. Still, he didn't pay her any attention.

The urge to turn around and walk out the door seized my legs.

You're not inexperienced, I assured myself. *Okay, so maybe you could have more experience under your belt, but this is how you get it.*

Judging from his mostly empty file, Bastiano Romano thrived on secrets. As far as I knew, he—and his presence at L'Oscurità—was the reason the bureau thought there would be something worth getting out of this cover, but he also fostered my hesitation.

Even after studying his file for weeks, I had thought I'd been ready to see him. To go toe-to-toe with him and come out as the unrelenting victor. I had been wrong. Just one glance at him, and I knew I was utterly, unequivocally fucked.

He was a beautiful monster—mafia royalty wrapped in a fifty-thousand-dollar bespoke Desmond Merrion suit. The tailored fit did nothing to hide his towering build or the sheer muscled width of his chest. His hair—so full and dark in its costly short gentleman's cut—spoke of the hundreds he must have parted with to get it.

His eyes were dark, but the expression they held was darker, the variety of sinister I would expect from the Devil himself. Absent of emotion and horribly indifferent, they pierced my very soul and left me feeling irrevocably bereft.

His defined cheekbones were cut like the sharp edges of an executioner's blade, and coupled with his perpetual, derisive sneer, he gave the impression that he knew just how much better he was than all of us and it amused him greatly.

But this was different.

This was him taking my plan and twisting it in his favor in *his* way. With *his* skill. As if it had been *his* idea in the first place. He wasn't kissing me back, but he dominated me regardless. I felt it in the pounding of my chest. In the weakening of my legs. In his refusal to Kiss. Me. Back.

He reached an arm around my waist and pulled me closer, still not returning my kiss. His palms explored my hips, curved up to the side of my breasts, then lowered to my ass. He gripped a cheek and squeezed, pulling my body forward and into him, grinding my core on the side of his thigh like he owned me.

His taunts didn't go unnoticed. Neither did the audience. I got it. I'd kissed him without his permission, so he touched me without mine. And still, he didn't kiss me back. My lips remained pressed to his lifeless ones, and his hands continued to knead my ass, both of us waiting to see who would cave first. His hand slid from my ass to my front, dipping beneath the hem of my dress.

I took a step back and tore my lips away, mentally cursing myself for using such a stupid, unoriginal, and clichéd approach. I was better than this, but he had made me sloppy. I was lightheaded from his presence—the heavily intoxicating smell of whiskey, oakmoss, musk, and aged ambergris. Drunk from the power he radiated. And dizzy from the viscous tension coursing through my veins.

We waited in silence as Aphrodite tucked tail and ran, silently disappearing into the crowd while our eyes locked in a power struggle he was bound to win.

He already won, I reminded myself as I took another tiny step back, hoping he didn't notice.

He did.

Amusement touched his eyes before it fled like an alley-cat, darting away before I could even process it. Only when Aphrodite was gone from the bar did he return his attention to the bartender's back, dismissing me again, like he had earlier. Like I was worthless.

I felt the dismissal in my gut.

"That's it?" I kept my voice low and carefully concealed the emotion in it, hoping I didn't sound as breathless as I felt.

He didn't respond. I was Aphrodite now, except he had actually looked at me, taken me in, deemed me inferior, and disregarded me. I felt like a flea. A pest. The minnow I had mentally accused Dana, his ex-girlfriend, of being.

In this moment, I knew that Wilks had been right to some degree. I needed the power of my last name. This legend had no chance of surviving otherwise. Not with this apathetic jerk involved.

I took a seat on the stool next to him, far enough away that I felt like I could breathe a little again. "Ariana De Luca," I introduced myself. "But you can call me Ari."

He didn't react. Not physically, at least. But I felt his attention as he spoke, still not facing me. "That's an interesting last name."

"It's just a last name."

He curled his fingers around his glass. "Sure. In the same way Romano is just a last name."

"It is, isn't it?"

That got to him. He turned to me, giving me his full attention and, with it, the full force of those devastating eyes. This was it—my moment to succeed or fail epically. I leaned over the counter, aware of how high my short dress rose, and grabbed a bottle of top-shelf amaretto and sour mix.

Leaning closer to him, I held steady eye contact as I

poured sour mix into his glass, followed by the almond whiskey. My hand covered his, and together, we swirled the glass, mixing the whiskey sour with the steady movement.

I held my breath as he took a sip of it, downing a finger in one impressive gulp. His Adam's apple bobbed as he swallowed, the movement far more erotic than it should have been. I forced myself not to avert my eyes.

"How'd you know?" Whiskey coated his lower lip. His tongue swiped across the skin, cleaning it in a way that ripped the air from my throat and left me fatally winded.

I tried and failed to tear my eyes away from his mouth. "I tasted it on your lips."

The same lips I couldn't stop staring at.

I was being unprofessional. I was getting drawn in by his allure, and I had no excuse. Bastiano Romano was about as delightful as a positive STD test result, yet here I was, distracted, intoxicated, and engrossed. The equivalent of spreading my legs and begging for gonorrhea.

"Are you in the habit of coming into bars and putting your lips on random strangers?" He paused, disdain passing over his features. "Anyone ever tell you you're a classy gal?"

And on top of his lack of charm, he was a full-blown jerk.

I held back my scowl, forcing myself to pretend he didn't affect me. "I don't recall ever asking for your opinion."

"I don't recall giving you my consent."

"And I don't recall you pulling away."

He laughed at that, but his laughter was drier than sandpaper. "This has got to be the worst job interview I've ever partaken in." He slowed his words, his tone dripping with condescension. "Have you ever had a job?"

I ignored his jab and leaned away from him, feeling

exposed and three steps behind. "How do you know I want a job?"

"You looked around when you entered the place, but you stopped as soon as your eyes landed on me; you just fixed me a whiskey sour with amaretto; and you have the tip of your resume hanging out of your purse."

Jesus Christ, he had made me as soon as I'd entered the room. Did he notice these details about everyone or was it just me? I bit back a scoff at my arrogance. Surely it wasn't just me, but the alternative was almost unbelievable. I was a trained FBI agent, and even I sometimes missed things. Granted, Wilks usually assigned me to such insignificant cases, I had virtually no experiences I could brag about.

I studied his eyes, wondering what they took in. "Are you always this observant?"

"Only when I'm breathing." He finished his drink and slid the glass my way, a silent demand for me to make him another drink.

I wondered if he was accustomed to ordering people around or if he just thought he could with me. Either way, the assumption that I would be at his beck and call pissed me off enough for me to not pour him another drink, though I should have for the sake of my cover.

He took in my defiance without concern, and when his mouth curved up into a scoff, I braced myself for the impact of his impending words. "Do you always force yourself on all your potential employers?"

He was trying to make me sound pathetic, and it worked. Christ, I hated his guts. Meanwhile, he remained indifferent, barely gathering the energy to spare me a glance in between sentences.

"No." I swallowed my irritation and tried to salvage this

impossible situation, reminding myself how much I wanted to prove myself and get better assignments. "But I'm an opportunist. I see an in, and I take it."

"And I'm your in?" He let loose a mocking laugh. "For what? The job?" His warm whiskey breath caressed my ear as he leaned closer and whispered, "Or something else?"

I placed a firm hand on his chest and pushed him away. He didn't budge an inch. I pushed again. Still no movement.

Lowering my hand, I racked my brain for a way to save face and came up empty. "The job. I got your attention, didn't I?"

He leaned back of his own accord, his face instantly serious. "There aren't any bartending openings here."

He was lying.

We both knew this.

The fact that I had to make him the drink he'd been waiting for was proof of that, but this was just another test. For what? I didn't know. I just had to hope for the best.

I tucked a strand of hair from my face and leveled him with a determined stare. "Make one."

"Why should I?"

"I did you a favor."

He scoffed. "Chasing off a mafia bunny? Hardly a favor. Unless you've taken a bullet for me, I don't owe you a thing."

Like I'd ever take a bullet for him.

"You're a real piece of work." The words slipped out.

What the hell. Stop talking, Ari, I begged.

"As if I give a fuck." He turned to me, stood up, and inched closer until his chest brushed my arm. "The door's that way. Drink's on you."

My jaw dropped. He wanted me to pay for a drink that *he* drank in a bar that *he* ran? He was unbelievable.

He placed his finger underneath my chin, pushed upward until my mouth shut with an audible snap, and started to walk away. Instinctively, I grabbed his arm, my fingers unable to wrap fully around the sheer width of his forearm.

The warmth of his skin burned my palm. He could have easily pulled away, but he didn't. He stopped; turned to me; carefully removed my fingers from his forearm like I'd caught an infection I didn't know about; and with a hand on each side of my bar stool, leaned forward, capturing both of my eyes with his.

I could feel his breath on my lips as he spoke. "I don't hire people I don't know, Ariana *De Luca*"—he emphasized my last name—"so why the fuck do you think I would make an exception for *you*?"

He said it like I was a curse.

Like I was nothing more than a nuisance.

Like the dirt on this floor held more worth than I did.

A lesser woman would have cowered. She would have cried ravaged tears. She would have weakened beneath the insults that cut deeper than words, carried by his supremacy and cemented by his self-righteous authority.

Instead, I steeled myself and inched closer until I could feel his lips feathering mine. His eyes widened in genuine surprise, the first reaction from him that hadn't been birthed from his inexplicable disdain for me.

"I'm the best." My voice barely reached a whisper as I reveled in his scent and the intoxicating notes of bergamot, blackcurrant, and Moroccan jasmine. Something this sinful shouldn't have smelled this delicious. "And this isn't your goddamn bar. So, you have fun explaining to your *boss* why you let the best slip through your fingers, while I have fun getting a job at your biggest rival. I hear The Dominic has a bullshit-free working environment."

I grabbed my purse, threw a couple hundred-dollar bills on the bar counter, and turned to leave, allowing my entire body to brush against his as I left. It was a badass exit as far as I was concerned, and I was proud of myself even if I was leaving without a job. I'd probably get pushed to desk duty for this, but at least I had my pride. Well, what was left of it.

He stopped me when I stood no more than a foot away, his hand placed on my hip. I didn't dare turn around. I could feel his breath on my neck as he closed the distance between our bodies.

With his front pressed entirely against my back, he brushed my long hair behind my ear and whispered into it, his voice full of condescension. "Silly, misinformed girl, L'Oscurità is mine in all the ways that matter. If you think you know a thing about me, you're more foolish than I already think you are."

For a split second, I wondered what had happened to him that taught him to treat people like this. I swept the thought away as soon as it came, chastising myself for thinking sympathetic thoughts in the first place.

Pressed completely against him, I felt unnerved. But I was too stubborn to allow his insult to go unanswered. "Back left corner. Blue button down. Black jeans. You're serving a Brillat Savarin with a Mourvèdre when a Counoise would work better. White dress, blonde hair at my six o'clock is eating her braised and confit lamb with a glass of Viognier when a Meritage is more appropriate."

I leaned back, pressing myself harder against him until I could feel his erection firmly against my back, and I was sure he could feel every curve of my body. It was erotic, sexy, and so fucked up, I refused to process it. "I could continue, but I'll spare you the depths of your inadequacy. But have fun with *your* restaurant. Great place you have here. It certainly doesn't need me."

I jerked away from his touch, forcing myself to ignore the brutal beating of my heart and the breaths that struggled to flee my lips. I had hardly walked two steps from him before he called after me.

"Wait," he demanded, and like a glutton for punishment, I did. "Saturday. Three o'clock. I have no tolerance for tardiness."

And just like that, I had a meeting with the most petrifying man I had ever met. I had a feeling that Bastiano Romano could ruin me if I let him.

Duty eats free will for breakfast.

—Daryl Gregory

ARIANA DE LUCA

The thing about being a woman was that, even in the twenty-first century, we were constantly being underestimated. And I could give you at least a dozen instances where that had been a good thing for me.

For instance, during our annual baseball game last year, the guys at work had decided it would be a good idea to divide me and my coworkers up into teams based on gender. Losers had to buy the winners two rounds of drinks at Simzy's, the local Manhattan pub that sold a short glass of piss-tasting beer for a whopping fifteen dollars apiece—high stakes given our measly pay.

But having vaginas hadn't stopped us from winning. In fact, we dominated in a game that, eight months later, was *still* being talked about around the office. And if I were being honest, none of that bothered me. It was a *perk* of being underestimated. Like a hustler owning her mark, we had made fools out of the FBI boys and would continue to do so.

Every.

Single.

Year.

I expected to be underestimated by others, but not my boss. Wilks knew my history. He had access to my case files, entrance scores, and college transcripts. If anything, he was the one person in the world who knew just how capable I was. And still, he never treated me like he would my partner Simmons—or any of the other men in my department.

When it came to receiving the best assignments, being underestimated was the worst thing that could happen to an FBI special agent, particularly an undercover one. I got the low-level drug dealers and the occasional white-collar criminal with the prowess of an accountant; Simmons got the top-tier criminals and even once nabbed an FBI most wanted. If this kept up, in ten years, I'd be pushing papers behind a desk, and Simmons would be running this unit.

This had to end somewhere.

I preferred it end now, with a cover that didn't require me to sludge around all day in a bar with zero confirmation of intelligence access. Drawing in a heavy breath, I tried my hardest not to yell at Wilks.

"You look like you've swallowed a lemon." Simmons took his time scanning me up and down.

"Do you have to be here?"

I couldn't deal with Simmons right now. Not with the memory of Bastiano Romano's lips pressed against mine burning my brain. It'd taken everything in me to push the thought away and focus on my assignment.

Simmons sat in one of the two chairs in our division head's office, his ankle casually resting on the opposite knee and his back pressed against the black leather, the posture too relaxed for my liking. I, on the other hand, stood off to the side of the mahogany desk in the center of the room like an uninvited dinner guest with no placemat.

He was the picture of indifference, and why would he give a damn? He no longer had to go undercover. Worse—before that, he had been assigned the legend of a multimillionaire, wannabe Gordon Ramsey, whereas I had an interview with the Devil himself for a job I was far too overqualified for.

I ignored Simmons and stared Wilks straight in the eyes, not wavering for a second. "This is bullshit, Wilks."

"Have you always been so confrontational, De Luca?" Wilks' voice never strayed from his trademark of one part calm and two parts condescension.

I resisted the urge to cringe at the address. No one in this office but my FBI-mandated shrink and Wilks, who vetted me, knew my last name was more than just a last name. It was a connection to one of the five greatest crime syndicates this country had ever known. To everyone else, it was just an ugly coincidence.

But Wilks and I knew the truth.

The Romano family could never know I was the illegitimate princess of the De Luca family. I shared half of Angelo

De Luca's DNA. Not like the De Lucas knew I existed, but that was the point. I wanted to keep it that way, and going under with my real name and being called De Luca tempted fate. On the bright side, Wilks only called me by my last name when he was messing with me.

Unfortunately, he messed with me a lot. He thought we had a father-daughter relationship, when in reality, he always sat on the tippy top of my ever-expanding shit list for giving me the worst assignments despite the fact we both knew I could do better.

Simmons muttered, "Women," under his breath.

I ignored him, because it was best not to egg him on after his recent divorce. "Give me anything else, Wilks." I leaned forward, pressed both of my palms on Wilks' table, and looked him in the eyes so he knew I was serious. "*Anything*. It's not too late."

And it wasn't. Anyone else could take my place. I had no idea why Wilks acted like this legend couldn't wait a second longer. Yeah, the Romanos engaged in pretty bad things, but it wasn't like the FBI just suddenly learned of them. They'd been around for generations, along with the other four major Italian mafia syndicates in North America—my family's included.

Behind me, Simmons chimed in unhelpfully, "There's always Depravity."

The Romano family owned and frequented a strip club named Depravity. It had popped up in Rogue's place when Asher Black, the alleged former Romano family fixer, made the transition from hitman to straight-laced businessman, taking the strip club and transforming it into a high-end nightclub.

And as far as we knew, Depravity was clean. There might

have been some meetings that went down there, but we couldn't connect the club to any illegal activity, no matter how hard we had tried.

And we had.

Over and over again.

Hell, Depravity even paid their taxes correctly and on time. Going undercover at Depravity would have been a fool's errand, exactly what Simmons was trying to imply I was. That, or he was still bitter over his cheating wife. Both were likely, given the current state of our relationship. He didn't treat other women like this. Only the ones who beat him in every test at Quantico.

Most men saw me as a pretty distraction. Simmons saw me as competition, and I did nothing to assuage the idea. He didn't like having a partner he knew nothing about, and sharing my past sounded as appealing as adult diapers.

We hadn't gotten along since the day we'd met. That was six years ago, back when there hadn't been a speck of dust on my Degory University undergrad degree and I had just graduated from Quantico as the youngest member in my class at the ripe age of twenty-two.

"Stop," Wilks bluffed. He encouraged this kind of juvenile behavior from us because it gave him an opportunity to assert his authority. He flexed his fingers, his poker tell when he got excited about a good hand.

I didn't back down. "Come on, Wilks. Anything else. Fly me to the South in the middle of the summer in a turtleneck, sweatpants, and a fur coat if you have to. Anything but this."

Aunt Nadia had once said I could convince someone to take their own life. I couldn't even convince my boss to take a chance on me.

"You're being dramatic."

Wilks was probably right, but I was sick of these jobs. I wanted the real assignments. The ones that didn't require me to dress skimpy, flirt my pretty little face off, and bat my long lashes to get what the FBI needed.

On my last undercover assignment, I had come too close to sleeping with a small-time drug dealer, who only fell under FBI jurisdiction because he'd crossed state lines by buying his drugs along the border of Indiana and pushing them in Chicago, Illinois.

Right on the border of the Camerino and Romano syndicates.

If we hadn't taken care of him, the Camerino or Romano families would have, and it wouldn't have been pretty.

I swiped my hair away from my face, my movements jerky. "With good reason. A bartender at L'Oscurità?! You had me as a stripper—"

"—retired stripper—" Simmons interjected.

"—for my last gig. You promised that I'd get a better legend this time around."

We called our covers legends. Sometimes, we called field agents in our division legends, too, but not many people had the clearance to know who is a legend and who is an analyst here. And when we became our legends, the FBI techies erased all traces of our affiliation to the FBI. The only people who could vouch that I was, indeed, an FBI agent worked on this floor with me.

"This *is* a better gig. You'll bartend regularly at L'Oscurità and keep your eyes and ears out for any intel that might be useful. Nothing trying. Nothing too dangerous. Just your eyes and ears."

"I can handle dangerous just as well as Simmons."

"And I believe you, but the fact of the matter is we nee—"

"Any other assignment, Wilks." I lowered my voice. "Please."

He placed both hands on his hips. No hand flexing. Just that somber expression I hated from him. "Drop the legend, *Ari*."

I reeled backward because he was right—even though I'd started my next legend, I was still trapped in my last legend. The confrontational Midwestern stripper, too stubborn for her own good. I'd thought I'd shed it. I really had.

Wilks turned to Simmons. "Clear the room." When Simmons left, he continued, "Have you seen Dr. Clemson?"

I stuttered out a ragged breath. "No."

"You're young. It's always the young ones who have trouble pulling out of their legends."

"You're being condescending."

"I'm not. It's happened to me and countless others who came before and after me. If you don't become your legend, you're not doing your job well. Everyone has trouble shedding their legends after abandoning a cover. That's what your therapy sessions are for."

I fixed my eyes on a spot beside his head, doing everything I could to not look guilty. "I have an appointment scheduled."

It didn't help that I never received the type of assignments that would give me real experience.

"Don't lie. It doesn't work on me." Wilks relaxed in his seat and shuffled some files out of the way. "I'll put Simmons on another case. You won't have to deal with him. Dr. Clemson will be your handler on this case under the guise of therapy sessions."

He paused a beat. "This is the last time you show your face in the office until the assignment is done. Hell, you shouldn't even be here now." He softened his voice, and I had to swallow the emotion bubbling in my throat. "Go see Dr. Clemson, and when you're done, I'll call you on one of your burners. Then we'll talk."

"About a better assignment?"

"About your problem."

And fuck, that was the last thing I wanted to hear. Because he was so right. I did have a problem. My legends consumed me, and when an assignment ended, I couldn't seem to differentiate between my legends and the real Ariana De Luca.

Deep down, I feared it was because I didn't actually know who I was.

6

Only enemies speak the truth;
friends and lovers lie endlessly,
caught in the web of duty.

—Stephen King

BASTIANO ROMANO

I showed up late.

Two hours, to be exact.

It was a dick move, especially since I had nothing better to do. I had spent the extra time working out, shopping for shit I didn't need from a copycat *Sky Mall Magazine* I'd stolen off a plane years ago, and jacking off in the shower.

Pointless endeavors.

My body was already in prime condition, I had no fucking clue what I would do with a serenity cat sleeping pod, and I was still craving pussy more than I was my fist.

But Ariana De Luca didn't seem to know her place, and it certainly wasn't anywhere near me. If I hired her—and that was a big if—I needed to train that spine out of her until she wilted like a limp noodle like the rest of my employees.

My phone rang as I flicked on the left signal of my car.

"Yes?" I answered Gio's call.

"Your mom's coming into town."

Irritation fused with excitement. Ma coming meant having to see her, but it also meant getting to see my little sister Tessie. A fair trade.

I rolled my neck, enjoying the way it cracked, and drove my Jag into the parking garage beneath L'Oscurità—probably the only parking garage in the city with great signal thanks to the tech division of Asher's company. "When?"

"Soon. We need to talk about rodents."

I caught his meaning. "Fine."

I hung up and checked my texts. One from Uncle Vince. Another from Elsa. I deleted Elsa's text, then cursed myself for acting so rashly. It could have been about Everett. She texted me again with a one-hundred-thousand-dollar wire request. Definitely not about Everett. Reminding myself I'd find a way to screw her over later, I sent her the one hundred thousand dollars and emailed her the confirmation link, along with links to a dozen porno sites known to cause viruses.

Sending the money to her put me in a bad mood. Seeing her name put me in a bad mood. Everything related to Elsa pissed me off. I slid my phone into my pocket and took my time walking to the entrance of the bar.

Nothing irritated me more than people who thought they could bulldoze their way into my life, take what they wanted, and expect no repercussions. Ariana De Luca ticked each of those boxes. On top of that, the other night, she'd worn a bandage dress which reminded me of something Elsa would have worn after New York had tainted everything I loved about her.

When I got to the bar entrance, Ariana was waiting outside in the late spring heat, a bustle of New Yorkers sparing her no attention as they walked past. My eyes, on the other hand, honed in on her immediately.

It wasn't because she was attractive. She was, but I didn't give a fuck. She was little more than a nuisance with a body and face that happened to make me look twice. It was her mouth that proved lethal, but I wouldn't exactly call her a worthy adversary.

Just a pain in the ass who happened to be right.

L'Oscurità needed a new bartender and finding one who demonstrated competence was taking longer than I had initially thought it would. Ariana De Luca happened to be the first candidate who knew her shit and was attractive enough to work at L'Oscurità.

Plain and simple, that was all that mattered.

Never mind the fact that her last name was a stain on this planet and belonged nowhere near my family, even if she wasn't one of *those* De Lucas.

She would get her interview, and if all went well, she'd undergo a brief training period. But as soon as I found a bartender who didn't piss me the fuck off, I was firing her faster than she could say, "I want a severance package."

She straightened from the wall as soon as she saw me, opening her mouth, no doubt an argument on the tip of the harpoon she called her tongue. "I thought you had 'no tolerance for tardiness.'"

"I have no tolerance for people who make *me* wait. How long you had to wait is of little importance to me."

"Oh, don't worry your grouchy little head off. I only had to wait a few minutes." Her voice was a satisfied croon, and she failed to hide her smirk. Hell, I wasn't convinced she had even tried.

I told myself that I didn't care, but I was already making a mental note to check the exterior cameras when I had the time. If she was telling the truth, she would have had me waiting for two hours, and Christ, that tore through my indifference and pissed me the hell off.

I unlocked the bar, turning on the lights as we entered. The bar didn't open until six thirty at night, so we had about half an hour before my employees were due to arrive. Ariana scanned the room, taking it in while it was empty.

Everything was black—from the floor to the booths, tables, and stools. All set amidst the backdrop of the gray on gray patterned walls. White crystal chandeliers hung from the high ceilings, casting a dim light over the bar.

Even without the buzz of a crowd and the seductive lull of the soundtrack we had exclusively produced for the bar, the atmosphere was edgy. Sexy. Erotic. A total waste of splendor given the quality—or lack thereof—of my present company.

Ariana trailed a finger over the bar top. "Word has it you run the other side of L'Oscurità. The restaurant." She turned to face me, her eyes flaunting an unflinching dare. "Yet, here you are. It must suck wanting all this control over your life but having none." She had no idea. "Piss off your *boss*?"

There was a potential rat that needed terminating, but I couldn't exactly tell her that. Instead, my eyes narrowed. Most girls went for sultry. Seductive. Desperate sex appeal. Hell, sometimes I even got the ass-end of the spectrum. Those so afraid of me they'd tuck tail and run at the sound of my last name.

But Ariana De Luca? She stood in front of me, her own brand of unwavering valor and unnecessary provocation. She was challenging. Combative. Argumentative. Fearless. I understood these qualities, but not on her and certainly not at my expense. She was poking the goddamned lion and loving it.

But she'd learn not to.

I didn't bother with a response, instead walking past her and toward my office. She hesitated for the briefest of moments before she trailed behind me. I sent a text to Giuseppe, my head chef, to set up the interview course, a selection of dishes that Ariana had to pair with a limited selection of wines.

It was a test no one had yet passed, and once she failed, the message would be clear—I had given her a chance and found her lacking. I would still hire her, sure, but I would break her spirit first.

ARIANA DE LUCA

One second.

That's how long it took for me to open my big, fat mouth and pick a fight with Bastiano Romano. I had done it the second I saw him, pissed off at having had to wait for two hours—one hundred and twenty damn minutes—for him to show up. I had antagonized him again when we entered the bar.

And now, standing awkwardly by the door of his office while he completely ignored my existence, I was tempted to pick another fight. After all, I liked nothing about this situation, about having to go undercover with my real name, and having to put up with *his* callous, miserable ass made it worse.

A pregnant lapse of silence passed. Bastian sat in his seat, the chair pulled arm's length away from the desk, thighs far apart, staring at his phone. I waited several more minutes for him to invite me in, to offer me a seat. He didn't.

Another lapse of silence—loaded to me, but likely meaningless to him. I sighed, bit the bullet, and took a seat across from him at his desk.

"The fuck do you think you're doing?" His voice cut through the silence like a bullet slicing through skin.

"Sitting," I offered, dragging out the two syllables in a way that exposed what little I thought of his intellect.

"That's top of the line nubuck leather." He eyed where my body pressed against the seat. "If I wanted something cheap on my chairs, I would have gone with polyester."

I waited for the ball to drop. For his full lips to curl up in a smile and his mouth to form the words, "Just kidding!" But he didn't. Christ, he was serious.

My ass didn't budge from the chair. We stared at one another, our resolves locked in an inescapable impasse. A knock sounded at the door. I didn't dare look, and neither did he.

"What?" he barked, his cold eyes still on mine.

"Your meal, sir," came a voice, wrapped in hesitancy and delivered with caution.

Sir.

Not Bastiano.

Not Bastian.

Not Mr. Romano.

Sir.

My God, he was like this with everyone, commanding supremacy like it was reasonable to demand. Like he ran the world instead of a restaurant and bar in New York City. I couldn't imagine the balls it took to act and think like Bastiano Romano.

My eyes involuntarily dropped to his crotch. I couldn't see it past the bulk of his desk, but it was like my body had a mind of its own. His eyes instantly narrowed, whether at my defeat or the direction of my sight, I didn't know.

In the background, I heard the same voice whisper, "Uh, sir? I have to get back to the dining service."

With his eyes on mine, Bastiano snapped, "Then leave already."

"But the food—"

"Leave it in the break room."

The sound of a cart creaking filled the air, loud but not nearly as loud as the tension between us. As soon as whoever had come was gone, Bastiano stood and left, not bothering to talk to me.

Gritting my teeth, I reminded myself of the greater good to dealing with Bastian's bullshit. Plus, I wanted better assignments, and nothing screamed unqualified like flunking a simple interview.

I stood, following after him like a mindless puppy. I suspected that was the point of his game—to drill into me that I was less than him, merely a minion meant to follow his every command and do his bidding, even when he didn't speak or ask anything of me.

And because I loathed that feeling, I took a seat as soon as we entered the break room, not bothering to wait for him to offer one. The chair was plush leather that curved around my body when I sat. It was larger than the other chairs and boasted a taller back. Clearly, it was the one meant for him.

But as soon as I sat, the waiter, who had been standing off to the side, pushed the cart, which was more like a traveling table with silverware and a tablecloth, in front of me. He left quickly after, passing a stone-faced Bastiano on the way.

When the waiter was gone, Bastian closed the door and locked it. The daunting click sent a shudder down my spine. I watched warily as he took his time approaching me, a look of indifference pasted on his face.

He removed his suit jacket, revealing wide shoulders and a broad chest; took his time sitting; placed a cloth over his lap; loosened his diamond-plated Stefano Ricci tie; unlinked his Jacob & Co. cufflinks; tossed them onto the table like they hadn't cost him more than a hundred thousand dollars; and carefully rolled up the sleeves of his tailored white button down until they sat midway up his generous forearms.

Meanwhile, I sat there, bathing in silence and feigning patience—all while pretending I wasn't affected by his impromptu strip show. He was taking his damn time because he could. Another power play, but from him, I would expect nothing less. I might have taken his seat, but he had won the battle.

Finally, he spoke. "The wine is in the wine cart by the door."

He expected me to get it. Of course, he did. I sat still for a moment, my back relaxed against the better chair as I childishly relished in my smaller victory and pretended for a short-lived second that I had another choice.

He was removing the lid off one of the silver-lidded dishes on the table when I got up. He paused what he was doing, giving me his full attention, no doubt reveling in my obedience. In my submission.

My humiliation.

And for the first time since becoming an undercover agent, I truly had no idea what to do. I was used to letting the legends react. Allowing my covers to dictate my feelings, words, and actions. But I wasn't a legend right now.

I was Ariana De Luca, and while I had no clue what that entailed, I figured I could allow myself to act on instinct. But instinct wanted to fight. And pride wouldn't allow me to shut up and take Bastiano's torment.

I was going to get the wine cart. Truly, I was. Until I wasn't. Instead, I found myself walking to his side of the table, hovering above him. He pulled his seat back, angled it toward me, and pushed forward until I stood between his thighs.

His thighs were spread lazily apart, the tailor-made qiviut slacks pulled tightly across his powerful thighs. His strong forearms rested on each arm of the chair, and his lips twisted into something between a smirk and a sneer. He looked both devastatingly handsome and entirely entertained.

I was about to confront him, and he was amused. I wanted to hit him hard with the things I knew and he didn't. The FBI had been siphoning the online job applications for the bartending gig, leaving only the unqualified applicants.

Which meant I had this job.

Though he was acting like he had an alternative, the truth was he didn't. However today went, this job was mine. We both knew this, but I couldn't tell him that I did. And at that realization, the fight in me died a painful death, murdered in my throat and buried beside my indignation.

"Well?" He arched a perfect brow, so damned smug and rightfully so.

I pivoted before he could see the pink hue of my cheeks and revel in my embarrassment. This whole situation was a disaster. I couldn't be too combatant. I needed this job. But if I wanted to survive it, for my sanity's sake, I couldn't just take his shit and pretend I liked the stench.

Beside me, someone banged on the door. I glanced at it, my embarrassment heightened when I caught sight of Dana and another employee through the glass panel on the locked door. They were trying to get into the employee room, but at the sight of me, they stopped and stared as I approached the cart.

I could feel Bastiano's amusement from across the room as I obeyed him in front of an audience. My anger flared. We could have easily done this job interview in his spacious office, but he knew what time it was and had deliberately chosen a public area—at a time when employees were showing up—to publicize my humiliation.

"Problem?" he asked, and even though I couldn't see him, I could hear the satisfaction in his voice.

My fists tightly clasped the bar of the cart, and I tried with all my might to transfer my humiliation into it and ignore the crowd. When I turned around and pushed the cart to him like his personal fucking maid, I had a saccharine smile pasted on my face. Like I wasn't fazed by his radical brand of assholery.

"None at all." Keeping the smile on my face felt like stepping in quicksand and giving my consent to sink. "Forgive me. I'm used to being around gentlemen who'd never let a lady exert herself."

The wheel of the cart wobbled, and my smile faltered. The amusement on his face increased.

"If this is your idea of exerting yourself, perhaps the exercise will do you more good than harm."

I opened my mouth to respond, a witty retort resting heavily on the tip of my tongue, but I forced myself to swallow it. I couldn't win this fight. The best I could hope for was for it to end already and minimize my casualties.

I pushed the cart a little faster, hoping he wouldn't notice my eagerness to end this interview and see it as a victory. Each squeak of the wheel was a blemish in my armor, adding to my demise and his building pleasure. By the time I reached the table, I felt like I had lost a proxy war.

"These are our bestselling dishes. Find me a wine pairing for each one." He deliberately lifted the remaining metal lids slowly, each dish's revelation bringing conceit to his eyes.

A 'nduja and guanciale charcuterie.

All-belly porchetta.

Duck confit.

These were all dishes that were best suited for red wines. He had given me a limited selection of whites. *Jerk.*

"These pairings shouldn't be too hard for someone of your talents." He leaned back in his seat, making me feel like a zoo animal on display. Was it too much to hope he wouldn't throw rocks at me and demand I perform?

"Not at all." I forced an indifferent expression on my face as I inventoried my poor selection and poured a glass of wine in front of each dish.

Gewürztraminer for the charcuterie.

Crémant for the porchetta.

Marsanne for the duck.

They were good selections. Not what I would have normally chosen, but the best given the circumstances. I sat down, my fingers clenched in fists at my sides as I watched him languorously cut into the porchetta, deliberately taking his sweet time.

I was sitting in *his* ten-thousand-dollar chair, dressed to kill in a fitted cocktail dress the color of coal, my hair pulled up in a French chignon that had taken an hour to perfect, my makeup flawless and natural.

I was educated and witty, well-read and gifted in almost everything I had ever tried. I looked like I belonged on a goddamned runway in Milan, and in a war of words, I knew I could hold my own.

Yet, in front of him, my entire existence felt inadequate.

Futile.

My heart struggled to escape my chest as I waited for him to cut the tiniest of pieces off the porchetta. He added a bit of a roasted rosemary potato to the fork and dipped it in the peach glaze, his movements measured and painstakingly slow.

And just when I thought he was finally going to feed himself, he lifted the fork in my direction. My eyes widened as he waited for me to accept the offered bite, a convincing look of indifference pasted on his cold face.

Just do it and get it over with, I begged my pride.

I leaned forward, excruciatingly aware of the way the table dug into my cleavage at the movement. His eyes dropped to my breasts for a short-lived second, but it was enough to quicken my breath. I forced myself to ignore my audience—him more so than his employees—and opened my mouth for the bite.

He made me wait there, my mouth open, his fork suspended in the air, before he allowed the cold metal to touch the tip of my tongue. He broke our tense eye contact to watch my mouth wrap around the fork. When his eyes dilated and his nostrils flared, I leaned back, trying to put as much distance between us as possible.

Everything about the situation was erotic. My nipples pebbled painfully against the bare fabric of my dress. My pulse felt tangible. A light sheen of sweat coated my neck. And I knew that, if I were to touch myself, I'd find myself dripping wet.

For him.

The man who came from a family of monsters.

The man who was, quite probably, a monster himself.

And only after I let out an involuntary moan—whether at the taste of the food or the indecency of being fed by him, I didn't know—did he speak, "This is the quality of food we serve at L'Oscurità." His lips formed a derisive sneer as he met my eyes with unrelenting judgment. "No bartender worth hiring would ever pair a porchetta with a glass of Crémant at a three Michelin star restaurant. Not even on the bar side."

He tossed his napkin onto the table and stood. The tailored fit of his pants showed off a massive hard-on he didn't bother hiding. I couldn't even process the fact that I had given him an erection before he left the room, leaving behind his suit jacket, one-hundred-and-fourteen-thousand-dollar cufflinks, and what little dignity I had left.

War is a duty... The only real choice is whether you accept it, and what you fight for.

—Rick Riordan

ARIANA DE LUCA

It took a solid minute for me to pick up my jaw, but as soon as I recovered, I tore out of the break room like my life depended on it. I passed Dana and another waitress on the way out. Both of them were frozen in place, and I totally understood where they were coming from.

If I didn't need this damn job, I would have allowed

myself more time to gather my wits, too. But I needed this job, and Bastiano Romano was the only man who could give it to me. And that meant chasing after him like a One Direction groupie hungry for Harry Styles' *drumstick*.

I entered his office without knocking. A clever retort rested on the tip of my tongue, but it died at the mere sight of him standing in front of his desk. His pants were down at his ankles, one palm flat on the desk and the other wrapped around his cock.

His very long, very hard, very *pierced* cock.

I stuttered to a stop, desperately trying and failing to tear my eyes away from the sight. His eyes had been closed, but when the door slammed open, they shot to mine. And he didn't bother stopping.

I watched, mortified and turned on, as he slowly stroked himself, his grip firm and his eyes running down the length of my body. I meant to take a step back. Truly. Which was why I was horrified when I found myself walking forward.

First one step.

Then another.

And another.

Until I stood on the opposite side of the desk, close enough to touch him if I leaned far enough forward.

This was more than inappropriate. The door remained wide open. Anyone could walk by and see us like this, but I couldn't bring myself to care. I was too mesmerized. By his strokes. By the pre-cum glistening at the very tip of his cock. By the barbell that winked at me from the head of his cock. By the way his tailored shirt hung loosely around his muscled thighs.

I knew I hated his goddamned guts, but at that moment, I couldn't remember why.

What would Ariana do? my cover asked me.

I didn't know, so I followed my instincts, but instinct told me to stay.

Stupid, stupid instincts.

Bastian arched his brow, daring me to tell him I didn't want to see this. Daring me to touch him. To join him. He was shameless in his actions, taking his time with each stroke even with an audience. His palm swiped over the pre-cum, distributing it past his piercing and down his length with an alluring downward stroke.

I swayed forward, drawn by his erotic magnetism. If anything, his cock got harder the closer I came. My nipples pebbled under my dress. I knew he was staring at them. That, or the way my breasts heaved with each breath I forced myself to take.

Desire felt heavy on my tongue. I hated him, yes, but I wanted him all the same. Did that make me weak? Perhaps. But for the life of me, I couldn't remember the last time I had wanted anything this bad.

"Pull up your dress," he commanded, still rubbing the erection *I* had given him.

His voice snapped me out of my reverie, sending me into the land of reality.

What the fuck am I doing?

I took a step back. Then another. The backs of my knees hit an office chair, and I stumbled backward, the impossibly tight pencil skirt of my short dress rising up and tearing as my panty-clad ass fell onto the chair.

"That works, too." He let out a soft, amused laugh, causing humiliation and lust to surge through my veins.

I hated whoever made him this jaded that he couldn't treat me with the decency any other person would give me.

You have two legs and can walk right out of here, but you're not. You want to see this.

I couldn't even process where these thoughts were coming from as Bastian groaned in front of me. His hand formed a fist around the base of his cock. He thrust forward, shamelessly fucking his hand.

His eyes fixated on the space between my thighs, no doubt noticing the wet spot on my white panties. I hastened to get up and away from him, but he was coming, and I couldn't pull my eyes away as he shot thick ropes of cum onto his empty desk.

His eyes closed, and for a split second, bliss colored his handsome features. This was the most peaceful I had ever seen him. The most approachable, too. But when he was done, his face sobered.

His eyes opened and landed on mine with eerie precision, and I knew I wouldn't like what he was going to say.

"The fuck are you still doing here?"

"How are you feeling?"

Appalled.

Furious.

Like a pawn in everyone's life—Bastian's, Wilks', Ariana De Luca's.

I still didn't feel like I had an identity. Not with all my past covers muddling my mind and my current legend assuming my real self.

I said none of these things as I sat in Dr. Jennifer Clemson's office, a fancy building in the better part of Manhattan. She used this office for her non-FBI clientele, though she saw her FBI clients in another office outside the FBI building. It was what made her the perfect debrief shrink for legends.

FBI shrinks were a lot like plastic display fruit. Like the fake fruit, I came to these meetings to keep up appearances, but I'd never actually bit into them. I could pretend, but the effort and energy could be better spent on maintaining my legend, so I didn't bother.

I arched a brow, pasting indifference on my face as I curled my toes to release my frustration. "How do you think I'm feeling, Doc?"

I'd been putting this meeting off for a reason. The overload of frustration I felt near Bastian only strengthened my resolve to avoid Jenn. My best friend. My therapist. A conflict of interest, you'd think, but she was a consummate professional. And she could always see past my carefully-crafted barriers.

She leaned back in her seat, relaxing her posture. "Confrontational."

"That's not a feeling."

She ignored me and nodded at my head. "I see you've dyed your hair back."

I sighed, running my fingers through the waist-length strands. "My last legend was a stripper, so Wilks had me go peroxide blonde. Blue contacts, too. I ran color corrector through my hair as soon as I was done. Threw away those damn contacts and burned the trash bag for good measure."

Every legend came with a new appearance. Truthfully, I was addicted to this. I was addicted to the adrenaline and thrill that came with becoming a new person. And it wasn't because I had Daddy issues or hated who I was, though the first was arguably true. It was because I loved the idea that I had the power to be whomever I wanted.

But lately, I had forgotten who I truly was. Sometimes, I forgot what I really looked like—exotic blue-green eyes; cascading, wavy hair that wasn't quite brown or blonde; and a tall, hourglass body, courtesy of the hand-to-hand training my combat instructor had me doing.

I fidgeted with my hands. "What do you know about my current legend?"

"Not much. I'll be briefed later this week. Being your handler..." She crossed her legs and made a circular gesture between us. "This was all very last minute."

I nodded, expecting as much. I considered addressing my concerns on why this legend felt more last minute than the rest but dismissed them as paranoia and, unfortunately, inexperience. Just because I'd never been on such a rushed assignment didn't mean it never happened. Wilks sheltered me. An unfortunate fact. I wanted the kiddie gloves off, so I couldn't complain when it happened.

"The assignment began." I ran a finger through my hair and averted my eyes. "I went au naturel." I kept out the part about using my name. She'd learn soon enough, and I didn't want to be there for her pity when she did.

"That's dangerous."

My eyes darted to hers. I studied her body language and stiffened at what I found. "You know," I accused. "How?"

Only Wilks and the first shrink the FBI had appointed me knew what my last name meant.

She met my eyes, unfazed. "Wilks briefed me on your last name when you first started working here."

My nails dug into my palms. Who else had he told?

"And you've kept this secret from me for six years?"

"As have you."

She leaned forward and slanted her chin on her delicate fist. A pen rested in her other hand, poised readily over her navy-blue spiral notebook, though I had never once seen her write in it.

I suspected she was about to shrink me, so I spoke before she could, "It's not exactly something I'd shout across the rooftops, especially given where I work."

"Fair enough." She tilted her head and did a thorough job of scrutinizing me. "So, how do you feel, keeping all of these secrets?"

"Like it's my job." I turned the tables. "It's your job, too."

"Are you reminding me to keep your secret?"

"No. I'm reminding you of who we are."

"And who are *you*, Ariana De Luca?"

You have no idea who you are, the little piece of me that had been torn apart by all my legends and pieced together all broken and mismatched insisted.

I pasted a paper smile on my face and ignored my inner demons. "I'm a special agent for the Legends division of the FBI."

"That's not who you are. That's *what* you are."

I sighed. "Can you drop the shrink act and just be my best friend right now? I need to process the fact that my best friend knows that I'm," I lowered my voice despite the otherwise empty room, "a De Luca."

Jenn snorted. "Everyone who knows you in your office knows you're a De Luca, Ari."

I sat up from the couch, alarmed.

She rolled her eyes. "They just don't know that you're one of *those* De Lucas."

It was my turn to roll my eyes as I laid back down. "I'd hardly call myself one of them. They don't even know I exist."

Thanks to my mom, who had done all she could to hide my existence until her dying breath.

"Fair enough. By the way, it's not a shrink *act*. I actually *am* a shrink, something you seem to forget every time you step into this office."

I laughed, latching onto her lighthearted words to shift the conversation. "Well, shrink, am I cleared for my next legend?" I crossed my fingers behind my back, unsure whether I was hoping she would clear me or hoping she wouldn't.

"Of course, Ari."

I nodded, stood up, headed toward the door, and turned to face Jenn when I reached it. Thanks to my last legend, I hadn't seen her in a while, so I took the time to observe her. With blonde hair, a freckled face, and giant doe eyes, she looked too innocent for a job which required facing other people's demons.

And I wondered, not for the first time, how she was my shrink despite the apparent conflict of interest. I figured that I should finally ask, just in case this legend was my last. Pretty likely considering Bastian hated my guts and the whole De Luca thing.

"Not that I'm complaining," I began, "but I've always wondered how you're my shrink. I mean, everyone in the department knows we're best friends. Isn't that a conflict of interest?"

"After Emma Stevens retired, I'm the only psychologist in the region with the clearance to know you're a legend."

"Fair enough." I paused a beat, noticing the amount of weight she had lost while I was away. It was slight, but I had always been one to pick up on details, and I cared enough to ask, "Are you alright, Jenn?"

"This job—our jobs—takes a toll on us. We age a lifetime in a year, and I'm supposed to help the agents process it, but sometimes I forget I need to process it, too."

My fingers clutched the doorknob tighter. I understood what she meant, because I danced around the topics during my sessions, never digging deep into my problems—and there were so, so many problems. I should have taken the time to unravel them and heal, but I could never bring myself to.

"I'm here for you. You know that? Say the word, and we can quit our jobs and run off to the Caribbean. You'd have to pay for it of course. I make less than a lemonade stand."

Jenn laughed, closed her notebook, uncrossed her legs, and stood up. When she walked over to give me a hug, I let her, relaxing into the familiarity of our friendship—the longest one I had ever had with anyone.

"You're always worrying about everyone else." She gave me a sly grin that immediately had me wary. "You should worry about yourself, Ari."

The way she said it, like she knew something that I didn't, caused me to narrow my eyes. "Why?"

"Have you seen the Romano family?" She paused. "Bastiano Romano has a reputation. Maybe it's all rumors, but even if one percent of it is true—good luck, girl. You're going to need it."

I hated that, for the first time since I'd met him, I'd finally pushed Bastian out of my mind for a minute, and she'd pushed him right back inside.

But she was right.

Bastiano Romano was first and foremost a Romano. And the Romano family was tight-knit. Secretive. Intense. Impenetrable. They had their lives locked in a vault—booby-trapped, rigged to blow, heavily guarded, and padlocked from the general public despite the recognition their name garnered worldwide. If you put anyone up against them, I would have bet on the Romano family to win every damn time.

Including against the bureau.

But I was a De Luca, and depending on which side of the law you sat on, that was the closest a girl could get to invincibility.

It is the duty that separates men from boys.

—Aporva Kala

BASTIANO ROMANO

Motherfucker.

Dildo breath.

Cum stain.

I sorted through my inventory of curses as Gio and I sat in a corner booth at the bar, waiting for Uncle Vince to show up. I loved my Uncle Vince. The man got me like no one else did, but he was always goddamned late, and no amount of love made tolerating his tardiness any easier.

Especially when I marinated in the company of Gio while he was in rare form.

"How about her?" My dad pointed to a girl sitting alone at a center table.

With her dark hair and heavy Italian features, I recognized her immediately.

"Gio." I raised my eyebrows and shot him a glassy stare. "That's my cousin."

"So? The British do it."

"Not for a few hundred years."

I caught a flash of skin as a girl approached the table, adjusting the neckline of her dress along the way. She'd gotten a few feet from our booth when Dana moved to intercept, narrowing in on her like a frat boy at a two-for-one lap dance sale.

Earlier today, I had demanded she escort any mafia bunnies she saw out of L'Oscurità. I was using my ex-girlfriend as my personal bouncer, but I couldn't care less about the ethics of the situation. All that mattered was she'd do it.

And I knew she would because she was fucking obsessed with me.

Her obsession started the moment she saw me. It was one of those things you could just tell. Shortness of breath. Glazed eyes. Difficulty breathing. Sometimes, there was even wheezing involved. She was either severely allergic to me or obsessed with me.

Her obsession would likely be a problem down the road, but when that time came, I'd fire her, slap a restraining order on her perky ass, and move on to the next hostess. Only this time, I'd hire her without having fucked her.

See? I was capable of personal growth.

"Gio." My voice remained firm, as unwavering as always. Not that he gave a damn. "Ten mob bunnies in half as many days? You've got me walking around like I'm Hefner reincarnate."

He needed to get it through his thick skull that I'd never be interested in the Romano business. He'd taken Elsa from me, and the only reason I still talked to him was for my sister Tessie and because it had been Elsa's choice to accept the bribe.

Gio, my uncles, and the rest of my family risked their freedom on a daily basis. For what? Money? We had enough. We could legitimize our businesses today, and the generations of Romanos to come would still be filthy rich.

Gio took his lazy-ass time shifting his body, returning his wandering eye's attention from a low hemline to me. "How are you so sure it's me sending them your way?"

"It sure as hell isn't Uncle Eli or Uncle Frankie. They don't give two shits. And Uncle Vince would be straightforward about it. No pussyfooting."

He absently rubbed his arm, cocked his head to the side, and lifted a single brow. "Pussyfooting? What're you trying to say, son?"

A smile tugged at the edges of my lips. "Exactly what I said, Gio."

"Huh. I'd wipe that goddamn smirk off your face with my fist, but your mother is coming in with your sister any second now."

We shared a tired grin at the mention of the woman.

I ran a weary hand down my face. "Man, Ma hates blood. She married into the wrong family."

Not that hers was any better.

Gio laughed, despite the fact that neither he nor she had a choice in their nuptials. Maybe that—the lack of control even one of the most influential men I knew had over his life—was why I held so much disdain for the mafia business, even before Elsa and I broke it off.

I eyed my whiskey sour, the drink reminding me of my meeting with Ariana De Luca tomorrow. "You ever hear the name Ariana De Luca?"

Gio's eyes narrowed as he straightened, finally giving me his full attention. "You gunning after a De Luca now?" Disapproval radiated off of him in fierce, unrelenting waves. "Don't. They're batshit insane, and we don't need any of that right now."

Rumor had it the De Lucas hadn't been batshit insane for a while now. Not with Angelo De Luca ousted and his son Damian in his place. I didn't broach the subject, however, because the De Luca syndicate was a joke, and the Romano syndicate was anything but.

"I'm not gunning after anyone, Gio." I downed my drink.

The more I talked about the family business, the more I wanted a drink. At this rate, I was well on my way to becoming an alcoholic. Maybe I could eat away my frustrations instead. Consume my sorrows, get rid of my six pack—and the mafia bunnies that loved said six pack. Two birds. One stone.

Gio stared at me with sober eyes. "Because you're not in."

He meant the mafia, and while we both knew Romano blood coursed through my veins, we also knew I didn't want the responsibility the name brought. We didn't speak about it, at least not explicitly, and I suspected it would always be the elephant in the room.

But Gio had been known to drop some damn impressive

passive aggressive hints here and there. In other words, pussyfooting. It was why he sent those mafia bunnies my way, and it was why he would continue to do so. It was why he always wanted to meet at a Romano-affiliated business. And it was also why, thanks to Asher, he tolerated me working at L'Oscurità if I had to go outside the Romano name.

I ignored his words, fostering the silence like a five-star general preparing for a battle speech. We were at war with our eyes, each blink a clash of swords, each breath a chink in our armor.

He caved first. "Ariana De Luca. I'll look into her. See what I can find."

I nodded once, a brief affirmation of my victory.

Elsa sent another text, though I'd just sent her a hundred large. For the past eight years, I'd funded Elsa's life. I paid her mortgage, her car payments, her health insurance, her credit card bills, her groceries, and a monthly allowance most people wouldn't make in three years. Talking to her placed a giant cloud over an already gloomy day. How much money did one woman need?

Uncle Vince came in, drawing attention from the bunnies as he made his way to our booth and sat beside me. His eyes swung once to one of the bartenders on shift before returning to me. "Keep an eye on Graham. He's the one we flagged as a potential rat." His murmur drifted my way, soft but straight to the point.

Graham bartended here, which meant I'd be spending more time on this side of L'Oscurità. My mind immediately flashed to Ariana De Luca and her infuriating behavior, but I pushed the thought aside. Not the time nor the place.

I nodded to Uncle Vince and turned to Gio. "See? No pussyfooting."

Gio scowled. I smirked. Uncle Vince sighed. And between the three of us, it was likely that none of us had seen Uncles Eli and Frankie in a while. This was a typical night with the Romano family, except for Asher's absence. And the fact that my mom and little sister were coming to meet us.

My eyes swung to the door when I caught sight of my little sister Tessie, her hand clenched tightly to my mother's. She was all sunshine and smiles, her curly black hair a long, unruly mess that bounced with each excited step she took.

The minute she saw me, she took off in a sprint. She clambered clumsily over Uncle Vince and onto my lap as soon as she was within touching distance. I wrapped an arm around her waist to steady her and let out a soft laugh, one I reserved strictly for her.

When she was a baby, she looked nothing like Gio and me. So much so that I questioned her paternity. After all, it wouldn't have been a stretch with the strained relationship Ma and Gio shared.

But as time passed, the hue of her irises had darkened, her hair had transformed from honey to dusk, and she had grown far taller than most kids her age. Now, at eight years old, she was a Romano through and through—save for the fact that she spent most of her time living in Rossi territory. If it were up to me, that would be rectified immediately.

I leaned down, captured the tip of Tessie's ear between my teeth, and pretended to munch on it. "My favorite little bear. Just in time for dinner," I murmured softly into her ear.

She giggled, turning on my lap to face me, her lanky body barely fitting on top of mine. "People don't eat bears."

"You'd be surprised," I muttered, eyeing Ma as she reached our table.

She took her place next to Gio, and his arm came around

her so naturally, you'd think we were the fucking Brady Bunch.

"New haircut? It's nice," I said like the best fucking son ever.

I gave her the requisite compliment. As far as I was concerned, I could check out for the rest of this family reunion. Maybe even take Tessie into my office, watch the security feed with her, and make fun of what people were doing. People were idiots, which made people watching our favorite pastime. Well, it was mine at least. Tessie would learn.

"Thanks, Bastian." Ma touched the tips of her blonde hair, a faint smile on her lips and appreciation gleaming in her light blue eyes. "I cut nine inches off in September."

As in eight or so months ago.

Did I compare us to the Brady Bunch?

More like the fucking Lannisters.

Duty doesn't always fit comfortably.

—Shannon Hale

ARIANA DE LUCA

Screw this job.

Screw the FBI.

Screw L'Oscurità.

Screw Bastian.

I paced the length of my apartment, a nice but small flat close to the Wilton University area. The FBI had paid for it in cash for the year. If my legend ran over, I would be taking over the payments with the bartending salary.

It was two in the morning, but I couldn't sleep. I was wired. The sight of Bastian's cock was seared into my mind, and I didn't know what to think about what had happened. I had walked in on him, but he could have at least stopped.

Or you could have walked away.

I stuttered to a stop, hoping the Devil's advocate in my head wasn't me, the real me, the one peeping its head out now that I had finally assumed my identity. If you could call it an identity since I'd shoved myself under so many covers for so long, I still didn't understand who I was or what I wanted.

What if the real me turned out to be a horrible agent, a deviant person, and a sex-crazed woman with no boundaries?

Because I couldn't stop thinking about him. The way his cock looked, hard and ready for me, pre-cum dripping past his piercing. And my goodness, his piercing. I didn't know how I was supposed to feel about walking in on him.

My last legend would have taken advantage of the situation, and the one before that would have been pissed. But as Ariana? I didn't know what to make of it all. Bastian had humiliated me all day, but I liked the challenge. I liked the thrill that accompanied defying him, and better yet, I liked how he pushed me.

Fire met each opposition. We were an inferno set to combust, and we had convinced ourselves we were fireproof. We were going to burn, but each flame was gilded, each blister worth the agony.

I knew deep down my lack of resolve was shameful. My lust—pathetic. But fighting Bastian *felt* intense, and no amount of logic could control my feelings. He was a potent high I couldn't achieve with adrenaline, alcohol, or any other vice I could think of. And I recognized the signs of an impending addiction.

To make matters worse, I still hadn't received a call or email or *anything* to tell me that I had gotten the job. Dread settled in my gut as I paced, paced, and paced some more. The phone rang, and I knew instantly who it was.

Who else would call at two in the morning as if I were at his beck and call?

I clutched the phone tightly, my fingers whitening from the pressure. "Hello?" My voice was breathless, but I didn't have it in me to put on a façade.

Not after what had happened.

"Training begins Monday. Half past noon. Black dress. Sleeveless but not strapless. Cocktail. Mid-thigh. Cleavage light. We don't want you looking like you frequent street corners at night. No heels. You'll regret it. Hair pulled back. Make up light. Natural." His voice dipped lower. "And Ariana?"

The way he said my name, like a horrible, reluctant caress, had me struggling to breathe. I wanted to argue, yell, whatever, but I didn't have it in me in this moment.

Monday, I would be ready, but right now, all I could manage was a ragged, "Yes?"

"Don't be late."

If I knew what was best for me, I wouldn't show up at all.

I didn't know why I was surprised by his tardiness. But I knew I was sick of waiting. The doorknob taunted me, demanding I pick it. My hand pressed against the handle, and I swore I wasn't going to do anything stupid. Like barging into L'Oscurità while it was closed. But I couldn't resist the temptation. I twisted it slowly, testing the lock, and was startled when the knob turned all the way.

My legs stuttered to a stop at the sight of some of the most influential mafia figures in the country gathered at a table together. Giovanni Romano, Vincent Romano, Bastiano Romano, and Asher Black sat in one of the four-seat booths on the opposite side of the bar.

A young girl, who I recognized from my files as Bastian's little sister Contessa "Tessie" Romano, ran around the bar, weaving between tables, bumping into chairs and sending them flying different ways. She laughed when one of the chairs she bumped into slid toward Vince, and he made a show of pretending to fall forward into the table's edge.

I wasn't surprised when Bastian was the first to notice me, his eyes connecting with mine as soon as I stepped into the bar. His lips curled upward in a sneer, an ugly twist of the mouth that only served to make him more devastatingly handsome.

I steeled myself, forcing my body to hide my apprehension. He wasn't going to be nice to me today. I had no disillusions, but I needed him to know I wasn't backing down. We were already at war, and I was prepared to win. No matter the cost. That brief moment of vulnerability I had felt after watching him touch himself was just that—brief.

I took a defiant step forward.

His eyes narrowed, and he stared me down like a race car driver gunning for the finish line. "You're late."

Four sets of eyes turned my way, including Tessie's. She took off in a run toward me, her eager legs pounding on the floor with each step.

My jaw set, and despite the normal volume of my voice, it boomed in the empty bar. "I was outside."

Waiting.

Always waiting.

His sneer hid thinly-veiled amusement, and I knew he'd had me waiting outside on purpose. "Why?" He drew out the syllable. "The door's been unlocked the whole time."

Simple words, but they made me feel foolish, even though I knew why I hadn't checked the door—I wasn't supposed to draw unnecessary attention to myself. Like entering without being let in. I'd knocked, no one had answered, and that should have been that.

Still, my neck flushed red, and the unwelcome heat of embarrassment traveled up and down my body. I hated the way he made me feel. The way he could have me loathing him one second and lusting after him the next. Or worse—at the same time.

I ignored his question, praying he'd spare me his onslaught given his present company. "Are we training or not?"

I was dressed like he had demanded me to.

I had arrived when he had ordered me to.

And I had waited when I had wanted nothing more than to leave him hanging, my duty to the FBI and this country be damned.

If he said no, I would march up to Wilks and demand a different assignment for all I cared. This time, I wouldn't take no for an answer.

Bastiano's eyes had already returned to the stacks of paper on the table he sat at. "Wait at the bar. We're just finishing up."

They weren't just finishing up.

I waited at the bar, on a stool facing away from them, for half an hour. I suspected that was on purpose, too. After all, everything represented a power play with Bastian. I tried and failed to study the men in the reflection of the frosted mirror behind the bar.

Judging by the size and color of the paper I had seen earlier, they were examining several blueprints. Of what, I didn't know, but I was surprised to see Asher here. Word was, he had gotten out of the mafia a while back, yet here he was, sitting in a closed-door meeting with two iconic mafia figures and two other Romanos.

Granted, one of the two was eight years old.

Speaking of the younger Romano, Tessie perched on the bar stool two seats down from mine, her short legs dangling in the air, while her brother ignored my very existence from afar. Meanwhile, she stared unabashedly at me and had been for the past thirty minutes.

I kept silent, a tad ashamed that an eight-year-old girl

could make me feel so uncomfortable. Finally, I turned to her, and from the corner of my eye, I caught Bastian lifting his head to stare at us.

I did what I did best and ignored him.

"Can I help you?" I kept my voice low.

As annoyed as I was with Bastian, I didn't want to disrupt the meeting in the off chance I'd get any intel. Unlikely, given the distance, but I'd still try.

Gravity lined Tessie's face, her brows pinched together as she matched my low tone. "Finally." Her voice dropped even lower. "My brother is going to fire you if he finds out it took you this long to take my order."

She said it with a nonchalance someone her age had no business possessing, but I wasn't the least bit surprised. She was a Romano, and if she was anything like her brother, she was well on her way to developing a sharp tongue any politician would be jealous of.

A reluctant smile edged its way onto my face. "What do you want to drink?"

She scrunched up her nose, eyeing the selection of liquor on the top shelf. "Mommy says I can't drink soda. She says drinking soda is like drinking diabetes." She turned to me. "And I don't want diabetes. Uncle Benny has diabetes, and he always has to prick himself with needles. I hate blood. And needles."

By Uncle Benny, she probably meant Benedetto Rossi, the head of the Rossi crime syndicate. I hadn't known about his diabetes, and I made a note to pass the info along to the FBI during my next check-in, along with the fact that Asher was here in a meeting with Vince, Bastian, and Gio.

I scanned the selection of drinks. Her non-alcoholic, non-soda choices were limited to water and the sugary juices L'Oscurità used for mixed drinks.

"Water or juice?" I made my way behind the bar, suppressing a shiver as Bastian's eyes followed me.

I didn't have to look at him to know he was staring. As much as I hated him, I was aware of his every move, and a part of me thought that sentiment was reciprocated.

"Mommy says I can't drink the 'manufactured sugary crap' here either." She sighed, dragging the sound out in a way which emphasized her disappointment and tugged at my heartstrings.

I felt for the girl even as I stumbled a little in shock at her use of the word "crap." She was her brother's sister, through and through, manipulating my every emotion in her favor. Glancing at her doe eyes, the same mysterious, dusky shade as her brother's, I couldn't help but cave.

"I think I see some lemons back here. I can make you some homemade lemonade if you'd like." I grabbed a few lemons, sliced them in half, and began juicing them.

She furrowed her brows, and her eyes darted from side to side. When she spoke, I could barely hear her despite the silence in the air. "But lemonade has sugar in it."

I wiggled my brows. A wide grin spread over my face. "So?"

Her responding smile whipped the breath from me, a smile so wide and gorgeous, it was a tragedy she wasn't gracing the cover of a Gap Kids ad. "Now I know why my brother likes you so much!"

I froze, my hand halting on top of the sugar container. "What did you say?"

"Bastian. He likes you."

She was wrong.

So wrong.

But I entertained her regardless. "Why would you say that?"

"Duh! He keeps staring at you." She scrunched her nose up. "It's weird. And creepy."

And then she leaned forward, took the spoon from my fingers, added double the sugar I would have, and drank her lemonade like she hadn't just left me reeling.

In happiness or unhappiness,
living is a duty, and must be done thoroughly.

—Ellis Peters

BASTIANO ROMANO

My eyes drifted to Ariana De Luca, and I hated myself for it.

I had always been unflinching. Resolute. It was ingrained in my DNA, passed on from generation to generation by persistent Romano elders, used to either being handed what they wanted or taking it with unrelenting force.

But what I wanted right now was to look away and gain back the sliver of control I had somehow lost when she'd walked in on me stroking myself to the image of her lips around a forkful of food, pretending it was my cock on her tongue and not the overpriced rosemary-glazed porchetta.

Yet, no matter how hard I'd tried, I couldn't look away. It was just a sliver of control relinquished. A seemingly innocuous shard. But it was more than anyone else had ever stolen from me in eight years—enough for her presence to distract me and the memory of the wet spot on her panties to haunt my thoughts—and I wanted my control back.

Maybe I was being punished for living my life as a miserable jerk, avoiding my duty to my family as often as I could and treating everyone like they were personally to blame for Elsa's greed. Maybe this was the universe's way of punishing me—throwing Ariana De Luca into my life and making it so that I couldn't look away.

And I couldn't.

For the life of me, I couldn't figure out why.

The curve of her neck as she threw her head back and laughed at something Tessie said had my mouth watering. I wanted to sink my teeth in her neck, draw blood, and revel at the sight of the vibrant red dripping down her otherwise untarnished skin. I wanted to steal back the sliver of control she'd taken from me—and then another sliver, just because I could. Her blood would smell like revenge and taste like the filthy things I wanted to do to her. I could almost taste it now.

I was a sick fuck, and I needed to look away before I convinced myself that I could blur the lines with my future employee, never mind the fact the lines had already been blurred when she'd taken unconscious steps closer to me and I came in front of her.

I tore my eyes away from her, promising myself that I wouldn't entertain my X-rated thoughts about her, let alone in the presence of my family.

Asher pulled a blueprint to the top of the pile. "How about we do it at Valentino's?"

I leaned back in my chair, counting down from ten as I eyed the ceiling.

Ten.

Must not punch Asher.

Nine.

Must not punch Asher.

Eight.

Must not punch Ash—

Gio, ever the sweetheart, was less tactful in hiding his irritation at Asher. He groaned, pounded a fist on the table, and barked, "Christ, Asher. Valentino's?"

The little shit was amused. Probably had his signature pretty boy, I'm-smarter-than-you-and-I-know-it smirk on his face, too. "What's wrong with Valentino's?" Asher drawled out, taking his sweet-ass time to form the question.

Nothing was wrong with Valentino's.

What *was* wrong was that it was Asher's ninth wedding venue choice of the day, and we had already planned security for the first eight choices. Granted, as soon as Asher suggested La Chiesa di San Valentino, I knew it was the best fit.

The Romano connection to the church dated back hundreds of years to the mid-1800s. When the prohibition era came, my great grandfather had tunnels built all over New York City and into the land past the boroughs.

There were tunnels connecting Valentino's to just about every Romano safe-hold establishment in the city, which meant the businesses connected to the tunnels served as safe entrances and safe exits.

The only reason I hadn't suggested it in the first place was because it would be a pain in the ass to fortify all of the entrances. We would have to deploy all of our soldiers to cover the ground and have Black Security, Asher's security company, cover the church's interior and exterior. But Asher never did things half-assed for Lucy. He was full-blown whipped and loving it.

Righting myself, I eyed Uncle Vince, who was usually the voice of reason in these situations. Gio and Asher fought. It was what they did. There was never any malice between them. They just liked to exchange words.

Gio fought because he couldn't understand the concept of someone not being intimidated by him, and Asher fought because he was a smug asshole that liked to fuck with anyone and everyone.

Uncle Vince usually intervened before someone bruised their ego (usually Gio), but when I looked at him, he wasn't paying attention. His hair frizzed outward, a tad untidy. A thin layer of bags lined his eyes, which was odd for him, but I figured we all were a bit fatigued from this drawn-out meeting. A soft smile ignited his face as he stared in the direction of the bar.

I followed his line of sight—right to Ariana De Luca and Tessie.

They were laughing.

Fucking. Laughing.

Again.

I hadn't held up this meeting on purpose, but an hour and a half had passed since Ariana had barged into the bar. She wasn't supposed to be laughing. She was supposed to be pissed, her eyes blazing so red it made my cock twitch. Instead, those luring irises—the color of Caribbean waters—glowed, and she leaned forward in rapt attention as she talked with Tessie.

And Tessie, the little traitor, was looking at Ariana *De Luca* like she was a backstage pass to a My Little Pony concert, or whatever the fuck kids listened to these days. Knowing Tessie, it was probably NPR.

Tessie and Ariana's laughter surprised me.

Hell, it blew me away.

Tessie was hardly a social recluse, but outside of the family, she wasn't exactly a social butterfly either. Down in Rossi territory, Ma kept her in a tight family- and friends-only circle that had yet to be infiltrated. In California, Tessie was homeschooled by a tutor, went nowhere without a family member or bodyguard present, and rarely spoke to outsiders.

Yet, she was laughing with Ariana *De Luca*.

Sure, I had run a background check on Ariana, and it had come up clean—she wasn't one of *those* De Lucas. But still, it was a little uncomfortable to watch the two already so chummy together.

Ariana was monopolizing my attention again, unwittingly stealing another bit of my control. If I didn't build a larger wall between us and soon, I'd possess no sovereignty over my own mind.

Forcing myself to ignore both Tessie and Ariana, I kicked at Uncle Vince's leg under the table. When he turned to meet my eyes, I gave a lazy head nod toward Asher and Gio, who were still going at it, Asher with a carefree smirk on his face and Gio with a slight frown.

Uncle Vince rapped a knuckle on the table once, then

pointed between them. "You two look like you belong on a marriage counseling ad."

"Only if I get to be the scorned wife." Asher leaned forward, nuzzled his face against Gio's shoulder, and made an exaggerated show of fake tears. "Oh, Dr. Phil, he's cheating on me. With another man."

Cue more fake tears.

He could be theatric for a stone-cold killer. When Asher and Lucy were attacked in their penthouse, Asher had his security guards play dead while he picked off his intruders one by one, toying with them, each death a taunt, each second he remained undetected in the dark a tease.

Me? I would have picked them off quickly. Efficiently, with little to no pretense. I didn't have Asher's patience, and I. Didn't. Give. A. Fuck. Since when has patience ever mattered?

Gio pushed Asher's head off his shoulder. "Fuck off."

I ignored the three of them, my interest drifting back to Ariana. I couldn't look away. *Why couldn't I look away?* As much as she annoyed me, she also demanded my rapt attention. Perhaps that was *why* she annoyed me in the first place. That, or her smart mouth and tendency to wage battles against me that she could never win.

I was the dark prince. Jaded. Devious. And a little too fucked up for my own good. I was the guy women talked about ten or twenty years from now, whispering in secret about how I'd given them the only orgasm they could remember only to never call them back.

Ariana De Luca, on the other hand, looked like she belonged in a jewelry commercial for wedding rings, standing between a slightly overweight golden retriever; some pathetic, clinically handsome sap, who doted on her every move; and their two-point-five blonde-haired, blue-eyed children.

When I'd first met her, I had dismissed her. After our last encounter, which ended with her on her back and my cum jetting onto the desk, I knew better. I couldn't deny her allure, something that couldn't be pinned down or described in a way that truly did her justice.

She was wearing a black cocktail dress.

Just like I'd asked her to.

Mid-thigh.

Just like I'd asked her to.

Light cleavage.

Just. Like. I'd. Fucking. Asked. Her. To.

Her obedience, unfortunately, was as much of a turn on as her defiance.

And I decided, then and there, that I wanted to fuck her.

Hell, perhaps I had decided that the moment she had served me a glass of Gewürztraminer with the charcuterie platter. The way her lips looked wrapped around a forkful of porchetta only sealed my intentions. Any day now, L'Oscurità would get an applicant worth hiring. When that day came, I would fuck Ariana, and then I'd fire her.

Problem solved.

My phone buzzed. Elsa. Again.

Asher leaned over Gio, plucked my phone from my hand, and answered. "Most women are capable of taking hints, but you're a special breed of desperate, aren't you, Elsa?" My lips tilted up in a ghost of a smile until Asher's eyes widened, and he said, "Oh. Hey, kiddo. Thought you were your mom. Yeah, he's right here. I'll hand the phone to him."

I'd already stood and pried the phone from his fingers before I dipped into my office. "Everett? Is something wrong?"

"Mom's gone again."

My fist nearly met the wall until I reeled it back. "Again? What do you mean again?"

"She left yesterday and didn't come back."

"Who are you with right now?"

"Nancy." His nanny. I trusted her. Vetted her myself. Then again, I'd trusted Elsa at one point, too. "I'm booking you a flight here."

It slipped past my lips before I could take it back. I couldn't fly to Alabama. That was Andretti territory, and we were at war. Everett couldn't fly here either, because for his safety, no one outside my inner circle could know he existed. Not while he lived in Alabama. Elsa didn't know why, but she knew something stopped me from going to Alabama and taking Everett back. She dangled it in front of my nose each time she wanted more money from me.

Are you sure you want Everett in New York? It doesn't seem like it.

That was all it took before another hundred grand popped into her bank account. She had the best bargaining chip in the world, and fuck that. My son should not have been a bargaining chip. Ever.

"Really?" The excitement in Everett's voice was a blade to my heart. "I'm coming to New York? But I have school!"

I bit back the relief as I took my out, no matter how much I wanted to see him. I'd bet he'd grown since I'd last seen him.

"Right." The apology in my voice couldn't be clearer. I hated that I was having this conversation in the first place. "Maybe next time. We'll convince your mom to fly you up here in your own jet. We can stay at your Uncle Vince's house in the Hamptons and go to the beach every day."

"Promise?"

"Promise." Fuck, I hoped I could keep it. "Now put Nancy on the phone, okay?"

A minute later, Nancy answered, her voice tired and aged. "Mr. Romano?"

"Where's Elsa?"

"Oh, she'll be back soon. I'm sure." She didn't sound sure.

"That's not what I asked. Where is Elsa?"

A beat of silence passed before she relented, "S-she went on a date, sir."

"Thank you."

I hung up and dialed Elsa's cellphone. Voicemail. Slamming my hand on the wall, I hung up. Any text or voicemail I left in this state would only hurt. She had all the cards. I was so damned sick of it.

When I got back to the table, Asher and Gio were still fighting over his wedding venues. I was tired of it all. My patience for their indecision far exceeded my normal threshold. My knuckles rapped the table once to gather their attention.

"Valentino's will work. We can send out texts an hour before the wedding with the location for each guest's arrival."

A question lingered in all their eyes, but I ignored them all.

My thumb traced the length of a tunnel on one of the blueprints. "One hidden guard outside each entrance, one at the entrance to check guest lists, one at the underground entrance to the church, and three dozen at the church dressed as wedding guests, along with your personal Black Security guards.

"You'll have at least a dozen undercover Black Security guards patrolling the exterior, dressed as beggars or hot dog vendors. That kind of thing." I made eye contact with Asher.

"I trust you'll be able to coordinate the rest of the details with your security team and event planner."

Without another word, I stood up, pushed my chair in, and headed to the bar, my message clear—get the fuck out. L'Oscurità was Asher's restaurant and bar, sure, but it was mine in all the ways that mattered.

Asher respected that.

My staff respected that.

My customers respected that.

If only my family would respect that.

When she saw me approach, Tessie casually slid her glass of contraband lemonade toward Ariana before her eyes lit up. She turned to me. "Are you done? I don't want Aunt Lucy to die, but you guys have been here all day!"

At Tessie's words, Ariana straightened up, and I cursed my baby sister's big mouth.

My voice was firm when I pointedly said, "Aunt Lucy's

not dying. We're going over the security for her wedding as a precaution. There's a difference." I added the last part for Ariana's benefit, because I didn't want her running to the cops about Lucy.

Tessie's intelligent eyes narrowed. "Are you using big words because you want me to stop talking? Because I know what 'precaution' means."

Of course, she did.

I leaned against the bar, a sour taste in my mouth as I spoke. "Sorry, kiddo. I've got to train Ariana. Her first shift is next week."

Tessie and I rarely saw each other, but I had a thriving business to run, employees to care for, and customers to think about. It sucked, but it was also the real world. I had a son in Alabama and a baby sister in California. Meanwhile, the Romano territory covered Eastern Canada and North-east America. And though I wanted to protect Tessie, with our blood, she'd learn soon enough how fucked up life could be.

Ariana looked between me and Tessie, her eyes briefly skimming my face before settling on Tessie's. "I don't see why you can't be here while I train."

Tessie leaned forward. Her eyes glowed as she nodded her head like one of those hula girl bobblehead dolls on the dash of a car going a hundred and twenty miles per hour. "Can I?" She pressed her palms together and intertwined her fingers. "Please, please, please, Bastian."

I wanted to spend time with my sister, sure, but I didn't want her here to witness my relentless battle with Ariana.

Battle.

Feud.

Foreplay.

Whatever you called it, it was inappropriate for an eight-year-old kid to watch.

But it was already hard to say no to Tessie once, and I couldn't say no to her twice, so I nodded my head. Tessie jumped off her seat like a flying monkey, clung to me tightly as I caught her mid-air, and pressed several sloppy kisses to my cheek.

I noticed Ariana's curious eyes on me as I shifted Tessie to my back. There was a question within those sea green depths, but I wasn't the type to ask. I was the type to demand. But I couldn't in front of Tessie, because I didn't want her to think it was okay for some fucker to treat her like that.

The hypocrisy wasn't lost on me.

As if I gave a fuck.

I began to speak in rapid fire. "You'll get a drink menu sent home with you tonight. Read it. Memorize it. Live it. You'll be expected to be able to make, describe, and sell everything on the menu by your next training session."

Her eyes advertised her hate for me like an oversized Times Square billboard. "And that is?"

I leveled her with a glare for cutting me off, the efficacy of my glare probably diminished by the adorable eight-year-old girl clinging to my back. "Tomorrow. Same time."

Ariana's eyes connected with mine, and she crossed her arms. "Would that be half past noon or"—she looked at her watch— "three past two?"

Ariana didn't let anything slide. Elsa had that same attitude. I'd liked it about her, so seeing it in Ariana pissed me off.

I ignored both her attitude and her question, unwilling to deal with any more bullshit today. "Blenders are in the back of the bar. Make sure the covers are on tight before you press any buttons. The covers muffle the sound, and no one wants to hear the help work."

She ignored the jab, unfazed by my brand of asshole. Something about that—and her—made me feel exposed. I wanted her to be like everyone else.

A coward.

Pathetic.

Weak.

Powerless.

But even thinking that, I knew she was none of those things. She either fought back or ignored me entirely, and that, in turn, unnerved me. I needed her to leave.

Now.

I pointed to a door past her shoulder and spoke even faster. "Ice is in the basement freezer. When it's your shift and you've been assigned the right-side shift, you'll be expected to bring ice up when the levels reach about twenty percent. There are extra bottles of alcohol stocked underneath the top shelf cabinets."

I opened one of the upper cabinets. "Always keep each bottle stocked. If there are only two left, you'll be expected to restock them from the basement. Except the Dom Perignon, Patrón, Grey Goose, Crown Royal, Hennessy, Ciroc, Johnnie Walker, Don Julio, Maker's Mark, Belvedere and Bombay Sapphire."

I pointed to the rows with those bottles and closed the cabinet before she could process the brands. "Those are our top sellers. You push those. Hard. And when they're down to five bottles, you restock. Always."

I pointed to the rows of tap levers. "Alcohol on tap is refilled by a vendor during pre-open prep. Additional rules will be in the employee handbook I emailed to you this morning, along with your initial offer, non-disclosure agreement, and contract. The offer expires at midnight. Any questions?"

It was a challenge. I had shot information at her quicker than most could retain it, but if she asked a question, it would be tantamount to admitting failure. And if I were being honest, neither of us wanted that.

I was very aware that Tessie was here and very aware of what I wanted to say if she wasn't.

I'll bend you over my knee.

Spank that perfect, round ass.

Show you what happens when you misbehave.

Our gazes locked, our resolves tangled, and I raised a single brow. Another challenge. My eyes narrowed as I read the unspoken words her eyes screamed.

You can't fool me, they taunted.

I know what you're doing, they mocked.

I see you, they destroyed.

Her eyes may have conquered me, but all those pouty, defiant lips gave me was a short, "None." She grabbed her bag, slung it over her shoulder, and returned her arresting gaze to me. "I take it that's the end of training?"

She looked at her watch again before she continued, "Huh. It took you two hours to do a fifteen-minute job. Funny. I never took you as"—her eyes dipped to my cock—"... incompetent." Her eyes lifted to Tessie's, and her voice transformed into something warmer than I would ever be on the receiving end of. "See you around, Tessie," she said, succeeding in calling my sister a nickname she refused to let me use.

And then she left, her swaying hips teasing me with each step she took towards the door.

Christ, who was this woman?

I was supposed to be breaking her spirit. It should have

been easier than this, but each move I made was met with fire, and each step I took reached an unexpected stalemate. If this were a game of chess, it would be a draw.

I had met my match with Ariana De Luca, and that made me want to defeat her, fuck her, then destroy her.

We don't choose our destinies,
but we must do our duties.

—George R.R. Martin

ARIANA DE LUCA

Nerves shimmied along the length of my spine, taunting me with each passing second. In all of my years undercover, this was the first cover that had me feeling woefully under-qualified. And I was under as my real name. As myself.

Well, as much of myself as I'd ever been.

"Ari." Graham stuck his hand out for me to shake. His blue eyes were welcoming, and his cropped dirty blonde hair reminded me of the California beaches I used to sunbathe at during my time at Degory University.

He looked exactly as handsome as he did in the picture in his file, courtesy of the New York DMV. Hell, everyone who worked here looked like they moonlit as models. It was an unspoken job requirement.

My eyes darted around L'Oscurità, searching for and failing to find Bastian before I planted my palm in Graham's hand and gave an Oscar-worthy fake smile. "Nice to see you again."

Graham had been training me over the two days since Bastian had given me the L'Oscurità Bartending Crash Course: Asshole Edition, and I was convinced he had a bit of a crush on me. I wasn't sure why. I'd done nothing to lead him on, and whenever he'd tried to steer the conversation away from work, I'd done my best to keep us on track.

Graham followed my wandering eyes across the room. "Still got the first day jitters?" A friendly smile eclipsed his face. His eyes crinkled in a knowing look. "I had them for a month. It's a lot to take in. Trust me, I was overwhelmed my first few days, too. But don't you worry." He let go of my hand. Finally. "I'll take care of you."

I didn't know what he meant by that, but Dana had told me, her straight white teeth gritted together, that Graham would train me during my week-long training period. It was clear that my presence here irritated her. That might have been a potential problem, but I had the advantage of knowing everything about her that her file had to offer—which was a lot. The only trouble Dana could offer me was drama. That was nothing compared to the dangers the Romano family posed.

I was tempted to ask Graham if any of the upper-level Romanos were around, but I settled on a short, “Thanks.”

Patience was the name of this game. Most undercover work existed in tandem with patience. Legends were supposed to wait for something to happen, and until then, we lived the lives we were assigned as if they were our own.

Some of my fellow legends had even started families while under. It wasn’t supposed to happen, but when the bureau expected us to live as our legends would, it included dating, and dating included sex and—sometimes—love. Or babies. You didn’t need love to make babies, and I was living proof of that.

So, even though I recognized at least a dozen faces in the bar as Romano *capitani* and *tenenti*, I couldn’t barrage anyone with questions like a detective would. Subtlety went a long way.

The other side of L’Oscurità was where the Romano members wined and dined, but the bar side was where they wined and wined and wined and wined. Someone would slip up. Eventually.

“So ” Graham fidgeted, sliding a hand in the pocket of his black dress pants and meeting my eyes with his twin blues. “I have two tickets to an off-Broadway show this weekend. I was wondering if you’d—”

“Oh, I heard about that!” I cut him off before he could ask me out. “My bestie and I really wanted to go, but I’m on shift all week and the next.”

Graham frowned. “Two weeks? When are your off days?”

“I have none.” I shrugged, feigning ignorance.

I didn’t have any off days because I’d mouthed off to

Bastian yesterday. He'd emailed me a schedule change, the alert pinging on my phone just as he'd materialized before me, a taunting smirk on his face.

A suggestive brow had been raised, daring me to open my email. I had, and that brow was still raised, urging me to challenge him. To finally cave and admit defeat. I didn't. I *couldn't.* That was pride, ego, dignity, and all the things that made us *us* speaking. Plus, he didn't realize it, but more time at L'Oscurità only gave me more opportunities to take him and his family down. His downfall would be my revenge.

Graham opened his mouth to respond, no doubt to offer an unwanted solution, so I spoke before he could, "What's that?" I nodded to the stapled packet of white printer paper in his hands. It was somewhat thick and bore the L'Oscurità logo on the front cover.

"A test. One hundred questions, a mixture of written response, true or false, fill in the blank, and multiple choice." At my look, he gave a small laugh. "Don't worry. We all had to do it. And it's okay to get a few wrong."

But it wasn't.

Not if Bastian would find out.

Bastian preyed on failure, and I had no doubt missing a single question was tantamount to failure in his eyes. I didn't know whether to be appalled or flattered that he expected so much from his employees.

That he expected so much from me.

Appalled, I decided.

Bastiano Romano appalled me.

My anxiety raced at L'Oscurità. I needed to control it, of course, even as I tried convincing myself my lack of experience meant nothing, my last name wouldn't get me killed, and Bastiano Romano wouldn't be spending his evening watching me take this test through the security camera diagonally above me.

The buzz of my phone pierced the silence. My legend's phone. Not the burner. Yet, no one but Jenn had my number, and she wouldn't call unless it was an emergency. I pulled out my phone, glanced at the caller ID, and tensed when I saw Jenn's name.

Pressing the green button, I raised it to my ear. "Hello?"

"De Luca." Wilks' voice only heightened my panic.

He hadn't called me after my meeting with Jenn like he'd promised. My eyes burned holes on the door as I resisted the urge to glance at the security cameras. I considered whether or not the Romanos had set up a microphone surveillance system in here and decided not to risk it.

Pasting a light smile on my face, I toyed with a loose

strand of hair. "Dr. Clemson, it's great hearing from you. I'm glad you were able to reschedule the appointment."

"You're not able to talk freely?"

"No, I'm afraid not. I'll miss you, though!"

"Got it." He shuffled around, and I could hear his breathing through the line—not as fit as he'd used to be. "Your cover with the Romano is very important."

Okay… He didn't call me to tell me something I already knew.

I raked my fingers through the tangles in my hair. "More important than the last time we talked about it?"

"More important than it was a second ago and only getting more important."

I leaned against the seat and ran a hand over the back of my neck, squeezing out the stress while racking my brain for something that would make sense in the context of this conversation in case of a mic. "I'm sorry to hear that your cat is getting sicker. I know exercise is extremely important for animals. Thank you for letting me know. I hope she's okay. Does it change our appointment times?"

Translation: What happened? Does it change the assignment?

Wilks heaved out a heavy breath. "Nothing you need to worry about."

I let a forced giggle slip and rolled my eyes like we were gossiping. "You and I both know that's not true." Beneath a curtain of my long hair, my fist clenched the phone. "It sounds awfully urgent all of a sudden. You've always known your cat was at risk for… diabetes. Why are you going into the doctor now? Why not last year? Or a year from now?"

Translation: The FBI has always known about the

Romanos. Why am I going undercover now? Why not a year ago? Or a year from now?

"There was a confirmed Andretti sighting in Manhattan. It's why I had you doing this now of all moments."

I immediately straightened up from the seat and dug my heels into the floor, forcing the freak out away from me, trying not to question my inexperience. "A vague diagnosis or an actual diagnosis?

Translation: Andretti member or an actual Andretti?

"Low- to mid-level. Non-blood relation."

Usually, given the notorious border disputes between the Andretti and Romano families, this wouldn't have been a big deal, but New York City was the heart and soul of the Romano family. There had been a storm brewing for years, and I felt stuck in the middle of it without shelter.

"Anything else I should know?"

"Our C.I. says there's a hit out on an unknown big name. Higher ups in the Romano family are covering up who the hit is out on, but there's already been at least one body that's had to be cleaned. No concrete evidence. Just the word of our C.I., who didn't see anything, but you should be careful regardless."

I hadn't known what I was walking into, but this was immensely worse than what I had pictured. This meant iron-clad guards were up for people who already had their lives hidden below impenetrable layers of secrecy.

My eyes burned greater with the need to peer around the room for more security measures. "And the appointment?" I asked, holding my breath for I didn't know what.

I wanted to be done. To be reassigned. I was torn between proving to myself that I could handle Bastiano Romano and begging not to have to. My stomach churned with the weight of my conflicting thoughts, and I was tempted to vomit the lunch I had eaten before my shift.

I'd chosen to be an undercover agent because desk assignments bored me, but I'd rather be pushing papers in a cubicle than buried in an unmarked grave somewhere in Jersey.

Wilks' breath came through heavy on the other end. "Remains the same, but—"

Footsteps pounded outside the door, and I straightened up. "My boss is coming. I have to go."

I hung up before Wilks could speak, his "but" lingering in the air like a noose around my neck, one whose knot I couldn't unravel. Graham's head peeked inside the doorway, and he looked both ways.

"I could have sworn I heard talking in here."

I faked a guilty smile and waved my phone in the air. "My doctor called to change my appointment time."

"Don't let Mr. Romano see you with that while you're taking the test. He'll think you're cheating."

My eyes burned with the need to roll them. God forbid I piss off Master Romano.

Graham raked his gaze over me and continued, "Are you okay?"

"I'm fine. No medical emergencies to worry about." At his face, I straightened. "Oh! You meant the test. Yeah, I'm on question eighty-six." I rested my back against the leather chair again.

Bastian's chair—mostly because it was the most comfortable one in the room, but also because I could.

Graham walked over to where I sat, placed his palm on my shoulder, and leaned over my head to peek at my test. "You're almost done? Damn, Ari." A whistle soared past his lips. "It normally takes a lot longer for us mortal folks."

I eyed where Graham's hand rested on my shoulder. Unlike Bastian's touch, it repulsed me. Bastian and I fought. We were never-admit-defeat cataclysmic, can't-be-in-the-same-room-without-fighting disastrous, tear-your-clothes-off hungry.

What we weren't was a hand on the shoulder. Obviously, Bastian jerking off in front of me was far less innocent than Graham's hand on my shoulder, but it certainly didn't feel that way.

Bastian was porchetta-feeding, verbal-sparring, eye-fucking, thought-stealing, breath-robbing. He was I-dare-you-to-fail unrelenting, fight-me demanding, can-you-or-can't-you provoking, tell-me-you-don't-want-me goading, lift-your-skirt-up taunting.

Graham was hard to get a read on, but I knew without a doubt he—and no other man—would ever be any of those things. Anything that set Bastian apart from other men only served to remind me how woefully unequipped I was to handle this legend.

The hand on my shoulder squeezed again. Graham was either super comfortable touching others or too comfortable touching me. The first was innocent enough. The second would result in a broken wrist. Depending on which I settled on, there could be hell to pay.

"Ariana," I corrected. Boundaries were never a bad idea, I reminded myself, even though I'd introduced myself as Ari to Bastian. "No one calls me Ari."

Wilks and Aunt Nadia did, but Aunt Nadia had breathed her last breath a few years ago. I'd been under at the time, but Wilks had allowed me to break my legend to attend her funeral. I buried her beside my mom's grave. Wilks and I had been the only two in attendance, and he'd never even met her.

Maybe Wilks had been there for me. Or maybe he had been there to see if my legend could have been preserved. The latter still seemed more likely to me. I didn't want to die alone, but I didn't know how to die loved.

"Sorry, Ari." Graham palmed his face. "Shit, *Ariana*. Ariana. Ariana," he repeated like Ariana was the hardest name in the world to figure out. "Got it."

I held up the test booklet, giving it a small shake. "I have the written response questions left. I should be done soon..."

Silence lingered in the air as I waited for him to take a hint and leave. At my dismissal, a flash of discouragement darted across his face before it was gone as quickly as it came. As if he expected me to fall at his feet. I kept my features passive as I reassessed him. He didn't seem malicious, but many people didn't until they unleashed their anger.

Since its creation, men and women had floated on and off the FBI's Most Wanted list like it was the world's most famous revolving door, and many of them had seemed unassuming to those closest to them.

If I had a dollar for every time the neighbor of a killer said, "I never would have guessed," I'd quit my job at the bureau and buy a penthouse somewhere in the city. So, I let my suspicions of Graham fester.

Suspicion was always warranted.

Suspicion was always safe.

Suspicion was unlike love in those regards.

Graham stared at me a moment longer before he nodded. "Come get me when you're done." Just like that, an easygoing smile painted his face.

It sent an eerie chill down my spine.

100. Two customers walk into the bar. They introduce themselves as Aaron and Alex before ordering two whiskey neats. As the night wears on and you talk to them, you begin to realize that Aaron is Alex's father, but Alex is not Aaron's son. How is this possible?

I snorted a laugh. The rest of the questions had been about New York state health code laws for restaurants, emergency procedures, and restaurant protocol. This had Bastian written all over it.

"What's so funny?"

I turned to the door, waving Tessie over when our eyes connected. Her eyes were red-rimmed, and she sucked in a sniffle. Tears brimmed at the edges of her eyes, refusing to fall past her long lower lashes. It wasn't my place to pry, but the least I could do was be here for her.

"What's wrong?"

She made her way to the seat across from mine, bit her

bottom lip, and rubbed at her eyes. "I don't want to talk about it."

I took in her face for a moment before I shrugged, giving her space. Like I'd said, it wasn't my place to pry. "Okay."

Her eyes widened. "You're not going to force me to tell you?"

"Why would I do that?"

"Bastian does. He says it's because he cares. I say, it's because he's mean."

"You'd tell me if you want to." I paused. "Is he mean to you?"

She considered this for a moment, her head tilting back. The wheels turning in her head were practically visible. "No, I guess not. He's mean to almost everyone else, but he's not mean to me."

I give her a teasing smile. "You're lucky. He's mean to me."

"What did he do to you?"

Pushed the boundaries of my sanity each time we were together.

Made me question my chastity.

Made me question my loyalties.

Obviously, I couldn't say that, so I winked at her. "For one, he just tried to trick me. Question one hundred." I pointed to the test packet while I wrote my answer in the answer booklet.

Tessie grabbed the test packet, her eyes skimming the page before she smiled proudly. "Alex is a girl. She's Aaron's daughter."

I quirked my lips and closed my answer booklet. I'd come to the same conclusion. "Smart girl," I praised.

She shrugged. "Mama's friend is named Aronne, but it's spelled A-R-O-N-N-E. And his daughter is named Alessandra, but we call her Alex." An uncomfortable look crossed her features.

I assessed her hunched shoulders. "Is Alex your friend?"

"She's mean to me. Whenever I get good grades, she calls me a nerd. When mama gives me new clothes, she tells me they're ugly. I don't like to hang out with her, but I have to see her when she's home."

"She lives with you?"

"Sometimes. Her daddy lives with me, but she lives with her mama most days."

I forced my face to remain neutral when the pieces fell together. Aronne was her mom's boyfriend, and Alessandra was his daughter. The bureau knew about the live-in boyfriend, but we didn't know who he was. Now, I knew his name. At the expense of a tear-stricken eight-year-old girl. If ever there was a moment to hate my job, it was this one.

"I'll let you in on a little secret." I crooked a finger, and she leaned closer, excitement wiping sadness from her eyes. "When people are mean, they're usually just jealous."

She leaned back abruptly, and her jaw dropped. "Alex is jealous of me?!"

I gave her a casual shrug and winked at her.

She settled back in her seat. "I don't want Alex to be jealous of me." Determination unfurled across her face. "I'll just have to be super nice to her, so she knows it's okay to be nice to me."

I sighed. Tessie was so innocent, it hurt my heart. If only the rest of the world shared her mentality. I'd be out of a job, and I wouldn't even mind.

"How'd you grow up to be so good?" I prayed that she'd stay that way. That she wouldn't follow in the footsteps of her family. That she'd grow up, go to college, and follow whatever *her* dreams were rather than the ones her family laid out for her.

Oblivious to the terror for her future that shot through me, she shrugged and paused. "Wait a minute. If people are mean because they're jealous, does that mean Bastian is jealous of you?"

I forced the negative thoughts away and laughed. "Oh, totally."

"Spreading lies, De Luca?"

At the sound of Bastian's voice, my eyes shot toward the door, and I took him in. No amount of time in the world could ever prepare me for seeing this man. It was sinful how attractive he looked in a suit, each of the three pieces perfectly fitted, his tie straight, and his rare Patek Phillippe watch barely peeking out past his suit sleeve. If he made his way to us, I'd bet I could smell the distinct, addictive scent of aged ambergris and oakmoss on his skin.

I hoped he didn't make his way to us.

I glanced at Tessie, tempering the heat that threatened to eclipse my face. "It's definitely not a lie. He's jealous of me."

Tessie squealed. "Oh, my gosh! Bastian was just mean to you!" She turned to her brother and pointed an accusing finger. "You *are* jealous!"

His eyes shot to mine, and his pair of treacherous orbs waged a silent war.

You'll pay for that, those persistent eyes promised.

You don't know who you're messing with, they lied.

Say something else, they challenged.

I was becoming an expert at reading his face, but he was becoming an expert at reading mine, too. What filthy, forbidden secrets were my eyes betraying?

I've never met a man like you before, they undoubtedly divulged.

I want you, they terrorized.

In another life, I'd give in, they admitted.

I didn't know where that had come from. In what world would I give in to my desire for a mobster? None. That should have been my answer.

"Aren't you supposed to be working?" he finally asked when the tension between us simmered too high. His eyes narrowed on the space between me and his sister, no doubt drawing conclusions I didn't want them to draw. A frown touched his lips as he continued to flay me with his words, "It can be an unfamiliar concept for... *slower* people, but it's really not that hard to get."

He drew out his words purposefully, as if I couldn't understand them otherwise. "If you work, you get paid. If you don't, you get fired." He turned to his sister, who was beaming at me like she suddenly had all the answers to the universe. "This is a perfect example of what not to be when you grow up."

And we were back on familiar ground, where he was the asshole boss, I was the illicit employee, and we ignored the fact that this job and Tessie liking me intertwined us when the last thing we needed was a reason to be closer together.

12

Self-development is a higher duty than self-sacrifice.

—Elizabeth Cady Stanton

BASTIANO ROMANO

"I invited Ari to my party." Tessie tucked a strand of hair behind her ear before her tiny fingers returned to the keys. "I like her."

I tapped her lower back with my fingers until she straightened her posture, her shoulders pulled back and the melody already smoother. "Keep your back straight. You're not a sloth."

"What's a sloth?"

"A type of animal." I moved her fingers over the right keys on the living room piano. "What party?"

She still played the song wrong. "My half-birthday party."

I stared at her. I couldn't tell if she was serious.

My head shook as I mimicked the hand movements she needed to learn. "You're not having a half-birthday party."

"Why not?"

"For starters, they're not a thing."

She crossed her arms and drew her lips into a pout. "But you're never in California for my real birthday parties."

Fair point.

You've missed too many of Everett's, too, my self-loathing reminded me.

I uncrossed her arms and placed her hands back on the piano for the millionth time during our lesson. "Fine, we'll have a half-birthday party."

She shrugged, and her fingers lifted off the keys until I *tutted.* "I already told Miss Luna to plan it for me."

My sixty-year-old housekeeper Luna favored Tessie over me. Not that I blamed her, but she could at least feign loyalty.

"You're not inviting Ariana De Luca."

"Why not?" She played the wrong keys again.

I gave up on the lesson, letting her do it her way as I said, "She's my employee not your friend."

"Why can't she be both?"

"Fraternizing with the help is a disaster waiting to happen."

From her spot on my staircase, one of the maids narrowed her eyes as she scrubbed the flooring on her hands and knees.

Tessie tilted her head to the side and stared at me, one

hundred percent giving up on the piano lesson she'd begged me for. "What does fra—fratur… What does that word mean?"

"Doesn't matter."

"I'll look it up."

"You can't pronounce it, and you can't spell it. How are you going to look it up?"

"Miss Luna will teach me after she plans my party and Ari shows up. I'll show her my unicorn collection in my room after she tells me what it means."

No.

Ariana De Luca would not step foot in my penthouse.

It simply was never going to happen.

I'd wanted to fuck her, yes, but something about her had me holding back. I normally trusted my resolve but not with her. If I had it my way, she'd be on her back with me inside her. I needed to trust my gut with this one and stay away.

"The restaurant," I bit out.

"Huh?"

"You can have your party at L'Oscurità. We'll close it down for you."

"Asher would do that?!"

"No, *I'll* do that." I paused a beat and relented, "But Asher would, too."

She flung her arms around my waist and peeked up at me. "I'm still inviting Ari."

Clink!

Clink!

Clink!

The bane of my existence strolled into my office without knocking, a metal food cart clinking before her. It was day four of her seven-day training period, and she was already overstepping her boundaries.

Hell, she'd overstepped them before she'd even been hired, but I had been too busy overstepping mine to screw my head on straight.

"Do you see that wooden rectangle over there?" I pointed to the door and continued before she could reply. "That's called a door. It's for privacy. You knock on it before invading someone's personal space."

She pushed the cart until it rested beside my desk and met my eyes. "Oh, so that's what that thing is."

She was infuriating.

Infuriatingly beautiful.

Infuriatingly witty.

Infuriatingly off-limits.

I closed my browser as she set my lunch on my desk. "You're testing my patience."

"I wasn't aware you had any."

I gestured between us. "What do you call this?"

"Inadequately rewarded labor."

I leaned back in my chair, eyeing Ariana. This was the woman my baby sister was smitten with. An irritating infatuation I wanted to snap between my fingers like a broken pencil. I'd sprinkle the remains over Ariana's food and feed it to her for lunch.

Ariana De Luca was all curves, backbone, and guts. I saw the appeal. Truly. But after Elsa, I was done caring for women. Then, after the Dana rebound turned fiasco, I was done fucking my employees, and Ariana simply wasn't worth it.

I tilted my head back, watching her set up my dinner on my desk. "If you want a higher paying job, go get it. I'll—"

"Find my replacement by the end of the day?" She snorted. "Good luck with that."

She was right. I still had the job listed on all the big job-hunting sites, and someone worthy of my attention had yet to apply. That didn't mean she had to know that.

The corner of my lips curled up until I exuded smugness I wished I felt. "No need for luck." I pulled up a random employee file and read, substituting my restaurant-side bartender's name for a made up one, "Candy Lane. Late twenties. Clean record. Gorgeous. Dad ran a bar. Lots of experience. Speaks English, Spanish, French, and German." I shifted my eyes to her. "I'd bet I could have her here, pen in one hand and contract in the other, by the end of the day."

She paused, her hand stilling on the silverware she'd just placed in front of me. "What are you willing to wager?"

My eyes narrowed as she called my bluff—who the fuck was this girl? "What do you want?"

Her answer came instantly, like she didn't even have to think about it. "Job security, my pick of hours, the shift of my choice, and a pay raise."

Liar.

I didn't let her words impress me as I raked my gaze over her frame and raised a brow. "Is that really what you want?"

She skimmed my body before her eyes met mine. "There's nothing else you could offer me."

I grinned, reluctantly, debating whether or not I could hire an actress to bartend for a short time—at least long enough for Ariana to see and lose. "Fine." Hole, meet shovel. "And if I win?"

"You won't."

I couldn't wait to drown her with her confidence.

My eyes returned to the screen as I continued reading Emily's employee file, "Candy Lane is TriBeCa born and raised, has a bachelor's degree in Communications, and is pursuing her MBA part-time at Columbia, which she assures will not get in the way of her bartending hours." I cocked a brow at Ariana, noting how easy bluffing came to me.

She laughed and began pushing the cart to the door. Once she reached the threshold, she turned to me, a smirk lining her full lips. "I didn't know Emily changed her name to Candy Lane. Would "Lane" be the last name or does the stripper of your fantasies have two first names? Like the Mary Jane of your delusions? Fancy."

This girl.

I didn't bother holding in my laugh. "When'd you make me?"

"It wasn't you, per se. It was the file. It was obvious you were talking about Emily."

"You've been here four days. How was I supposed to know you know Emily that well?" I tilted my head slightly. "How do you know her, by the way? You've never had a shift on the restaurant side."

Something flashed in her eyes. She smothered it like cheap condiments on a curbside hotdog. "You know, your Royal Highness, if you'd leave your throne every now and then and talk to your subjects, you'd be surprised by how much you'd learn."

"Are you telling me how to run my business?"

"I'm telling you how to run Asher Black's."

"I sign your paychecks."

"Speaking of, I look forward to my raise."

She left before I could answer, but it wouldn't have mattered if she'd stayed anyway. I didn't have anything to say. Ariana blazed into my life uninvited, infatuated my sister, and left me speechless. If she kept this up, I wouldn't recognize my life.

Elsa pushed her way into my mind, the word betrayal tattooed up and down the milky skin of her arms.

Is that really a bad thing? I heard the ghost of her whisper.

ARIANA DE LUCA

"Something interesting happened today."

I jumped, surprised, and the glass I'd been cleaning fell. Bastian caught it before it hit the floor, and when he handed it back to me, our fingers brushed and lingered.

I pulled back and scowled at him. "You shouldn't sneak up on people." I hated when people snuck up on me, though it rarely occurred. "You never know what might happen."

"Worried about me?"

"Worried about my paycheck."

"Right. Your unearned pay raise. Speaking of, are you going to ask me what happened today?"

"I'd rather guess—you finally grew a conscious?"

"Ha. Ha." He tilted his body, blocking out the rest of the bar, where no one bothered to hide their staring, least of all Dana. "Actually, I asked Emily how long she's known you,"—*Oh, shit*—"but she says she's never even spoken to you."

Truth was, I had read her file, and it'd been too tempting not to call Bastian's bluff yesterday. I'd been sick of his constant threats against my job and, for the sake of my cover, needed to secure my place here, but perhaps it'd been at the expense of my cover. Oh, how I hated irony.

I leaned a hip against the counter and eyed Bastian up and down, my faked nonchalant confidence never wavering. Did the way he filled out his obnoxiously expensive suit intimidate me? A little.

But I didn't show it as I spoke with a relaxed voice, "I never took you for a sore loser, Bastian."

"It's Mr. Romano." He leaned forward. "Deflection isn't your strong suit."

"But it's yours?" I took a step closer to Bastian as Dana began the trek over to us. "'Deflection' implies there's something to deflect against."

He leaned toward me, lessening the already small gap between us. "How did you know all that stuff about Emily?"

I cocked my head slightly to the side. "Have you always been a sore loser?"

"I don't lose. It's my tenacity you're reacting to." His eyes narrowed. "Now, answer my question."

"Bastian?" Dana approached us from the side, her eyes drifting to the negligible space between us. "I was hoping I could talk to you." Her face hardened as she shifted her gaze to mine. "Am I interrupting something?"

I took a step back. "No, not at all."

Not at all, Dana. Not at all.

Before Bastian could stop me, I walked to the other end of the bar, putting as much distance between me and Bastian as I could without quitting, and ten minutes later, when I gathered the courage to glance their way, Bastian was still staring at me. A shiver trailed down my spine. I had a feeling he'd be watching me closer from here on.

I didn't know how I found myself sitting in L'Oscurità during my free time. One minute, Tessie had come barreling at me at work, and the next, I'd agreed to come to her half-birthday party.

A half-birthday party.

I didn't even know that was a thing.

I scratched the side of my face with my middle finger as Bastian stared at me from his seat across from me.

He cocked a brow up. "Real mature."

So far, it'd been just me and Bastian to arrive. Miss Luna, the sweet Italian lady with the graying hair and chaotic choice of wardrobe, had left as soon as she'd finished setting up, giving Tessie a parting kiss on the forehead on the way out.

Bastian and I had been painfully civil since Tessie was here, but she'd left for the bathroom ten minutes ago and hadn't returned. My eyes dipped to the unicorn tattoo on his cheek. Tessie had planted it on his face the second the party had begun, and I couldn't take him seriously since. The monster brought to his knees by an eight-year-old girl.

Who would have thought?

"I see that look on your face, and I can assure you I am no less inclined to make your life at L'Oscurità hellish with or without this ridiculous temporary tattoo on my cheek."

My lips quirked up, and I didn't bother hiding my amusement. "Sure." I paused a beat. "Interesting choice of words. Hellish. Do they let unicorns into hell?"

He ignored me.

"What I wonder is why," I continued. "Why would you need to make my life a living hell? Do I bother you? I know you're insufferable, but you're more respectful with everyone than you are with me. Why is that?"

I shouldn't have asked that. In undercover work, the only reason to get this close—to draw this much attention to myself—is if I have plans to sleep with the mark. I didn't. With Bastian... I had this sinking feeling, if I were to sleep with him, I'd be ruined.

I wanted to say I'd never consider it. I wanted to claim I had enough self-preservation to tamp my lust. But I knew, if he were to make the first move, I'd give in.

Not because I had a duty to the bureau but because the attraction between us was the most palpable thing I'd ever felt. It was only luck that it'd benefit my job. The bureau loved its honeypots, and I stood in a place where I had an opportunity to discover my real self for the first time in my life. The only thing stopping me was *him*.

Bastiano Romano was a truly awful person.

I had so many firsts to give, and I couldn't give them to someone like *him*.

He studied me before answering. "Perhaps they've earned my respect."

"Avery Adams, the guy who wears velcro shoes on his days off because he struggles tying them, has earned more respect than I have?"

"A pity hire." He shrugged. "Then again, so were you."

I couldn't believe half the shit he spewed. But this conversation was a one-off. The only opportunity I'd have to confront him on neutral ground.

So, I pressed harder. "Have you ever stopped to think that there are no reasons to treat me poorly?"

"Have you ever stopped to consider I don't give a fuck?"

"You cannot be that insufferable."

"It's cute you think you can tell me what I can and cannot be." He leaned forward. "You clearly have this grand idea that humans should be good people when the reality says otherwise. People are incapable of anything other than greed and betrayal. That's a fact. Perhaps you should get out more. Your naivety isn't endearing."

I have been out, I wanted to scream. *I've pretended to be a stripper. I've sailed the Amalfi coast with Swiss bankers. I've been to political rallies in third world countries, been fake arrested in Arizona, and lived dozens of lives through aliases.*

But you've never lived your own life, I couldn't help but remind myself.

And there was the truth.

I'd lived every life but a normal one.

Hell, I hadn't even been to a movie theater before.

How could I?

Growing up, my aunt had never been home, I'd spent my college years focused on school and rebelling against friendships, and every year since I'd graduated had been spent under various covers with the bureau. I'd lived more days of my adult life undercover than as Ariana De Luca.

The tears surprised me. They rose within me and lined my lower lashes, but I didn't let them slip out. I couldn't give Bastian the satisfaction of my tears. No matter what, he couldn't see my weakness, because he'd attack them. Of this, I had no doubt.

I felt his eyes on me as I failed to force down my tears. One slipped past my lashes, slid down my cheek, and splashed onto the table like a

"You look prettier when you cry," he said quietly, almost absentmindedly.

It took a second for his words to register.

Was he serious?

Who said shit like that?!

I rose from my chair so quickly, it flung behind me. Amusement drowned those black orbs he had for eyes as I leaned over the table and got in his face. "Who fucked you up so much that you can't even spend five minutes acting like a decent human being?"

Anger spread across his features before he tamped it down. "Being a decent human being is overrated," he spat like the very idea disgusted him.

"Treating people with respect and dignity keeps us civilized."

He leaned forward, and his breath fanned my face. "Fuck being civilized."

I try to get a handle on my pulse. He was so close.

Leaning back, I crossed my arms. My eyes raked his body with condescension pasted on my face. "You may dress in fancy suits, style your hair with thousand-dollar cuts, and look like a GQ centerfold, but nothing will change the fact that you are a miserable person."

I'd done it. I'd gotten myself fired. Why couldn't Ariana keep her mouth shut?

You are Ariana, dumb ass.

Great. I was quickly becoming my least favorite legend.

Instead of firing me, he lifted an amused brow. "Are you flirting with me?"

Flirting?

He called *that* flirting?

If this was his idea of flirting, I didn't want to know what his idea of foreplay was.

I shook my head, disbelief fueling every movement. "Never."

A sniffle caught my attention from the restroom attached to the break room. I fled for the door. Tessie had gone in twenty minutes ago. Had she heard us fighting? Why hadn't I checked on her when she'd been gone for too long? I kicked myself and her brother for distracting me as I swung the door open and took in Tessie.

She sat on the tiled floor, her shoulders hunched and quivering as her arms stayed wrapped around her bent knees. I felt Bastian behind me, but I ignored him as I took a seat beside Tessie and leaned her head on my shoulder in a side hug.

"Oh, honey." Pressing a kiss to her forehead, I wrapped an arm around her shoulder. "What's wrong, Tessie?"

"Mommy said she can't come, and Daddy won't answer the phone," she stuttered between sobs and shuttered breaths, and I swore, I broke for her.

Because I got it.

I understood how it felt to not see your mom or your dad and to have no one growing up. It was almost worse that her parents were alive and she still felt abandoned by people who had the means to be with her whenever they wanted but chose not to.

It wasn't lost on me that Bastian, despite his flaws (and there were many), always seemed to put Tessie first. If anything, that was the one and only thing I admired about him.

I tilted Tessie's chin up, so she looked at me. I couldn't make her parents' absence any better, but maybe I could distract her from it. "Wanna know a secret?"

She hiccuped, her eyes wide and round and so damn sad. "Yes."

"You're the coolest girl I know."

"No, I'm not."

"You are. For instance..." I turned to Bastian, who stared at me with such an intense look in his eyes, I had to look away. "Your brother, who is a big stubborn meanie—"

"I know." She finally gave me a tiny smile. "He's the biggest meanie, but I love him."

"Well, you got your big, meanie brother to wear a unicorn tattoo on his face. I think that makes you the coolest girl ever, and if I could hang out with you every single day, I would."

She gave her last sniffle. "Do you mean that?"

"Yes."

Her shoulders straightened. "What about in outer space?"

"Duh."

She held her head up and widened her eyes. "Underwater?"

"Of course."

"At the movie theater?"

I quirked my head to the side and admitted, "I've never been."

"You've never been to the movie theater?!" Her small gasp hitched on a hiccup, and my lips quirked up at the sound.

"Nope, but I'd love to go sometime. With someone special and as cool as you." I nudged her shoulder with mine, and her smile took over every inch of the room.

Bastian took that as his cue to walk our way. Our eyes met as he took a seat on the other side of Tessie, his body brushing against my arm as he grabbed Tessie's hand and intertwined his big fingers with her tiny ones.

His eyes said the words he'd never say out loud.

Thank you.

A temporary truce.

One more destructive than any fight we could ever have.

13

Of two duties we must choose the greater,
though of two sins we must choose neither.

—Richard Baxter

BASTIANO ROMANO

There weren't too many people in the mafia community. I lived in a big city, but my world was small. Though I didn't understand normal, I understood this little world like the back of my hand.

My mom had never physically hurt anyone. Not with her own hands, at least. But she'd been an absent mother at best and an unfaithful wife at worst. She'd turned a blind eye to the countless number of times her family had harmed, injured, and killed people, regardless of whether they'd been guilty or not, and had even encouraged—though not ordered—a death or two. Maybe she'd never done anything truly bad by her own hand, but all those little things made her a bad person.

Gio, on the other hand, had been more active in his transgressions. He had no qualms about murder, and he'd done exactly so without remorse in the past. He was an active Romano *caporegime*, who'd made an extracurricular activity out of killing to protect the family and fucking every decent-looking girl in the city. No amount of love I held for him or donations to charity to ease his guilt changed the fact that he was. Not. A. Good. Person.

Tessie, however, was the sunshine of our lives. Perpetually happy and radiating purity, she'd never had a malicious thought towards anyone—probably wasn't capable of it. When confronted with adversity, her solutions always involved unity, working together, and the type of rainbow-full-of-unicorns bullshit only someone with truly moral intent could conjure. Sure, she was young and people changed, but goodness—true goodness like she had—wasn't something that would go anywhere anytime soon. If ever.

Everett, despite being raised by the female equivalent of an ass-faced wildebeest, was exactly the same way. Pure. Good. Incapable of horror.

Point was, in my world, people were usually black and white. Good people were good, and bad people were bad, but so few delved into the grey area in between. I was one of those people. Ariana De Luca was one, too.

I was an asshole, and she was combative. I was the type to

continue jacking off when interrupted, and she was the type to watch it and enjoy. I'd let my family's indiscretions go uncontested time and time again while she had a secretive past she hid, and I knew—I just goddamn knew—it wasn't a good one. She knew things she had no business knowing, and I had no reservations when it came to spying on my employees or anyone else for that matter.

But in her cards-too-close-to-her-chest, take-no-shit, and answer-to-no-one crusade, she'd managed to be kind. To the staff. To the customers. And most importantly, to my sister. I wasn't as nice as her, but I had my hard limits. Killing was one. Treating Tessie and the women I loved nothing less than the way they deserved to be treated was another.

I liked to think that, so long as I didn't do anything truly bad, I could exist in this murky grey zone for the rest of my life and feel pretty damned content about it. If the pendulum swung too far one way, I'd just swing it the other way.

And that was exactly what Ariana De Luca was doing, too.

Day One of her training period, she'd served me a dish for lunch that had gotten sent back to the kitchen by a customer. A bite had been missing from the corner of the Miyazaki wagyu, which she'd tried to conceal with a piece of broccolini.

I'd insisted she return it to the kitchen, and in front of a Zagat food critic, she crossed her arms and decried my failings to the homeless population of New York City, as if the solution to world famine and hunger hinged on not wasting the three-hundred-and-fifty-dollar six-ounce steak.

Day Two, she'd taken my five-thousand-dollar Eames executive chair to the break room to nap on, and when I had demanded Ariana to return it, she turned it into a "unicorn" chair for Tessie to do her homework on, complete with an ice-cream-cone-turned-unicorn-horn and a makeshift tail made from cooked spaghetti noodles.

"But you can't take Uni from us, Bastian!" Tessie had shouted when I'd accidentally stepped on the ridiculous spaghetti noodles hanging from the back of the chair.

Us, she'd said, as if she and Ariana were a unified front.

Squashing Uni's tail, of course, had made me the bad guy.

Ariana: 2. Bastian: 0.

Day Three, Ariana had compiled in one of my crystal decanters—turning my sister into a thief when Tessie nabbed it from my office—all the alcohol waste from my customers. I'd spit it out when I poured myself a glass that night, and Ariana hadn't missed the opportunity to point out that it'd taken no more than fifteen minutes to fill the thirty-ounce container.

"Maybe if you made better drinks, there'd be no waste. You could end the water crisis." I'd pointed out, to which Tessie—as if I'd insulted them both—argued, "Stop pretending you care about people and actually care about people."

What. The. Fuck.

Ariana was turning Tessie into a new age hippie environmentalist under my own nose.

And Day Four—*fuck Day Four*—Ariana had managed to wrangle an unearned pay raise, win her pick of work hours, and secure her employment at L'Oscuritá. All while making a fool of me.

I was down four now, and that was four times in a row she'd proven herself to be no stranger to the inner workings of Hell. But yesterday, after four consecutive slights to me, she'd decided to swing the pendulum from evil to virtuous, confusing the hell out of me.

I couldn't fight someone good.

Even I wasn't that far gone.

And today, she still hadn't swung her pendulum back to evil.

Ariana eyed the door for the third time in three minutes. Tessie sat in front of her, oblivious, but her presence alone was a signifier of mine. After our confrontation the other day ended with her dodging my questions and the follow up ended in an unspoken truce, I figured Ariana was dreading seeing me. She kept looking at the door like I'd enter the break room any second now.

Interesting.

I watched on the security monitor as Tessie pointed to something in her textbook. Ariana stood, grabbed a white erase marker, and began writing on the whiteboard we sometimes used for employee meetings.

It was her lunch hour, and she'd been spending it tutoring Tessie. The Mother Teresa act baffled me, and it didn't escape me that she not only gave my sister unsolicited help but also looked happy doing so. Not to mention she had no way of knowing I was spying on her, taking in her good deeds with no clue how to process them.

Tessie hadn't been born for most of my relationship with Elsa, but Dana had met Tessie plenty of times while we'd dated, and she'd never lifted a hand to help her. My mother and father foot the bill for Tessie's private tutoring, various extracurriculars, and so on, but that wasn't the same as honest-to-God, hands-on helping. I tried to help as much as I could, but I lived several states away from Tessie for most of the year. Limits bound me, and they were almost as asphyxiating as Gio's expectations of me. If I could, I'd be there for Tessie and Everett every day. It killed me that the two hadn't even met since they were both too young to remember.

But Ariana held a fancy degree from a top-five university,

worked a dead-end job as a bartender, and helped the eight-year-old sister of her asshole boss with the little free time she had during her breaks. None of it made sense to me.

So, here I was, spying on Ariana when I should have been spying on Graham. Vince had sent over a dossier a few days ago, listing supposed allegations against Graham and a proposed schedule that would make it easier for me to keep watch over him.

I may or may not have switched Ariana's schedule to match Graham's—two birds, one stone and all. In my defense, she warranted looking into. Nothing she did made sense. She was too educated to be here, too combative with me despite the fact that I was her boss, and too idiosyncratic, exhibiting behavior none of my sizable staff ever had. If I had reason to look into Graham, I certainly had reason to look into Ariana De Luca.

With that in mind, I slipped on my suit jacket, grabbed the Graham dossier, and headed to the break room.

"Can you adopt me?"

The fuck? I froze, just short of the doorway.

An awkward laugh crept out of Ariana's lips. "What? Why?"

"Mom went back home yesterday, so I might have to go back soon. I don't like it in California. The beaches are cool. So is Disneyland when I'm allowed to go. But my mom is never home, Aronne and Alex are really mean, and they live with us, so Alex never stops bullying me."—*Wait, she never told me that*—"Plus, I never get to see my dad or Bastian." She took a deep breath. "I know you hate Bastian—"

"I don't hate your brother..."

Unconvincing.

"—but he's the best big brother ever, and I miss him."

Back at ya, kiddo.

I waited for Ariana to shit talk me.

She didn't.

"Remember when I told you that people are usually mean when they're jealous?"

"Yeah?"

"I was wrong. People are mean for lots of reasons. Jealousy is just one of the big ones."

"What's another reason?"

"Because they're scared, angry, sad—it can be anything, really."

"How do I do anything about it if I don't know what's wrong?"

I dipped my head a little past the bend, just out of sight.

Ariana shifted in her seat before I slid back behind the wall, and I could picture her turning to Tessie and reaching for her hands. "Sometimes, there's nothing you can do but do your best to be kind to others and hope that, one day, they'll be kind back."—*What a crock of bullshit.*—"But other times, you have to stand up for yourself. It's up to you to know when to do which. You're smart. I trust your judgment."

"If I stay in California, do you think Bastian will visit me?"

"Have you ever asked him?"

"No. I'm afraid he'll say no."

Fuck me. I was the worst brother ever.

"If he says no, he's stupid."

Fair assessment.

"Yup!" Tessie giggled. "Will *you* go to California with me? You can come if Bastian visits me!"

And that was my cue to interrupt.

Ariana expertly dodged the question, "Did you know I

used to live in California?" She glanced at me as I entered. "I went to school there—Degory University."

Boring.

I placed a hand on Tessie's shoulder and spared Ariana a cursory glance. "Did you take a class on how to name drop at Degory?"

She ignored me, her head tilted on the dossier in my hand.

Nosy, nosy girl.

Graham's name was printed in the corner. The font was small, but I had no doubt it was legible for her, so I casually tucked the file under my arm, narrowed my eyes at her, and asked, "No comeback?"

She tilted her chin up at me, defiant as always. "Comeback? What are we? Eight?"

Tessie's head swung to Ariana, her hair whipping my side. "Hey!"

"You're right, sweetie." She patted Tessie's arm. "You're much more mature than your brother."

I rolled my eyes. "Time to go, Tessie."

"It's Contessa. You can't call me Tessie. It's a child's name."

Lately, Tessie had it in her head that nicknames were for children. The fact that she was still a child was, apparently, lost on her.

"Funny. I missed when you turned eighteen." I rolled my eyes. "You let Ariana call you Tessie."

"That's different. She's cool." *Ouch.* "Plus, she lets me call her Ari, and she made me a unicorn chair."

A damn unicorn chair.

Who could compete with that?

"Fine, *Contessa*, let's go."

She turned, hugged Ariana, and skipped out of the room. I followed after her but stopped short of the doorway.

And just because Ariana was right—Tessie was far more mature than I was—and I was maybe a little jealous of her relationship with Tessie, I turned, said, "You have right shift," and left.

The right-side bartender was responsible for the heavy duty, back-breaking tasks, like restocking alcohol and ice, and was usually given to the more muscular bartenders. Was this an asshole move? Probably. But I had no problem with my pendulum swinging in the direction of evil.

I matched Tessie's pace out the door and into the town car.

When she settled into her seat and clipped her seatbelt, she turned to me. "I like Ari. She doesn't talk to me like I'm a kid."

"Just be careful, kiddo. She's a De Luca."

If I were being honest, I didn't mind Ariana's friendship with Tessie. My problem here wasn't with Ariana. It was with the fact that there would be a time, probably soon, when Tessie would leave for California or Ariana would stop working at L'Osuritá, and the closer the two got to each other, the bigger the heartbreak for Tessie.

And that was the last thing I wanted.

Tessie met my eyes. "She's not one of *those* De Lucas."

"So?"

She shrugged. "Well, I like her anyway."

She looked out the window for the rest of the ride home.

Sometimes having courage means
the hardest tasks fall onto your shoulders,
and those leave the biggest scars.

—C.J. Redwine

ARIANA DE LUCA

"I'm serious. I've got nothing on the Romanos. Nothing."

It disappointed me to admit it, but it was the truth. My only saving grace was that it was Jenn in front of me and not

Wilks or Simmons. Plus, what did she expect? It hadn't exactly been long. She didn't have to look so appalled.

She shrugged, placed her pen and notepad down, leaned back on her chair, and kicked her legs up onto her coffee table. "Fair enough. It hasn't been that long anyway." Her intelligent eyes studied me, her usually intense scrutiny far more manageable after my exposure to Bastiano Romano. "So, how are you?"

"Fine."

"Anyone giving you any trouble?"

Bastian's face instantly popped into my mind, and I forced myself not to flinch. "Nothing I can't handle."

In fact, Bastian had been remarkably absent during the rest of my week-long training period. He hadn't even finished my training. Dana had, and it had been awkward and uncomfortable, to say the least.

Bastian and I had a few run ins, sure, but it was only because I'd been appalled by the amount of waste his restaurant produced and talking to him while serving his dinner couldn't be helped.

Today was the last day of training before my first official shift tomorrow, and as far as I knew, Bastian wouldn't be involved. There were already whispers around the staff that he was spending more time than usual on the bar side of L'Oscurità, whispers they somehow attributed to me, though I suspected the timing of my hiring and his increased presence was a coincidence and nothing more.

Jenn clasped her hands together and laid them on her stomach. "There's something you're not telling me."

My chest tightened, and I forced myself to remain calm. Jenn knew nothing about my unhealthy fixation with Bastian. My unhealthy, *unprofessional* fixation, which all but screamed inexperience. And since the bureau was usually inclined to encourage a honeypot scheme, I wanted to keep it that way.

But Jenn was an expert at reading human body language. It sucked to have a psychologist as a best friend. It sucked even more when you wanted to tell your psychologist best friend about the man giving you problems, but she was also your FBI handler, and that man was one of your targets.

For someone who preferred simplicity, my life could be pretty damned complicated.

I drew out my next breath, taking extra time to answer. "The girls are kind of catty." Truth. "The boys are overly flirtatious." Double truth. "The work is... tiring. I swear, I can't feel my arms." Triple truth.

In fact, my back was killing me, my feet ached from being on them all day, and I hadn't been able to feel my arms since yesterday during training, when I was asked for the second time that day to carry one hundred and fifty pounds of ice up the steepest set of stairs I had ever seen in my life.

Not so fun fact: The average American bar sells five hundred drinks a night.

L'Oscurità sells five thousand.

Ask me how much ice that is.

Ask me.

I. Fucking. Dare. You.

"There's a nice massage spa on fifth."

"You mean the one that charges four hundred dollars an hour?" I looked around Jenn's fancy office. "I'm supposed to be on a bartender's salary, and even if I wasn't, my FBI salary *combined* with my L'Oscurità salary isn't that pretty either." I sat up, winced at the sharp ache in my back, dug through my purse, and tossed my new insurance card her way. "Speaking of keeping up my cover, you can start charging these sessions to my fancy new insurance, courtesy of L'Oscurità's health plan."

She looked down at the card, and her posture sagged a bit. "I can't believe they had you go under with your real name."

I stared at the framed doctorate degree on the wall behind her, the picture of her and her mom below it, then the row of thick psychology encyclopedias on her bookshelf. My eyes continued to travel across the room, darting everywhere that wasn't Jenn. "Well, they did. Too late now."

Translation: Why didn't you give me a heads up? Did you know? Did you oppose their decision? Did you fight for me? *Why didn't you say anything to me? Why?*

Translation of translation: I was still bitter. Probably would always be.

The heavy weight of her eyes burned my skin. "And how do you feel about that?"

Cliché.

Even for her.

I sat up and gathered my things, happy I only had a minute and thirteen seconds left in the session. "Does it matter?"

"Yes."

I finally gave her my eye contact. "To who?"

"To you."

To you.

She was supposed to say, "To me."

We had been friends since I had joined the bureau six years ago, yet here we were, with a rift so big between us, I could barely see past it anymore. So, why did it feel like only I could see it? Why did it feel like I was in this alone?

I stood up, put my jacket on, grabbed my purse, and

headed to the door. I stopped once I reached it and turned to face her. "Look, there's nothing I can do about it now, so I'm not going to think about it. I'm just going to keep my head down, focus on doing my job, gather as much intel as I can, and try to stay safe."

Did that sound as impossible as it felt?

"You're late."

Dana's eyes narrowed on my dress, a figure flattering black number that usually made me feel like a Bond girl. But right now, I couldn't feel anything past the ache in my feet let alone focus on how I looked. The rest of me, thankfully, was numb.

She took a step forward and raised her voice, the sound of it echoing in the employee break room and likely into the hallway, though I suspected that was her intent. "If you're going to be late, don't bother showing up at all. That's not the type of business we run here."

We.

As in Bastian *and* her. Her words weren't lost on me, considering he managed the restaurant and she was a hostess for the bar. That, and the fact that I was actually eleven minutes *early*.

Which meant Bastian must have been close, and she wanted to make me look bad. Not surprising at all. Dana was a goner as far as he was concerned. Her head was shoved so far up his ass, I was surprised she could still see clearly.

I ignored her, took a seat on Bastian's chair, and tried but failed to push aside the memories that invaded me as soon as my ass made contact with the buttery leather. The phantom image of Bastian feeding me annexed my mind like an unwelcome apparition.

She watched as I grabbed my Kindle out of my bag and began to read as if she wasn't still lingering by the door. After all, I had—I checked my watch—nine minutes and forty-nine seconds before my training shift began.

I hadn't even gotten through a page before Tessie came in, barreled past Dana without sparing her a glance, and climbed onto my lap. Dana wavered in the center of the room as Tessie shifted in my lap until she was comfortable (and I wasn't).

She grabbed my Kindle from me. "What are you reading?"

I covered her eyes and snatched it back from her. "Nothing appropriate for an eight-year-old girl."

Still, Dana hovered, uncertainty plain and clear on her face. "You guys know each other?"

Tessie looked up at Dana and squinted. "Who are you?"

"Dana." She fidgeted. "We've met. I-I dated your brother."

Speak of the Devil.

Bastian entered the room, his presence as demanding as a heart attack. His eyes narrowed on Tessie's lanky body covering ninety percent of me before he turned his powerful gaze to Dana. "What are you doing here?"

If I were being honest, I was relieved that it wasn't just me he acted callously toward.

Dana gestured weakly in my direction. "She's late."

"No, she's not. Her shift starts in six minutes. Yours, on the other hand, started twenty-four minutes ago."

Silence hung in the air, sifting through the tension like an Olympic skier weaving through an obstacle course. Gold. This was pure gold. I mean, I could be mature about it and not enjoy Dana's suffering, but part of me still believed people got what they deserved and enjoyed when it happened.

"But... She..." Dana raised a futile gesture in my direction. "I—"

Bastian lifted an impatient brow. "You...?" He crossed his arms, and his face was cold as he leaned against the doorframe, his movements almost too casual. "I hope you don't talk to our customers like that. I wouldn't want them to think I hire illiterate staff members."

Jesus.

I was glad that, for once, I wasn't on the receiving end of his wrath.

A red flush spread across her cheeks. "I'm sorry. It won't happen again." Her head lowered, marking her defeat, and she left the room in haste, taking with her half of the eleven precious minutes I'd had before my shift was scheduled to start.

I sighed, placed my Kindle back into my bag, ignored Bastian—because fuck him—and stared at Tessie. I kept my voice gentle and soft, so her brother couldn't hear me speak. "What was that?"

Tessie and I had gotten along during the past week, sure,

but she didn't strike me as the type of kid to just clamber onto my lap out of the blue. She had an ulterior motive, and I would probably be the worst FBI agent in the world if I couldn't figure out the intentions of an eight-year-old.

Tessie's eyes were wide and innocent before a small grin slipped past her lips. "I wanted to make Dana mad." She paused, her brow furrowing in concentration. "I don't like her."

"Why not?"

She eyed where Bastian was still standing, arms crossed like an impenetrable fortress, and leaned forward to whisper in my ear. "She's mean. I never get to see Bastian, and when she dated him, she always tried to send me away from him."

Dana was jealous of the time that rumors made her think I spent with Bastian, and Tessie was jealous of the time Dana had once spent with Bastian at her expense. The irony wasn't lost on me, except Tessie was an eight-year-old child, and Dana had no excuse for her petty behavior. That, and the fact that everything seemed to revolve around Bastian, even though he clearly didn't give a damn about anyone but his family.

I leaned back and studied Tessie's face. I didn't like her brother. Hell, I could hardly tolerate him on the best of days. But I liked Tessie. She was exactly the type of innocence I had wanted and vowed to protect when I'd first joined the FBI.

I kept my voice low, so only she could hear. "People like Dana—or any other girl your brother is with—don't matter to him like you do. Whether he tells you it or not, you're his favorite person in the world."

I disliked her brother, her family, and everything they stood for, but that didn't extend to Tessie. She was pure.

At least, for now.

Maybe in a decade or two, things would change, she'd follow in her family's footsteps, and I'd be the one called upon to arrest her, but until then, she was just a kid. Innocent. Pure. Protected.

She bit her lip. "Really?"

I nodded my head, my smile eclipsing her hesitant one. I'd been honest. I could say a lot of negative things about him, but I would give Bastian this—he loved his family, and he loved his sister most.

I could see it in the way he paid attention to her, doted on her, and talked to her in a manner I'd never seen him use with anyone else. It was a pity she didn't realize this, but she'd figure it out, and when she did, she'd realize how lucky she was to have a family who loved her—even if it was composed of criminals and the biggest jackass I had ever met.

After all, that was more than I could ever say for myself.

Bastian's lips formed a small grin. He looked human in the same way celebrities often did—alive and on the same planet as me, yet so far out of reach. "Tessie, you done talking about me?"

"No."

He rolled his eyes. "Too bad. Ma's here to pick you up."

She reluctantly got off my lap, waving a slight goodbye to me before she wrapped her arms around her brother's legs in a short hug and walked out the door. Bastian stayed in the room, silent for a moment. I met his eyes, my stare unchallenging for once.

I wondered what he saw when he looked at me. The heavy slump of my shoulders? The way I slouched on his seat to dull the ache in my back? The way my legs crumpled to the floor in a lazy, sore mess that I couldn't find it in me to hold up?

I had no doubt he noticed, inventoried, and processed it all.

That was the type of man he was.

But his expressionless eyes met mine and stayed there. "Why didn't you defend yourself?" He meant against Dana.

A tired sigh slipped past my lips. "I don't bother with insignificant things."

We both froze at my muttered words, the implication clear and heavy in the air. I bothered with him. *He* was significant. After all, we were always at war, engaged in a never-ending battle, with wits and lust as our weapons of choice.

I longed for my bed. Not my fake bed in my fake apartment. My real one. The one with the wine stain in the corner and the scent of coffee beans infused in the mattress from when my aunt had made me her ridiculous organic coffee stain remover, and I hadn't had the heart to tell her those words put together made no sense, let alone in a stain remover.

I longed to bury my head in my Tempur-Pedic pillow and wake up a year from now, when the humiliation finally lessened and Bastiano Romano was just a memory I couldn't shake but didn't have to confront.

I waited for him to say something.

To deepen my mortification.

He didn't.

Instead, he nodded his head and turned to the door, but before he left, he shifted to face me. "Oh, and Ariana?"

My palms felt clammy. "Yes?"

Silence drifted between us.

He looked like he wanted to say something important, but he settled with, "Now, you're late."

ARIANA DE LUCA

"You're coming with me," Bastian stated as he strolled into the main area of the bar.

Not a question.

A statement.

Like I had no choice in the matter.

"Excuse me?" I continued to set up the chairs for opening later, not bothering to face him.

"Who works for whom here?"

"Have you ever been to Brunei?"

"Yes."

I blinked dumbly for a few seconds before I recovered. "Good. Then you'll be able to recognize a dictatorship."

He set a hand on the chair I grabbed, so I'd stop moving. "The thing about dictators is, they don't care what their subjects think... They will, however, punish those who don't follow their orders without hesitation." His voice dipped lower. "Would you like to be punished, Miss De Luca?"

Wow.

Those words actually came out of his mouth.

Instead of fighting him, I pulled my shoulders back and tipped my chin up to stare at him. "You're insufferable. In any other company, human resources would have a field day with you."

"Good thing *I* am human resources."

He turned and walked out the door without waiting for my reply. I barely had time to grab my phone and sweater before I chased him down the street, running at him like a jilted lover. He didn't stare at me as I caught up to him, and he slid into his car without opening the door for me.

I pulled the handle of the flattened sports car, and instead of opening outward, it shot upward, nearly hitting me in the face. Amusement gleamed in his eyes as he watched me struggle to slide into the car in my short dress.

I didn't know how he got his massive frame in here without looking ridiculous. The passenger seat had probably been set for Tessie or something, because it had been pulled as far forward as it could go.

My knees bucked against the glove compartment as I stared at the dozens of buttons in front of me. Bastian could have taken pity on me and moved the seat back, but he didn't. He started the car and drove off, stopping at a light to eye the top of my thighs as my short dress rose up in my position. My panties peeked out of my dress, but I couldn't do anything about it, and he wasn't a gentleman enough to put me out of my misery.

To fit the sleek aesthetic of the car, none of the buttons had labels on them. There were no buttons on the doors either. I twisted a random knob, and a screen slid out of the center console. I pressed a button, and cold air blasted me in the face.

Finally, Bastian pushed the rectangular button nearest to my hand. His knuckles brushed against mine. I sucked in a breath and moved my hand away as fast as I could without looking like I was running from his touch.

The seat moved back. I bit back a groan as I stretched my legs.

"I hate your car," I told him.

"Duly noted."

We pulled in front of a building. Tall, shiny, and expensive—like most things in New York. Bastian slid out of the car, handed the keys to the valet, and actually opened my door for me. I took his proffered hand, waiting for him to use it to push me or something.

He didn't. He'd merely lifted a finger, signaling the valet to wait as he lifted the front trunk of the car, pulled out a pair of Louboutins, and handed them to me. Nude colored, six-inch pumps with the signature red beneath. I'd fall in these if I hadn't gotten experience in high heels as a stripper.

"Wear these."

Another order from him.

I shot him a wary look before slipping them onto my feet. He gripped my elbow to steady me. This felt like some fucked-up fairytale. Except, instead of Prince Charming sliding a glass slipper onto her feet, Cinderella got an unapologetic dictator who ordered her to slip on Louboutins as he watched the skirt of her dress rise. At least they were a perfect fit.

When I righted myself, several inches taller now, Bastian's hand found the small of my back. He led me into the lobby of the building as I tried to convince myself this wasn't weird. A blonde with a model's figure greeted us with a smile. Her hand reached out, but Bastian ignored it as he stepped past her.

I sent her an apologetic stare as she scrambled to catch up with us. She ignored me. Rude. The elevator pinged and opened as soon as Bastian pressed the up button. The elevator ride to the top floor—sandwiched between the starstruck blonde and the leery Bastian—felt like torture.

With his hand still on my back, Bastian led the three of us into an office at the end of the hall. People stared with wide eyes as we passed their cubicles, the blonde trotting behind us to keep up.

He didn't knock as he opened the door. A man sat at his desk. When we entered, he looked unfazed, ending his call without a goodbye.

"A pleasure as always, Mr. Romano." The man leaned back in his seat, looking powerful with his strong build and salt-and-pepper gentleman's cut. His eyes raked my body as we approached, blazing a path down my legs and settling on my feet with an intrigued gleam in his eyes.

So, Dictator Charming had a reason for the heels. He had wanted this man distracted, and he got it. I was Bastian's pawn, and I expected nothing less from him.

"I'm sorry, Mr. Bennett," the blonde behind me started.

"Leave, Felicia." Mr. Bennett waved his hand toward the door. "I don't have time for your stuttered apologies."

She left, and I felt a little bad for her, even though she'd ignored me. Mr. Bennett stood, and instead of offering us a seat, he rounded the table and leaned against it. My instincts told me it was to get closer to me.

I'd been led into the lion's den by a wolf.

"You'll understand if I cut straight to the point." Bastian's hand lowered on my back, so it rested just above my ass. "My patience is spread thin these days."

Mr. Bennett's eyes studied the Bastian's hand placement on my back. He couldn't see how low it was from his angle, but I was sure he knew as he spoke, "You want my company to lower the price per barrel of beer for nothing in return. The answer is no."

"A ten-million-dollar a year account would piss off your share holders." Bastian's hands lowered even more, sprawling across my ass. "Remember them?"

I hated how much I reacted to his touch. My thighs squeezed together. I knew Bastian felt the movement because his eyes flicked to me as Mr. Bennett's narrowed between my legs. I should have turned around and walked away instead of standing here like a pawn in Bastian's twisted games.

One man wanted me; the other wanted to use me.

"Fine," Mr. Bennett finally relented, his eyes never leaving my body. "A bargain it is. What do you want?"

I couldn't believe I distracted him this much. Mr. Bennett's eyes kept drifting to my legs in these damn heels.

"A twenty-percent reduction in fees and priority selection of inventory." Bastian's finger toyed with my thong through the thin fabric of my little black dress. "What would you like?"

"I want her."

Bastian's fingers dug into my body as he grit out, "Out of the question."

"Not for an entire day. Just for an hour. Those lips look like they'd put a Hoover vacuum out of business."

"You will not disrespect her."

Mr. Bennett ignored him and jerked a thumb in the direction of his desk. "Sitting on this chair all day while working past midnight bores me, and Felicia on her knees beneath my desk isn't cutting it anymore. She has thin lips, she couldn't fit a straw down her throat let alone my cock, and her legs look like stumps in heels. You know how it is."

Bastian stepped forward, tucking me a little behind him, shielding me from Mr. Bennett's eyes as he spoke, low and deadly, "I warned you not to disrespect Ariana once. You didn't listen. I'm killing the contract."

Bastian had been silent as Mr. Bennett spoke, something simmering beneath his surface. I didn't know what I expected him to say, but it wasn't that. Bennett Brewery supplied most of our tap beer. This was our biggest account.

Bennett had been an asshole, yes. I hated him, duh. I hated Bastian for bringing me here as his pawn, too. But he'd just stood up for me. Against a man who essentially made our bar business what it was.

For the first time, uncertainty swam in Mr. Bennett's eyes. "She's just a woman. One girl. This is... this is both of our businesses. Ten million dollars of inventory you'd have to replace."

"Her worth is none of your business, and I have dozens of suppliers who could take your place in a heartbeat. Good luck explaining to your share holders how you lost a ten-million-dollar account because you think with the wrong head."

Bastian turned and led me out of the room, his hand still on my back, keeping me in front of him, a barrier between me and Bennett. The car already waited for us when we reached the valet stand. Bastian helped me into the car, got in on his side, and started the engine.

We sat in silence as he drove for a few minutes.

"I'm sorry," Bastian finally broke the silence, his words surprising me yet again today. "The restaurant and bar both keep over one hundred-people employed. This is... *was* our biggest account. Stephen Bennett raised the price per barrel of beer last month, and I needed him to lower it or I'd have to make cuts elsewhere. Most likely in the staff hours. I brought you here because Stephen loves gorgeous girls with sexy legs, but I didn't expect him to be an ass to you. You didn't deserve that."

"*You're* an ass to me," I pointed out, my mind unable to process that he'd just called me gorgeous and sexy in one sentence, and he'd done all that for his employees.

It put Bastian in a different light.

One I wasn't ready to shine on him.

"True," he admitted. "But it's different when you like it."

I narrowed my eyes. "You are delusional."

"You kissed me when we first met."

He had a point, so I kept my mouth shut and stared out of the window.

As we drove past shiny building after shiny building, what he'd just done sunk in.

He'd ended our biggest contract because of me.

For me.

15

Ever notice that the whisper of temptation can be heard farther than the loudest call to duty?

—Earl Wilson

ARIANA DE LUCA

About an hour before my shift ended, Vince, Gio, and another man had come into L'Oscurità. The tailored suits on Vince and Gio could pay for my New York City rent for the next two years, but their companion—a John Doe—looked like he couldn't afford two months of utilities for my tiny apartment.

I had tried to study them from my perch beside Graham, but they'd gone inside Bastian's office and hadn't left since.

The bar was closed, most of the staff had already left, and still, not a peep from the office. Under the guise of helping a busboy with table cleaning duty so he could get home early to his pregnant wife, I positioned myself at the center of the bar, where I had a direct line of sight to the hallway that led to the office door.

"Dana," Graham called from the entrance as the busboy slipped past him. He had a jacket in one hand and his car keys in the other. "I'm leaving. You wanted a ride?"

Dana, who sat at a bar stool, no doubt waiting for Bastian to show his face, looked between me and the general direction of Bastian's office. Indecision marred her pretty features before she finally heaved a sigh, her desire to avoid walking in her high hostess heels winning.

"Ari?" Graham turned to me and raised a brow.

When I realized I'd been cleaning the same table for about ten minutes, I straightened up, my fingers clenching around the rag, and said the first lie that came to my mind. "I'm alright. I'm catching a movie with a few friends at the 24-hour theater a few blocks from here. Thanks, though. Drive safe."

He nodded to me and opened the door for Dana, who gave one last lingering glance in the direction of the office, narrowed her suspicious eyes on me, and left with a soft huff. The door slammed shut behind them, leaving me alone with just the men behind the door.

As soon as Graham and Dana left, I tossed the rag with the other dirty rags, washed my hands, and made my way to the small section of the hallway that laid between Bastian's office and the employee break room—close enough to Bastian's office to hopefully hear, yet close enough to the break room that, should I get caught, I could say I was on my way to the break room to gather my things to leave.

I'd done something similar yesterday when Bastian had almost caught me eavesdropping on his phone call with someone.

Everett.

I needed to find out who Everett was. I made a mental note to pass his name along to the bureau.

My phone felt heavy in my hand as I pretended to text. Several security cameras lined the hallway, so I needed to look like I was doing something. My ears remained alert, and I heard a voice speak behind the closed office door.

"Y-you've got it all wrong." From the hesitancy, I suspected this was the man I hadn't recognized. The John Doe.

"Are you calling us liars?" This voice was firmer. It wasn't Bastian's. I'd heard a wire tape of Vince's voice, and this didn't sound like him. Gio's voice, maybe?

"N-no. O-of course n-not."

My breath hitched. Just listening to John Doe's voice gave me anxiety. I didn't have my service weapon. It remained hidden under my apartment sink in a fake detergent bottle with a false bottom. For this legend, the bureau had only approved me to carry it if I suspected I was in imminent danger—beyond the hostile working environment.

And for the first time since I started the legend, I wished I had it with me.

I didn't think they would kill him. Not here, where they had so much to lose. But maybe they'd leave, and I would have to follow them without the safety of my Glock 22. The thought made my skin crawl, and I switched from fake texting to fake talking on the phone to keep my eyes alert.

"Quit being a little bitch." This came from Bastian, his voice so deep, gruff, and distinct, I would recognize it anywhere. "You haven't paid us. Either you lost the money or you skimmed it from us. Which is it, Bianchi?"

I made a mental note to pass along the name to Jenn during our next session, along with whatever I could grasp from this conversation.

Bianchi's voice was a soft quiver. "I'll get it t-to you. I promise."

A smoother voice spoke this time. Firm. Self-contained. Deadly. *Vince.* "You have a daughter, don't you?"

Bastian feigned a laugh before chiming in. "What was her name? Mara? Maria?"

"M-marta." I strained to hear Bianchi's barely audible voice.

I felt for the guy. I could barely handle one Romano, and he had three in front of him—taunting him. I paced as quietly as I could, pretending to speak into the phone with animated hand gestures. In reality, I wanted to be closer to their voices. I could barely hear them as it was.

Another laugh tore free from Bastian's throat. This one so dark, it sent a chill down my body traveling through each limb. "Marta." He tsked. "Right. That's what it was."

"Didn't you fuck her, son?" Giovani Romano toyed with his words, deliberate in their delivery. "How was she?"

I winced at his crass words, empathy for Bianchi gripping my heart. I was trained not to feel empathy while undercover, and even though I knew Bianchi had to have known what he had gotten himself into with the Romano family, I couldn't help but sympathize.

After all, my mom had gotten in way over her head with the De Luca family before she'd become pregnant with me and ran away. As far as I was concerned, Bianchi could have been my mom, and Marta could have been me.

"I've had better." Bastian's dry words spoke of boredom I wonder if he felt, and something about his indifferent tone relieved me.

I hated myself for it.

"Marta." Vince's calm demeanor was eerie, like warning tremors before a life-shattering earthquake. "I remember her. Sweet girl. Too bad."

A long pause swept the air before Bianchi spoke again. "Too bad?"

Vince's words had been vague. Nothing I could arrest him over. Still, the threat remained clear. I wouldn't wish Bianchi's position on anyone.

Vince ignored Bianchi. "I'd forgotten what she looked like. Oh, wait. Didn't you see her the other day, Bastian?"

They were teasing Bianchi. It was cruel, but I would expect nothing less from the infamous Romano family. If my mom hadn't run away from the De Luca family and hidden my existence, would I be Bastian or Bianchi in this scenario? Would I be the heartless monster or the tortured victim?

I refused to be either.

"Hmm... I don't remember." The door muted Bastian's playful voice, but the delivery was no less effective. He was either a phenomenal actor or a sadistic fuck, who enjoyed causing pain.

I was betting on both.

They were monsters.

All of them.

Undercover at the bar, even for just a week or so, I had lost sight of that. I had humanized them, attributed them with the normalcy of the restaurant business, and saw Bastian for nothing more than an jackass who only had a heart when it came to his sister and family.

That was a mistake I vowed to never make again.

The three of them were having too much fun with this. With toying with this poor man. Short of Vince's short drawl, I would have believed this excited them. That they were eager to taunt and intimidate Bianchi.

They hadn't actually said or done anything illegal. Yet. Unless I wanted to blow my cover, which would destroy my career at the FBI, I couldn't do anything about them. I was hopeless. *Helpless.* And damned if that didn't make me feel worthless.

Gio cleared his throat. "Why don't we look at the security footage?"

Oh, shit.

His words stopped me, and I struggled not to sneak a peek at the security cameras. My grip on my phone loosened, and I dropped it, trying and failing to catch it. It fell to the floor with a soft thud, and when I bent to pick it up, the door swung open.

My hands were still on the floor and my ass in the air when Bastian stepped out. His eyes locked on mine with eerie precision, and I succumbed to the fury in them.

They were lethal.

Vibrant.

Irate.

If death had a face, it would be Bastian's.

And he was glaring right at me.

BASTIANO ROMANO

In the restaurant business, people say if you've earned a James Beard award, you've made it big. That it's something to be proud of. Something to put on your trophy shelf, add to your LinkedIn profile, or whatever your typical doleful sap did.

But I had not one, not two, but *three* James Beard awards for top restauranteur. Three fucking James Beard awards, and I was taking care of some pitiful schmuck from the armpits of the Lower East Side.

This sure as hell didn't feel like making it big.

Tommy Bianchi thought he could get away with skimming money from my family and knocking up my second cousin. We were pissed about the money, sure, but that wasn't enough to warrant a visit from me, Uncle Vince, or Gio—let alone the three of us together.

Any other day, and it would be a lowly Romano soldier raining punches down on his head. But Tommy Bianchi had made the mistake of tossing the money he had skimmed from us at my cousin and telling her to find the nearest clinic when she'd told him, with tears in her fucking eyes, that she was pregnant.

Gio, of course, was affronted, never mind the fact that he had just recently tried to pawn that same cousin off on me. Uncle Vince, on the other hand, was absolutely livid, and that made him lethal.

You couldn't tell it just by looking at him. But I knew him well enough to know that the hand he rested in the pant pocket of his tailored Tom Ford suit was clenched and the casualness of his tone concealed thickly veiled rage.

Uncle Vince leaned against the edge of my desk and crossed his legs at his ankles. "Marta." He tilted his head to the side. "I remember her. Sweet girl. Too bad."

I fought the urge to sigh. We were toying with Bianchi. It was supposed to be fun. It was supposed to satisfy the vengeance my cousin rightfully deserved. But I was bored. Bored of it all. This life. This job. This conversation.

Couldn't they take care of him and be done with it?

Bianchi's head faced down, but I could feel the tension in his body. It permeated the room until the air was so thick, it suffocated me almost as much as my duty to this family. A line of sweat trickled down Bianchi's nose and dripped onto the wood, soiling the Macassar ebony milled onto the floor.

Another second passed.

Another drop of sweat on my hundred-thousand-dollar floor.

Another irritant.

Another reason to leave.

I could walk out the door right now. Gio and Uncle Vince didn't need me for this. But I didn't want another lecture about the importance of joining the family business from Gio, and I didn't want to disappoint Uncle Vince.

Decisions, decisions.

"Too bad?" Bianchi's voice was a squeak. Fitting for a pest. He played the arrogant playboy well until he came face to face with the real wolves.

Us.

His tail tucked between his legs suited him, I supposed. The same way white paint suited a clown.

"I'd forgotten what she looked like. Oh, wait." Vince turned to me. "Didn't you see her the other day, Bastian?"

I smothered a smirk. I made fun of Asher for being dramatic, but the truth was, he had learned that from Uncle Vince. He was mostly straight forward, but he was still a Romano. And everything with the Romanos was a production.

If Vince set up a meeting with me, it couldn't just be at his or my place at a regular hour. It had to be pitch dark and in the middle of nowhere. The more fog the better.

"Hmm..." I paused, drawing out Bianchi's suffering. "I don't remember." The corner of my lips tilted upward at the shudder of Bianchi's shoulders.

Pathetic.

Gio cleared his throat and walked around to where I sat behind my desk. "Why don't we look at the security footage?"

I pressed a button at the bottom corner of my desk, and the wood slid back before the screens glided up and out of my desk's false top. An image of Ariana on the phone filled one of the screens.

Gio nodded his head toward the door, a gesture for me to see what was up with her. I stood, relieved to be out of here. Maybe I could salvage this night. Deal with Ariana, then head to Rogue to find an easy lay.

I strolled past my desk, ignoring the pathetic waste of oxygen on the floor. Turning the knob, I pushed the door open, and my eyes landed on Ariana's ass. She was bent over at the waist, her round ass facing away from me, but I could still make out the generous curves.

Her head lifted, and her vivid blue-green eyes locked on mine. I didn't bother hiding my irritation at having to spend my night dealing with Bianchi. Maybe it was because her position—bent over before me with her curved ass in the air—made her look so vulnerable. Or maybe it was because I was sick of holding back with everyone.

I wasn't sure why, but for the first time in my adult life, I let my walls down.

I let her see my rage.

My incurable fury.

Do your duty as you see it,
and damn the consequences.

—George S. Patton Jr.

BASTIANO ROMANO

Her eyes widened as she studied me in silence.

"I was on the phone, but I was just leaving." Her tone remained casual, but I caught the slight breathlessness. The tantalizing way her chest moved up and down with each inhale and exhale.

I took a step forward, and she lifted herself, teetering off balance when I took another step toward her. With her equilibrium still wavering, she quickly spun around to leave, but my arm shot out and pressed against the wall, blocking her path.

She turned further to avoid touching me. A smirk graced my lips at her new position. She faced the wall now, and I let my other arm press against the wall on her other side, effectively caging her in.

She could have ducked under my arm or pushed it aside, and I would have let her.

But she didn't, so I took a step forward.

Then, another.

And another.

With every step I took, she moved with me until her front pressed flush against the wall. I stopped when hardly a millimeter separated us. Her heavy breathing occupied the air surrounding our bodies.

Music to my fucking ears.

I moved her hair from her shoulder, letting my finger linger on her skin longer than necessary.

Her head fell forward, and she pressed it against the wall. "What are you doing?" Her husky whisper gripped my cock and wouldn't let go.

The flashes of her parted lips as she'd watched me shoot jets of cum on my desk did nothing to soothe my erection.

I ignored her question in favor of my own. "What are you still doing here?"

Even though I'd been absent while dealing with my best man duties the past week, I knew the employee schedule like the back of my hand, and almost an hour had passed since she'd been scheduled to get off work.

My only employee with the habit of staying late was

Dana, and my glance at the surveillance cameras had already told me the leech was long gone.

Ariana, on the other hand?

Her body begged me to take her. To lift her dress, pull her panties to the side, tug on her ponytail, and sink my teeth into her neck as I buried my cock inside her soaking wet pussy.

Yet, she didn't strike me as the type to stalk the men she was attracted to—and I had no doubt she was attracted to me. The sexual tension simmering between us burned hotter than a volcanic eruption on the sun.

Once upon a time, I'd been prepared to propose to a woman with whom I'd thought I had incomparable sexual chemistry.

I was starting to realize that comparing Ariana to Elsa was like comparing a stove fire to a forest fire. Elsa was the flickering flame above the stove; Ariana was the blazing inferno that consumed the forest, chased predators from their home, and rained ashes down from the sky.

But our chemistry—the need for us to touch one another—couldn't be why she stayed late.

Which led me to why I left for the hallway in the first place—to figure out why the hell she was still here. Her reasons were most likely innocent, but I wasn't one to assume. One wrong move, and I could hurt a lot of people. I had my family to think about.

I considered my options. I could ask nicely, but that never got shit done. I could keep an eye on her, but between my standard deep background check, Gio investigating her last name, and my attraction to her, I was already doing that.

I settled on asking impolitely, catching her off guard, and using my body to lure an honest answer from her.

I looped a finger around a lock of her hair—successfully taking her off guard—and tugged gently. "Well?"

She shuddered under my touch, and I relished in the power I held over her. I should have stepped back. She was my employee, and I needed it to stay that way until I could find a replacement.

Plus, until I fired her, this was a human resources disaster just waiting to happen, and despite the fact that he could afford one, I doubted Asher would appreciate a lawsuit.

But it had been a long day, and I was sick of holding myself back for everyone. And I wasn't above using my body to fluster her.

"I think I was stood up."

"You think?" I didn't bother smothering my amused smirk.

"He was supposed to pick me up and take me to the movies, but it's almost four, and he's not here."

Boring.

My amusement waned. She had a date, and it sounded like something out of a G-rated Disney flick. Until I remembered what she'd said to Tessie. Ariana had never gone to the movie theater before.

I'd love to go sometime. With someone special and as cool as you.

She could have been lying to Tessie, but I doubted it. Which meant she thought whoever she had plans with was special.

I took a step back, releasing her from my hold and almost regretting the fact that, other than her hair and shoulder, I hadn't taken the opportunity to touch her.

"He did you a favor by ditching you. The 24-hour theater is where fifteen-year-old boys go to get laid when their parents are home and they can't afford a hotel room. Did you choose the place or did he?" I paused, and a rude laugh slipped past my lips with ease. "Are you sure he's eighteen?"

She scowled, turned to face me, and opened her mouth to respond, but I cut her off. "That was rhetorical. I don't actually give a shit." I took another step back, finally an appropriate distance from her. "I have better things to do with my night."

I didn't.

It was four in the morning, and all the hottest models were probably long gone from Rogue by now. If I left L'Oscurità, I'd be alone with nothing to do.

But I sure as hell didn't want to go back into the office, and if I stayed in this narrow hallway with Ariana any longer, I would probably end up balls deep inside her.

Hell, her nipples were still hard and poking out of her dress. She could pretend to hate me all she wanted, but I knew she craved me.

Which was why I also knew this conversation had to end.

Now.

But when I was halfway to the door, she called out, "Wait."

And because I didn't actually want to be alone, I did.

ARIANA DE LUCA

This was a mistake.

Everything about this situation was a mistake.

Going undercover with my real name.

Leaving Bianchi with Giovanni and Vincent Romano.

Being alone with Bastian.

But it was the hand I had been dealt, and I needed to make the best of it. And that meant keeping Bastian here, so I had an excuse to keep an eye on Bianchi's safety. Or maybe I'd get lucky and witness an after-hours crime I could testify to seeing.

Either way, my plan depended on Bastian staying. Bastian, who had just been delivering Bianchi's suffering. Bastian, who was perhaps the most unpleasant person I had ever met. Bastian, who couldn't care less about keeping me company. Bastian, who I was way too attracted to for my own good.

He turned to me, a sheen of curiosity coating his eyes. "Well?"

I fixated my gaze on the bar. "Have a drink with me."

"Why?"

A surge of helplessness flooded my body at his indifferent tone. "Because I just got stood up, and it's the gentlemanly thing to do."

"I'm not a gentleman."

He was right, but he was also wrong. Bastian, for all intents and purposes, didn't just look like a gentleman. He *was* one. He had been educated at the best boarding school the country had to offer, was a Wilton alumnus, had the distinct wardrobe of an upper east side point-zero-one percenter, and could be so chivalrous, it did unmentionable things to my ovaries.

The problem was, his chivalry only extended to his family, and beyond them, it was like none of us little people existed. A few days ago, he had patiently held the door open for a solid two or three minutes while Tessie had taken her time packing up her backpack before heading out of the break room. I had been right behind her, but as soon as she passed the doorframe, he closed the door.

Right. On. My. Face.

My eyes lowered to the floor, and I dragged the uncomfortable moment out before I finally gathered the nerve to look him in the eyes. "Be one for me."

My words surprised even myself, but they were an honest plea. A little bit of vulnerability I allowed myself to brandish because it was me and I was doing my best at pretending to be myself.

Maybe I was being foolish, but for some reason, talking to Bastian came as naturally as breathing. And the odd thing was, organic moments like these were gold for legends. When undercover agents entered a legend, they aspired to achieve the ability to instinctively be their legend.

Yet, here I was with Bastian, my words and actions effortless and natural in the face of the mafia prince of one of the cruelest criminal dynasties to have ever graced the United States of America.

The tension in the air—one part hostility and two parts mistrust—shifted. The mistrust remained unaffected, but the hostility loosened until the only thing left between us was caution and desire.

Bastian led me to the bar, and I followed closely behind. Surprise trickled through my body as he took his position behind the bar and began to make us drinks. He grabbed two glasses, dried them off, and topped them with ice. I let loose a bitter laugh when he poured the amaretto in them and filled the rest of the cups with sour lemon mix.

He took a seat next to me, his eyes flickering briefly in the direction of the office. "When you were in front of the office, did you hear anything?"

My pulse thrummed in my veins. I placed my glass on the table, so it wouldn't slip through my fingers as I forced myself to keep my voice casual. "Are you accusing me of eavesdropping?"

"Not of eavesdropping intentionally." He arched a brow. "Unless you did." The way his eyes stayed on me, so intense and unapologetic as the scanned my face, unnerved me.

I backtracked, considered my options, and decided to go with the half-truth. I gave a convincing wince and admitted, "Some parts. When you guys were loud."

"What did you hear?"

"You were threatening someone's daughter."

"We were *reminiscing* about his daughter," he corrected, traces of an untethered smirk gracing his lips.

I rolled my eyes. "What did he do to deserve that?"

He considered me for a moment, his eyes slowly roaming my face with far more patience than I possessed. "My cousin is pregnant with Bianchi's baby. When she told him, he tossed some bills at her face and directed her to the nearest women's clinic."

Ice coursed through my veins, and I winced. If my mom had told my dad she was pregnant, would he have done the same? Or worse? Would he have forced my mom into something she hadn't wanted?

Growing up, I'd never known how to feel about my mom keeping me a secret from my dad. On one hand, I wanted to give him the benefit of the doubt. That he wasn't the monster my aunt had told me he was. On the other hand, I wanted my mom's sacrifice to mean something more than just a mistake.

It was worse that I couldn't confront her about it. She had died the same day she had given birth to me, and her sister—my aunt—had raised me in a small town in New Jersey, where she taught me to hate the De Lucas and all things that strayed on the wrong side of the law.

The sympathy I had for Bianchi died a transient death.

I took a long swig of my drink and muttered, "What an asshole."

Bastian barked out a surprised laugh and nodded his head. "Of the gaping variety."

"That's just gross."

A rare playful gleam glazed his eyes, making him seem almost human. "Tell me honestly, how much of an asshole do you think I am?"

"Honestly?"

"Of course."

"The worst. Like, at least a twelve on a scale of one to ten."

"And Bianchi?"

"A different type of asshole."

"If we're different types of assholes and he's gaping, would that make me puckered?"

"Oh, my God. How much have you had to drink?"

He laughed, and I reveled in the fact that he could be playful.

Gross, but playful.

I had the sinking feeling this was a one-time thing. That I had caught him off guard. Maybe something had happened today to make him crave this type of companionship. Maybe it was the delirium of the early hour. Maybe I was filling in for someone else. Or maybe, like me, he was sick of feeling so damned lonely all the time. Either way, I knew the likelihood of catching him like this again was slim to none, and I wanted to preserve this moment and take advantage of it.

Whether for selfish reasons or my sense of duty, I didn't know.

Bastian's glass had been emptied, but he didn't make a move to clean up and leave. "Why are you here, Ariana?" His words doused me like a bucket of ice-cold water flipped over my head.

"What do you mean?"

"Why are you a bartender? As you like to slide into every conversation, you went to Degory. You graduated top of your class, too."

Degory was the West Coast's answer to Ivy League schools. I saw nothing wrong with being a bartender, but I understood what he meant. What was the point of pursuing a premium education only to get a job I didn't need a degree to do?

"I don't slip it into every conversation." It was valid, but I ignored his question anyway. "You actually read my resume?"

"I vet every employee I hire and all the ones I don't." His voice was miffed, as if the mere suggestion that he ran the restaurant anything but perfectly disturbed him. "Are you ignoring my question?"

I took a moment to think before I spoke, threading the truth into my cover like Wilks had taught me, "I don't know why I'm a bartender. In fact, I don't know what I'm doing with my life in general. Maybe I never have. I know what my family wants me to do,"—Aunt Nadia had been all for my career at the FBI and would probably have been delirious with excitement if I took any of the mafia syndicates down a peg, even if it wasn't the De Luca family in particular—"but I don't know what *I* want."

I downed the last finger of my drink. "I guess, until I figure it out, I'm just going through the motions, trying not to disappoint anyone along the way."

He turned to me and opened his mouth to say something but faltered, the most uncertain he had ever been around me. "I feel the exact same way."

His words left me reeling.

"But you have L'Oscurità."

And the Romano syndicate.

Was it possible he didn't want anything to do with that side of the family business? That maybe, like me, he was just going through the motions? I wanted to confide in him. To explain that I was floundering because nothing about my life was black and white. But just like I couldn't choose myself over my duty to my country, I couldn't tell him who I really was and what I really did.

And I was struck by my desire to confide in him.

By this fleeting moment of camaraderie we shared.

His eyes didn't leave mine as he spoke. "L'Oscurità is mine and it isn't. But even if it was entirely mine, I don't know if I would want it."

"So, what *do* you want?"

"I don't know, Ariana. I don't know." He paused a bit before he admitted, "I want a lot of things I can't have."

A connection between us lingered in the air like the morning fog above the California coastline. When I had gone to Degory, I used to wake up early to run through the fog. The cold mist against my skin felt like being kissed by mother nature, but this time, it was Bastian I wanted to kiss.

I leaned forward, my intent clear in my eyes. This was wrong, so taboo I could hardly fathom it, but I wanted this more than I could remember wanting anything else. And for a startling second, it looked like he wanted me, too.

He leaned forward, and finally—*finally*—his lips were almost brushing mine.

The sound of footsteps drummed their way into my ears, and Gio and Vince interrupted us, entering the main bar area with Bianchi trailing behind them like a meek lamb being led to slaughter. Bastian straightened up instantly and leaned away from me. The movement was small, but it spoke volumes.

His voice dipped low, so only I could hear. "This conversation changes nothing."

But it did, and we both knew it.

Do not forget duty.
But choose love when you can.

—Cinda Williams Chima

BASTIANO ROMANO

"As your best man, I feel the need to insist that you tap out of this one."

My arms squeezed Asher's head, flaunting my Anaconda Vise hold because I could.

He grinned, brushed off my millionth innuendo about

calling off his wedding, and twisted out of my grip. "That one wasn't even creative."

If Niccolaio were here, he'd be on my side of the rifts, so I felt the need to double up on the jokes. I didn't actually want Asher to cancel his wedding, but it was my obligation as his best man to pretend marriage sucked and was the end of everything good in the world.

Hell, it had been for my parents, so maybe there was some truth to that.

Not that I thought Asher and Lucy were anything like Ma and Gio.

Or me and Elsa for that matter.

I swung my leg around Asher's torso, wrapped my arms around his elbows, and held him in a Full Nelson hold on the wrestling mat. "Seriously, though. You're off your game. Tap out, Ash."

He straightened his left arm and rapped his flat palm against the mat three times. I tightened my hold for a few seconds because I couldn't resist, and then I released him from my grip.

As soon as he escaped my hold, he straightened up and gave me a blasé shrug. "Pre-wedding jitters."

I popped a brow up. "Second thoughts?"

"More like excitement."

I followed him to the refreshments and towels area of the home gym in his penthouse. "Aww, you're so cute, Ashy. Let's go get our nails done, and you can tell me all about it over pink lemonade martinis and scones."

"Fuck off, asshole." He paused. "Everyone knows you eat scones with tea, dumbass."

I laughed, loud and in his face, but I couldn't help but wonder what the type of love that Asher and Lucy shared felt like. In most ways, Asher was the same person I had always known him to be. The only difference was, he had someone to share his life with. But Lucy? She got to see a side of him that none of us got to see, and I was sure that Asher shared the same privilege with her. A part of me wanted that, but that part was buried deep down, below my forced indifference and the duty I had to my family.

Asher tossed a bottle of water and a clean towel my way. "Are you on steroids or what?"

I drank half of the bottle in one gulp. "What are you talking about?"

"That had nothing to do with pre-wedding jitters. You actually got the best of me, fair and square."

"*Actually?* That's awfully arrogant of you." I slapped his stomach with the tip of my towel. "Maybe you're not as good as you think you are."

The truth was, aside from the five or so hours of sleep my body needed to function, I was either at L'Oscurità or the gym. Gio was a bust to hang out with nowadays since he couldn't catch my hints that I would rather talk about literally anything else but mafia business.

Vince was MIA at random hours of the day, doing God knew what. I was worried, but I wasn't sure it was my place to confront him about his absence.

And Uncle Frankie was busy being the head of the Romano syndicate. Hell, I couldn't even remember the last time I had seen him. Uncle Vince's birthday, maybe? He'd be at Asher's wedding, but I probably wouldn't catch a peek past his security.

Asher, who was usually my go to, had Lucy, and while I figured they'd eventually come up for air and hang out with the family more, I didn't want to push them out of their honeymoon phase prematurely.

Niccolaio was, like always, in hiding. With the five-million-dollar bounty his brother had placed on his head, I had no clue if he was attending Asher's wedding or even in the state still, and while I would be down to hang out with him, it just wasn't worth risking his safety. Plus, I figured if my family were currently doing everything they could to keep Niccolaio's presence here a secret, hanging out with me wasn't exactly low profile.

Everett lived with Elsa in Alabama.

Tessie had a strict schedule—home school, sleep, food, and extracurriculars. When she could actually hang out with me, L'Oscurità usually confined me with work. Ma, on the other hand, already left for her home in De Luca territory. Truth was, even when she was actually around, Ma wasn't—and had never been—great company.

Which left *me.*

Alone.

Being alone wasn't so bad when I had Asher and Niccolaio for company, but having a big family I loved and still feeling alone was fracturing for the soul. Not to mention the fact that I had a son I hadn't seen in years.

Which was why I had caved and had a drink with Ariana De Luca last night.

I didn't even want to think about last night. Thinking about how much I'd shared with her made me want to build a thousand-foot-high fortress around myself and live the remainder of my life in an Ariana-free safe zone.

And that, in turn, made me feel like a pathetic loser for being unable to process my emotions.

Nothing about the situation was pleasant.

Asher shook his head and let it go. "So, we got security down for the wedding, and the wedding list has been finalized. Are you taking a plus one?"

"No."

A boyish smirk crossed his pretty boy face, and it reminded me of when we were younger. When I didn't have the weight of my family's expectations on my shoulders. Before Gio and Elsa had betrayed me, and I could call my dad "Dad" without wanting to throw a punch in his face. Back when Ma got pregnant with Tessie and still lived in New York with us, unhappy but at least pretending to be in a relationship with Gio.

"Are you sure about that?"

"Tell me he didn't." I ran a hand down my face. "Tell me Gio didn't set me up on a blind date with a mafia bunny at your goddamned wedding. For Christ's sake."

"I won't tell you, but it doesn't make it any less true."

I swung a fist at the nearest punching bag, which happened to be bright pink and had a picture of Asher's face taped to it. When it stopped moving, I noticed the bruises photoshopped on his face and smirked. "Lucy's?"

"She won't take the picture down."

I followed Asher out the door and into the hallway of his penthouse. "Remind me to ask her to make me a copy. I'll frame it on my desk."

"Consider it done," Lucy said from behind the kitchen island.

Asher wrapped an arm around her waist from behind and leaned forward to kiss the side of her forehead. "Remind me why I'm marrying you?"

"Definitely for the sex."

I took a seat on one of the island stools. "You two are disgusting."

Lucy winked. "Maybe you'll find love at my wedding. I hear your dad set you up with a date."

"Fuck you both."

Asher squeezed Lucy's waist. "Sounds fun, but double dipping isn't my thing."

Lucy turned her head to face him. "Isn't that a food thing?"

I smirked. "Yes, but it's also an Asher-and-I-take-turns-with-you thing."

Lucy was a pretty girl, but I didn't want her like that. Messing with Asher was just too fun to pass on an opportunity.

Asher leaned around Lucy, grabbed an apple off the counter, and threw it at my head. "Talk about double dipping Lucy again..."

I caught the apple and took a bite, feeling relaxed for the first time in a long time. "You started it."

"And I'm ending it, children. How is it that you two shed ten years from your ages every time you're around one another?" Lucy reached across the island, grabbed the apple from me, and cut around my bite. She threw the chopped pieces into her pan. "A gentleman, by the way, wouldn't make such crude jokes."

Asher apologized, but I just smirked, remembering a past conversation with Ariana.

A gentleman would.

I'm no gentleman.

Be one for me.

My smirk slipped. I wasn't delusional. There was something there between me and Ariana. I was the magnetic field, and she was gravity, pulling us closer together, strengthening the link we shared.

Problem was, this couldn't happen. Secrets shrouded her, and I couldn't afford any risks. Her combative nature proved volatile, and the last thing I needed was for someone to rock the boat. And most of all, she was my employee, and I was her boss.

My duty chained me, each responsibility another link in a never-ending chain that tightened its hold around my throat with every passing second. Did I really need to remind myself of this?

"Where'd you go just now?" Lucy reached for my hand from across the table and pinched my skin.

I shook my head, focusing on the present. Asher had left somewhere, probably to shower, and I hadn't even noticed.

I was off my game, and I needed to rectify that.

Cocking my head to the side, I studied the mixture in her pot and dipped a finger in. It burned the tip of my middle finger, a big F U to me, but perhaps I needed that. "I need to fire an employee."

Lucy narrowed her eyes and swatted my hand away. "You've never had a problem with that in the past."

I tasted the apple mixture, dried my hand on a paper towel she offered me, and took a seat on the bar stool. "I've also never been set up on a blind date by my dad at my best friend's wedding. There's a first time for everything."

"Why?"

"He thinks if I marry a mafia bunny, I'll be forced to strengthen my connection to the family business."

Lucy knew about the Romano business. She just didn't care.

She shook her head. "No, I meant, why are you firing the employee?"

"She's causing problems for me."

"For you or the restaurant?"

"For me."

"What's she doing exactly?"

Distracting me.

Confusing me.

Turning my world upside down.

I shifted in my seat and replied, "She's rude."

"To the customers?"

"To me."

Lucy furrowed her brows. The confusion on her face had discomfort traveling through my body.

"Not grounds for firing unless she's damaging the business by hurting your feelings." She cocked a brow as if to say, "Well, is she?"

"She rearranged the furniture."

"In the bar? I didn't notice anything different when I stopped by before opening hours yesterday."

"The break room. She took the chair from my office and put it in there."

Her lips twitched. "And what did she do with that chair?"

"Turned it into a unicorn."

Laughter erupted from her thin frame. "Are you high?"

"Not an actual unicorn. She stuck a cone on the top of the chair with frosting and tied spaghetti noodles to the back of the chair at its spine."

"Changes to"—she snickered—"the break room don't count."

"She's argumentative."

"Last I checked, it's a restaurant, not a dictatorship."

"Well, she—"

"Bastian, what's really going on? You're grasping at straws here."

I paused a beat. "I'm attracted to her, and employees are off limits."

There. I'd said it. Not the whole *it*, but the part that wouldn't leave me bare.

"You're not going to fire her."

"Excuse me?"

"You're not going to fire the poor girl because you can't control your penis." She tilted her head to the side, goddamn comprehension filling those flawless features of hers. "...unless it's more than your penis you can't control."

Fuck me sideways with discount lube. Why couldn't Asher marry someone dumber?

"No one under eighty says penis. It's dick or cock. And I don't know what you're talking about."

Was I proud of lying?

Only if it worked.

She crossed her arms. "Don't play dumb."

"He's not playing." Asher strolled to the fridge with just a towel around his waist. "He *is* dumb. Not an act." A few droplets of water slid down his chest, and I caught Lucy eyeing them.

I grabbed my wallet and keys off of the counter and slid them into my pockets. "And that's my cue to leave."

From the door, I heard Asher ask, "What's his deal?"

Lucy giggled. "He's in looooooove."

She was joking and so far off, but it didn't change the fact that Ariana De Luca had caught my attention. I wasn't in love with her. I wasn't even in like. But she intrigued me, and that was more than anyone had done since Elsa.

But if it was just intrigue, why did I feel so fucked?

As soon as we entered L'Oscuritá's bar, Tessie ran straight to Ariana and wrapped her arms around her legs. The buckets of ice in her hands wobbled while she tried to steady herself from the impact of Tessie's body.

Her thin arms flexed when she hauled the buckets onto the counter and returned Tessie's hug. "How are you, Tessie?" She straightened her back, allowing a slight wince to escape before that perky, just-for-Tessie smile transformed her face into the centerfold of my fantasy *Playboy* spread. "I've been looking forward to seeing you all day."

"Really?"

"Of course."

I approached them, needing to stop the love fest. Tessie didn't need someone in her life who would leave.

Ariana squinted at me when I was half a foot away. "No one has ever quite looked at me like you do."

"And how is that?"

She glanced down at Tessie before her eyes met mine and her voice lowered. "Like you're not sure whether you'd like to kill me or kiss me."

Our eyes held, and I didn't know if mine were the capturers or the captives.

Tessie jumped up and down, breaking our trance. "Kiss! Kiss!"

Fuck my life, I needed space. Distance from this... this... this what? What was she? Whatever she was, it was messing with my fucking head. Tessie. Everett. I had two priorities. Just two, and I couldn't focus on them with her around.

I hardened my stare, trying to convey to Ariana with my eyes that I'd rather kill her. "There's a customer at the bar, and the ice is melting."

She took a few steps back, wincing with each movement. "Hatred paralyzes life."

Love releases it.

She wasn't talking about us. She was talking about me. As if she knew me. Was I paralyzed? I sure as hell felt stuck. But her voice had been a whisper, almost as if she'd been talking to herself.

And she was quoting Martin Luther King, Jr. I was struck for the millionth time by the fact that she could've been doing anything other than manning a bar with her life. Maybe it was hypocritical. We both had Ivy League-level degrees, and while she bartended, I managed a restaurant. Two sides of the same coin.

Tessie tugged on the edge of Ariana's skin-tight dress. "What's wrong?"

"What do you mean?"

"You keep scrunching your nose all funny."

"Don't worry about me, sweetheart." She placed a hand

on Tessie's shoulder. "I've been carrying ice all day. My back is just a little sore."

Guilt surged through my veins.

Distance, Bastian. Distance.

Being an asshole counted, right?

"Put some ice on it." I nodded toward the ice bucket and laughed. "Looks like you've got plenty." I settled a hand on Tessie's lower back and led her to my office.

She was scowling by the time we stepped foot past the doorway.

I cocked a brow. "What?"

She crossed her arms. "You are such a jerk!"

"Because I expect my employees to do their job?" It bothered Ma that I talked to Tessie like she was an adult, but I wasn't in the habit of babying people. That included my sister.

"You don't have to be mean about it! I bet Everett doesn't know how mean you are!" She speared my gut, turned around, and headed out the door.

"Where are you going?" I called after her.

"I'll be back."

Had the age of adulthood changed since I was a kid?

I shook my head and, unable to help myself, pressed the button for the security monitors to rise. Ariana was halfway up the basement stairs, carrying another massive load of ice. Did I feel guilty? Unfortunately. Feelings felt as dumb as they sounded.

But then I leaned against my chair, the ache in *my* back noticeable as Tessie returned and scrambled onto that damn unicorn chair. The ergonomic unicorn chair that my ass was supposed to be planted on, sans cone, frosting, and spaghetti.

Tessie removed plastic wrap from the straw of her juice pouch and poked the top of the cardboard with her straw.

"You shouldn't be drinking that."

"Why not?"

"Too many preservatives and added sugar."

A smile teased her lips. "Are you going to tell on me?"

"Maybe. Serves you right. You've been consorting with the Devil lately."

"What does 'consorting' mean?"

"Fraternizing."

"Nice try. I know what 'fra-tit-er-ni-zing' means now."

"Fra*ter*nizing," I corrected. "But I like your version better."

She wrapped her lips around the straw sticking out of the contraband juice pouch, the joke (thankfully) lost on her. After a stare off, which I lost, Tessie took another victorious sip. "Stop looking at it like I can't drink it."

"You shouldn't."

"There's no extra sugar. It's freshly squeezed from *Squeezed!*"

"That place on Fifth?"

How was she getting gourmet juice from a bougie juicery several blocks over?

"Yup!" she popped the 'p.' "Ari brings me one every day and leaves them in the break room fridge for me."

Of course, she did.

I sighed, drawing out my exhale. She couldn't make this easy on me and let me hate her in peace. While Tessie pulled out her homework, I eyed the camera. Ariana was still hauling ice up the stairs, a different load this time. Each slow step she took visibly strained her body.

There was that damned guilt again.

ARIANA DE LUCA

The bar got rowdy late at night. I understood it. People came in to wind down, and the later it got, the more drinks people bought. It usually wasn't a problem.

Always let someone on your shift know where you're going.

Don't travel to empty areas alone.

Those were two rules we'd gone over during training. I'd noted them back then, but I'd never really adhered to them. My training gave me comfort, but when it came to actually using it, I realized I couldn't. Not because I physically could not, but because if I did, I would blow my cover.

Bartenders didn't have a background in mixed fight styles. I needed to act like a bartender. Not an agent. I hadn't told Graham when I slipped out alone to go to the stock room and grab more paper towel rolls.

Rules number one and two? Broken.

Because of the way the bar's entrance laid on the side and the basement had been converted into a cellar for drinks and ice, a stock room had been built into the alleyway. The path was lighted and the bar had bouncers inside and at the door, so with my training, it felt safe to slip around the corner into the alleyway.

I thought nothing of it as I used my key to let myself into the stock room. Grabbing as many rolls as I could hold, I turned to leave and realized I'd let the door shut with my key on the outside lock. To prevent theft, the door had an auto-lock feature, not that a portable saw wouldn't shred through the wooden door easily.

I set the rolls down on a shelf and turned the door handle. No movement. I patted it. Nothing. Scouring the room for something to pry the door open, I came up empty. Fuck. I slammed my palms onto the wood and shouted out, hoping someone could hear me.

Relief swept through my body as the doorknob twisted open, but I faltered when I caught sight of the man on the other side. I recognized him from the bar. Not an enforcer, but sometimes he'd drink with that crew as they entered. He looked dangerous, but I knew I could take him on... I just could blow my cover.

I balled my fists and held them in front of me, ready for a fight in case I needed to. He laughed, throwing his head back at the sight of my fighting stance.

"Cute." He shut the door behind him. "I love it when they fight."

I swallowed as I watched the door swing shut, locking me in here with him. "You don't want to do this."

"I love it when they try and talk me out of it, too." He took a lazy step forward.

"You won't get away with this. Think about it. There are hundreds of people in the restaurant and the bar. Witnesses."

He *tsked.* "He said. She said. Unless they actually see this happening, no one can prove a thing."

His truth settled into my bones as he circled around me like a shark ready to attack, and I scanned his body for weak points, somewhere I could launch the first strike. I didn't need to. The door swung open, and there stood Bastian. He leaned against it, using his body to keep it open.

His arms crossed as he took in the scene, his eyes quickly assessing my body and stance before lifting to the man. "Look at her again, and she will be the last beautiful thing you see."

He talked as if he owned me. I understood why. He was laying claim to me, knowing his status would ensure this man wouldn't pick a fight with me anymore. Not that anyone would disobey an order from Bastiano Romano regardless. Still, his compliment had my lips parting, and he knew it because his eyes shifted and narrowed on them.

Beautiful. He'd called me beautiful.

You're supposed to be gathering intel, I reminded myself. Except so far, L'Oscurità had been painfully absent of intelligence. Perhaps Asher Black had truly gone clean and, with him, his restaurant.

"Sorry," the man muttered. He shoved me forward as he stalked past me, bumping his shoulder against my back, and out of the door.

Bastian caught me before I fell, but the movement caused him to let go of the door, trapping us both in the storage room. Oh, goodness. I chased the door, but it had already shut. Trapped. With him of all people.

My fist connected with the door as I yelled for help. I raised my fist again, but he caught it.

"You'll sprain your wrist," he explained, as he rubbed the redness away from the first hit. It was almost as if he cared. "I don't have the time to rework the schedule because you want to act foolish and petulant."

Right.

There it was.

The real him.

I tore my hand away and paced the length of the room. Mostly because I was starting to feel claustrophobic with him taking up so much space. He was 6'4" and 220 pounds of muscle at most. He shouldn't have taken up that much space, but he did.

"You're freaking out," he remarked, leaning casually against the door that trapped us.

"We could be here all night."

"Are you dumb?"

I stopped and stared at him. "Excuse me?"

"Always let someone on your shift know where you're going, and don't travel to empty areas alone." He crossed his arms. "Two simple rules that exist for a reason, yet you seem incapable of comprehending them. If I hadn't come..."

I cut him off, "I would have been raped by one of *your* regulars who likes to hang out with *your* people." It was the first time I'd made a reference to his mafia dealings. Subtle, but the reference hung in the air and caused it to thicken.

Bastian's jaw ticked at the word rape, and he unfolded his arms. "He'll be dealt with."

"How?" I knew he wasn't going to incriminate himself here, but I was genuinely curious.

"By someone with more intelligence than you." His words lacked their normal bite, but his eyes looked irate. If it were anyone else, I'd say he cared.

"Thank you."

I suspected it wasn't the answer he'd been expecting because he opened his mouth to say something but stopped.

He dipped his head in a nod. "You're welcome."

I leaned my head against one of the shelves. It dug into my scalp, but I ignored the sting. "It was stupid." I knew I could have taken that guy, but it would have broken my cover. I shouldn't have put myself in the position. "I'll be more careful next time."

"Good."

Great. I was trapped in here with a neanderthal. I couldn't process silence or one-word replies. It was like sending a long text and receiving "K" in return. Only uncivilized people did that.

Silence settled into the tight space. I considered organizing the storage for something to do, but it was already organized, so I hummed the tune to Jeopardy and looked around for something to help us get out of here.

Paper towels. Toilet paper. Printer paper. Receipt paper rolls. Paper napkins. Lovely.

"Why a unicorn?" he asked.

I swiveled to face him, not sure I heard him right. "What?"

"You turned my chair into a unicorn. Why a unicorn?"

"Because your sister reminds me of them. She is one of a kind, beautiful, and resilient. She sees the magic in life."

"The magic?"

"If you don't believe in it, you'll never find it."

"You believe in magic?"

He looked amused, his face filled with a condescending mirth. His lips lifted in some semblance of a smile, and I swore everything seized. He had dimples. Two of them. I wanted to reach my fingers up and poke them. I'd never do that, of course, so I shook my head in furious spurts.

"Not like wizards and witches," I explained. "I mean it like Fate and Destiny. That type of thing."

"You make the world seem prettier than it is."

"Funny, considering I don't see beauty when I look at it. But your sister does."

"She's young."

"Maybe. But I'd like to keep those rose-colored glasses on her for as long as I can. She laughs out loud without hesitating, speaks what she feels in her heart, and only thinks with good intentions. People who have lost those things don't realize their value until they're gone. People like us. It's up to us to protect those who haven't lost them, because only we know."

"We."

"Yes."

He could deny it if he wanted, but it wouldn't change the fact that I saw loss in his eyes. The kind of loss that always bled no matter how long the wound had closed. It stuck there no matter how he felt, no matter what he was doing, no matter what he would do. I didn't know who he'd lost—the files hadn't told me—but I knew what I saw.

Bastian had a protective instinct. His jaw had ticked at the word rape, and he'd not only saved me but also reacted to the fact that I needed saving. Like the idea that it could happen again unsettled him.

There could be no worse thing for me to realize about him. I'd always been drawn to people like that. Seeing protective instincts fractured a barrier I'd worked so hard to erect. How desperate was I for affection that I preened at the first inclination of feeling from someone who'd been an obstacle since I'd met him? Pathetic.

"You'll hurt Tessie if you leave," he remarked as if it would be so simple to stay away.

What a jerk. I turned from him and continued my search for something that would free me from this hell pit. Me. Not us. *Me*. I'd lock the door and leave him in here for all I cared.

"Come here," he commanded.

I ignored him.

"Come. Here."

I paused in my steps, goosebumps lining my arms at the authority in his voice. My body swiveled around to face him, but instead of letting him speak, I shook my head and asked, "Who hurt you?" His eyes narrowed as I approached, but I didn't stop. We stood foot to foot as I continued, "Because you act like someone who's been stabbed everywhere possible. Back. Neck. Thigh. Chest." I reached forward to jab his chest with my finger, but he caught it.

He didn't stop me as I stumbled forward against him. I had to use his chest to steady myself, mortified by the burn of my palms against his skin—even separated by his button down.

"Are you done?" he asked.

Fury built in my throat. Not at him. At me. That wall that had shattered couldn't erect itself again, and he looked... *different*. Something like pity filled his eyes. I tried to close my eyes and tune out what he said, wondering how this day had spiraled into a confrontation like this.

"I'm sorry."

My eyes flew open. Surely I hadn't heard that right.

He continued, "I'm sorry you were cornered today. I'm sorry you got attached to Tessie and will eventually see her leave for California. I'm sorry we fight. I'll offer you a trade."

"A trade?"

What could he possibly want from me?

"Yes. I'll be less... volatile," he toyed with the word, "if you start following the rules. They're there for your safety."

I couldn't wrap my head around this proposal. What did he even get out of it?

"Deal," I finally agreed.

He nodded once, turned, and kicked the door down like it was easy. The wood splintered and broke into a bunch of pieces. My mouth dropped open as I watched him step past the mess, wondering why he hadn't just done that in the first place.

The only thing that feels right
is as wrong as it can get.

—Maggie Hall

ARIANA DE LUCA

Since I'd met him, I noticed three things about Bastiano Romano—all of them nothing but trouble.

Firstly, when I thought I finally knew him, understood some semblance of his motives, and could at last prepare myself against him, he'd pull the rug out from under me, and

I'd be back at square one. Completely clueless. The worst part was, I wanted to know him for reasons I loathed to admit went beyond the call of duty.

Secondly, he answered to no one but himself. Asher may have owned this restaurant, but for reasons I refused to admit, the staff responded to, respected, and admired Bastian. He was horrible to deal with, yet for the most part, he treated his employees quite fairly and successfully ran one of the most impressive restaurants and bars in the world. Still, the fact that he was always in control of everyone and himself disconcerted me at best.

Thirdly, Bastiano knew how attractive he was, and he used it like it was another weapon in his already impressive arsenal. I rarely saw Bastian at the bar side of L'Oscurità, but when I did, our eyes always found one another's, and his smoldered, searing through me and invading my space like knock-off T-shirt vendors outside a Lakers game.

But despite the fact that I'd rarely seen him lately, I felt him. I felt him when I tutored Tessie in the break room, and she stared keenly at me with eyes identical to her brother's. I felt him when he stepped into the room, and the hairs on the back of my neck stood up like a dog raising its hackles. And I certainly felt him each time I hauled hundreds of pounds of ice from the basement, thanks to the right-side shift I should have never been assigned.

I should have cashed in my pick of shifts I'd won from my bet with Bastian, but I was just thankful he'd chosen to drop the questions on how I knew about Emily. So, I lifted my last load of ice for the night, dropping it almost instantly as my back gave out.

I leaned my head forward, pressing it against the wall. "Fuck my life."

"There's that can-do attitude." Bastian's presence flooded the room.

I forced myself not to groan. In this moment, I felt weak. Physically but also mentally. The last person who needed to see me weak was Bastiano Romano.

I kept my head facing the wall. "I know this is normal for us—you push, and I pull, or whatever—but can you not, *Mr. Romano*? Just for today. Because I can't. I just can't." My shoulders and back ached, and my legs were struggling to hold my bodyweight as it was. He'd already taunted me yesterday, and if he poked the bear right now, I swore I'd bite him.

He took a step closer. "Bastian."

"What?"

"Call me Bastian."

I kept my forehead pressed against the wall, not daring to risk a glance at Bastian. The electric tension that swam between us whenever we were near each other was nothing short of dangerous. "What is this?"

My brows pressed together as I tried and failed to decipher his tone. It didn't have the bite he usually reserved for me. Did he feel guilty seeing me like this? I doubted it. The man was colder than an ice cube frozen in an igloo in the South Pole.

He continued his approach. "Maybe I feel a little bad."

"What happened to—" I deepened my voice and mocked, "'this conversation changes nothing?'"

"It didn't."

His voice was closer, and still, I didn't turn. I probably should have—having a conversation with him while staring at a wall reached a level most would consider weird—but I couldn't.

He continued, no trace of mocking in his tone even

though I knew he was mocking me, "I was human when I said that, and I'm human now. Humans tend to help when they see another in peril."

Disbelief ransacked my frame, and I let loose a huge laugh. "Help? You put me in this situation. How are you going to help?"

I shuddered when the tip of his fingers brushed my neck, but I didn't pull away. "What are you doing?"

He didn't answer. Instead, he gathered my hair and repositioned it to the side, exposing my neck. His thumb brushed along the slender nape once, twice, and a third time—harder. I held back a moan, my mind reeling and my breaths shaking.

His hands shifted over my shoulder.

No way.

He was massaging me.

Bastiano Romano—of the freakin' Romano crime syndicate—was massaging me.

I leaned into his touch as his hands trailed down my back. I'd thought I couldn't afford the four-hundred-dollar-an-hour massage Jenn had suggested, but this... This felt even more out of my means.

I didn't stop him, but I should have. Each day I stayed here tugged me deeper under the spell of this cover. This had never happened before. Sure, some covers changed little pieces of me, but none of them had possessed me before. I'd never lost myself in an assignment. Maybe it was the people—Bastian and Tessie—or maybe it was the fact that I was my own cover. This was *me* I lost myself in.

Okay, maybe it was a little Bastian, too.

One hand gripped my waist, holding me still as he pressed harder into a knot below my shoulder. My front teeth dug into my lower lip, refusing to show him how good this felt. His hand splayed out across my waist, the sheer size of it consuming my skin as his other hand worked on my knots.

My eyes pressed shut, and I caved. I balled my hands up.

"Harder."

The plea slipped out like powdered sugar passing through a sieve, my broken clumps spreading into tiny little pieces before they fell to the floor beside my resolve. I did *not* just beg that. Except I did, and I couldn't take it back, so I tried to keep quiet as he continued.

He stopped entirely before he started up again, harder this time, giving me what I refused to admit I wanted. His breath fanned the exposed skin of my neck, and I dug my nails into my thighs until little crescent grooves formed on the flesh.

"Bastian, this isn't a good idea."

My body defied my words, meeting his fingertips, begging for more. I dropped my neck to the side, and he slid his palm along my shoulder and up the nape, caressing it. If I closed my eyes and let myself forget about everything—forget about where we were, who we were, and the hate we shared for one another—I could have convinced myself that we were lovers, fogging up the tiny room with our lust.

And fuck, it felt so good. I'd never had vices before, but I imagined fighting them felt like this, and giving in...

It'll feel better, that lurching in my stomach whispered.

She's right, my heart agreed.

Truth was, I needed this. My back ached. My feet hurt. No amount of physical activity at the bureau prepared me for hauling hundreds of pounds of ice and vodka up and down the stairs all day long.

That's definitely why you haven't moved, I rationalized

before I hesitated, reached up, and lowered the straps of my dress. The fabric dropped, and I caught it before it fell past my waist. I gathered the top of the dress together and held it bunched against my stomach, my bare breasts pushed against the wall. The coarse texture drew my nipples into hard peaks that demanded attention, but I ignored them like I ignored rational thoughts.

I faltered for an explanation before fumbling out, "It feels better skin-to-skin."

Really, no explanation existed to justify this. Body aches could be eased by a hot bath, not a private topless massage from someone affiliated with one of the city's most dangerous crime families. And the prick who put me in this situation in the first place.

Bastian muttered something under his breath, a cross between a groan and a swear, but his hands returned to my bare back as he leaned down to whisper into my ear. "Tell me to stop."

Stop?

How could I?

I wanted this. I wanted him. Rationally, I knew I couldn't. I wouldn't. I had a responsibility to fulfill, an oath I'd sworn to uphold, and nothing about this situation possessed an ounce of the integrity I'd once prided myself in.

But maybe if I gave in just one time, I could shed myself of the desire scratching at my throat and get on with this legend without falling apart. I latched onto that poor logic like it would absolve me of my sins and leaned against Bastian's touch.

"Don't stop," I begged.

His fingers paused against my skin, and I arched my head

back, seeking his eyes. They looked torn—so unlike his normal cocky, self-assured attitude—before his eyes met mine and narrowed with lust. He reached out and guided my head until my cheek rested flat against the wall.

My fingers pressed against the brick, failing to hold onto something as his fingers slid down my back, dragging the dress' fabric with them until it laid pooled around my ankles. The wait pained me as he trailed kisses from my neck to my spine, his hands following his lips' descent down my body.

"Spread your legs wider." The gruffness of his voice scratched at my insides, churning lust in dizzying circles, and I knew, if he were to reach around me and slide his fingers into my panties, I'd be wet and ready for him.

Fucking hell.

I obeyed his command, and his hands rewarded me by tearing at the bottom of my panties until they hung open, not a care in the world that I would either have to work in ripped panties or without any at all. The opened-mouthed kiss he pressed to my ass cheek preceded the bite he gave me, his teeth sinking down on my flesh until pain sent jolts of lust straight to my clit.

I shifted, agitated, needing more but unable to bring myself to ask for it. A *smack!* echoed in the room, and it took me a moment to process what had happened.

He'd slapped my pussy from behind, light but firm against my swollen clit. "Stop moving. Palms flat against the wall."

I placed them against the brick, but I couldn't stop my movements as he leaned forward and licked a trail down my slit from behind. His hands gripped my hips on either side when I jerked forward. He kept me still as his tongue slipped past my lips, skating across my clit.

"What?" I faltered as he stood.

I'd convinced myself I didn't want this, but now that he'd begun, I couldn't fathom stopping. Ever. Instead of leaving, Bastian ignored my question and yanked my panties until they tore at my hips, leaving angry red marks on my sides. Then, he stood, grabbed each of my hands, bunched them together behind my back, and bound them tightly together with my panties.

"When I say stop moving, you stop fucking moving. Got it?"

Holy fuck.

This man could ruin me.

If anything, his words forced more wetness to escape my lips. I couldn't even hate myself for this, because I'd *tried*, damn it. I tried to hate him. I tried to force into myself that bone-deep, soul-consuming, will-crushing hatred that usually came easily when it came to my marks, but with Bastian, it never stuck.

The cocky attitude and demanding behavior only made me want him more. I'd met a litany of men who knew what they wanted, but I'd never met a man who could actually take it. That take-no-shit dominance drew me in like bait on the tip of a fishing rod, and that man I'd connected with and almost kissed when I was supposed to be spying on his family? That was the side of him I wanted to hold me... after the side of him who forced me to serve him in front of a crowd fucked me harder than I'd ever been fucked.

I had issues.

"Got it?" he repeated, his body pressing me against the wall, his hard cock digging into my back.

"Yes." My moaned words parted my lips and he slid two fingers in my mouth before he returned them to my bare ass.

He tested me by reaching between us and stroking a slick finger against my slit. I didn't move. His finger shifted to my clit, and he flicked it. The sharp pain nearly sent me forward, but I dug my nails into my palms and forced myself to stay still. I could almost feel his satisfaction unfurling.

"Good girl," he praised.

The tip of his nose traced a path down my neck to my shoulder before he bit down. Hard. Moving his hand back, he slid his thumb into my pussy, gathering my wetness, before he pushed it between my ass cheeks. I stiffened, unused to the sensation as he used my own wetness to tease my backside.

"Never been touched here? You innocent little thing." His condescending tone should have pissed me off. Instead, it fueled my lust, and I needed the hate-fuck he all but promised me each time he provoked me.

He leaned down, plucked a melted ice cube from the bucket of ice, and slid it up my ass, the tip of his finger with it. I screamed out, shocked by the cold and his roughness, clinging onto him for strength.

He slid his finger deeper. "Are you on the pill?"

Oh, God.

This was happening.

Holy fuck.

I could hear the zipper of his pants lower, and I relinquished all semblance of control I had. My heat melted the ice cube, and he used the wetness to slide his finger in and out, adding another finger until I gasped at the fullness. My hands jerked, fighting the restraints, begging to touch him, until my lust ripped the panties binding my wrists. They fell to the floor in tattered scraps like scattered evidence in a crime scene.

I didn't allow myself to question this.

Bastian slapped my clit again when I didn't answer, his voice rougher and impatient as he repeated, "Are you on the pill?"

"Yes!" The words struggled to squeeze past my lips as I panted and rubbed my clit against his fingers.

His free hand latched onto my hair, and he used it to pull my head back until I stared him in the eyes. "I'm going to fuck your tight little pussy raw until you come on my cock." His thumb returned to my backside, and he teased my entrance. "And then, I'll fuck you harder, and when I come, I'm going to pull out and leave a trail of my cum from your pussy..." He pushed the tip of his thumb into me. "...to your ass." His harsh laugh filled the air when I cried out. "Who knew you'd be so needy?"

"Fuck you." I tilted my head to the side and nipped at the hand holding my long locks back.

He hissed out and tightened his grip on my hair. "You are so goddamned difficult. You know that?"

"Shut up and fuck me already." The more we talked, the more time I had to convince myself that I shouldn't do this.

And hell, I wanted to do this.

My taunt broke his little restraint. He spun me around until I faced him. My eyes dipped down, taking in his erection. He'd unzipped his pants and lowered his black boxer briefs. His piercing glared at me from the tip of his long, thick cock before each of his palms met my shoulders, and he guided me down.

I let him, taking my time to lower myself to my knees. "What are you doing?"

"You're going to thank me for massaging you." He stroked himself, running his fist up and down his length.

Once.

Twice.

A third time.

Placing his free hand on the back of my head, he guided himself to my lips and traced them with the head of his cock.

"You're the reason I needed a massage in the first place." My tongue brushed his piercing as I spoke. I arched a brow, nodded at the buckets of ice behind him, and taunted, "The ice is melting. Are we doing this or what?"

"Open." He groaned out when I took him into my mouth and squeezed my arm as I reached down to play with myself. "Stop."

"What?" I tried to ask around him as he thrust into my mouth.

His piercing hit the back of my throat. My nails clawed a path down his pressed slacks as I struggled to keep up with his pace. He ran his fingers through my hair and yanked a little, tilting my head so our eyes met as he spoke.

"Right now, your pussy is mine, and you don't touch what's mine unless I tell you to." He arched a brow, daring me to argue with him. Almost like he wanted me to fight him. Truth was, our fights fueled our lust, drove us straight off a cliff, into this unknown territory that frightened me and clouded my rationality.

He pulled out and pushed back in, his movements rough and jerky, like he couldn't wait to slide back into my mouth. This attraction between us had grown into a boulder I couldn't stop, and I knew I should have stopped this.

Sleeping with people while undercover happened. It came with the territory. But this? I couldn't control myself if I tried, and *that* was dangerous. I had a job to do, and if this snowballed any further, the bureau would lose this once-in-a-lifetime opportunity to take down the Romano syndicate.

I couldn't let that happen.

Bastian pulled out of my mouth, stroked himself once, and let go. His cock smacked my face, jerking me out of my thoughts.

I peeked up at him past my lashes with furious eyes. "What the hell?"

He looked unapologetic as he ran his hand up his length and toyed with his piercing. "You were distracted."

"So, you spanked me with your cock..."

"Yes."

"You don't apologize for anything, do you?"

"I hear an awful lot of talking and very little fucking."

My god, he was such an bastard. It escaped me why I still wanted him. Time and time again, he gave me reasons to run the other way, and still... I remained fixed to the floor, my legs like stubborn roots, unable to move. Transfixed by a man who could snap my neck with a twist of his wrists and leave the mess for his family to clean up.

I stood and met him face-to-face. "You don't need to be an asshole."

"I'm not an asshole. I take what I want, and you dislike it. There's a difference."

"You're in denial if you don't think you're an asshole."

"Call me an asshole again, and I'll have to fuck yours."

I reached up on my tip toes, leaned forward, and whispered, my lips brushing his with each syllable, "Ass. Hole."

He placed his palms on each side of my head and kissed me, backing me into the wall. His tongue slipped past my lips, deepening the kiss as he stroked the roof of my mouth and ground his cock into me.

"So. Damn. Needy." His lips didn't leave mine as he spoke.

He lowered his hand to my pussy, gathered my wetness, brought it up to my face, and smeared a line down my cheek. Amusement danced in his eyes as he pulled back. "The evidence is spread across your cheek. You can call me an asshole all you want, but you and I both know you want me. So, what does that make you?"

I opened my mouth to answer, floundering for something to say. This wasn't a game. Life wasn't a game. But being near Bastian felt like a round of wins and losses, and him? He was always the victor.

Standing to face him, I took a step to him, but he met it, leading me back into the wall. His hand slid to my pussy, and he dipped his fingers past my folds. I should have been embarrassed by how easily his fingers slid in. I should have been a lot of things, none of which included riding his fingers like he was a wild horse.

I leaned my head back as he twisted his fingers and added a third finger. The door to the hallway creaked open, and I swung my head to the curved stairwell. Bastian didn't bother covering himself as footsteps descended, but my mouth dropped a bit as I tried to reorient myself with Bastian's fingers still inside me.

"Ariana?" Dana's voice flooded the room as Bastian added a fourth finger.

"What the hell are you doing?" I whisper-shouted, but he didn't stop, and I didn't stop him. If anything, my hips met his thrust and begged for more.

"Ariana?" Dana repeated, her voice more irritated.

Bastian's palm met my clit as his fingers slid in and out of me. His other hand covered my mouth when I moaned out his name, my body not caring that Dana stood at the top of the stairs, separated only by the thin drywall that ended at the bend. All she had to do was walk half a flight, and she'd see him finger fucking me.

He bit down on my neck, then flicked his tongue out, and I knew he'd leave a mark. Inside. Outside. Everywhere. If anything, I think he enjoyed the audience. His ex-girlfriend, no less. He was fucked up, and I was fucked up for loving it.

Dana huffed out a breath I heard from all the way down here. "I know you're in here, Ariana. I'll tell Bastian you're taking a break down there."

Bastian laughed against my throat. My skin muffled his mirth as he ground his cock against my belly. I reached forward and stroked him. My hand glided up and down easily, the skin still slick from my spit.

His mouth met mine, and his tongue flicked the roof of my mouth as he thrust into my hand. He pushed my palm away, removed his fingers from my soaking pussy, and slid inside me, hard and fast and bare.

No words.

No warning.

Nothing held back.

My eyes widened, my breath hitched, and I nearly screamed in surprise as I came around his cock within his first thrust.

Pounding into me harder, he bit my earlobe and murmured, "You may think you hate me, but your body hasn't gotten the message. It wants to be mine. It *thinks* it's mine."

"Hello? Are you down there? You know how hard it is to walk these steep stairs in heels!" I filed Dana's complaints under the Things I Give No Fucks About tab.

Bastian's piercing hit my G-spot just right. I cried out, unable to hold it in. I had half a second to process his smirk before he pulled out, leaving me empty as my core spasmed, and I almost fell to my knees. He waited until I lost my footing to catch me.

"What was that?" Dana took her first step down the stairs.

The *click! clack!* of her heels sped my pulse.

"Nothing!" I faltered for an excuse as Bastian held me up while I rode my orgasm out, feeling so empty without him in me as I clutched his shoulders for dear life. And damn, he looked like he knew it, too. "I s-slipped and spilled ice everywhere. Just c-cleaning up the mess!"

Did that even qualify as sex? He'd made me come and pulled out midway, staring at me like the control he had over my body amused him more than finishing off would. He wanted me to want him back inside me. It felt like a power play above all else, and as much as I wanted to hate him for it, I'd never felt more liberated in my life.

I leaned against the wall and slid down, trying to catch my breath. Bastian's eyes dipped to the way my breasts heaved. He rubbed himself, his movements unapologetic. Jets of cum shot out of him without any warning.

My eyes widened when I realized he was aiming at my face or hair—that jerk. I leaned forward in a hurry, connecting my mouth with his cock, and taking all his cum, much to his amusement, like he'd planned it this way all along.

He pulled back and parted my lips with his thumb. His cum pooled in my mouth pushed to the edges of my lips, nearly spilling past my lower lip.

"Swallow," he ordered, his voice low. Barely a whisper.

My glare spoke of refusal, but my mouth closed, and I swallowed. Didn't even think twice until Dana's second footstep shot me into action. I pulled up my dress straps and discarded my ripped panties. Bastian pried them from my fingers before I could toss them and rubbed the lace on his cock, drying himself, then pocketing my panties when I tried to retrieve them.

"I'm taking a break," I finally shouted up to Dana. I figured I couldn't get in trouble for it, considering my boss stood in front of me, tucking himself back into his pants while the taste of him lingered on my tongue.

"Where's the ice? It's getting crowded." Dana sounded pissed but also satisfied. Like she took joy in my failures. "I'll have to write this up." Fucking delusional. She held no authority. The most she could do was report this to Bastian, and well...

I shifted my eyes to him, took in his mirth, rolled my eyes, and shouted, "The machine's messed up, and I have most of the spill cleaned! It'll be a minute."

"Fine."

Her footsteps halted, and I closed my eyes and sagged against the wall. The relief swept up my back as I listened to her retreat. When the door slammed shut, I straightened up and faced Bastian, who looked so unaffected, it riled me.

The pain in my back flared as the adrenaline and lust cleared. I rubbed at the base of my spine, ignoring the pounding of my heart as Bastian's eyes drifted to my hand, and his brows furrowed. It couldn't be concern I saw. Probably amusement at the pain he'd caused.

I swiped a finger at my lips. "I'm gonna go, um, to the restroom. I'll get the ice in a bit. Promise."

I strode away before he could answer, not making eye contact with him as the ramifications of what we'd just done punched me in my gut. The gut filled with Bastian's *cum* of all things.

Almost kissing was one thing.

Blowing him in the bar's cellar? Worse.

Liking it? Unbelievable.

Bastian's eyes burned my back, and he muttered, "Fucking hell, I need a drink."

You and me both, Bastian.

But not together.

Definitely not together.

19

We all know duty better than we discharge it.

—John Randolph

ARIANA DE LUCA

I smoothed out my hair and clothes before I stepped out of the basement, then passed Dana on the way to the restroom. Her lips tilted upward as she watched me from her perch at the edge of the bar, a pen in her right hand and a complaint form in the other.

She'd lied.

Graham had a complete handle on things, and I'd only

been retrieving the ice because we didn't have a big crowd at this hour.

What a cow.

In the restroom, I fixed my hair and makeup, washed my cheek where Bastian had swiped my wetness onto, cursed the breeze from my lack of panties, and headed back out. Graham nodded to me as I passed him. I dipped down the stairs, my back aching with each step, and took in the empty cellar.

Nothing.

The buckets of ice had been emptied and sat stacked on the rack to the side.

I bounded the steps and ducked to the back of the bar. Dana passed, her smirk from earlier gone and a scowl lining her perfect features. I lifted the lid to the ice freezer.

Full.

What? Did Bastian...?

No, he wouldn't.

Graham passed me and tapped my shoulder. "You're welcome."

"Oh." Of course, it was Graham. I squeezed his hand and smiled. "Thank you."

"No problem."

A throat cleared, and we both turned to face Bastian. "Whiskey. Neat." He looked so irate for someone who'd just come in my mouth and watched me swallow it.

I turned to Graham. "I've got this."

He nodded and headed to his end of the bar, where he pretended to be busy.

I kept my voice low as I spoke. "It's not even five."

"I don't actually want the drink. I just want him gone."

My eyes widened for a fraction, and I took in his face, wondering how in the world we got here. "Why?"

Bastian couldn't actually be jealous.

He didn't seem capable.

He adjusted his cufflinks, not bothering to give me his full attention. "Because you're here to work, not fornicate with employees. Unless it's me."

"Are you trying to piss me off?" I leaned across the bar. "It's not working. I find your jealousy... entertaining."

"It's not jealousy. It's fact. You come here to serve drinks, not fuck every employee you see."

"Is the hypocrisy lost on you?" I raised my chin and glared at him. "You nearly fucked me."

Gosh, when had I ever been this crass?

He looked too entertained by the irritation trailing the length of my spine, and his eyes flicked to my lips before returning to my face. "I'm not an employee. I'm your boss, and if you cared about your job, you'd start acting less like an interrogator and more like an employee."

Interrogator.

He couldn't know my intentions, but the word still thrummed my pulse. Enough to make me back off. A little.

I cocked my head to the side and eyed him. "What's got you so worked up?"

"Blue balls," he said as if he hadn't just come in my mouth. No way was he ready for another round already. His eyes dipped to my chest, drawing heavy breaths from me. "I'm going to head to my office, jerk myself off to the image of your lips around my cock, and come into your panties." *Good. Grief.* "Don't look so appalled. I know your bare pussy is still wet for me. I bet it's dripping down your legs as we speak. You should control yourself before a customer sees. We wouldn't want them to think you're unprofessional." He shifted his eyes to the door, where a group of enforcers had just walked in.

"You've got customers, and I've got your panties to make a mess in."

And then, he left.

The worst part?

I still wanted him.

I didn't know how I could look Jenn in the eyes after what had happened yesterday, but it came surprisingly easy. Maybe because I laid horizontally on the couch across from her, splitting my time between staring up at the ceiling and peering at her sideways head.

"And that's all the updates you have?" She cocked her head to the side and skimmed her eyes down my body, showering me with uncertainty, the way she did so well.

I should have told her about Bianchi and the way Bastian, Vince, and Gio had threatened him. Instead, I'd given her the lightest debriefing possible. Mundane day-to-day tasks. Silence on all fronts. Nothing to report.

It seemed like she suspected otherwise.

I nodded, spreading nonchalance across my features like whipped butter on a bread loaf. "That's all."

She let out a soft *hmm* before crossing her legs. "You seem different."

I looked down. "Did I gain weight? The food at L'Oscurità is so good. I can't help myself."

"That's not it, and you know it." She tapped her pen on her chin, though her notebook laid somewhere on the desk behind her. "You've got this flush to you."

"A flush?" My eyes shifted to the clock. Fifteen more minutes, and I could leave. I considered my options and decided I didn't want to look defensive. "Hmm..."

"Hmm?"

I shrugged. "Yeah. Hmm. I mean, I don't know what I'm supposed to say to that." The smile I cracked didn't elicit a reaction from her.

She just studied me from behind her horn-rimmed glasses we both knew she didn't need but wore to be taken seriously on the job. "Is there something you want to tell me?"

"No."

"Wilks had a check in with the informant, who said there are rumblings of an Andretti in Romano territory. I'll ask again. Is there something you want to tell me?"

"Jenn, just spit it out already. What are you saying?"

"I'm saying I think you're keeping something from me, and I'll have to note this in your file."

Would it kill her to look more remorseful?

"What? Jenn..." I straightened up from the couch I laid on. "You're my best friend. You'd write me up for some crazy thought you have in your head?"

"It's not a crazy thought. It's a professional opinion. You

and I both know I have to note down everything I see. I can't make exceptions. Even for you."

But I was her best friend.

I drew in a shaken breath. "This is insane. You could unleash a hailstorm upon me. They could pull me from this legend."

On second thought, that shouldn't have been a bad thing. I could finally take a break and catch some distance from Bastian, but if I were being honest, I didn't want to. What a mess.

Jenn shrugged and set down her pen. "I'm not writing you up. I'm making a simple note in my report. It'll be eyes only for Wilks."

"But—"

"The alternative is to lie on my report, which would risk my job." She popped a brow up, reminding me of the strict business psych professor at Degory that everyone hated. "Are you asking me to risk my job?"

No. I'd never ask that… but it occurred to me that, if it were a Romano in this situation, speaking to another Romano, there'd be no discussion. Loyalty to one another came first. They blurred the lines without thinking twice when it came to protecting one another.

As my best friend, I'd thought Jenn would at least hesitate before doing something like this. This struck deeper than the confines of our friendship. It struck a chord in my life, in every day I've spent living. I'd thought having this duty as a law enforcement officer and protecting my country would fulfill me.

It didn't.

Truth was, I knew my colleagues did amazing work, but I personally didn't feel like I protected anyone, and even though I had hordes of colleagues and a best friend who I knew, deep down, truly cared for me, I felt lonely. But tending bar at L'Oscurità, that loneliness had slipped away, and I hadn't noticed it until now—sitting before someone who was supposed to be my best friend but unable to recognize her.

She stared at me. I stared back, cataloging her unforgiving features. Each second that passed deepened the rift between us until the fissures became too broken to mend. I wanted to grab some thread and stitch together the pieces of our friendship. I also wanted to run away and start fresh, in a place I didn't have to question everyone's motives. Where I could just live and be me, whoever that was.

I'd once joked that we could run away to the Caribbean together, except this time, when I pictured it, I didn't see her beside me.

Jenn sighed, stood, straightened out the wrinkles on her corporate America pantsuit, and reached out a hand to me. A fucking *hand*. Like we were standing in the Oval Office or something.

"I think we should call it a day. It was lovely to see you again, Ari."

I took her hand in mine, and she latched her grip tightly as she shook. My eyes darted around the room, wondering what the hell was going on, waiting for Ashton Kutcher to pop out from under her table to tell me I'd been *Punk'd*.

But nothing happened.

And it wasn't until I walked out of the building and made it to L'Oscurità for my shift that I realized one of the many things that was off. The vase I'd given Jenn a few years ago for Christmas had been replaced with another.

She hated that vase. That was the point. A gag gift, something for her to laugh at every time she replaced the floral arrangements she was obsessed with and saw the way they clashed with the bile-yellow porcelain.

But she'd never replaced it, and it stood as a token of our friendship year after year, a testament to the distance between us that could expand but never quite keep us apart.

Turned out, that had been a lie, too.

Avoiding Bastian didn't lessen my lust. It clawed its way up my body, moving from my core to my head, filling me with crazed thoughts. I no longer recognized this woman who couldn't control her desire.

Hell, I think our attraction surprised us both. Because I hadn't seen Bastian with another woman since we'd met, and me? I'd wake up each night, soaking wet from dreams of what would have happened had Dana not interrupted us. Would he have fucked me rough and fast or slow and long? I'd never know.

I didn't know what I'd expected after what had happened in the basement, but it wasn't this. Him acting like he couldn't care less that I'd had my lips wrapped around him, his Prince Albert stabbing the back of my throat. Me wondering when I'd have an opportunity for it to happen again, followed by a litany of destructive thoughts that, if I thought about it, stemmed from whatever the hell was happening with my friendship with Jenn. One of many reasons legends weren't supposed to have contact with their friends.

I turned away from Bastian for the twelfth time since my shift started tonight, forcing myself to focus on finishing my shift and leaving without another impromptu... whatever that was in the basement.

Graham nodded his head in Bastian's direction. "What'd you do?"

I used my towel to dry off a beer glass, then handed it to him. "What do you mean?"

He passed me another wet glass. "He likes you. He doesn't like anyone."

I set the glass down and met Graham's eyes. "He doesn't like me."

"No?"

"Nope." Rolling my eyes, I returned to drying the glasses.

"Then why'd he carry a hundred and fifty pounds of ice up the stairs for you in a fifty-thousand-dollar, one-of-a-kind suit?"

I froze. "That wasn't you?"

He laughed. "I like you, sweetheart, but not *that* much."

I shook my head and pushed aside the hair from my face, searching Graham for any signs of deception. "But you said, 'you're welcome' the other day. Why else would you say that?"

"Because you were in the basement for a really long time. I covered, like, thirty minutes of your shift, Ari."

"Oh."

But that meant Bastian actually carried the ice up for me, and that meant Bastian had a heart buried somewhere in that asshole exterior. The consequences of that proved fatal.

Graham tilted his head and narrowed his eyes. "Come to think of it, wasn't Bastian down there with you? I saw him leave after you did with the ice buckets in his hands, but I don't remember seeing him enter after you left."

I racked my brain for an excuse. "Yeah, he yelled at me for being late the other day. Gosh, he's such a jerk."

I was never late, but Graham was, so he wouldn't know that.

Graham took the last glass from me. "Hey, well, he did bring the ice up for you..."

I didn't need the reminder.

It was easier to write Bastian off when I thought he had no depth, when I thought he was just a jerk I couldn't stop lusting after. But when he did nice things without taking credit for them?

This dangerous territory scared me.

And the truth was, it should.

20

The world is full of beauty, as other worlds above, and if we did our duty, it might be as full of love.

—Gerald Massey

BASTIANO ROMANO

"Are you in bed?" I drew my phone closer to my ear, so I could hear her answer better.

"Yup." Tessie popped the P and inhaled like she was on the verge of finishing a marathon, which came out like a squeaky Darth Vader through the line. "How ironic coming from you."

I rolled my eyes, though she couldn't see me. "Do you even know what irony is?"

"Yes! I totally do! It's the antonym for wrinkly."

I shrugged. At least she knew the definition of antonym. "Get to bed, smart ass. It's late."

"You just cursed."

"Because I'm an adult, and I can. Stop changing the subject."

"I couldn't sleep."

I swore, dragged my palm along my jaw, and considered yelling at Gio for not checking up on Tessie. "And now?"

"I guess I'm okay. Why can't I stay with you? Daddy snores."

"Your room is on the other side of the brownstone. Not even on the same floor."

"It's scary!"

I pulled up my calendar and browsed through the events and tasks lists, narrowing in on the early piano lessons she had tomorrow. "Tell you what... you can stay over tomorrow or the day after. I'll work it out with our dad. Okay? Just go to bed."

"Fine." After a beat, I could still hear her breathing on the line. "Bastian?"

"Yes?"

"I love you." She sounded fractured, fragility concealing the strength she usually wore every day like her favorite light-up shoes.

"I love you, too, Tessie," I murmured in Italian.

"It's Contessa."

I rolled my eyes and hung up on her, knowing she'd probably stay up for at least another hour if I stayed on the line. I wanted to help her. I did. But I wasn't in the right state of mind. I'd spent too much time hunting, tracking my prey, waiting for a vulnerability to attack. If Graham was the mole, he didn't seem to be leaving any tracks. I struggled to find something. Anything.

My blue balls didn't help either.

The week since my Prince Albert had kissed the back of Ariana De Luca's throat had sent me spiraling to control my sex drive. Like I was back to my preteen days, where all the action I'd gotten happened between the pages of a Playboy magazine or consisted of feeling a girl up in the back of the boarding school gym. The gush of women Gio tossed my way didn't stop flowing, but if anything, my already non-existent interest lessened.

I could have had her. I'd been buried deep inside her. But when I fucked her, truly fucked her, it wouldn't be with a time constraint and her reservations looming over our heads. What happened last week didn't count. You didn't eat the appetizer and call it dinner. What I wanted—what I needed—was to savor each taste of the main course and stay for dessert.

I wanted Ariana, and perhaps it'd happen. She worked later than the rest of the crew, staying odd hours while all the lazy assholes left her to do most of the closing work. Her bonus at the end of the month would reflect her extra hours and effort, straight out of the paychecks of everyone else on her shift.

That also meant I could count on her to be out there right now—to tease, prod, and poke until she snapped, and we tumbled to the floor and hate-fucked our attraction out of our systems. Then, I could move on, hire someone new, and gather some more distance between Ariana and Tessie, who grew increasingly attached to her by the second. Hell, I'd rip

Everett away from Elsa had he not already gotten attached to the witch.

I grabbed a few manila files to look at when I got home, secured my desktop, double checked that I had nothing laying around, and locked my office door on the way out. In the bar, I'd expected to find Ariana wiping down the tables or lifting the chairs.

They had been cleaned, yes. But Ariana hadn't left. She sat at the bar, nursing an open bottle of vodka between her dainty palms. And not one of the small bottles. A bottle too big for her petite hands to fully grip.

A great chunk was missing from the bottle, more than someone her size should be drinking. She had her eyes closed, her head facing the ceiling as she hummed a melancholic melody that made me want to play along with my piano keys.

Instead, I approached her, set my stack of folders beside me on the bar top, and nodded to the bottle, though she had her eyes closed and couldn't see me. "That's coming out of your paycheck."

She peeked an eye open. "Are you always such an—"

"Asshole? Have you ever read a book with the same line over and over? It gets boring." I didn't relent as she closed her eyes and drew in a chest-shattering sigh. "Come on, De Luca. You can be more original than that."

"I don't want to be."

"Okay. Care to explain why you've drunk your way through"—I eyed the four-thousand-a-piece bottle of Diva vodka—"a grand of vodka?"

She swiped a lock of hair away from her face, like the single strand was the source of her anger. "It's my death-iversary."

I opened my mouth to ask her what the hell that meant,

but she continued, more forthcoming than she'd normally be, thanks to the vodka. I'd let her speak, because her secrets bothered me. I wanted to untangle them all until I reached the center where only she existed.

Fuck, these weren't thoughts I should be having.

She set the bottle down on the counter and traced its rim with the tip of her finger. "My mom died today."

Shit.

"Ari—"

"For once in your damn life, just let me speak."

Fierce eyes met fierce words. I stared into them, taking in all she'd let me see before relenting. She needed this. Clearly. Knee deep in liquor and lashing out was a state I saw too often in this bar.

I nodded. "Fine."

I'd let her have this. She looked like she needed it, and contrary to popular belief, I wasn't a complete asshole. I unbuttoned the top two buttons of my button-down shirt, removed my cufflinks and placed them in my pocket, sat on the stool beside her, and gave her my full attention—knowing this wasn't my typical protocol with employees.

Normally, I'd fire their asses for drinking the inventory; write a severance check on the spot, so I wouldn't have to see them again; and call them a cab to avoid a lawsuit.

Her lips connected with the rim of the vodka bottle. She tilted her head back and swallowed. "My mom died today. Twenty-nine years ago."

I racked my brain, thinking back to her employee file. Fuck. Ariana turned twenty-nine today...which meant her mom probably died giving birth to her. I opened my mouth to say something, but there was nothing to say.

I understood hating birthdays. Mine was in a week, and I

already knew how it would go. A quirky call from Tessie. A text from Gio, Uncle Eli, and Uncle Frankie. A text from mom if I was lucky. A visit from Uncle Vince, and a gag gift from Asher. I'd spend the night alone, and aside from a few texts, it'd be any other day.

Ariana set the bottle down and turned to face me, her eyes clear for how much she had drunk. "I don't have a single memory of her. Not one." Her laughter surprised me, punching me in the throat, where everything had been bottled up since I'd met her. "Granted, I don't have a single real adult memory anywhere. Not since college. You know, I have a job —a job some would consider good and honorable—but I don't feel either of those things. I don't know who the hell I am or what I want to do with my life, and now I'm twenty-nine, feeling like my life has spiraled into something I can't stop or recognize."

I didn't know what she meant by that for her, but her words resonated with my life. I was thirty—thirty-one in a week—and I didn't feel like life went beyond the motions. I had a family I refused to let down but no desire to do the things they wanted from me. A job I liked but didn't love. A sister and son I adored but rarely saw.

My life stood at odds with the type of man I was—an unapologetic taker. But how could I take what I wanted if I didn't know what I wanted or how to get it?

Besides her.

I wanted her.

I slid the vodka bottle away from Ariana, considered taking a swig, but decided one of us needed to be sober. "There's always a way to stop things. To live life on your terms and only yours."

It never ceased to surprise me how I could dish advice, but

I couldn't take it. Asher or Niccolaio would come to me with questions, and I'd always have answers for them but never for myself.

Ari swung her head back and forth, the movement a little sloppy. "Maybe because you're Bastiano Romano, but for us normal people, there's not always a way to take what we want. Not even close."

"What does being Bastiano Romano mean to you?"

"It means you're ruthless." She leaned forward and poked my chest, the tiny digit not even moving me a centimeter. "It means you can do whatever you want, create the future you desire, and make the choices you want to make. It means full autonomy of your own life, and I fucking hate you for it."

She was so far off, it almost pissed me off.

"Careful," I warned. I grabbed her finger when she went to poke me again. "You know nothing."

"I know this: you jerked off in front of me without a care in the world; you dangle me around, making me wait hours and hours for you with little consideration for my feelings; you got me to do your bidding from day one; you threaten people like Bianchi, because you can, and even if he deserved it, most people wouldn't be in the position to do so and get away with it, but you are; and you touch me when you want, but worse, you make me want it, too. You do these things, and I hate them, yet I can't stop thinking about you. You've made me wake up wet and aching for you dozens of times, and each time, I slip my fingers between the folds of my pussy, mortified by how wet you make me, and make myself come, pretending it's you, but it doesn't live up to the real thing. What if I want to be that to another person? What if I want to be irreplaceable? That's not the kind of thing you can just *make* happen."

I knew she was drunk, but it didn't lessen the impact of her words.

She dreamed of me.

She fantasized about me.

She thought I was irreplaceable.

Shit. Shit. Shit.

Dangerous words from a dangerous woman, who saw more of me than I'd thought she did. But I doubted she saw the inside, past the shiny exterior. The inside, where nothing existed. No wants. No desires. Nothing. A hole where dreams and aspirations should have lived but didn't, because what I truly wanted—my son—was so far out of reach, I couldn't even dream of it.

"You don't want to be me."

"Fine," she agreed. "Maybe I don't. But I want to know that, if it were my one true desire, I could."

Her confessions made her bare before me, but they didn't make her weak. The opposite, actually. She was strength and vulnerability, intertwined so thoroughly, I had no clue which was which.

I ran my palm across my jaw and stared at the vodka bottle before taking in the way she gave me all of her attention. "You strike me as the type of person who can do anything." Maybe it was because I doubted she'd remember this in the morning, but honesty felt like the right approach here.

"Really?"

"I don't lie."

Except to myself.

She sighed, closed her eyes, and stood. "I do. I'm probably the biggest liar you've ever met."

I doubted that.

Whatever the fuck that meant escaped me as she stood. I half expected her to leave. Instead, she grabbed my hand, and I let her slide it up the skirt of her dress, wondering how far she'd take this.

She used my hand to push aside her lace panties. My nails grazed the lips of her pussy. I didn't move them. Just let them sit there as every cell in my body warred with my head.

"Touch me." Her eyes spoke of no uncertainty. Just sheer, unfiltered need. Her tone was a decibel short of begging, but one look at her, and I knew she wasn't going to.

I swiped a finger between her lips, gathered her wetness, brought it to her mouth, and slipped my finger inside. "I make you so wet."

"Sometimes, I hate you." She latched her lips around my finger and sucked, so damned greedy for us to happen.

"You hate that you want me. Don't confuse the two."

"Maybe." She sighed around my finger, and I knew then and there, with that vulnerability so bare before me, she was too drunk for this to continue. "Bastian," she groaned out, making it so much harder for me to stop. She said my name like it wasn't just a name but a breath—an extension of her, like I was already inside her.

I slipped my finger out of her mouth and helped her steady herself. "You've had a lot to drink. Let's get you home."

"Yeah, okay. I think I'm sleepy anyway." She leaned into me, letting me support her weight as we walked to my car. "You're such a fucking asshole sometimes, but when you're nice, it confuses me."

You and me both.

Thing was, she might have called me an asshole, but she wasn't sweet, soft, or kind herself. She was hard. Strong. The makings of a warrior. And I'd only ever seen her softness near

Tessie... and now. When alcohol had reduced her barriers to nothing.

She rattled off her address, though I remembered where she lived from her employee file. I helped her up to her apartment and into her bed when we got there. The place was bare, devoid of personality, and the cabinets even emptier. No Advil. No sports electrolyte drinks. Nothing to combat the brutal headache she'd no doubt have in the morning.

At the very least, I supposed food could help. She had nothing in the fridge and a lone carton of ice cream nestled in the back of the freezer. I grabbed it, a spoon, and a napkin, then headed into the bedroom. She laid on her mattress, her dress thrown to the floor, her body all curves and lace, her eyes closed and limbs sprawled across the bed like limp noodles.

When I entered, her eyes shifted to me, and she took in the carton of ice cream. "Ice cream is cheaper than therapy."

"Probably."

"I hate therapy."

I dimmed the lights, then turned back to her with a raised brow. "You've been?"

Was it wrong to take advantage of her forthcoming state? Probably. Did I care? Not in the slightest. There were worse ways to extract information.

Her eyes drifted shut. "Yes. I still go, because I have to."

"You don't have to do anything," I reminded her.

"Yes, I do." She opened her mouth wide.

I sat beside her on the bed, my body putting a giant dent in the shitty mattress. "What are you doing?"

"I want ice cream, but I don't think I could move my arms if I tried."

"Because of the ice shift?" I needed to get her off that shift. It was an asshole move, even for me.

"You're such a jerk. My body hurts. I thought I was fit, but of course, you ruined that conception, too."

"I tend to ruin things," I allowed, remembering the many nights I'd stayed awake, wondering whether or not what happened with Elsa was my fault. "But usually not without reason."

"Yeah? What's your reason for making me carry a hundred and fifty pounds of ice up and down a giant flight of stairs multiple times a day?"

"Punishment."

The answer came easily.

"For what?"

Making me want her.

Instead of saying that, I opened the ice cream, scooped some into the spoon, and fed her. Her lips wrapped around the cold metal, and I drew it out, my movements slow and labored. The metal sliding past her lips brought back the image of her tongue flicking my Prince Albert. My cock jerked to life, and the lingerie on her body did nothing to help it. This woman could wear denim-blue tarp and look fuck-hot.

"Mmm." She groaned and closed her eyes. "Definitely cheaper than therapy."

I scooped some into my mouth when she opened hers for another bite.

Her mouth dropped open. "Seriously?"

"I can't stop who I am."

"Who you are is an asshole. That's my ice cream. I bought it."

"Remember what I said I'd do last time you called me an asshole?"

"Yes, please." She leaned back onto the sheets, her lingerie-clad body arched toward me. "I hear an awful lot of talking and very little fucking." She threw my words at me like a pro, something like excitement sparkling in her eyes before they drooped as she yawned.

Christ, I hoped she didn't drink like this in front of other people.

"You're a high-functioning drunk. You know that?" I tossed the empty ice cream carton to the side when she yawned again. "You should sleep, or you'll feel it when you wake up."

"Are you leaving?"

I stood and readjusted my clothes, along with my unapologetic erection. "Yes."

"It's late."

I eyed the clock. Nearly five in the morning, but I didn't really have anywhere to be until my meeting with Gio at four. "Are you asking me to stay?"

"I'm just saying, you brought me home, it's late, and I don't think it's safe for you to drive while tired."

I watched her struggle to get the covers over her body. "So, you're asking me to stay..."

She gave up on the sheets before I leaned forward and swept them over her body. "Yes, I'm asking you to stay. Happy?"

Not really. Aside from Elsa, I'd never spent the night with the women I'd slept with, so spending the night without the sex would be a worse idea. This complicated things. I didn't do complicated.

But it was late, and I was tired, so I kicked off my shoes, tossed off my suit jacket, unbuttoned my shirt and slipped it off my torso, and slid my slacks down my legs.

She peeked an eye open, her eyes widening as she took in

my tattoos, eyeing the one with Everett's name beneath my ribcage. "What are you doing?"

"Getting in bed with you. Do you expect me to sleep on that couch?"

"It pops out into a bed."

"If your bed mattress is this shitty, your couch mattress will be worse."

"Blame my shitty salary."

"Your 'shitty salary' is double what any other bartender in the city would make. Not to mention the tips you make as the most attractive bartender on the staff."

"You think I'm attractive?"

"I fucked your mouth, slid my fingers up your ass, and had my Prince Albert pressed against your G-spot. What do you think?" I slid under the sheets, reached out, and pulled her closer, so her body pressed entirely against mine.

"What? I—" She let out an alarmed breath, but I buried my face in her neck and closed my eyes, because fuck it.

If I was doing this, I was doing this the way I wanted to.

I pressed my lips to the delicate skin at the back of her neck. "Shut up and sleep."

For once, she listened to me, relaxing against my chest without any protest. I told myself it meant nothing. I may have told Ari I wasn't a liar, but I'd left out one thing.

I was good at lying to myself.

If I were to remain silent,
I'd be guilty of complicity.

—Albert Einstein

ARIANA DE LUCA

"You ready for Asher's wedding?" Gio rapped his table as Bastian walked past it and gestured for him to come over.

I ran a rag over the bar's countertop as Bastian approached them, my eyes down on the table but my ears perked and ready for intel.

Intel.

Gosh. I even hated the word. Two syllables that ground into my soul. Especially after Bastian had gotten me home safely—without taking advantage of me—even though I'd spilled a little too much to him the other day.

Drinking that much while undercover was dangerous. I had no excuse, but my birthday always hit me hard. Back when she'd been alive, my aunt had even known not to call and wish me a happy birthday, not that she'd been able to get in touch with me with my covers intact.

I'd woken up to an empty bed and hadn't had a chance to thank Bastian. Eavesdropping on him and his dad certainly didn't qualify as a thank you, but I did it anyway… and felt bad about it, I realized.

"Yeah. You know if Nick's going?" Bastian took the seat across from his dad.

I racked my brain for a Nick in any of the syndicates' files and came up empty. Niccolaio Andretti, perhaps? But he was a myth. Bureau folklore. The mafia equivalent of the Lockness Monster. The former heir to the Andretti throne, who'd disappeared one night, never to be heard from again.

The Andretti and Romano family had been feuding for generations. The last place an Andretti, let alone an Andretti royal, would be found was New York City, deep in the heart of enemy territory.

Gio fiddled with his phone, then peered up at his son. "If he can swing it, I'm sure he will. You know how he and Asher are. But I sent Ash a text to double check. If he goes, we need to make sure the security is good enough to protect him."

Bastian drew out a breath and skimmed his eyes across his dad's face. "I'm handling it, so you know it's good."

"That's not what I meant."

"Isn't it? I'm not in, so you question everything I do."

"I meant, Niccolaio's family can be ruthless."

Niccolaio Andretti.

The confirmation left more questions than it answered. It made no sense. The rivalry between the Andretti and Romano families spanned centuries. So much bloodshed had passed between the two. I couldn't picture a world where an Andretti and Romano occupied the same room, let alone the same city.

Then again, Niccolaio Andretti hadn't been seen or heard from in years. The bureau had lost track of him for a while, and Bastian's warning look to Gio only strengthened my suspicions. Niccolaio Andretti lived somewhere in New York City.

Holy. Shit.

"So can we."

Gio pocketed his phone. "You call running a bar ruthless?"

"Belittling it doesn't change the fact that I've done enough for this family to justify my status. Don't question it again."

Gio stared at his son. Silent. "Take every precaution in planning the security detail."

"Nick and Asher are family." Bastian nodded. "We don't take risks. Family. Duty. Honor. Above all else. Protected at all costs, no matter how large. You taught me that."

"I did." Approval gleamed in Gio's eyes as he took in Bastian's face. "Nick says he won't miss the wedding. Be sure to increase the security. Vince says the bounty on his head raised to five million dollars."

And suddenly, everything made sense. The bureau had always wanted to take down the mafia. Of course. But they'd sent me now, of all moments, in response to bodies dropping in the city and whispers from their informant of something going on in the Romano territory.

If Niccolaio Andretti, the missing Andretti heir, was hidden in the city with a five-million-dollar bounty on his head, the logical conclusion would be the Romano family had given him safe haven. I didn't know or understand why, but judging by the way Gio and Bastian talked about Niccolaio, the Romano family cared about him.

The road before me forked, and I stood, splintered in two impossible directions. It should have been a no brainer. I'd tell Jenn the intel during our next session, she'd pass it up the food chain, and someone with more power than both of us would make a decision.

Except my heart demanded I rethink this. It remembered the way Jenn had treated me. What was it Bastian had said?

Family. Duty. Honor. Above all else. Protected at all costs, no matter how large.

In theory, the bureau had that. We'd all taken the same oath, swore the same promises, and followed the same rules. But at the end of the day, being an agent didn't entail loyalty to one another or even the country. It entailed loyalty to a chain of command—whoever played the game of politics best and had the power to pull my strings.

If I were being honest, the mafia had more integrity, and it blew me away. Mom had run away from Angelo De Luca, the former head of the De Luca syndicate, because he'd been dangerous. A beater. An asshole. The type of man who killed without remorse.

After she'd died giving birth to me, my aunt raised me to hate anything and everything mafia-related. The hatred she'd taught me led me to joining the bureau, and here I was, holding a kernel of information that could hurt the Romano syndicate but hesitating to use it.

Everything I'd ever been taught demanded I give it to the FBI to take down the syndicate, but my heart refused, begging me to consider the alternative—I had a choice whether or not to say something.

And it might not have seemed like a viable choice to an outsider, but now that I'd seen the syndicate in action, I knew they weren't as bad as they'd been made out to be. They had a code of honor and a way of protecting the ones they loved at all costs. More than I could say about me.

And somewhere between the beloved and the outsiders stood people like me. People who had wormed their way into the syndicate and managed to form a connection. I hadn't had the opportunity to thank Bastian for the other night, and it was probably for the best.

Otherwise, I'd have to confront the idea that a second side of Bastian existed. One who took me home and acted like a gentleman—albeit his filthy version of a gentleman.

But you trust him, I couldn't help but admit.

I trusted the man who'd ended a contract for me. Who'd later protected me against one of his own. Who'd made me promise to stay safe. Who brought me home, tucked me into bed, and fed me Ben & Jerry's when I drank too much.

Dangerous territory.

Bastian eyed the ceiling for a few drawn-out seconds. "That bounty will prove troublesome. We should set a counter bounty on Ranieri Andretti's head. Either he'll give in and remove the bounty or he'll raise it, in which case we'll do the same. We all know which syndicate has the most money." His low murmurs made it nearly impossible to hear, but I'd been trained in surveillance.

I was a rat.

A damned good one.

Goosebumps lined my arms. It never felt good to be ashamed of your identity. Of the very thing that defined you. But hell, I hadn't even passed the name Everett along to the bureau yet. Surely part of me still had limits.

Gio swept his eyes around the bar as he spoke, "Or we'll have killed the Andretti syndicate's boss."

Bastian shrugged."The position belongs to Niccolaio anyway."

"Niccolaio still cares for his brother."

"His brother doesn't deserve the sentiment."

"If you were in Ranieri's position, at eighteen or so years old, and you'd just seen Asher with a gun near your Uncle Vince's dead body, would you not have drawn the same conclusion? The same assumption?"

Silence.

"Irrelevant." Bastian stood, looking powerful in his tailored suit. "Uncle Vince wouldn't have let anyone sneak up on him. That's the difference between a Romano and an Andretti. We're the hunters, and they're the hunted."

He left, and every part of me warred over what to do with the groundbreaking intel I'd just discovered. Niccolaio Andretti had a bounty on his head for killing his uncle, and he'd been hiding in Romano territory.

The bodies dropping all over the city? They had to be connected to the bounty on Niccolaio's head. Which meant a thread of evidence connecting those bodies to the Romano and Andretti families existed. The bureau would just have to find it... if I told them to look.

Don't do it, my heart warned. *They don't care about you. Even Jenn would give you up in a heartbeat for her job.*

I'd been cleaning the same spot for the past ten minutes, but I didn't care. Because the realization struck me hard.

Perhaps everything I'd ever been taught was wrong.

And my job in the bureau?

I was slowly coming to terms with the fact that I didn't want it anymore.

BASTIANO ROMANO

People are made to be resilient. We overcome cancers, hurricanes, heartbreaks. We are fighters, scavengers, survivors. The experiences we endure teach us to be better versions of ourselves...but for some people, better doesn't exist.

Only bottom.

Graham Filth scraped the lowest point of the barrel.

I knew Graham was a rat. I could feel it as sure as I felt breaths escape my lips and trouble in the air. Worst of all, I couldn't prove it, no matter how much time I spent watching

Graham. And like an acne-faced fifteen-year-old exploring PornHub for the first time, I'd spent a lot of time watching.

But it wasn't like I had something else to do with my time. The restaurant business demanded a lot from me, but the bar side—much less. The security for Asher and Lucy's wedding had been planned, Tessie spent most of her time getting tutored, and my family duties started and ended with confirming Graham as the rat.

For the twentieth day in a row, I watched Graham go about his day-to-day work schedule through the security cameras. Restocking the alcohol. Taking orders. Mixing drinks. Retrieving the ice—I hadn't taken Ariana off ice duty, but I figured I'd let it slide since it was a little fucked up in the first place. I could admit I was an asshole, just like she liked to call me one.

All this watching, and nothing happened. Some more orders. More drinks. A few texts when he should have been working. A food break midway through his shift. Chatting with Ariana, his body a little too close. More texts. More drinks. More talking to Ariana. Still too fucking close to her.

Ari, Ari, Ari.

I didn't know what I'd do with that woman. Feisty. Witty. Sex on heels. She defied all expectations, and I decided the night I'd taken her home that I'd have her, fuck her six ways till Sunday, and release her. I traced the resume on my desk. A viable new hire to replace Ariana De Luca. I'd been sitting on it, debating, trying to keep away from Ari.

Not anymore.

Movement on the screen caught my attention. Graham leaned a hip against the counter and flicked Ariana's nose, like he was Zac Efron and life was a C-grade Disney flick. She laughed and shoved him before returning to a customer.

And then he did it. Graham's hand slipped into his back pocket, and he pulled his phone out. I didn't even notice at first, but it was a different phone. He lifted his gaze, his eyes shifting left and right before they dipped down again and his brows pressed together, like he was confused by something on the screen.

I toggled with the keyboard, zooming in as close as the camera would let me. Not close enough. Despite the 4K quality, his phone screen remained pixelated. I drafted an email to Niccolaio, asking him to enhance the quality, before considering he was still in hiding. The rest of the tech guys we had on hand would take longer, but they'd do, so I sent the file to them and called up Gio on an encrypted line.

He answered on the first ring. "Your mom's driving me nuts."

"What's new?" I studied Graham as he wiped the bar counter down and winked at Ariana. The fucking rat. "I may have something."

"And?" Gio's impatience had my jaw ticking.

"Graham has a second phone. Possibly a burner. I sent the video to our techies for enhancing."

"No need. I'll arrange for someone to swipe the phone and pull up records with the cell phone company."

"Good. We'll put this rat business to rest before Asher's wedding, and I can return to running the restaurant side."

"Not quite."

The fuck?

"What now?"

"I'm getting word from our informant that there's another person in the bar."

"Impossible."

Why now? Aside from Ari, my staff had been with me for

ages. But I trusted Gio's intel. I trusted the Romano Syndicate. And that meant believing another rat existed.

Gio's voice left little room for debate. "I need you to stay there."

"And go hunting for rats," I finished.

"Exactly."

I swiped a hand over my face, unable to hold back my anger. Not what I had in mind for my birthday, but there was nothing I hated more than a rat.

22

Love can flourish only as long as it is free and spontaneous; it tends to be killed by the thought of duty.

—Bertrand Russell

ARIANA DE LUCA

I'd never been a fan of birthdays.

I had no parents, and while I loved my aunt, she'd never wanted children. She didn't know how to care for them. I felt that as each birthday passed with little fanfare, like she didn't know what to do.

When I'd turned twelve, a neighbor had asked her if she had plans to throw me a birthday party, and she'd looked so flustered by the idea. She ran to the grocery store, bought me an array of Barbie party paraphernalia I was too old for, and threw me my first birthday party with the neighborhood children as guests—all of which were at least five years younger than me.

I hadn't minded. I knew she'd tried. I knew I'd stuck a knife in the middle of her plans for life. She had ambitions in her law firm, and I'd been an obstacle the second she'd taken me in, yet she loved me anyway.

I was grateful for her sacrifices.

Truly.

But understanding how woefully she'd been prepared for me didn't lessen the sting of a birthday without parents each year. It didn't help that my mother died on my birth date, giving birth to me, so it always felt wrong celebrating my life on the day of her death.

I had this baggage, but Bastian didn't. His parents were both alive and healthy as far as I knew, yet he didn't look particularly happy as he sat in the corner of the bar on the day he turned thirty-one.

Maybe, like Tessie, he had issues with his parents abandoning him on his birthday. I'd seen his Uncle Vince stop by earlier to wish him a happy birthday and the chirpy call from Tessie, but that had been it.

Loneliness bled deep. I knew that better than most, and I felt the craziest desire to cure his. I told myself it was because I still hadn't thanked him for getting me home safely as I ducked into the fridge in the employee break room and pulled out a juice pouch from *Squeezed!* Tessie would understand.

Making my way back behind the empty bar, I ignored

how unnerved I felt at being the only one still here. The staff had left at closing. Graham had given Dana a ride home, and I'd offered to do closing tasks myself.

I cut the top of the juice pouch off, dumped ice into a whiskey glass, and poured the juice over the little square ice cubes. When I set the glass in front of Bastian, I told myself it was a thank you for taking me home.

Nothing more.

I was such a fucking liar.

My fists clenched, and I watched the same hands that had been in me curl around the glass as he brought it to his lips.

"What's this?"

"Your nightcap."

"It's juice." He narrowed his eyes on me and studied my posture. "You buy these for Tessie."

We'd never fully acknowledged my relationship with his sister. I wanted to keep her out of this. Of us. Of this entire world. The little ray of purity in my otherwise dark world needed to stay pure.

But I was coming to terms with the fact that Bastian wasn't entirely bad. I didn't need to protect her from her own brother, and maybe I didn't need to protect myself from him either. Everything I thought I knew had been twisted during my time undercover. I felt like a baby taking her first steps, experiencing things for the first time.

I didn't say anything as he took another sip. I slid a step back to go back to the bar, but he stopped me with a hand on my wrist.

"Thank you."

My eyes dipped to his fingers on my skin. "For what?"

"For the drink. For keeping these juice pouches on hand

for Tessie. For keeping her company and helping her with her homework and school, but—"

"Happy birthday," I cut him off before he said something that would piss me off.

Why did there always have to be a *but*?

I knew if I'd let him continue, with the way his parents had abandoned him today and how lonely he looked, we'd fight. For once, I didn't want to fight. Not after I'd come to terms with the fact that this cover had changed me. He'd changed me. Or maybe I'd always been this way, and I was just discovering myself.

Bastian ignored me. Of course, he did. "You can't be friends with her."

This wasn't happening. I'd come to the realization a few days ago that Tessie might have been my only friend nowadays, and he wanted to take her away from me?

Over my dead body.

I hoped my glare burned holes in his clearly underdeveloped brain cells. "So, I'm good enough for you to fuck, but I'm not good enough to be friends with your little sister, who seems to spend more time with me than you or anyone else in your family, by the way. You sure have a way with kids."

His eyes flared, and anger consumed them, like maybe my words had cut him deeper than I'd intended them to. I should have given him a stiff drink. And spit in it. Anything but the juice pouches I used my own money to buy, taking my very little personal time to get, walking to Fifth Avenue despite my mounting back pain, because I already loved that little girl so much, I wanted her to be happier than I could even fathom.

"That's not what I meant, and you know it. People come and go. That's life. But Tessie's not like us. She doesn't have to be like us. We can shield her from this world for as long as we can." I opened my mouth to retort, but he cut me off, so damned unapologetic, "And don't deny we need to shield her from you, because the reality is, you're not always going to be in Tessie's life, so spending more time in it now will only make it harder when you leave. Or *she* leaves for that matter. She doesn't even live in this state."

Why was he so torn up about it? Yes, she lived in a different state. People still built relationships long distance. Siblings grew up and moved to other states. Sons moved away from fathers, daughters from mothers. Life happened. We just had to adjust.

But at the same time, I knew he had a point, even if I wanted to resist it. I was sent here to take down the very people she loved. I wasn't doing her any favors by befriending her, but I couldn't bring myself to cut the strings. I liked her. I liked the normalcy she gave me. Some days, I pretended she was my sister, and I had a chance to give her the life I never had.

How fucked up was that?

I shook my head. "Tessie doesn't need to worry about me hurting her. You, on the other hand—"

"I'm her brother. Nothing you say will change the fact that blood ties us together. I could live across the world, and I would still be her brother."

He believed it, so I believed it. Simple as that. If I were being honest, he really seemed like a good brother. But it also seemed like he repeated it because he wasn't so sure. Like, somewhere along the way, the distance between him and his sister had made him uncertain of his place in her life.

I tilted my chin up and tore my wrist away from him. "I came here to be nice to you and wish you a happy birthday. Are you so miserable that you have to stomp on that, too?"

"Yes."

The earnest dip of his brows. The flare of something undefinable behind his eyes. The tense set of his shoulders. I'd walked onto a minefield with that question, and there was no backing out now. Not unless I wanted to get blown up, and even I couldn't pull off splattered intestines. I couldn't erase his reply from my memory. My self-preservation demanded I try, but I didn't.

"I don't know what to say to that."

"Do you want to know what I think?" He didn't wait for my reply. "I think you're miserable, too."

I should have been pissed off. Nice people didn't say things like that. Polite people didn't either. Civilized people didn't confront other people's demons like they had a right to pick fights with them.

"Well, I think you're trying to pick a fight with me because it's your birthday; you're alone at your bar that closed an hour ago; no one in your family is here, including your sister; you're wondering how you reached thirty-one with no one to chase away the loneliness; and you're so fucking bitter, you can't think straight."

I knew this because I felt the same way.

Living in a city of millions but always alone.

Always bitter.

"There she is."

I narrowed my eyes, not waiting to take the bait but biting into it anyway. "There who is?"

"The real you."

"Oh?" I hated his certainty and wished I had it. "And who is that?"

"You're a biter. Once you latch on, your jaw clamps down, and there's nothing anyone can say or do to get you to release.

You decided from the beginning you would hate me. I'm okay with that. It wasn't like I treated you like royalty. But the thing about being bitten is, it means nothing if I have a high pain tolerance. I don't need you to like me for L'Oscurità to maintain its success." His eyes raked a path down my body before he met my eyes once more. "I don't need you to like me for us to fuck either."

I knew he was deflecting, turning this conversation away from him, trying to swim from the deep end to the shallow end as quickly as he could. I wouldn't let him.

"You're disgusting and crass, and this has nothing to do with me and Tessie."

"Except it does. You and I aren't made like everyone else. You like to bite; I like to be bitten. But other people? They can't handle the pain, the anger, the aggression, the never-ending stream of bullshit life has piled onto us. Tessie is a strong girl. She's smarter than most kids double her age, and she always will be. But the one thing she is not is a fighter, which means people like us have to take the hits for her. And I'm okay with that." He cocked a brow. "Are you, Biter?"

Always.

I would always be okay with protecting Tessie.

I wanted to tell him she didn't need protecting from me, but that'd be wrong. If I succeeded in my assignment, I'd strip her of everything—her family, her money, the life she'd grown up in.

She did need protection from me.

I swallowed away my hatred for myself. This should have been easy. It should have been black and white. Romanos—bad; FBI—good. If only it were that simple. It'd be easier to stomach who I was and what I did to others as I weaseled my way into their lives and lied until I destroyed them.

"Your opinion is duly noted." I swiveled on my heel and headed for the break room, hellbent on getting out of here before he could see me break down.

The first tear slipped past as I grabbed my things from my locker. I swiped at it with the back of my hand, my movements jerky and angry. I had identity issues, yes, but surely this wasn't me. I wasn't the girl who cried when the mean boy pointed out all her flaws.

I'd thought I had a spine.

"Don't cry."

I swung my head to Bastian. He stood at the door, his arms crossed as he leaned against the archway.

His voice was harsh as he spoke, "Biters don't cry."

"Maybe I'm not a biter." I certainly didn't feel like one as my voice wobbled, and I swayed a little to the right.

"You are, but you're lost."

"How do you know?"

"Because I am, too."

I swallowed the thickness in my throat and shook my head. "I don't understand."

"I've been asking myself why someone with a double major from Degory University would spend her time bartending for an asshole she can't stand. You could have any job you want, not just because you have a fancy degree but because you're smart. I see it in you—that unshakeable drive people are born with and can't be taught."

He gestured down his body, and I followed the path of his hand, taking in the three-piece suit only status could buy. Not a hair or thread out of place on him. The perfect golden boy with the perfect golden cufflinks. "I was born with a gold-coated spoon dangling from my lips, and I have an education most can't fathom let alone acquire. Give me any Fortune 100, and I'd run it easily. But I don't. Why not?"

"How drunk are you?"

I couldn't fathom why he was telling me this.

"I'm not drunk," he dismissed. He took a step closer. "That's a cop-out, and you're not copping out of this conversation." Another step. "We're the same, Ariana De Luca," he accused, his voice so seductive, it was like he was calling me his lover. "We have the mafia last names—and don't even deny that." It was the first time he'd ever said the word *mafia* around me, and he didn't even give me time to marinate in the severity of that. "We have the Ivy League education." Another step. "We have the bone-deep, mouth-frothing viciousness that cannot be faked. I see it in your cold eyes." He stepped in front of me, tipped my chin so I stared into his eyes, and whispered against my lips, "And we are both so very lost."

"I'm not lost," I tried to deny, but I knew in my bones I was.

I didn't want this job anymore. Not the bartending one, but the one with the FBI. I didn't want to lie. I didn't want to pretend. I didn't want to know my fake covers more than I knew myself. I didn't want to die alone. I didn't want to betray the people around me.

You'd think with my job, I would be a fighter. I wasn't. They taught us to run in the bureau. When our cover was blown, we ran. My cover wasn't blown, but my heart had been torn to shreds by the truth in his words, so I did what I did best.

I turned and ran.

23

To exact revenge for yourself or your friends
is not only a right, it's an absolute duty.

—Stieg Larsson

BASTIANO ROMANO

Giving myself time to fester on how close Ariana's words had hit home would have made me hate her, so I didn't. She'd hit the truth. I was angry and bitter. Not just because I rarely saw Tessie but also because I never saw Everett.

No number of private investigators or bribery had given

me success in unlocking a secret I could blackmail Elsa with. I'd exhausted all options, but I refused to come to terms with the idea that Everett would never live with me.

"Oh, this is gorgeous." The mafia bunny slung her arm around my shoulder, dipping her head back and fawning over every little detail of Asher and Lucy's wedding.

I'd forgotten her name as soon as she'd told me.

Not that it mattered.

Gio had set this "date" up, and I wasn't going to make a scene during Asher and Lucy's wedding. I had my limits. I wasn't that bad. I'd give them their special day without interfering. I had a spine, but today it happened to be as tough as a limp dick. And they said romance was dead.

"When we get married, can we do it here?"

She batted those 99-Cents Store lashes at me and gripped my shoulder with those stick-on nails. She was missing one. The middle finger. It fell off on the car ride because I'd insisted on taking the motorcycle despite her protests.

This woman was delusional. Every mafia bunny knew about Gio and Ma's arranged marriage and figured they'd be next. Fat chance in hell I'd ever get married unless it was a farce to somehow help me get Everett back.

"Have you seen the flowers? Oh, they smell so good."

She plucked one from a table and shoved it under my nose. I plucked it from her finger and shoved it under *her* nose, not-so-accidentally smearing her lipstick in the process.

"Oh, Bastian. You smudged my lipstick, silly!" She reached into her clutch for her lipstick and pulled the plastic tube out. "Excuse me while I fix this in the restroom."

I loosened my shirt collar when she left and slid my suit jacket off. If I had to sit through another mind-numbing second of that, I'd probably get arrested for murder, and I wasn't in the mood to pay anyone else off right now.

Freddy, Asher's new assistant, who'd replaced the batshit insane Monica, made eye contact with me as he strode my way. I stood and met him halfway, hoping the mafia bunny would forget about me when she returned to the spot I was at and didn't see me.

Freddy cut straight to the point when he reached me. "The front desk security at your penthouse has been trying to get ahold of you. I just got off the phone with them since Mr. Black is your emergency contact."

"My phone ran out of batteries earlier." I'd been on it all day, hoping the bunny would take a hint and disappear. They never did. "What did they want?"

"A woman is there, and she refuses to leave before she sees you. They've asked if you'd like them to call the police." His crisp tone never wavered, the consummate professional, a huge step up from Asher's last batshit insane executive assistant.

"Who is the woman?"

"I believe they called her Elsa."

I forced the breath to escape. "Did they mention what she wanted?"

"Just that she insisted on seeing you and is making a fuss at the front desk. They've taken her into the security room for holding."

"Thank you. Let Asher know I've left and will talk to him when he comes back from his honeymoon. Don't tell him what happened." At Freddy's reluctance, I added, "He just got married. He doesn't need to worry about my problems on his honeymoon. I'll tell him everything when he gets back."

Freddy nodded once and left after that, all business,

moving on to his next task as I made my way to the exit. I was one of the few who'd actually arrived at the church. Everyone else took the tunnels, but since I'd arrived with the mafia bunny from Hell, I'd wanted the quickest route to the venue.

I passed Vincent on my way out.

Vincent latched onto my arm as he examined my face. "Going somewhere? They haven't cut the cake yet."

I bit back a cringe and pulled my motorcycle keys from my pocket. "Elsa is in town. My penthouse security has her in holding."

His eyes scanned my face, looking for something I hoped he didn't find. He looked exhausted. Hopefully not from me. "Do you need anything from me?"

"No," I answered, a little distracted. If Elsa was here, where the fuck was Everett? "Just enjoy Asher's wedding." My lips quirked up as I forced myself to look more light-hearted than I felt. "Hopefully it'll only happen once."

He barked out a laugh and patted my upper back, the natural gesture reminding me of how easy our relationship was and how much I valued it. "You need something, you call me, okay?"

"Okay," I promised, not sure if it was a lie or the truth.

I moved to leave, but he latched onto my arm again and stared into my eyes as one hand cupped my cheek like he used to do when I was a kid. "It won't always be like this. This version of Elsa will be a distant memory, and you'll have Everett with you. You'll see your son again."

I took a step closer and furrowed my brows. I needed to get to the penthouse, but that look on Vince's face… He knew something, and it unnerved me.

"You know something I don't, Uncle Vince?"

"I know plenty you don't, but you trust me." He took a

step back and patted my arm as if he could brush away his cryptic words. "You should go see that girl. Love you, son."

I nodded, shaking away the odd conversation because he was right—I did need to tend to Elsa. I brushed past the bunny on her way from the restroom, ignoring her calls as the security guards opened the double doors to the exit for me. Slipping the helmet on, I slid onto the motorcycle, turned on the engine, did a few revs, and took off.

By the time I got to the penthouse, I'd run through a million doomsday scenarios in my head. The Andretti family had discovered Everett. He'd been kidnapped. A ransom had been demanded. Those tiny fingers had been sent to Elsa in a box. Each thought more fucked up than the last.

The night guard led me to the security room where a frazzled Elsa yelled at one of the guards on shift. She wore a long-sleeved mini dress and an obnoxious row of bangles, which made clattering noises as she waved her arm and continued to berate the guard. She looked like a Southern Belle like I looked like the face of a Born-Again Christian pamphlet.

"Do you know who I am?! I used to live here! This is not how you should treat me! Give me the respect I deserve!"

I leaned against the doorway and crossed my arms. "Respect is earned, and the only thing you've earned in your entire life is the A you got after sucking Professor Ronson's dick."

Yeah, there had been rumors. I hadn't believed them at the time, but now I wasn't too sure.

"I didn't—" Her green eyes cut to the guard she'd been yelling at after he snickered. She inhaled deeply, then exhaled and turned back to me, swiping a hand at her cardinal-colored hair. "Can we speak in private?"

"Can you behave with some semblance of dignity? You're embarrassing your gender."

She met my eyes with a glare, both of us hating one another so much for two people who used to be in love. I didn't know why she hated me. She was the one who'd fucked me over. Everything I'd done to her since had been in response to that.

Her shoulder brushed my chest as she walked past me and into the hallway. I led her to the stairwell.

She turned to me with a pout on her face. "We're not going to the penthouse?"

"No."

"But—"

"No." I shut the door behind us, ignoring the bang as she flinched. "The penthouse is for people who matter. You don't. Speak or leave. Those are your only choices."

She spoke after a reluctant second. "I need money."

"Where is he?"

"Huh?"

"My son. If you're here, where's Everett?"

"He's with the nanny in Alabama."

"You left my son in another state while you flew off to New York?"

"Easy for you to judge! You don't even see him!"

"I don't see him because his toxic, coldhearted bitch of a mother keeps him away from his own father. Do you even know his nanny's name?"

Her eyes darted to the side, and she licked some gloss off her lips. "Of course, I do! What kind of question is that?"

"The kind of question I ask a woman who abandons him to go on overnight dates with strange men."

Her eyes met mine, and she cocked a brow, confidence

returning to her. She pulled her shoulders back, took a step closer, and licked her lips. "Are you jealous?"

Was she Snoop-Dogg high at the moment? She looked like she could be in one of his rap videos. Extra #2. The girl who sucked his dick and winked at the screen. Classy.

I stuck a finger to her forehead and pushed her back. "The only jealousy I feel is toward men who have never had the displeasure of meeting you."

Her arms crossed, and she kicked at the floor. "You don't have to be so mean."

"Is there a point to your visit?"

"I need money."

"I wired you three-hundred-thousand dollars yesterday."

"Yeah, but I need more."

"What could you possibly need more money for? There's only so much plastic you can get implanted into your body." When her eyes darted around the stairwell, I hardened my voice even more. "Whatever lie you're conjuring in that fucked up head of yours, I'll see past it. The truth. Now."

Her sigh drew out of her like the creak of a bed, slow and reluctant to carry weight. "I borrowed some money from someone, and now he's asking for some back."

I made a mental note to direct my investigators to her spending habits. They'd found nothing in the past, but perhaps this could be a new lead, one that would lead Everett back home to me.

"How much?"

"Not much. Just a hundred thousand."

"And the rest of the money I've given you?"

"I spent it. I have bills to pay."

I grabbed her arms and tore the sleeves of her dress off.

"Hey!" she shouted and tried to push my hands away.

I ignored her protests as I scanned her arms for track marks. There were none. She wasn't on drugs. That didn't explain her spending. How much damned money could this woman spend? I could feed a hundred orphanages with the money I gave her each month, all because she continued to hold Everett over my head, and I'd rather send her money than risk her not feeding our child.

"Are you gonna give me the money or what, Bastian?" The Southern accent thickened with her impatience.

"You flew all the way here to ask me for money. It must be important."

Wariness lined her eyes in an instant. "No. I just need it now."

"I'll give it to you."

"Okay—"

"After I see Everett."

I watched the decision war in her eyes. She knew I couldn't go to Alabama. She also knew if she took him to any other territory, including mine, I'd rip Everett away from her and find some hole to bury her in. That was how deep my fury for her ran, and I didn't bother to hide it.

I didn't know why it shocked me when she took a step back and said, "Never mind. I don't need the money. I'll figure something out."

My eyes narrowed on her. "Figuring something out better not entail starving or neglecting my son."

"You're less of a father to him than your own father is to you," she seethed. She'd always been jealous of my relationship with him.

"You harm one hair on his head, and Social Services will be on your doorstep so quickly."

"They'll take him away. You'll never get him back."

"There is no shortage of people I can buy off, Elsa. Surely you, of all people, know this."

The real threat wasn't Social Services. It was the Andretti family. As soon as they discovered Everett existed, his life was at risk, and maybe I wouldn't get to him in time to save him. I couldn't risk that.

But I didn't tell Elsa that as she huffed out a breath and stormed away with her ripped pink sleeves flapping in the wind like her loose pussy lips.

And I swore, if I had to die trying, I'd get Everett back from that lunatic.

The grand essential to happiness in this life are something to do, something to love, and something to hope for.

—Joseph Addison

ARIANA DE LUCA

I didn't see Bastian the following day. Probably for the best. I wouldn't have known what to say if I had. I just wanted to finish my shift in peace and give myself time to think about turning in my badge to Wilks.

Turning in my badge.

I couldn't believe it had come to this. I didn't know much about myself, but I knew giving up went against my very nature, because every time I thought about it, frustration and anger and resentment would bubble in my throat, practically demanding I continue with my legend when my heart fought so hard against it.

When the bar closed, and everyone had relegated closing duties to me before I'd even had a chance to volunteer, Vincent Romano entered the bar alone. No security guards trailing behind him.

Just him.

I coiled walls around my mind, everything in me alert as the head enforcer for the Romano family strode my way. His bespoke suit and tailored button-down spoke of money, but he looked worn out.

Fine lines of wrinkles piled onto his forehead like rippled sand dunes in a desert. His cheeks had sunken in a little. He looked like my aunt after her cancer had sucked the soul out of her. Though he had vibrant dark hair, it had lost most of its fullness, and that fit body of his had lost some of its mass since I'd last seem him, too.

I shouldn't have, but I lowered my guard. A little. It was the eyes. Vincent Romano had a hardened exterior, but when he looked at me, those clear blue eyes spoke of kindness. Putty. I should have been hard as a rock, but this cover had turned me into putty.

If I were being honest, I liked it. I didn't want to be hardened or jaded. That wasn't a way to live. Look at Bastian. I'd never met a man so on edge, and he seemed miserable.

I ran a rag along the bar top and gave Vince a slight smile. "It's just me here. I think your nephew left a while ago. I haven't actually seen him today."

"I'm not here for him. I'm here for you."

I froze and stared at him, doing my best not to look flustered. "Oh."

"You're pretty well-spoken for a Degory alumna."

My lips quirked up. Who would have thought I'd be sitting alone in a bar, passing lighthearted jabs with the enemy of my family?

"That's what people tell me. Can I get you anything?"

"A scotch, please, darling." He coughed a little, and I considered getting him a glass of water instead. He really did look bad.

I poured a glass of top-shelf scotch and slid it his way, genuine concern etching my brows together as I set the bottle beside his glass and asked, "Are you okay?"

He let loose a long sigh. "I'm old."

Not really. I'd say late fifties. Maybe just short of sixty. Not even retirement age in this country.

I stood there, waiting for him to say something. When he didn't, I tried to break the awkwardness I felt. "I'm just about done closing up..."

"Stay. Please." He kicked the leg of the chair next to him, sliding the bar stool out for me.

I stared at him a moment, studying the tired lines under his eyes before nodding. "Yeah, okay." I grabbed a bottle from beneath the bar. It was an old bottle of vodka I'd filled with water for when customers bought me shots, but I needed to stay sober. Topping a glass with ice, I capped it with the fake vodka and rounded the bar to take a seat beside him.

My marks usually let their guards down when they thought I was drinking beside them. I had no doubt Vincent Romano was always on high alert, but it didn't hurt to be proactive.

"What's your favorite thing about living?"

"Pardon me?"

"If you had to choose one thing to do before you died, what would it be?"

"I'm...not sure." I floundered for an answer. I'd been asked all sorts of questions as a bartender but none like that one.

"You can't think of a single thing?"

"I—" The compounded lies in my life compelled me to answer with the truth. "No. I'm still figuring myself out. What I like. What I dislike. My family's gone, so I wouldn't be able to spend time with them. I'm not in a relationship. Other than Tessie, I don't really have any ties to people. And anything other than spending time with somebody feels unworthy of the last few moments in my life."

"I knew I liked you."

I let loose a laugh that I hoped didn't sound as alarmed as I felt. "With all due respect, Mr. Romano, you don't even know me."

"For the purposes of this conversation, pretend I do."

"Umm, okay..."

He laughed a little, and it shook his frame. He seemed so different than what I'd thought a head enforcer would be, from the awful stories my aunt had told me about Made Men and the damage they'd done to my mom's life.

"I'm a grown man. I don't pussyfoot. I'll say it. I like you. No, not like that. I like you as a person."

"Why?"

I didn't even like myself.

I mean, I liked the vain things—how I looked, my intellect, the way I cared for other people and animals, the weird skills I'd acquired under my various covers. But the darker parts of me, the parts that could betray others like they meant nothing… they were not worth liking.

"My son, Asher, got married today."

That was why I hadn't seen Bastian today.

Thank you, Asher Black.

Words I'd never thought I'd feel let alone think.

Vince practically inhaled the rest of his scotch before he continued, "His wife Lucy is wonderful."

"Congratulations." It sounded like an unenthusiastic question, so I repeated my congratulations and tacked on, "Asher must be so happy."

"He is. So am I. When I leave this world, I want to know my family is okay. Asher… he'll do great things, as will Lucy. They've both got great heads on their shoulders."

"I think some would say Asher has already done great things."

Black Enterprises was a Fortune 100.

"They'd be right, of course. But now he's found someone, and that makes all the difference to the parts of his life that truly matter. You were the one who said it seems insignificant to spend the last moments of your life without someone."

"I did," I allowed, feeling uneasy at having my loneliness rubbed in my face. Not that I thought he'd meant it like that. It just never got easy to swallow my solitude.

Vince poured himself some more of the scotch. "I'm not married. Never have been. That's a lonely life. I've loved a woman, but we never married. I'd rather Asher live a humble life with someone who made him happy than the life of a billionaire entrepreneur with every material object at the tip of his fingers except someone who matters. Fortunately, he doesn't have to choose between the two because he found Lucy."

I didn't know where he was going with this, so I nodded my head, took a sip of my fake vodka, and said, "Mhm."

He matched my sip with his own. "My brothers...They're of a different generation. Jumping from woman to woman and living an emotionally distant life doesn't make them unhappy. Their goals are different. I don't have to worry about them in that way. This lifestyle was meant for them, not my nephews and sons. Not Bastian."

My eyes jerked to his. "Bastian seems miserable, but it gives him no right to project that misery onto others. He's not a nice person, and it makes him unpleasant to be around unless Tessie is there as a buffer. Even that is debatable."

He nodded, but a fond smile spread across his face. "You'd be hard pressed to find anyone who disagrees with anything you just said." He turned to stare at me. "Has he told you about Elsa?"

"No."

I hadn't heard her name from the files either.

"Ask him about Elsa."

"You won't tell me?"

"It's not my story to tell."

"It's not my business anyway. I'm just an employee."

"We both know you're not."

My eyes darted around the room. I didn't know how to take that. What the hell did that mean, and how would Vincent Romano know anything about me and Bastian? Bastian and I weren't anything to know about in the first place.

I settled with a question. "Why are you here?"

"Closure."

"What closure can I offer you? I don't mean to be rude, but I don't know you."

“Word of advice, darling—it’s never too late to get closure. Life happens. You live one second; you die the next. If there are loose threads when that time comes, you’ll take them to your grave, and everyone you know and love will hurt for it. If you care about the people in your life, you handle your business when you can.”

“I don’t have anyone in my life.”

“We both know that’s not true.”

“I’m not sure what you’re getting at.”

“Tessie told me about you and Bastian.”

“She’s a kid. Eight.”

“And she’s bright, but she’s not my only source of information. I have eyes and ears everywhere, little De Luca.”

I stiffened like a corpse, unmoving as I took in the way he said my last name and what, if anything, his intonation implied. Swallowing my uncertainty, I asked, “What do your eyes and ears tell you?”

“That there’s something between you and my nephew.”

“He’s not a nice person.”

“Bastian isn’t a nice person, but he’s a good one.”

“We don’t... We’re not ”

“I know.”

I turned to face him. “You know?”

“I know who you are, Miss De Luca.”

It was reflex to reach for my hip, where my weapon would have been holstered if I wasn’t undercover.

Vince’s lips tilted up at the movement, and he gave me a knowing smile. “I wouldn’t be who I am if I didn’t have eyes and ears everywhere. I knew who you were the second you entered this bar. In fact, I knew who you were before that. Not much happens in the syndicate world without my knowing, including the mistress of the De Luca boss giving birth to a baby girl named Ariana De Luca."

"I-I—" I couldn't form words as I struggled to accept the information he dished me.

Was this where I begged for my life? Did he want me on my hands and knees, pleading for mercy? Fear strangled me, and I gasped for breath.

He placed a hand on my shoulder. "Breathe."

His touch only made it worse, and I coughed, hacking air out of my lungs in my struggle to breathe.

Breathe, Ari. He's right. Just breathe.

He knew I was a De Luca, but that didn't mean he knew I was an FBI agent. I could make him see reason about my family ties. The De Luca family and the Romano family didn't have a blood feud like the Andretti family did with them.

And blood feuds… they could only be paid in kind. An Andretti *caporegime* had died, which meant a Romano *caporegime* had to die to end the feud. That was Gio, Eli, or Vince. I couldn't see any one of them dying, so the feud would never end. Generations and generations of unborn Romano and Andretti children, destined to fight one another until their dying breath. It was sad and pointless.

"I've never…" I swallowed my hesitation, wishing yet again that I had more practice in the field, more practice guarding my fear and emotions. "I've never met a De Luca."

"I know." He paused a beat. "You have a brother."

"My aunt told me he's about my age."

"Yes. He's taken over the De Luca syndicate from your father."

I knew this thanks to the FBI files, but of course I couldn't say that, so I nodded my head and kept my mouth shut.

Vince continued, "He's not a bad kid. He's rebuilt the syndicate in ways your father never could. Years of neglect are hard to unravel, but he's done a great job. He has a good head on his shoulders."

"Why are you telling me this?"

"Have you ever considered visiting him?"

Have I ever considered dying?

"No."

"He wouldn't hurt you."

"How can you be so sure?"

"For one, it'd be stupid to harm an FBI agent. Too much heat."

I froze once again, shocked by his knowledge. My identity had been wiped, like it was each time I entered a new legend. The only way he could know that was if there was a mole in my division.

I laughed a little, forcing out bits of noise I hoped sounded amused. "You're funny."

"Yes, I am, but I'm not right now."

"I don't know what you're talking about."

"You'd think a legend would be better at lying, but I suppose you've only had small legends up until now."

Oh, god. How much did he know?

I didn't answer. I couldn't. I felt stripped to the core by a man who looked so fragile right now but could tear me apart and feed me to the whales in the Hudson River.

He drained the last of his drink and didn't pour himself another one. "I'm an old man. My time has long come. It's not in my interest to harm you when you've yet to harm my family, and I know you wouldn't."

He couldn't possibly know that. I'd only just come to this decision. I needed an extraction now. I needed to fumble out an excuse to leave, call Wilks on the emergency burner phone, and beg for an extraction team to save me.

"Sometimes," he continued, "the people furthest from a situation see it clearest. I've been watching you since you came to L'Oscurità, and I've been watching my nephew. Have you heard of Jupiter and Ganymede?"

He didn't wait for my answer. "In Roman mythology, Jupiter captures Ganymede and makes him his lover. I know my nephew. I know he seems difficult to love, even like, but he isn't. And you may not want to admit it, but there's something there between you two. You feel like he's captured a piece of you, and you can't shake it off. You've tried because of your last name, because of your duty to the FBI, but no matter what, you can't shake it off. Do you want to know why?"

"Why?" I breathed out, too breathless, my mind reeling, trying to contain everything bubbling near the surface of my heart.

Fear.

Truth.

Warmth.

"Because he didn't capture you, little De Luca. You captured him. You are Jupiter, and he is Ganymede. He revolves around you, whether he knows it or not, transfixed by the way you've captured his attention, by the way you fight back, by the way you differ from every woman he's ever loved or hated or been betrayed by, by the way you are with Tessie, and by the way he wonders how you would be with Everett."

Everett.

Who was Everett?

I couldn't process his words. There were too many things packed into them. I didn't love Bastian. I didn't even like Bastian. We fought and volleyed insults back and forth until our only truce came along in the form of Tessie, yet another thing we couldn't agree upon.

But you told him about your mom, and he told you about his pain.

I ignored my thoughts and breathed out the only question I could latch onto. "Everett?"

Vince ignored my question. "You are Jupiter, and he is Ganymede, revolving around you like you are his planet, and he is your moon."

"Jupiter is a man."

"You're finding shallow excuses to deny something you know in your heart is true."

"Why? Why are you saying this to me?" I didn't want to push my luck, but I needed to know. "Why aren't I buried in a shallow grave or whatever you do with people like me?"

"I just wanted you to know, when all is said and done, you have my blessing."

"For what?"

"To heal him. To save him. To cure him. To be his family when I cannot."

25

Love is a better teacher than duty.

—Albert Einstein

BASTIANO ROMANO

When Tessie was six, I'd left for Missouri—the closest I could get to Alabama without actually entering Andretti territory. Missouri laid in the southernmost portion of Camerino territory.

Marco Camerino had met me at the border of Missouri, near Tennessee, and we'd hatched a plan to get Everett back. He'd sworn on his life he wouldn't let anyone know Everett existed, and I trusted him. He was the heir to the Camerino syndicate, yes, but he was also my best friend from boarding school.

We spent about a month in Missouri, failure after failure until a gnawing dread chewed at my gut. This unshakeable feeling that something was wrong, and I couldn't stop it. I'd called Elsa, forcing myself through a gritted conversation until she assured me Everett was fine.

Then I'd call everyone else in my family, one by one until I reached my mom, and she told me Tessie had gone to our cabin in Big Bear with our cousin. I dropped all my pride and begged my mom to make sure Tessie was okay.

She wasn't. My cousin hadn't noticed Tessie had slipped out the back door to chase a squirrel, and Tessie had broken her foot on a log far into the wooded backyard of the secluded cabin we owned.

The temperatures had dropped so low that night, and by the time they'd found her in the snow, Tessie barely had any breath in her.

I had that same feeling gnawing at my gut now.

That bone-deep, heart-chilling feeling of doom.

Tessie sat in the break room, drawing something on the walls in what she swore was washable marker. She assured me she was fine, which I saw with my own eyes. I texted Everett, who told me he had tutoring in a few minutes and would video call me later.

Gio and Ma replied within an instant, and Uncle Frankie and Uncle Eli's security teams confirmed their safety within seconds. I debated for another minute before shooting a group text to Asher, Lucy, and Vince.

My eyes shifted to Ari as I waited for their responses. She hadn't looked at me all day. Not because she'd been busy. It was like she was actively avoiding all things to do with me, her eyes darting around the restaurant every few seconds like a skittish shelter dog.

My phone rang as I took my first step to her. Asher. He'd just gotten married, and it was supposed to be a happy occasion, but I couldn't shake this feeling. It wasn't Elsa's visit. If anything, that excited me. It renewed my hope for some blackmail material to loom over her head, something to get Everett back in New York.

I answered Asher's call, feeling a little guilty that I'd interrupted his honeymoon. "Honeymoon going that bad?" I joked.

"We're not on our honeymoon." His words had a bite to them.

My back stiffened as I paused my path to Ariana and straightened. "What? What happened? Are you okay? Is Lucy okay?"

I knew.

I just *knew* something was wrong.

"He's gone."

"Who's gone?"

"Vince."

Laughter bubbled in my throat. This had to be a joke. Vince was the one Romano I could depend on to always be there. He couldn't be gone.

"Did you check with his security?"

"Of course. He's just... gone. Look, shit went down with Niccolaio. Something to do with the bounty. I don't know. It's not looking good. No one has seen Vince."

I heard a clock ticking. Not here. Physically. But inside me. My gut feelings never failed me. We'd found Tessie in time, but Vince... how long had he been missing? Questions shot through my mind, each coming faster than the next. A minute longer, and Tessie would have been dead. How long did Vince have?

Silence.

I finally bit out, "I'll be right there."

After hanging up, I texted Tessie's babysitter and strode to Ari. "I need to go. Tessie's babysitter is coming in fifteen minutes. Can you watch Tessie until then?"

Her brows dipped together, her eyes skimming my face, searching for something. "Of course. Is everything okay?"

I didn't have time to explain, so I gave a half-assed nod and left for the break room. As soon as Tessie turned to me, I said, "I have to go."

"Where?" She drew the cap of her marker into her mouth and spoke around it. "You look funny."

I couldn't tell her about Vince. She'd freak, and I didn't want her worrying, so I lied like a jackass. Even though I felt the time ticking in my gut.

"I'm fine." Bouncing a curl of hers, like I'd do if things were fine, I continued, "Asher just called me. He needs my help with something. Ariana will watch you until your babysitter gets here. If you need anything, find Ari behind the bar."

"Okay!" The cap fell out of her mouth when she spoke. She flung her arms around me and kissed my cheek when I lifted her in a hug. As soon as I set her down, she turned back to the wall and drew a smiley face on it in yellow marker that had the word *permanent* printed on the side. "See you later!"

I shook my head but didn't bother dealing with the marker as I left. When I got to Asher's penthouse, Lucy had a pot of tea on the kitchen island, but it had lost its steam. Dozens of Asher's security team milled in the living room, taking up every inch of space. Sitting at the bar was Lucy, Asher, Niccolaio, and Vincent's head of security.

I tossed my keys and phone onto the counter. "What happened?"

"Vince is gone. He slipped past his security team." I opened my mouth, but Asher cut me off. "Don't ask how. We all know he's resourceful. What we need to focus on now is finding Vincent. We can deal with the rest later. Okay?"

I nodded and took in the massive three feet by three feet map on the kitchen island. They'd set tacks all over it in red, green, yellow, and black. "The green is where he most likely is, the yellow is where he could be, and the reds are a long shot. The blacks are where you've already searched?" I confirmed.

We'd done this before, usually when we were hunting people who hid in our territory. Not Vincent. This had to be a joke. Every fiber of me believed this was a joke. I knew what I'd felt earlier though.

That dread.

I didn't share it with everyone else. They needed their hope, and I needed... I needed to find Vincent and figure out the rest later. Why did it always take losing someone to realize how much you loved them?

The clock ticked in my head.

Louder.

Louder.

Telling me I was too late.

Tick.

Tock.

ARIANA DE LUCA

I'd been worried about dealing with Bastian, but I didn't need to be. He'd been emotionally distant after Vincent had visited me, leaving me to stress over every word Vincent and I had shared.

He knew I was a De Luca.

He knew I was an FBI agent.

Why hadn't I asked for an extraction? Why was I waiting?

Because you're wondering if he's right. If you're Jupiter, and Bastian is Ganymede.

Ridiculous thoughts.

Especially since I was so unbelievably pissed at Bastian—once again. Tessie's babysitter had left hours ago, my shift had ended around ten, and I didn't want to leave Tessie here, even with the staff to watch her.

I'd had Tessie call her parents and brother, but no one picked up.

Tessie pocketed her phone and looked up at me, so adorable and oblivious. "Do boys kiss girls on dates?"

I cleaned the marker from the wall with one of those magic erasers with the buff bald guy on the box. "Sometimes."

She grabbed a magic eraser from the box and began to tear it into tiny pieces. "I want to go on a date."

"Maybe when you're older." I plucked what little remained of her eraser from her hands, swiped as many pieces as I could off the ground, and tossed it.

"Carrie left to go on a date. She said he was super cute."

Carrie was Tessie's babysitter, and I'd kill her right after I killed Bastian for leaving Tessie here.

"Come on." I took Tessie's hand, helped her into her jacket, and gathered all her knick-knacks into her bright pink backpack. "I'll take you to my place."

"Where's Bastian?"

I wish I knew.

Instead, I gave a half-truth. "I'm sure he'll call when he's done. It must be important."

She shrugged and followed me out the door. I almost felt like a kidnapper, but there was no way I was leaving her alone in L'Oscurità with no one I trusted to look after her. Plus, it pushed my luck to even be here.

Instead of heading to the subway, I hailed a cab, so Tessie and I could sit in comfort while we headed to my place. I wasn't even sure if she'd ever taken public transportation here or in California.

The cab took his time sifting through the New York traffic. By the time we pulled up to my apartment, Tessie had fallen asleep with half her body on my lap. I paid the driver and eased Tessie up and into my arms, carrying her and the backpack up the stairs and into the elevator easily thanks to all the ice I was used to carrying up and down the basement stairs.

I managed to unlock the bedroom door with one hand and

slide Tessie into bed without waking her up. She sprawled out, making it hard to slip her jacket off. I worked it off her shoulders as gently as I could, then took her shoes off without even stirring her.

After sliding the sheets over her body, I showered, prepped for bed, and grabbed the spare set of blankets and a pillow from my bedroom closet. Pulling out the shitty mattress from the pull-out couch, I sunk into it with the blanket and pillow and fell asleep.

I woke up to the sound of pounding. My hands immediately reached for my gun before remembering the closest one sat hidden under my sink in a fake container. I cursed before Tessie's face flashed in my head.

She was asleep. Bastian probably stood on the other side of my door. Only he would find it appropriate to wake everyone in my building up at—I glanced at the clock—three in the morning.

I peeked through the peephole. Yup. Bastian. Unlocking the door, I swung it open without a word. Bastiano Romano was the type of man who took up more room than he did space, and standing in the doorway of my apartment, he filled up every inch of my place with his presence.

People considered me to be skinny, yes, but I'd never felt small until this moment—standing before a pissed off Bastiano Romano as he glared at me with so much hatred, I had to pinch myself to make sure I hadn't been petrified.

"What is your problem?"

I crossed my arms. "What's *my* problem?" It was so easy to forget all of my problems, actually, when Bastian stood in front of me, and we argued. "My problem is you, standing in front of me at three in the morning, waking up all of my neighbors."

"I can assure you, the people who live in this building are the type used to three A.M. wake up calls." He took an uninvited step into my apartment and shut the door behind him with his foot. "You kidnapped my sister and took her to a meth lab."

"There are no meth labs in my apartment building," I protested. I met his step with my own, and we stood nose to nose, my head tilted up and his dipped down. "You mean, I protected your sister from being left alone in a bar unattended because she has no responsible adult presence in her life besides me."

He looked like he could have punched the wall. "You could have called."

"We did. You didn't answer. Your dad didn't answer. Your mom didn't answer. Great adults she has in her life." I folded my arms across my chest like a shield. Instead of protecting me, the movement drew me closer to him. His skin burned the backs of my forearms.

"You don't understand."

"Enlighten me."

He opened his mouth. Closed it. Opened it again. Instead of telling me what the hell was so important he had to ditch his baby sister he supposedly cared so much about, he asked, "Where is she?"

"Sleeping in my bed. It's three in the morning, and you will not wake that little girl up after ditching her."

"Fine."

We stared at one another, both of us at a weird impasse. I took the time to study him. Bags under his eyes. His usually neat hair stuck up in several directions. Wrinkles littered all over his untucked button down. I didn't know what to make of this version of him.

Pity and this overwhelming desire to help him filled me. I had to be insane. Certifiable.

I gentled my voice. "What happened?"

Why?

Why had I asked that?

Why did I care?

Why?

Just why?

You are Jupiter, and he is Ganymede, revolving around you like you are his planet, and he is your moon.

Maybe Vince had gotten it wrong. Maybe Bastian was Jupiter, and I was Ganymede, revolving around Bastian, unable to pull away from his gravity. Gosh, Ganymede was such an idiot. He needed Jesus and an intervention.

Bastian's anger still simmered waves of heat around us. He looked like he sought an outlet; I didn't know if I could give one to him.

"He's gone." The words ripped out of him, escaping his lips and clawing its way into my throat.

I felt his pain to my very core, and I couldn't explain it. I didn't even like Bastian as a person, so why did I feel his pain like it was my own? Nothing about us made sense. We were supposed to fight, and fight, and fight, and fight. He wasn't supposed to massage me. He wasn't supposed to listen to me grieve my mom's death. He wasn't supposed to help me home and tuck me in. He wasn't supposed to carry hundreds of pounds of ice for me.

He was supposed to be the villain in the story, and I was supposed to be the hero. Never once did I consider it'd be the other way around.

Then, don't betray him.

I shook the thought away. I'd already committed to leaving

the bureau. I just didn't know how. But tonight, for just one night, maybe I could feel like the savior for once.

I took another step closer and reached up and touched his face. "How can I help? Who's gone?"

His jaw ticked, his efforts to keep himself in control visible. "Vincent."

I worked to tamp my reaction. "When did you last see him?"

"The night of Asher's wedding."

And I'd seen him after that. Had I been the last person to see him? It couldn't be a coincidence that Vince had visited me just before he went missing.

Why are you here? I'd asked him.

Closure.

What else had he said?

That I had his blessing with Bastian.

To heal him. To save him. To cure him. To be his family when I cannot.

Those weren't the words of a man prepared to live. They were the words of a man preparing to die. But I couldn't tell Bastian that. He'd never understand without me explaining the whole conversation to him. The one where Vince had revealed he knew all my dirty little secrets, all my destructive lies entombed in one deceptive package.

Instead of telling the truth, I buried myself in a deeper hole, one dug by guilt and filled with remorse. "Stay."

"Excuse me?"

"It's late. Your sister needs her sleep. I'm guessing you're going to wake up to search for Vincent in the morning, and you're going to need your sleep. I have a pull-out couch. The mattress is awful, but it's better than waking Tessie up, driving to your place, and falling asleep just to wake up hours later. So... stay."

"Where will you sleep?"

"The couch bed is big enough for the both of us."

He nodded his head, his eyes thanking me instead of his words. The relief in his shoulders only dug the guilt deeper beneath my skin until my fingertips burned with the need to scratch at it.

And when we both dipped under the covers and he wrapped an arm around my waist like he couldn't help himself, I felt like the worst person in the world.

Not Jupiter.

Not even Ganymede.

Apate.

The goddess of fraud and deception.

26

Why must my duty require me
to break my own heart?

—Rachel Hauck

ARIANA DE LUCA

Days Missing: 2

I woke up to an arm around my waist and stayed as still as my breathing would let me. I'd lost feeling in my right hand. Inching it up into the air, I shook it lightly, trying my best not to wake Bastian up.

"What are you doing?"

My eyes darted to Tessie at the base of the tiny hallway.

She tilted her head and stared at Bastian beside me. "Is that my brother?"

I considered lying for a second. "Yes."

"Oh. Can you wake him up? I'm hungry."

"I'm awake." His voice vibrated against the back of my neck, and he moved his arm from me and stretched, like he woke up next to women every day. "Luna will have breakfast for you when we get to my place."

"Where were you last night?"

My head cocked to Bastian, taking in his face. I could read it in his eyes. He didn't want to tell Tessie, but he didn't want to lie.

I made the choice for him. "Can you help me pick out my outfit for the day, Tessie?"

"Okay!" She ran off to my room, and I heard my closet door open before I even shouted my permission.

When I turned to face Bastian, he didn't just have his thank you projecting from his eyes. It sat on the tip of his tongue, too. "Thank you."

"I'm still mad at you. You don't want me near Tessie, yet here we are."

His sigh heaved past his chest. Heavy. Like it took everything in him to exist. "I'm going to sound like a hypocrite, but I need a favor."

I eyed him warily. "Fine."

"Until we find him, everyone will be looking for him. My mom, my dad, my uncles, Asher, everyone who works for them, me... Everyone. I clearly can't trust Tessie's babysitter, and..."

"And you trust me. The woman you wanted to keep away

from your sister." Even as I said them, my words held no real bite to them.

I didn't take it lightly that Bastian trusted me with Tessie, a fact he'd be reluctant to admit had Vince's absence not changed everything. In fact, he still didn't admit it. That was okay. I had my secrets, too.

I could never tell him about that night with Vincent.

Even as tearing the city apart looking for Vince tore him inside.

I was his Apate, not his Jupiter.

Never Jupiter.

"I'll do it."

Of course, I would.

I loved Tessie.

Sure, that's why.

"I can pay you."

I shook my head. "I don't want your money."

Bastian paused for a moment, staring at me like I'd just said something bizarre. He stood and pulled up his pants, which I hadn't even seen him remove last night. "I'll have someone cover your shift, so you can come back with us and get set up with the security."

It wasn't lost on me that, just as I'd committed to leaving the FBI, I'd been given an unheard-of opportunity into Bastiano Romano's penthouse. Who knew how much intel the place held?

None of it interested me.

I wanted to help Tessie.

Nothing else.

I was such a mess.

"Security?"

"Your own badge to enter and exit the building, a key to the penthouse, and biometrics. Do you have a car?"

I raised a brow. "Do you pay me enough to own a car?"

"You won't need a parking spot in the garage then. It'll be quick. A few scans, and you're good." He rattled off a text message as he spoke. "They'll have the key and badge ready for you by the time we get there."

Tessie ran out into the hall with a giant duffle bag that fit my entire wardrobe in her hand. "I'm ready. I got your clothes."

"What?" I went to grab the bag from her.

This was enough clothes to stay the rest of the month. No way would I sleep over at Bastian's. Letting him spend the night on my couch after he scoured the city for an uncle I knew was either dead or soon-to-be dead was one thing, but moving into his place... even as I thought it, I knew I wouldn't fight it.

I didn't want to be his Apate.

"Good idea." Bastian nodded and grabbed it from her hand before I could. "You'll probably need all this until..." He trailed off and glanced at Tessie.

I turned to her. "How did you know to pack the bag?"

She looked so proud of herself. "I ear dropped."

"Eavesdropped," Bastian corrected.

She turned to him. "Who are you and everyone looking for?"

"Whom," Bastian corrected again, like he was buying time. He glanced my way, shot me a shut-up look, and turned back to his sister. "Adult business."

"But—"

"Do you want breakfast or not? We might not make it back before Luna leaves if you keep talking."

She shut her mouth then opened it again. "It better be pancakes."

It wasn't. It was strawberry chocolate chip flaxseed waffles, which Tessie promised she liked better. She gobbled them down, unaware that her favorite uncle had been missing yesterday. Then again, Bastian was unaware that I might have been the last to see him, and I wasn't about to confess anything.

Bastian showered, changed, and left before Tessie finished her breakfast. Luna cleaned up the dishes and left, too. The concierge sent a few security guys up with some portable tech. They took my fingerprint, retinal scan, and breath scan.

My fucking breath.

Tessie watched from the kitchen island, her little feet dangling off the barstool. She kicked the side of the island just to watch her shoes light up before looking at me. "Are you going to tell me what's happening?"

"What do you mean?"

I knew what she'd meant. I just didn't want to be the one to tell her. For one, it wasn't my place. I also didn't want to be the one to break that news. I knew in my gut this wouldn't end well.

Vince wasn't just missing. He was either already dead or about to die. I'd seen that look in his eyes, the sunken-in cheeks, the way he'd sought out closure. He'd been preparing to die. I just hadn't realized how soon.

Tessie kicked the island again, and her shoes flashed a kaleidoscope of colors onto her ankles. "Everyone is freaking out. I called Daddy while you were breathing into that thingymabob, and he seemed scared. I think. I don't know." She scratched at her shoulder. "I've never seen him or Bastian scared. Except once."

I nodded my thanks to the security team as they finished packing up their stuff, handed me a badge and keycard, and let themselves out. I considered answering Tessie's question, but again, it wasn't my place, so I redirected it.

"What happened that one time?"

"It was a few years ago. My cousin took me to our cabin in Big Bear. There was a squirrel outside. It looked hungry, so I grabbed some food from the kitchen and snuck out the back. It ran away from me when I tried to feed it, so I chased it. I tripped on some wood and broke my leg. It was snowing. I was too far from home. I called for help until I fell asleep. When I woke up, I was in the hospital. Daddy, Bastian, and Mommy were all in the same room. I hadn't seen them in the same room for a while, but they all looked scared until the doctor told them I'd be okay."

"Were you scared?"

"No. I didn't know what was going on, but the doctor was right. Everything was okay."

"Are you scared now?"

"No. I don't know what's going on."

I grabbed her hands and kneeled a little, so we were face to face. "Good. I'm going to tell you the same thing the doctor told you. You're going to be okay. No matter what happens in life, no matter if you break your leg and get too cold, no matter if everyone is acting funny around you, no matter how you feel in one moment, you will be okay. You have so many people who love you and want you to soar, and you are the smartest little girl I've ever met. If anyone is going to be okay, it's you."

She flung her arms around my shoulders and dug her nose into my hair. "It's Uncle Vince, isn't it?"

I pulled back and studied her. "Why do you think that?"

"He snuck into Daddy's house after Asher married Lucy. He told me to never be scared because he's always with me, but he's not here now. I talked to Bastian, Daddy, and Mommy this morning. Uncle Frankie and Uncle Eli called me, too. Asher and Lucy are with Bastian. Where's Uncle Vince?"

My heart broke for the little girl who'd never have another second with her favorite uncle, who didn't realize the last time she'd seen him would be the last memory she had of him, who was too young to feel this kind of heartbreak.

I shoved down the tears I felt building behind my eyes and whispered, "Close your eyes."

She did.

I grabbed her hands and held them tight. "Think about Uncle Vincent, all the favorite things you've done with him, and every memory he's given you. Can you do that?"

I wished I had a memory of my mother. Just one to keep me warm at night when I tossed and turned, and my life felt like a chaotic mess I couldn't fix. The thing about love is, it hurts when you lose it, but it hurts more to never have it in the first place.

Tessie nodded her head, her eyes still squeezed shut. "Yes."

"If you can hold on to those memories and those feelings, he will always be with you." My voice broke.

My mom was *never* with me.

Tessie peeked an eye open. "Promise?"

"Promise."

My heart broke for her, but it broke for me, too.

BASTIANO ROMANO

The city lights left the alley behind Depravity unscathed. I barely made out the scattered trash and cigarette buds under the dim moonlight.

A black cat hid in the corner, but I paid it no attention as I swung my leg at the dumpster container. It didn't move an inch. Pain shot up my leg, and the cat darted away like even it didn't want to remain in the shadows with me.

Another place empty.

Another place without Vincent.

And my gut—the gut that wouldn't shut up—whispered, *he's already gone. You'll never find him.*

Weeks ago, Vince had set Niccolaio up with a safe house to hide from the bounty on his head. Niccolaio had been attacked, and sometime before Vince had gone missing, he'd captured him.

Tortured him.

Accused Vince of betraying his location, then let him go when he'd realize his mistake.

And then Vince vanished.

No trace behind.

Not a coincidence.

Uncle Frankie expected all of us not to blame Niccolaio, but I couldn't. I got it. I did. He'd made a mistake, and Vince forgave him, so we should, too.

But it was easier to blame Niccolaio than myself, for not understanding why my own uncle left. And we knew he'd left. It was the only way he could have eluded his security.

Vince's voice teased me, the sleep deprivation sinking its claws into my head.

Tick.

Tock.

Tick.

Tock.

I kicked at the dumpster again, needing the pain to lap its way up my body and chase away the rage. The back door swung open, and a security guard peeked his head out. He took in my glare for a second before bowing his head, apologizing, and shutting the door to Uncle Frankie's club.

When my phone rang, I answered without looking and barked out, "The fuck do you want?"

"D-dad?"

Shit.

"Everett. I thought—" Nothing. No excuse. Just... *fuck.* "Sorry, kiddo." I leaned the back of my head against the brick wall, harder than necessary, but I deserved the pain. "How are you?"

In seven years, I'd never yelled at him. Never cursed at him. Never spoke to him in any way less than he deserved. All that love, all that tenderness, all that devotion up in flames.

If I were anyone else, my fist would be in my face, and I'd wake up with a black eye.

Everett's breathing grew ragged over the line. "Mom's acting weird."

"Are you okay?"

"Yes. Can I come home yet?"

I ran a hand down my face and bit back a swear. I wanted everyone home twenty-four-fucking-seven.

Him.

Vince.

Tessie.

This—always searching or waiting for the people I loved to be near me—chipped at my sanity, scattering a trail of my soul across the city with each step I took.

"I'll find a way, Everett," I promised, hoping I could keep it.

You can't, the distorted Vince in my head taunted. I needed sleep. *Time's running out.*

Tick.

Tock.

Tick.

Tock.

Too late.

ARIANA DE LUCA

I'd never let myself grieve my mom. I'd always felt that, if I took the time to hurt, I'd never stop. It made no sense. I'd never met the woman. I didn't know what I was missing out on, so how could I miss her?

The first tear slipped past my lashes as I stared at Bastian's bed. I'd tucked Tessie into bed in her room a few minutes ago, and I was supposed to be finding a place to sleep in this stupid two-bedroom penthouse with a million useless rooms but no guest room.

Leave it to Bastian to not want guests.

The second tear volleyed past the first as I kicked my duffel bag to the side of his bed, something like grief clogging my throat as I told myself it made no sense to grieve someone I'd never met.

The third tear chased the second as I stripped off my clothes and shrugged into satin pajama shorts and a thin camisole, trying my best to follow a routine. I froze, the shirt halfway down my midriff as I realized I'd been following a routine my whole life.

Up until I'd turned eighteen, it was school, homework, books, and sleep, trying my best not to get in my aunt's way. In college, it was school, homework, and doing my best to avoid people. At the bureau, it'd been burying myself in legends because I didn't want to confront my own life and sought an escape through my covers.

But here I was, Ariana De Luca for once, and I was tearing at the seams. A ripped dress I'd once loved and vowed to sew back together but had tossed in the back of the closet and forgotten before I could fix it.

The tears built behind my eyes. I could feel them pushing, pushing, pushing, trying to tumble past my stubborn irises, but I held them back.

You don't cry.

You don't cry.

You don't cry.

You are not Jupiter. You are not Ganymede. You are not Apate. You are Ariana De Luca, and you do not cry.

I was thankful for the crash that forced me to push aside my self-pity. Rushing to the living room, my right hand absent-mindedly patting my hip where I knew my holster wasn't, I had my other arm up, ready for a fight.

It lowered when I caught sight of Bastian and the tossed piano chair beside him.

He turned to face me, his eyes distraught and his voice so low, I struggled to hear him. "We're not going to find him."

No, you're not.

Instead, I kept my secrets carefully tucked in my gut, where they festered like a decomposed heart; crossed my arms; and swiped at my stupid tears. "You're unhinged."

He took a step toward me, and it struck me how much space his body took up. He could break me if he wanted to. "Do you fucking blame me?!"

I held my ground, my voice low but strong. "Tessie's asleep."

He opened his mouth but stopped, his gaze raking my body in my sheer pajamas and settling on my cheeks, which glistened with the tears I'd failed to wipe. Stupid fucking tears. Instead of picking and prodding at my weaknesses, he just stared at me. I felt broken, bare, and vulnerable before him, but I suspected he felt the same.

It happened before I could stop myself.

We eyed the door to the bedroom, where Tessie slept. I met his eyes and took a step toward him, pushing us both to his front door and into the hallway outside of his penthouse. His eyes flared, and then we were on each other, our lips attacking one another so quickly, I barely had time to shut the door behind me.

He tasted like demons. Ours. Intertwined. Mated in something we couldn't control.

I pushed my tiny shorts down my legs.

He pulled back and glared at me like there was nothing he hated more than me. "Take off your panties. Now. Or I'm fucking you with them on."

He hooked one of my legs around his waist, and my hands moved to push the lace down, but he was already pushing them aside.

"Too slow." And then he sunk himself deep into me.

My fingers dug into his back, unsure whether to pull him closer to me or push him further away. My wetness dripped onto his cock, the insides of my thighs, the hallway floor where anyone could see.

Each thrust was punishment for making him want me. The louder I moaned, the less controlled his movements became. He leaned forward and bit my nipple through my shirt, sucking it into his mouth along with the fabric.

A door opened down the hall. I swung my face to the right, saw the blurred shadow of someone through my lust-hazed eyes, and couldn't hold back the groan as Bastian's piercing hit me just right.

He didn't stop, not caring about the audience. It was just me and him as his neighbor retreated. It struck me, not for the first time, that Bastiano Romano could do whatever he wanted, but right now... he wanted me.

He bit the side of my neck and nipped his way up to the corner of my lips. His hands spread my cheeks, and he toyed with my backside, sliding his finger in and out to match the way his cock hit my G-spot.

"I could take this, too," he claimed, always so enthralled by the idea of taking from me even though, I realized, I'd give him everything in this moment without him asking.

"Do it," I dared him, diving deeper into this thing between us than I'd ever expected.

His eyes flared, and he set me down and urged me to my knees. "Beg for it."

I studied his face, the tick of his jaw, the hardened set of his eyes. He *needed* this. He needed to control me, so he could feel control in his life again. His temporary lack of power was the sickness, and giving him control of me was the cure.

And I would.

I'd give it all to him.

Not because I felt guilty, but because I was just as depraved as the people I lied to. I wanted Bastiano Romano. Any way I could get him.

"Beg for it," he demanded again, this time less gentle as he gripped my hair.

"Please."

"Not with your words." He fisted his cock and guided my head to it by my hair. "Show me how needy your tight little ass is for me." My hands gripped his thighs as he thrust into my face. "Your ass better feel tighter than your mouth," he goaded and pushed deeper into me until his piercing hit the back of my throat.

I wanted to gag but held it back, determination driving me to take all of him. Glaring at his taunts, I sucked my cheeks in, narrowing my mouth's hold on his cock as his balls tightened and hit my chin.

The wetness dripped down my thighs, making a mess in the hallway, where anyone could walk out and see me suck hungrily at his cock like it was my first meal of the day. I reached between my legs and tried to swipe the wetness off my thighs, but he swatted my hands, pulled out of my mouth, and spun me around.

Reaching down, he grabbed my hips and lifted. His fingers gathered my wetness from behind and used it to slide them into my ass. He spread my wetness then replaced his fingers with his cock.

I screamed out in surprise as he slid the tip of his cock into my ass, my spit and wetness making his movements embarrassingly smooth.

"Bastian," I groaned as he slid in and out of my ass, his movements slow as he prepped me.

"Tell me what you want."

"You. Oh, God, I want you."

He sank his cock all the way, and my groan echoed up and down the halls. My eyes darted from side to side, knowing his neighbors could hear my pleasure at this ridiculous hour and marveling at the fact that no one dared to enter the hall and cross Bastian.

I could practically feel their eyes peeking through the peepholes on their doors, their hands stroking themselves to the sight of us, watching Bastian's relentless movements as his nails dug into my hips and his cock sank into my ass.

"Touch yourself."

Hoarse. Rough. Gritted.

I could barely make out his words.

"What?" I breathed out through the haze.

"Three fingers. Inside your pussy. Now."

"I—"

"Stroke my cock through your walls. Make me come." I hesitated, and he growled, "Now."

I braced the wall with one hand and slid my fingers inside me with the other, gasping out when I felt him through my walls. *Holy shit.* We moved together as my fingers hit my G-spot each time I stroked his cock as he thrust inside of my ass.

Buried in this hostility was our unspoken need. I didn't know how it had happened, but I no longer loathed him.

I clenched around my fingers, and I knew he felt it from behind because he bit my shoulder. "Don't you dare fucking come."

I was so close, but I pushed the feeling aside. He had me obeying his every demand, giving him everything he asked of me and more. Like I belonged to him. And perhaps my body did, because he fucked it like he owned it, until even I believed it.

"Come," he demanded, and I let my body take over.

Traitor, the agent in me whispered as pleasure whipped a

frenzy in my core, pebbling my nipples into disloyal peaks that brushed against the wall with each thrust.

Apate, I accused as my head fell back on Bastian's shoulder, and my glazed eyes caught the security camera above us and I wondered if someone could see the pleasure on my face and the lies beneath my skin.

Ganymede, I hoped when the beginnings of an orgasm blurred my thoughts and I felt like I'd only be in his gravity and never my own.

Jupiter, I begged as he came inside me, marking me as his in a way that could never feel permanent enough.

I was no one and everyone at once.

A liar.

A con.

A traitor.

A distraction.

A savior.

His.

I rested my forehead against his shoulder, my arms clinging to him as he held me up while I tried to gather myself. He set me down, letting me fall a little before he steadied me.

Neither of us said anything.

My heart in my throat, I broke the silence first. "Tell me about your day."

I waited for him to tell me about his day. Why he beat up his piano and sought refuge inside me. He didn't say anything. Instead, he wrapped an arm around me, scooped me up as I wrapped my legs around him, carried me back into his penthouse to his room, and tossed me onto his bed.

I opened my mouth to speak. I had his cum dripping down my thighs, my satin shorts on the floor in the hallway, and the scent of sex all over my body. I couldn't sleep like this or in a bed with him.

Bastian cut my words off with a shake of his head, tore off his clothes until he stood in front of me in his boxers, and sank onto the bed until he hovered above my body.

He stared at me, looked me in my traitorous eyes, and whispered, "You're the only good thing about my day."

And for a second, as he ignored the ebbing redness of my tear-stained eyes and I pushed aside his grief over his uncle, I pretended I didn't have any duties, I'd never lied to this man, I didn't know anything about his missing uncle, I was not his Apate, and I was normal. That nothing tainted me and this crazy, fucked up man.

Nothing stopped us from being each other's.

Love is the bane of honor, the death of duty.

—George R.R. Martin

ARIANA DE LUCA

Days Missing: 3

I remembered the words Wilks had taught me my first day as a legend.

This job is about patience. It's about molding yourself into someone else. You flatline. Become dull. No threat. Then, you look for weaknesses. Because your enemy is still a human being. One weakness is all you need. Their weakness gives you hope, and your hope is the only thing you need for strength.

It wasn't hope I felt as I considered Bastian's grief. Like a gentleman—his version—he'd wiped himself off me with a wet towel last night before showering and joining me in bed. He'd been asleep since I'd woken up with his arm slung around me.

I stayed as still as I could because he looked exhausted, and I knew he needed his strength to search for his uncle I knew in my soul he wouldn't find. I toiled over the guilt, debating my options.

I needed to turn in my badge, but I couldn't bring myself to leave Tessie. Not with her uncle missing and everyone in her life searching for him. Until I left, I couldn't speak about Vincent. If I told Bastian about Vince's visit, our truce would dissipate. It'd lead to my secrets unraveling, and I didn't want to think about what would happen if he knew I was an illegitimate De Luca Princess and an undercover FBI agent.

"Bastian! I'm hungry!" Tessie called out, her voice growing louder as she neared.

I pulled the covers up, shifting her brother's arm away from me.

She didn't look surprised to see me in bed with Bastian as she entered the room in her pink Power Rangers pajamas. "Can you make me food? I can't find Luna."

Bastian peeked his head up. "Luna's off work today."

"Oh." She frowned and stared at me. "Bastian sucks at cooking. I hope you don't suck, too."

I shrugged beneath the covers, painfully aware I only wore my camisole and no underwear. "I do alright. What do you want?"

"Two mini pancakes with flax and almond butter, a mushroom and cheese omelet, half an eggs Benedict, and a blueberry and açaí smoothie."

Good lord. Rich people breakfast.

I popped a brow. "Is that all?"

She bit her lip and actually tried to think of more. "I think we ran out of almond milk, so I guess that's all." She turned to her brother. "Did you find Uncle Vince yet?"

Bastian's eyes shot to mine, the irritation growing until I shook my head in denial. His fault for having a smart sister. He sat up, and the sheets pooled around his waist. In the light, I could finally see his tattoos.

He had the name Everett inked onto his ribcage, bold and unapologetic. I wanted to bite down on the tattoo and ask who in his life was so permanent they'd earned the right to stain his skin.

An inappropriate line of thought with an eight-year-old at the door, so I tamped it and stared at the ceiling as Bastian spoke.

"We're still looking. Also, this is my house not the Ritz Carlton. You'll have cereal."

"But—"

"Or you could have oatmeal."

She shut up. "Fine, but I want Captain Crunch."

"Deal. Go change out of your pajamas and gather your homework, and I'll meet you in the kitchen."

I slid the sheets off as soon as she retreated, feeling way too self-conscious without my panties. He didn't bother pretending he wasn't looking as I walked to the en suite bathroom as quickly as I could without outright running.

I turned and glared. "Could you at least pretend you're not looking?"

It felt like a wall between us had been shattered yesterday, and we navigated this unusual territory with reservations, trying to discover what each other's limits were, but each second bridged the divide we'd once shared.

He laid on his side, his fingers absently tracing his Everett tattoo like they were used to doing so. "No." He tilted his head sideways, and I got the feeling he was prolonging this, trying to push aside the severity of Vince's absence for as long as he could. "Your ass is pretty hot, but it looks better with my dick in it."

"Your mouth is pretty nice, but it looks better shut," I shot back as I slammed the door on him.

The opulent marble floors chilled my feet. His bathroom could have housed two of my apartments, which didn't surprise me. He had a double sink, black clawfoot tub, and standing shower with a clear door and Aurora marble and pearl tiles.

Deciding I'd rather use his towel than go out there and ask for one, I stripped my shirt off and hopped into the shower. I jumped when I heard the door open, covering my breasts with my arms. He didn't glance at me through the glass door of his shower as he grabbed his toothbrush and brushed his teeth.

After ten seconds of staring at him aghast, I turned on the water to a warm setting and tried my best to relax under the spray. As soon as he rinsed his mouth, he turned to stare at me, his arms casually crossed and the backs of his thighs resting against the sink counter.

I tried not to be affected, failed, and endeavored to throw him off balance instead. "Who is Everett?"

"None of your business." He uncrossed his arms and took a step toward me. "I need a favor."

I barked out an uneasy laugh as he slid his boxers down in one quick movement, and his cock bobbed against his stomach, already hard. "Why would I do you a favor? You've never been nice to me."

I could have given in, allowed what had happened yesterday and the way we'd used one another to heal to truly change us, but I couldn't. Not yet. I'd let it shatter our boundaries and pull us closer, but I couldn't break down that last barrier. The tiny, breakable wall made of Elmer's glue and paste. Not while I knew what it meant that I had, quite possibly, been the last to see Vincent Romano.

"I'll return the favor."

"I don't want anything from you," I whispered.

A lie.

I wanted this life. Not the penthouse, the fancy bathrooms, and the prime New York real estate. I could do without those, but I wanted the little sister to talk to, the man to come home to, the idea that someone could actually depend on me like Bastian did now with Tessie.

I wanted to feel loved and wanted and trusted and *me*.

A version of me I could be proud of.

A life where the only duty I had was to make myself and the people I loved happy.

He opened the shower door and moved me aside, stealing the water from me. I shivered in the cold, my nipples pebbling and thighs shaking as I watched the water drip from his head down his chest, past the twin V lines, and to his erection.

Good Lord.

Showers were invented to watch water drip down Bastian's skin.

"Take care of Tessie until I return."

"That's the favor you want?"

I'd thought we'd already settled this. It was hardly a favor.

I would have done it anyway. Plus, he'd cleared me of all my shifts already.

My lips parted a little as I watched him kneel in front of me. "What are you doing?"

He kissed my inner thigh, bit down on the skin, and slid apart my lips. "Returning the favor," he said before he latched onto my clit, and I realized he knew I'd already agreed to take care of Tessie.

He just needed an excuse to touch me.

Yes.

This was the life I wanted.

Tessie had a burger in one hand and fries in the other as Bastian and I made our way to the kitchen, dressed, hair blow dried, and bodies a respectable distance apart.

Didn't matter.

I still felt him all over me.

Tessie bit into the burger and looked at us. "You guys took so long, so I ordered food."

A greasy burger and the equivalent of oil with a side of fries hardly constituted as food, but I supposed Bastian and I couldn't say anything after he'd screwed my brains out in the shower while Tessie waited for her breakfast.

He pressed a kiss to her temple, pocketed his keys and phone, and headed to the door. "Call me if you need something."

I waited for the door to shut before taking a seat beside her and stealing a fry. "Do you have schoolwork?"

She slid her food from me and inched away a bit. "I finished it."

I arched a brow. "Really?"

"Well, I'm almost done. I have piano practice."

"Is that piano yours?" I nodded to the piano behind us, to the side of the living room in the open-plan apartment.

He had the craziest place I'd ever seen. A two-story penthouse with a view of Central Park. Marble flooring in the foyer, bathrooms, kitchen, and stairs. Dark wood in the living room, floor to ceiling curtains, and a wall to wall window overlooking the park.

The piano sat to the side of the living room, beside the stairwell. It'd been maintained well, like the rest of the penthouse, but I couldn't picture him playing it. Or Tessie. She just didn't seem like she had the attention span.

Tessie shook her head, her wild hair bouncing back and forth over her face. "It's Bastian's. He doesn't play anymore, but he keeps it because he wants to teach Ever—" She stopped and took a bite of her burger.

"Who is Everett?"

"I'm not allowed to talk about Everett. I'll get in trouble."

"Not even for me?"

She thought about it for a few seconds. "No. I'm sorry. I don't want to get in trouble."

The guilt came instantly. I hadn't asked for the bureau. I had asked because I genuinely wanted to know more about Bastian. But putting Tessie in this position wasn't my best move. It was the reflex of a shameless undercover agent, used to extracting information from any source possible.

Sometimes, I hated myself.

I wondered if I'd ever shake away the parts of me I loathed.

The bed dipped and an arm wrapped around my waist late into the night. I'd been in a light sleep for hours, but I woke the instant Bastian's skin touched mine. I glanced at the clock. Four in the morning.

When I turned to face him, the dim light from the hallway lit up the side of his face. Exhaustion lined his features. He looked like he'd aged a year in a day, and defeat—

something I never thought I'd see on Bastian—looked inked on his skin.

"Sorry for waking you." Always the asshole, he didn't look sorry. "I don't think I'll be able to sleep."

"You look tired."

"My mind is racing."

"Vincent?"

"Still missing. I don't want to talk about it." His ankle locked around mine.

"Tell me about the piano." I let him pull my leg around his waist.

He'd taken off his clothes, so the only thing separating us were my panties, his boxers, and the Wharton School of Business shirt I'd stolen from his closet.

"Sometimes I play it. Sometimes I don't."

"Wow. So forthcoming. I think I'll go to bed now." I shut my eyes and hoped he'd say something.

"It's a relic of the past, and I can't part with it."

My eyes flew open at the confession. How tired was he?

I traced a path along his face, taking in the way he stared at me like I was the only thing in the room.

"I don't have any relics of my past," I admitted.

"I've seen your place. It's pretty bare. I just thought you're either a minimalist or suck at managing your money and should ask for a refund on your Degory degree."

I shoved his shoulder. "I just have nothing."

Both in my fake apartment and my real one.

"Does that bother you?"

I considered giving him a bullshit answer, but for once in my life, I wanted to be real.

Not a liar.

Not a con.

Not Apate.

"Yes, but only because I want the memories attached to the object. My aunt raised me, but she never married and was always at work. There weren't birthday parties and family Christmases. It was just us. Mostly me home alone, sometimes with a neighborhood grandma watching over me. I was given everything I needed, and I never asked for anything else. I always felt like a burden. Not because my aunt made me feel that way but because..."

I heaved a breath and relented. "Because my mom died giving birth to me, and that's the biggest burden I can think of. I literally killed someone before I took my first breath in this world. So, when it came to things like pretty dresses and toys, I never felt like I deserved them. And now, I'm just used to not having anything, but not having anything and not having anyone means there are memories lacking in places my soul needs them."

"You're lonely."

"I am."

I felt bare before him. More naked than I was in L'Oscurità's cellar. More naked than I was in my bedroom. More naked than I was in the hallway. More naked than I was in his shower. I'd stripped myself bare in all the places that mattered, and he could tear me apart right now, and I wouldn't be able to do a thing about it.

That barrier we'd shattered couldn't be replaced.

He didn't move as he whispered against my lips. "I see you."

"What do you see?"

"Everything." His thumb brushed the skin beneath my knee. "It's not your fault your mom died. You couldn't have predicted that. You didn't hurt her on purpose."

"I know that logically, but it's another thing to accept that emotionally."

"What will it take?"

"I used to think it would take time to heal. Now, I'm not so sure."

I'd confronted more about my past since I'd met Bastian than I had in the twenty-nine or so years before. The truth was, someone to fill the void that had swallowed me whole was what it took.

I hated that it was Bastian who did that because I'd never met a man who scared me more. Not because he could snap my body and discard of me as easily as a stale bag of chips but because despite every flaw he possessed—and there were many—he'd managed to crawl his way beneath my skin and sink hooks into me.

He hadn't even tried.

The Jupiter to your Ganymede.

What delusions of romance.

He pressed on a sensitive spot on the inside of my knee when my breath hitched. "It's never time. It's finding someone to fill the void."

"That sounds like experience talking."

"It is. Over eight years ago, I had a girlfriend I planned on proposing to, she turned out to be a bigger bitch than a pregnant two-hundred-pound Mastiff, and I was lucky enough to find someone else I love to fill the void soon after."

He loves someone.

A lump in my throat robbed me of air, filled with resentment and shock and all the jealousy I wished I could claw out of my body.

"And where is she?"

He avoided my question and tugged on the edge of the Wharton shirt. “I like this on you.”

I let him dodge the question. I wasn’t ready to hear what he had to say, but I opened my mouth, wanting to ask him what this was. What was happening.

As if he could read my mind, he tugged me closer to him and pressed a kiss to my shoulder. “Don’t question it. Just sleep.”

28

There is no duty we so much underrate as the duty of being happy. By being happy, we sow anonymous benefits upon the world.

—Robert Louis Stevenson

BASTIANO ROMANO

Days Missing: 6

"Play me something."

Ari and I sat on my kitchen island, a juice pouch in each of our hands. I'd spent the day searching for Vincent. She'd spent the day taking care of Tessie and, according to her, fielding Tessie's questions about Uncle Vince.

And at four in the morning, like clockwork, I'd come home and join her for a juice pouch. Our version of a nightcap. Sometimes, we'd talk. Sometimes, we'd make out. Sometimes, we'd do both.

I tossed my juice pouch in the trash. "You first."

"I don't play the piano." She tugged at the bottom of her shirt—my shirt—and I wondered if she wore anything underneath.

I'd figure out in a moment.

I tossed her juice pouch in the trash, too. "I know."

"Then... what?"

She let me lead her to the piano, and when I tapped its top, she gave me a dubious look before hopping on. I'd saved this piano for Everett, but every investigation I'd done into Elsa had turned up empty, and I could never get something to hold over Elsa's head. Not even with the money she'd supposedly owed to someone.

With Vincent gone and all our searches coming up empty, my hope had plummeted somewhere beside my soul, and that motherfucker was probably the size of a pea. Or maybe something smaller, like Elsa's heart.

I pressed a hand to Ariana's knees and nudged them wider. Her legs parted, and a smirk curved my lips at her lack of panties.

Such a beautiful distraction.

More than a distraction.

I shoved that voice down. The one that told me to take a risk with Ariana, that she wasn't Elsa, that I could trust her.

You already do trust her.

"I'll play the piano keys"—I curled my fingers around her

calf and spread her legs wider—"if your fingers play the same melody on your pussy."

"What?" Her lower lip dropped open a bit, amusing me.

I placed her hand on her pussy and rubbed her fingers in tiny little circles on her clit. "Are you slow today or is this a usual thing?"

She sighed and closed her eyes as she quickened her movements. "Always a jerk."

"Did you think you could change me?"

In some ways, she had. She'd gotten me to want her. I didn't just want to fuck her. I wanted her. Everything. Anything she'd give me. Dangerous territory, considering the last time I'd felt this way…

Only this time felt different.

Falling in love with Elsa was like jogging at the park; this with Ariana—and I refused to call it love—was like falling face first onto hot concrete on a cold day. I could pick myself off the ground, but then I'd be the assface with pebbles indented on his skin, so I figured I'd lay on the ground for a little and enjoy the heat before the consequences set in.

"I'd never be so arrogant." Ariana closed her legs, the movement nipping at my hand I had between her legs. "You're not playing the piano."

I nudged her legs open again and tilted my head. "You have been arrogant."

"Oh?"

"Where's the woman who worked her Degory degree into every sentence?"

"I never did that."

My eyes dipped to her legs. They were better suited for a Sports Illustrated photoshoot than behind a bar. She had tits that would make Katy Perry weep, and her ass resembled the after picture of a Brazilian butt lift testimonial.

But it was her mouth I wanted to fuck. Those pouty, plump lips that spewed challenges like peace was a foreign concept, like her mission in life was to start World War III. The lips that comforted my sister with sweet words and heartfelt reassurances. The lips that were there for me, silent when I just needed a juice pouch nightcap and vocal when the silence threatened to eat me.

I stared at those blow job lips and asked, "Are you calling me a liar?"

"Well, you said you'd play the piano."

I placed her hand back on her pussy and struck the first chord of Yiruma's "River Flows In You" harder than necessary. It vibrated the piano, and I knew she felt it in her core.

"Oh, God," she whispered, her free hand clenched on the piano top.

"Every time I hit a key, a hammer hits a string beneath you. It vibrates the string, and you can hear it. But if you're sitting on the piano, you can feel it."

I continued playing, hitting the notes harder than I needed to, letting the siren sitting on my custom Steinway ride out the vibrations. I played to the view of her stroking her pussy instead of the keys.

Her wetness slid onto my piano, but I didn't care. I'd make her lick it off later. She rubbed tiny circles on her clit and moaned out my name until I finished the song, picked her up, and carried her to our bed.

I laid on the mattress and sat her on top of me, so she straddled my waist. She tugged off her shirt until she was naked, her tight little pussy pressed to my chest, not caring that I was fully clothed.

I stuck two fingers inside of her, leaned back, and commanded, "Fuck my fingers."

Her hips jerked forward, and she looked so aware that I was watching her grind herself against my fingers.

"Filthy girl." I smacked her ass with my free hand. "Are you always this wet or is it just for me?"

"You," she groaned out, once again transporting me away from my reality.

The truth was, I spent my days searching for Vincent and my nights escaping that fact. Right now, she was the only thing keeping me sane.

Without her, I'd splinter.

29

To exact revenge for yourself or your friends
is not only a right, it's an absolute duty.

—Stieg Larsson

BASTIANO ROMANO

Days Missing: 10

I slammed Graham against the wall. It shouldn't have felt as good as it did, but I was in no mood to pull back. It wasn't Vince flashing through my mind as I roughed Graham up; it was every memory of him making a pass at Ariana.

That and the fact that he was a rat.

Smelled like one, too.

"I don't know what you're talking about. I swear." He dipped his head, his frantic eyes searching for an escape, but there was none.

We stood on the roof of his apartment building, twenty-three stories into the air. I had a height, weight, and muscle advantage on him. He stood no chance.

"Don't make me ask you again."

Every Romano in New York had scoured the city looking for Uncle Vince over the past ten days. We had Romano members searching the entire city, and the bosses of every syndicate except the Andretti syndicate had agreed to perform their own searches in their respective territories.

All empty.

People disappeared, sure, but a mafia *caporegime* didn't. Especially one for the Romano family.

"Please," Graham begged. "I don't know what you're talking about. I don't know where your uncle is. Why would you think I know?"

I looked at him. Really looked at him. I wanted him to be the one who'd taken him, so I could retaliate with my fists. But I believed him. I believed the fucking rat. I let go of him, and he dropped to the floor like panties on a stripper.

After zip tying him to a pipe, I left for Vincent's brownstone. We'd searched the place, but something felt off. Vincent was the best of us. He just wouldn't go missing. Not without leaving some breadcrumbs at the very least.

Vince's security team, some of the Black Security guards, and Gio searched the brownstone, but I hadn't been able to bring myself here. It made his disappearance real. I felt his absence every day, but seeing it in the form of his empty house haunted me.

Letting myself in, I searched every inch. Beneath the pillows. The mattress. The bathroom. The vents. Everything. And when I didn't find anything, I tore the house apart again, flipping every vase upside down, emptying out his fridge, opening his couch cushions, and checking the water tank of the toilets.

There, in the water tank, was a file sealed in a waterproof Ziploc bag. I pulled it out of the water, shook off the droplets, and pulled out the file. It had Graham's name written on the tab.

I opened it. Drops of water flung at my face, but I ignored them as I skimmed over the file. A background check. A de-pixelated copy of the image I'd sent Gio for rendering. The receipt to the burner phone, which was bought a block away from Vince's house. I read the rest of the file, checked the dates, then read it again.

I fired a text to one of Asher's men to cut Graham loose and deal with him.

Fuck.

Vince had put most of this file together about a week after I had hired Ariana. Vince knew Graham wasn't the mole. He'd planted the burner phone in Graham's pocket, then sent Graham a text through it during his shift, so I'd catch him with the burner.

He wanted me to think Graham was the mole.

Why?

What the hell was he up to?

ARIANA DE LUCA

Lucy Black had dropped lunch off today with red-rimmed eyes. She was supposed to be on her honeymoon. Not bawling her eyes out in New York City.

It was the first time I'd met her, and while I loved her personality, the circumstances cast heavy shadows over lunch. Tessie had picked at the lobster macaroni and cheese. Lucy hadn't even bothered eating, and I'd lost my appetite a bite in.

The only thing I seemed to be able to stomach these days were the juice pouches I capped the night off with next to Bastian. His presence should have made it worse. The guilt over my last visit with Vincent should have made being near Bastian unbearable. Instead, each time he left for the day, I craved the next time I'd see him again.

Issues.

I had more of them than *Vogue*.

When she'd left, Lucy had kissed me on the cheek and told me that Bastian was lucky to have me.

Like I wasn't his Apate.

When dinner time came around, I figured Tessie wouldn't eat much, but I had to at least try. She'd been okay the first few days of Vincent's absence, but when a week had passed and things hadn't turned back to normal, she'd started lashing out at everything and picking at her food instead of eating it.

"I'm making you lasagna. Lucy gave me the recipe."

"I'm not hungry."

She crossed her arms from her spot on the couch. I couldn't see her face from the kitchen, but I could picture her pouting.

"You haven't eaten breakfast or lunch. Please, eat this."

"No."

I strode over to her and kneeled in front of her face. "Remember what I said about everything being okay?"

"Yes. You lied."

"Close your eyes." Relief swept through me as she listened. I repeated the words I'd given her when her uncle first went missing, "Think about your Uncle Vincent, all the favorite things you've done with him, and every memory he's given you. Can you do that?"

Like last time, memories of my mother consumed me, except this time, it didn't hurt so much. I was the monster who'd healed in Bastian's home as his life crumbled around him. It was a difficult realization to stomach, so I pushed it aside.

Tessie nodded her head, her eyes still squeezed shut. "Yes."

"If you can hold on to those memories and those feelings, he will always be with you."

"You promised last time."

"Yes, I did."

She peeked an eye open. "Do you promise again?"

"Promise."

"Okay, I'll eat."

I gave her my best grin. "Want to help me cook?"

She nodded her head, and I lifted her up and carried her into the kitchen on my back. She was way too lanky, but I did it anyway. Plus, all my time on ice shift had prepared me for this.

I peeked over my shoulder at her. "You can brown the meat."

She slid off my shoulders, grabbed a little stool to stand on, and helped me stir the meat, light returning to her eyes for the first time in a couple of days. Both of us jumped a little when the door opened and Bastian walked in.

"Is everything okay?" My eyes darted to the clock.

Six in the evening.

He was ten hours earlier than he usually was.

He shrugged off his sweatshirt, tossed it onto a barstool, and kissed Tessie on the temple. "What are you guys making?"

I knew he was ignoring the question, and the undercover agent in me felt compelled to force an answer out of him, which was why I did the exact opposite. "Lasagna. Lucy stopped by for lunch and gave me her recipe. I hope she's not a shitty cook."

Tessie tilted her head back to look at me. "That's a bad word."

"And now you know not to say it," Bastian remarked.

He grabbed Tessie with one arm and let her cling to his body so she didn't have to stand on the stool. The three of us cooked the meal together, and it felt odd because it felt normal. Like we were a family.

I shook the thought out of my head as soon as I had it. I was Apate not Jupiter and definitely not family material. But I wanted this. A family. This love. More than I'd ever wanted anything else. I could never have a dime or a car or clothing on my back, but if I had this feeling, bottled up and relived for eternity, I'd die happy.

BASTIANO ROMANO

The weight of Vince's secrets sank my sanity. I couldn't keep looking for him knowing he'd lied. I needed, at the very least, some distance before I tried again tomorrow. I found that refuge in Ariana and Tessie.

Every time the guilt over not being outside searching for Uncle Vince threatened to bowl me over, Tessie would smile at me or Ariana would say something so unexpected, she'd become the center of everything.

"Stop," she whispered after we'd tucked Tessie into bed and read her a bedtime story with one of us on either side of her. "I can see your thoughts eating at you. Stop thinking about those things. Whatever they are."

"Impossible," I admitted.

Her eyes flashed with the challenge as she shut Tessie's door behind her, and she launched herself at me. Her lips found mine. Rough. Needy. Begging. She drowned the thoughts in my head until it was just me and her.

She pulled back and looked at me like she knew me—not the surface-level bullshit I'd been passing off for the past eight years, but who I really was deep down. This felt dangerous. Whatever we had between us had grown and snowballed into something too big to deny.

I trusted her.

I trusted her with me.

I trusted her with Tessie.

And if Everett were here, I'd trust Ariana with him, too.

It's dangerous, Elsa's ghost taunted.

It's worth it, assured the small part of me Elsa hadn't damaged.

I shook the thoughts out of my head and bent forward to kiss her again.

Fuck.

I was drowning without a shore in sight.

Duty is not collective; it is personal.

—Calvin Coolidge

ARIANA DE LUCA

Days Missing: 12

"Why is Contessa here?" Jenn had that stupid pen poised above her notebook again.

Tessie sat in the waiting room with a coloring book in her hand because I couldn't get anyone else to watch her, and I also couldn't miss this check-in. I'd long ago made the executive decision not to tell Jenn or the bureau about Vince being gone.

"Her babysitter is borderline brain dead and unworthy of a brain cell let alone the responsibility of caring for an eight-year-old child." I tossed a rubber band stress ball from palm to palm. "This legend is a dead end by the way," I lied.

It felt weird to lie and lead Jenn away from the truth. Not because I had a duty to the FBI but because Jenn was my best friend. Or, she used to be. We pulled apart with each legend, but this one topped the cake. I didn't think, once this was over, I could reconnect with her like we usually did.

My heart broke for our friendship, and I tried to latch onto a life raft, anything to salvage us.

"Can I say something off the record?"

Jenn leaned forward. "Of course."

"I'm swearing you to secrecy."

She put her pen and notepad down. "You can trust me."

"I need to help Tessie process something, but you can't add this to your report. She's just a kid."

Jenn's brows drew together, her concern genuine. "Yeah, of course. What happened?"

For a moment, it felt like us again. Jenn and Ari. Old friends. Nothing between us.

"Tessie's uncle is missing, and she isn't taking it well. She's confused."

"Her uncle is missing..."

"Vincent Romano," I relented.

The look on her face said it all. Telling her this was a bad idea. I tried to back-track.

"It's no big deal," I offered. "He's probably in Atlantic City gambling away more money than Nicaragua's GDP."

"Ariana," she said my name slowly, drawing each syllable

out. “You do understand that I need to note this in my report, right?”

I shot off of the couch. “You’re my best friend and handler. You can make the decision not to.”

She took in my stance and curled fists at each side of my body. “Fine. I won’t. Promise.”

This.

This was how it felt to not trust someone.

31

The first duty of love is to listen.

—Paul Tillich

BASTIANO ROMANO

Days Missing: 13

It wasn't a conscious decision to tell Ariana about Elsa and Everett. Like the trust we'd built, like the feelings we shared, like the way I'd come to rely on her, it just happened. One day, I hated her. The next, I couldn't live without her.

Her arms were the therapy I'd chosen, the hospital I

wished to heal in. I came home each night exhausted. I left each morning revived. Like magic.

She traced Everett's name on my ribcage, toying with the tattoo as we laid in bed.

"He's my son."

Her fingers on my tattoo froze, pressing down hard on my skin. I didn't even think she realized it.

"You have a son?"

"I'm not in the habit of tattooing random names on my flesh."

Her cheeks reddened. "I figured it was maybe a place or... a girl. An ex-girlfriend, maybe? Like how Jamie and Parker are both boy and girl names."

"I do have an ex. Her name is Elsa, and if I had her name tattooed on my body, I'd burn it off with acid."

I wasn't kidding. I would. And then I'd have to talk myself down from dumping her in the vat of acid, too.

"Is Elsa Everett's mother?"

"Yes. An unfortunate egg donor."

She propped her chin on my chest and stared into my eyes. Her eyes took their time studying me before she accused, "You hate her."

"Understatement."

"How did it happen?"

"Everett?" I pulled Ariana's body up, so she was half on top of me, her face close to mine.

"Yes, but also Elsa. People don't go from love to hate."

"Have you seen the divorce stats in this country?"

She winced. "You were married?"

"No, but I almost proposed."

"Tell me about it."

"I met Elsa in college. I was doing my master's at Wharton, and she was in all of my classes. The smartest girl in the program, but if you looked at her now, you wouldn't know it."

"So, you met in college and fell in love. Why?"

"She was the exact opposite of New York. No glitz. No glamour. She had the pretty face and the complete utter lack of makeup, the cowboy boots, and the Daisy Dukes. The wicked humor, the wit, and the intellect. She made me feel like I wasn't living in the world I'd been born in. She was easy to love."

And it had all been a lie.

Ari pressed a kiss to my jaw. "You were running away from this world."

"Yeah. And I ran straight into a trap. I've played it over and over in my mind, and I can't see me getting her that wrong unless it was a trap. She was almost too perfect. Too easy to love. I caught her with a five-million-dollar check in her hand on the night I was going to propose to her. My dad had paid her to leave me."

"So, you hate her, and you hate him."

My head shook. "I don't hate him. I think he helped me dodge a bullet, but our relationship has never recovered. I call him Gio. I haven't called him Dad in eight years."

"When it happened..."

"Exactly. I wish we could repair our relationship, but it's probably too fractured. I don't hate him, but I do hate her. She's the worst of this world, packaged into one fucked up, belligerent redhead."

"So, your dad paid her off. Where does Everett come into this?"

"About six months after we broke up, she showed up on my doorstep super pregnant. The dates worked out. We'd been having sex up until the day we broke up, and I'm an asshole, but I'm not a neglect-innocent-kids asshole. I let her stay in my penthouse. I wasn't about to get back together with her, but I let her stay in the room that is now Tessie's. We had a nursery built into my room. I could have made it work. Everett was born. I fell in love with him. We lived like this for years, and then one day, she vanished. Everett was five at the time, and she took him with her. I hired investigators, had Romano men scouring the city for him, did everything I could to find him."

"What happened?"

"She called me from an Alabama number a couple months later. She told me Everett wasn't mine. That she'd paid for a sperm donation as soon as we'd broken up so she could trick me, I'd be tied to her through him. She'd chosen a donor that looked like me just so she could fool me into believing he's mine. The dates lined up, and Everett fucking looks like me, so I never questioned it. After she hung up, I grabbed some hair from Everett's comb, had it tested, and she was right. We weren't a match. But it didn't matter. He loves me. I love him. I raised him. Everett is my son."

Ariana looked shocked, like the information was too much for her to take in. "And now? He lives in Alabama?"

"She's been leveraging money from me. I pay for her mortgage, her house insurance, her car insurance, her health insurance, her car payments, her groceries, her staff, everything. She gets a six-figure allowance each month, and she always wants more."

"Why? Why are you paying her? Why not get Everett back?"

"It's too dangerous. We're at war with the Andretti family. I know I've never talked about what my family does, but I'm sure you've heard whispers around the bar. The Andretti family... they're worse than us. Alabama is their territory. The Romano soldiers have been sworn to secrecy. Everett is our best kept secret. If the Andretti family know he's living in their territory, it can mean death for him, and by stepping foot in Andretti territory to get him, I'm risking the chance they get to him first. Any dirty cop or politician down there may be on their payroll, so I've sent my own investigators to find blackmail on Elsa."

"Have you found it?"

"No. I call her names, I call her stupid, but she's not. She graduated top of our class at Wharton. She's good at covering her tracks, especially when it comes to finances. I don't know what she spends the money I give her on. Maybe shoes. Maybe more cars. Maybe Birkin bags and Herve Leger dresses she loves to wear. Or maybe something I could use against her. But if that's the lead I have, it'll go nowhere because of how good she is at covering her tracks. Probably the only thing she's used her degree for."

"And Everett?"

"He's not happy down there. I'm not saying this because I'm biased. He wants to be up here. He wants to be home. Elsa is always gone, and they don't really have a relationship."

"That's awful. And lonely."

"And sometimes, I feel like it'll never be okay. One of the last things Vincent said to me was that it wouldn't always be like this, but I can't bring myself to believe him."

She shifted so she was completely over me now. "Then believe in yourself. If there's anyone who can get Everett back, it's you. I've never met anyone as capable."

I mulled over her words before returning the kiss she pressed to my lips. Hungry. Greedy for me. Everything about us defied logic. I'd been burned too many times. It made no sense to want her, but I did, and so I took her. At least for tonight.

I took her body like it was mine, and she let me, and when we were done, she begged, "Tell me a secret." Her voice was a whisper, soft and raspy in my ear, a plea just for me.

"This—here, with you—is the happiest I've ever been."

I know of only one duty, and that is to love.

—Albert Camus

BASTIANO ROMANO

Days Missing: 14

"Asher." I answered his call on the first ring, already running to my car from the run-down alleyway of the lead I was chasing. "Did you find him?"

"I need you at my place. We have something."

The line went dead as I slid into the car and broke every vehicle law in the state to get to Asher's place in under ten minutes. That sinking feeling I'd felt before I'd found out Vince had gone missing had never left. Ariana De Luca had just distracted me from it, playing house with me like we were in a 90s sitcom or something.

When I left the elevator into Asher's penthouse, dread was the only thing that pulsed through my body. We'd torn the city apart for fourteen days, each search fruitless, each day ending with dread and a drained soul.

It couldn't be as easy as a sudden lead on day fourteen.

Lucy met my eyes when I entered. Nothing but apprehension and resignation in them. I cut my eyes to Asher. Asher lived in a ten-bedroom "apartment" close to Lucy's school Wilton, but in this moment, it felt like a tiny studio apartment with no air to breathe nor room to move.

The suitcases Asher and Lucy were supposed to take to their honeymoon remained abandoned in the foyer. I stepped around them as I made my way to Asher and Lucy and sat on a bar stool.

"The line went dead." Asher raked a hand through his haggard hair. "I was on the phone with Niccolaio. Sounded like he had something, and he wanted to meet."

Behind me, the door opened, and Niccolaio walked in with his red-headed girlfriend Minka, who reminded me a little too much of Elsa. Physically at least.

Asher sprung up at the sight of them and shot out questions without a greeting. "What is it? Why did you call this meeting? Did you find him?"

Niccolaio ran a hand through his hair, the movement so natural I suspected he'd been doing it a lot lately. "No, but we need to talk. Dex tracked down that lead we've been following."

Dex was Niccolaio's neighbor and a tech guru. The lead he referred to was a burner Vince had been calling twice daily for the past few months. He'd had another burner, too, but that one had been thoroughly destroyed, so we'd focused on the one intact.

Niccolaio squeezed Minka's hand before stepping away from her. "And... God, Vince didn't want me to tell you guys this, but given the situation, I think I should."

I held back my anger. Fourteen days. Vince had been missing for fourteen days, and Niccolaio held something back from us?

Asher grit his teeth. "Spit it the fuck out already."

"Vincent has cancer. Late stage. The number belongs to his oncologist. God, Asher, he might even be dead already. I don't know how bad it is, but don't you see how he's been looking lately?"

I bit back a curse. I'd first noticed it when we were planning Asher's wedding security the day I'd first trained Ariana, but I'd been distracted by a phone call from Everett. I'd been so wrapped up in my own world, I hadn't considered it again. But I'd seen it, and I'd ignored it. It was worse than not seeing it at all.

Sorrow. Rage. Guilt. It consumed me as I forced myself to keep breathing. Asher's face had gone blank, but I knew he felt the pain. Vince had practically raised him. His shoulders tensed, and his fists clenched, but he said nothing.

Lucy held her head high, but she let fat drops of tears wet her cheeks. They splashed onto the floor. One by one. I watched them fall, so I had something to do that didn't involve violence as I waited for someone to say something.

Instead, a phone rang.

Niccolaio pulled his phone out, his eyes widening when

he took in the screen. "Holy shit, guys." He showed us the name on the screen. "It's Vincent."

We all sprang into action, crowding around Niccolaio as he accepted the video call. But when Ranieri Andretti's face came onto the screen, I nearly lost it.

Black hair. Green eyes. Niccolaio's same jaw. I'd never met him in person. Not with the war between our families. But I felt like I'd seen him before with how much he resembled his brother.

Ranieri opened his mouth, so fucking smug. "Hello, brother."

Niccolaio's fist clenched, but it stayed hidden from the phone camera's view. "Why the fuck do you have Vincent Romano's phone, Ranie?"

"It's Ranieri to you."

"Just answer the fucking question."

"You owe me a blood debt, and imagine my surprise when Vincent fucking Romano just offers himself as a sacrifice."

Shit.

I bit back the swear when all I wanted to do was scream. Blood for blood. The Romano family had taken a *caporegime* from the Andretti, so they would take one from us. The blood debt. The only way to settle this war.

And Vince had given himself up.

Of course, he had.

Not just because he had cancer, but because he—despite being the head of enforcement—believed in peace and sacrificing himself for family. I hated his loyalty right now. I wished he had Elsa's selfishness and self-preservation, so he'd at least be here. Safe.

"No," Niccolaio protested. "I don't accept his sacrifice."

Ranie smiled. Genuinely. A little too eager for the blood

debt to settle. "Well, it's not really your decision. Is it, Niccolaio? And I most definitely do." He leaned the phone against something and backed up, so we had a view of the room. Of Vince. "Any last words, Romano?"

A half-eaten steak dinner sat in front of Vince like the last meal prisoners on Death Row received. He had some bruises on his face, but they looked old and tended to.

Vince stared straight into the camera. "Is Asher there?"

Niccolaio passed the phone to Asher, who answered with a guttural, "Vince."

I didn't want to, but I cleared the room with Niccolaio, Minka, and Lucy to give Asher privacy. Tears continued to stream down Lucy's face, but she kept them silent as Minka took Niccolaio's hand and led him to the balcony.

Silence nipped at my sanity as we waited for Asher to finish.

"I know you blame him."

I kept my eyes on the door. "Niccolaio is the reason Vince is in this situation."

"It's not Niccolaio's fault your families are at war. It started long before him."

"Vince gave himself up to settle the blood debt. To remove the bounty from Niccolaio's head."

"Have you ever considered there's more to it? Maybe ending the war benefits everyone he loves."

She had a point, so I shut up. Lucy went in the room to see Vincent after Asher left. Ten minutes passed before I took my turn. Alone in the room, I had the damnedest urge to call Ari here. She'd been the distraction I'd needed for the past two weeks, and all I had left was the beat of my fingers against my thighs as I tried to prolong the conversation that needed to be had.

"You look like shit," Uncle Vince drawled.

"Thank you. So do you."

Yeah, tell the guy with cancer he looked like shit. Clearly, he and Gio had raised me right.

"How's the girl?"

"Elsa's still the bitchiest bitch of the East. I don't think that will change anytime soon. Or ever."

"I meant the De Luca girl."

"Oh. Her." I didn't know how he knew to ask about Ari, but I could either question it or give the dying man the answers to his questions. "She's... something else. She's been watching Tessie while I searched for you. Tessie likes her."

My throat felt full as I realized he wouldn't have an opportunity to say bye to Tessie.

"Do you like her?"

"What a convenient time to play matchmaker."

"Evasion. That's a yes."

"She's no Elsa."

"Well, I didn't think Elsa was a bitch either until her bitchiness throat punched me, and I had no choice but to pat her head and send her on her way."

"Remember when I told you about Jupiter and Ganymede?"

"The moon and the planet. Always revolving around one another. Ariana De Luca is not my Ganymede."

"No, she's not. You're *her* Ganymede."

"No, we're—"

"Stop fighting it. You have spent eight years lonely and miserable, penance you never deserved, and now you have an opportunity of happiness most don't have"—an opportunity *he* didn't have, I read between the lines—"and you'll brush it aside over fear and pride. I knew you were stubborn, but I didn't know you were foolish, too."

Only he could speak to me like this. I'd volley back at Gio, ignore my mom, give Tessie a run for her money, and continue the back and forth banter with Ari. But with Uncle Vince, there was this reverence.

He spoke, and I listened because I'd known from a young age that he saw parts of me I never understood myself. But, I realized, Ariana De Luca did, too. Which was how I knew Vince had a point.

Ganymede and Jupiter.

It sounded crazy until it didn't.

"This isn't supposed to be our last conversation."

He shook his head. "Life never turns out like it's supposed to, but I have a gift most don't. An opportunity for closure. I've stitched together the wounds my sins have left, made peace with the ones I've loved, but there's still you I worry for."

"You don't need to worry about me."

"I do. You don't see it because you're so used to it, but you're spiraling. I knew Graham wasn't the mole. It was Dana, but I used Graham to keep you at the bar because I saw you with Ariana. When you saw the burner phone, I told your dad there was a second mole so you'd have a reason to stay on the bar side."

I swiped a hand across my face. "You can't play God like that."

"It's not playing God if a human can do it."

That.

His wit.

The way he cared.

The way he saw me.

I'd miss that.

I couldn't live without it.

"Don't go."

"It's my time. I've made my peace with it. My only wish is you open your heart to the people who love you. Asher. Gio. Frankie. Eli. Niccolaio. Tessie. Lucy. Everett. *Ariana.*" Someone behind Vince shoved his shoulder, and he spoke quicker, his voice more urgent. "Promise me."

No, I wanted to say. *Only if you stay.*

"I promise."

ARIANA DE LUCA

For a legend, I'd never had a good radar for impending doom.

It happened when it happened, and I was more reactive than I was proactive. But tonight, I stayed awake in bed as I waited for four in the morning to come instead of catching a quick nap. Something kept me up. I couldn't pinpoint it. It was like gravity pulling me in a direction before I knew it was happening.

My eyes were open, and I was alert as Bastian pushed his way past the bedroom door. He stared at me for a second, his eyes almost relieved to see me, before he spoke.

"He's gone." His voice was guttural, raw, and everything wrong in the world. A lone tear trailed down his cheek, and he was the strongest man I'd ever met.

Bastian made my skin crawl. He made me second guess my confidence. He made me wonder if it was misplaced. He also inspired a sense of loyalty I couldn't shake. I couldn't hurt him. Not when he was already hurting so much, the pain so tangible in his eyes, I wished I could grab it and burn it.

I knew Vincent would die, and I'd felt like a traitor for keeping it to myself. He'd come to *me*. One of the most important people in his life had died, and he'd come to me.

"I… I don't know what to tell Tessie." He opened his mouth to speak. Closed it. Opened it again, then shook his head and stared me down. "I need you to help me forget."

Instead of telling him the truth, instead of confronting our demons, I met him at the door and let him use me to heal.

No words.

Just us.

And neither of us were ready to confront why he was here instead of with his family.

Our duty is to do our best to keep on living.
Even if our lives are not perfect.

—Haruki Murakami

BASTIANO ROMANO

~~Days Missing~~
Days Too Late: 1

"Open up, Bastian."

I heard Gio behind the door, but I ignored him. I could picture his face—identical to Uncle Vince's—pressed against the Diospyros wood that cost more than his soul. If ever there was a time I wished money could buy shit that actually mattered...

Gio continued, "Your girlfriend is worried. She says you won't come out of bed."

Ariana wouldn't tell Gio anything.

I kept my mouth shut, knowing he'd go away.

Staring at the ceiling, I warred with whether to push memories of Vincent away or draw them nearer.

Away, I decided as Gio's footsteps retreated.

The real duty of man is not to extend his power or multiply his wealth beyond his needs, but to enrich and enjoy his imperishable possession: his soul.

—Gilbert Highet

BASTIANO ROMANO

Days Too Late: 3

I pieced together every day of the past year, wondering the exact moment that Vincent had been diagnosed. When I couldn't figure it out, I reconstructed the year, again and again, giving up only to start again from when I'd first noticed something wrong.

The day we'd gone over Asher's wedding security plans.

But the most prominent memories of that day were of Ari.

Fuck.

I needed to do stuff. Get out of bed, maybe. People died. Life moved on. The sun still rose and set. The moon still did its orbiting shit. I still had a business to run. Only, I couldn't. Get. Out. Of. Bed.

Dana had been fired. An emergency restraining order had been bribed from a judge and slapped on her ass. Ari had gone back to work, pulling double shifts with Graham of all people while one of the bartenders took over Dana's hostess shifts.

Gio took over Uncle Vince's duties like nothing had happened. Asher returned to work the next day to put out some fires that had risen in his absence. Lucy probably sat in a lecture the day after he died.

I knew they all cared.

I knew they'd never just brush off his death.

I knew this, but I couldn't see past the fact that they were out living their lives while Vince didn't have a life to live. I would never get used to a world without Vincent Romano in it. My future had been rewritten, and I no longer liked how it looked.

My phone buzzed.

Another text. Probably from Ari.

I ignored it. I kept her at a distance while she took over my duties at L'Oscurità. Not because I needed space. But because I didn't want it. I needed her. Craved her. Wanted her to make me forget Vince, which was precisely why she couldn't be here.

I'd left the door locked and fell asleep that first night. It hadn't been on purpose, but when Ari hadn't been able to enter the room, she'd spent the night on the couch and left before I'd woken up. And the memories of Vince? They stayed intact in my mind. Locked up. Not pushed aside by fresh memories of a woman who changed everything.

Now, she was giving me space. She still texted. I answered sometimes, keeping my texts short. I'd promised Uncle Vince I'd open my heart, so naturally, I'd broken that promise that same day.

I heard Lucy's voice outside. Asher returned the conversation, and I ignored two people I loved as they approached the door. Pulling the covers over my head, I fell back asleep as they tried and failed to enter the room.

Alone.

Just me and Vince's ghost.

I told you you'd be too late, he taunted.

35

Your only duty is to your heart.

—Avina Celeste

BASTIANO ROMANO

Days Too Late: 5

The silence weighed my body down.

I woke to silence.

I ate to silence.

I slept to silence.

And the ghost of Vince's memory… He laid beside me.

Silent, but there.

At least he was there.

36

To love someone is madness, to be loved by someone is a gift, loving someone who knows you is a duty, but being loved by someone whom you love is life.

—Unknown.

BASTIANO ROMANO

Days Too Late: 6

I dry heaved and rolled off the side of my bed. Getting to my legs, I forced myself to the bathroom sink and splashed water on my face. The hunger pains had long since faded as my body grew accustomed to the lack of food.

I stared at the mirror.

Not only had my life changed, but I'd changed also. Stubble covered my cheeks, chin, and upper lip. My cheeks had hollowed out. Not by much, but the difference was visible. My boxer briefs hung low on my waist, and the ridges of my V and abs seemed deeper.

I needed food.

Soon.

Anything but the water bottles from my mini fridge.

Vince will never enjoy a meal again.

I couldn't force that voice away. My fingers gripped the sink's porcelain, struggling to keep my weight upright. Bright specks of white light clouded my vision, and I swore, Vincent's ghost I had thought was my guilt manifesting looked *real* beside me. I reached out to touch him but felt nothing.

You can't touch me. I'm not here. He took a step closer, goading me. *Because you were too late.*

I needed to sleep. Or food. Anything to exorcise these demons, this guilt, this all-consuming pain. Stumbling to the kitchen, I swung open the fridge, found it empty, then grabbed an expired granola bar from the pantry before making my way back to the bedroom.

The bite I took churned in my stomach. Crumbs fell to the sheets, but I ignored them.

You're pathetic. Vince's ghost smiled at me. *So bitter.*

I'm sorry, I tried to say, but it came out all warped and raspy.

When was the last time I drank water? This morning? Yesterday? I didn't even know the day.

Ariana caught me in a moment of weakness. I had the

granola bar in my hand, the door still open but my legs refusing to move as I laid in bed like a useless lump. She chose that moment to enter the apartment. I heard her footsteps and closed my eyes.

"You look like a mess."

I didn't respond.

"I know you're awake."

Still no response.

I tossed the granola bar onto the floor. My eyes peeked open, and I watched wordlessly as she slid under the sheets with me in her little black dress that smelled a little of alcohol, the food from L'Oscurità, and a strong scent of cologne that better not have belonged to Graham.

We laid in silence for a few hours until she turned to her side to face me. She cupped my face, and I braced myself against her whispered words.

"Tell me what you need."

"To forget," I whispered.

I waited for Vince's ghost to reply.

He didn't.

Instead, Ariana's hand found mine.

37

Duty makes us do things well,
but love makes us do things beautifully.

—Unknown

BASTIANO ROMANO

Days Too Late: 7

I didn't wake up alone. I thought I'd open my eyes to Vincent's ghost, but he was gone. The sheets pooled around my waist as I sat up. Ariana slept beside me, but I couldn't see Vince's ghost.

Nothing behind me.

Nothing to the left.

Nothing to the right.

Nothing straight ahead.

Just gone.

Maybe he was really gone, or maybe it was the granola bar I'd eaten. I was tempted to starve myself again, but my stomach churned at the thought. The fear that I'd forget what he looked like—each detail of his face I thought I'd see every day—gripped my throat.

I hacked out a cough, reminding myself he and Gio shared the same face. It didn't help. I couldn't look at Gio without seeing Vince, and because Gio was so far from Vince... I vowed not to look at Gio again.

A hand rubbed at my back until the coughing subsided. Ariana's hand. She hadn't left.

I kept my eyes on the wall as I asked, "Do you have a shift?"

"It's"—she paused—"eight in the morning."

Oh. Right. The bar didn't open until dinner time. I didn't even know today's date, let alone the time. Ariana stood and stretched her arms up. She'd changed sometime during the night because she wore my Wilton Rugby shirt and a pair of pink panties. The shirt rose, and I caught a peek of the lace caressing her hips before she lowered her arms and left the room.

She returned ten minutes later with a tray with peanut butter and jelly on toast and a glass of orange juice. "I stopped by the grocery store while you slept last night."

I stared at the food. If I took a bite, Vince's ghost would never return.

"You need food." She set the tray in front of me. "Please."

The orange juice tasted bitter, but I finished the glass off, taking my time so I wouldn't throw it up. I ate the toast slowly, studying Ariana the entire time. She looked as tired as I felt. Bags under her eyes. A little thinner than she already was. Shivering as she stood in front of me, refusing to sit until I popped the last of the toast in my mouth.

She grabbed the tray, set it aside, and took its place on my lap. "I talked to Everett." Her words shocked me enough to snap me from my self-loathing. For a second at least.

I wrapped my arms around her waist and anchored her when she fell to the side a little. "How is he?"

"You could hear for yourself if you'd pick up your phone?"

"How is he?"

"Sad. Not because of Vincent. I didn't think it was my place to tell him, but I did say you were sick. That's why you weren't answering your phone." She bit her lower lip. "Basically, he's been calling you for the past seven days, I finally caved and answered, and the first real thing I told him was a lie. Sorry."

"It's not your fault." I was a shitty dad. I gave Elsa a hard time, but truth was, I failed at parenting, too. "Did he ask who you were?"

"Yes."

"What did you say?" When she didn't respond, I pressed, "I'll need to know, so I don't contradict it."

"I said..." She looked away from me. "I'm your girlfriend."

The label fit us. We weren't in the fifth grade, where I'd bike over to her parent's house with a handful of roses I'd picked myself and stutter out the question. But if anyone deserved grand gestures, it was Ariana.

Open your heart to the people who love you... Promise me.

Vince's last words to me echoed in my head. Just his words. No ghost this time as he reminded me to open my heart up, and I tried with everything I could manage to follow my promise. He'd included Ariana on his list.

I tilted my head back and studied her. "Do you love me?"

An unfair question, at least now when I knew she worried about me. The question caught her off guard. She glanced to the ground and tucked a strand of hair behind her ear. I let the silence stretch out for a few seconds before I shook my head.

"Don't answer that." I already knew how we both felt. "Answer it when you're ready. When you know for sure."

She hadn't shattered my barriers. She'd broken them down one by one until they laid stripped away, and I hadn't even noticed until I looked around and saw only her.

Here I am, Uncle Vince. Being a man of my word.

I tipped Ari's chin up, so she looked at me. "I love you. Not just because you're amazing with Tessie, not just because you've helped out these past weeks, not just because you put up with me. I love you because you stare at my dimples when I smile. I love you because you genuinely care about people. I love you because you have so much fight in you. I love you because you're patient. I love you because you don't take my shit without dishing it back. I love you because your tongue is sharp but your heart is soft." She opened her mouth, but I shook my head. "Don't say it back right now. I want to hear it when you're not worried about me."

"Okay, but I *will* say it."

"I know."

She pressed her forehead to my shoulder, digging her nose into the crook of my neck and inhaling before pulling away. "You smell."

I couldn't remember how a shower felt. The day after Vince had died, I'd sat under the shower until the water ran cold, my entire body pruned, and my back ached from the tile. Hours soaked in soap and water, and I still hadn't felt clean.

Ari pulled away from me and grabbed my hand. "Come on."

I let her lead me to the bathroom and slide my boxers down until I stood naked on the marble flooring. She stripped her dress off and leaned over the clawfoot tub to run the bath. Her breasts swayed as she stood, and I pushed aside the grief, the frustration, the anger, the sadness, and focused on her.

The way she made me feel.

The way she made me want to change.

The way she consumed my life.

I slid into the tub as she grabbed a razor, hand towel, and shaving cream from the sink counter. She hung the towel on the side of the tub and sat on the edge until I sunk deeper into the tub and leaned against the backrest. She slid in next, straddling my waist, the razor in one hand and the shaving cream in the other.

"Hold this."

She placed the razor in my hand, pumped shaving cream onto her fingers, and spread the lather across my face. I closed my eyes and enjoyed the feel of her. Her ass against my cock. Her breasts pressed against my chest. Her fingers on my cheeks.

Her breath fanned against my face. "Stay still."

My eyes popped open, and I watched as she set the shaving cream bottle aside and lowered the razor to my skin. She bit her lower lip, her eyes concentrated on the movements of the razor against my cheek.

I reached up and gripped her narrow waist. "You've lost weight."

She swiped the razor against the hand towel and returned it to my face. "So have you."

"I haven't been eating."

"I know. We ran out of groceries today, but I've been leaving a meal in front of your door every day. It's always there when I get back."

Another reason to love her.

Told you, Vince's memory agreed. No taunts. Just genuine happiness for me.

I traced the outline of her rib, enjoying the way she jumped and her bare pussy rubbed against my stomach. The jolt of pleasure flashed across my face, and her hand shook. The razor nicked my skin, but I didn't care.

She was so beautiful.

My fingers skimmed her ribs again. "Have you been eating?"

"I've been pulling doubles. More like triple shifts. We're understaffed with Dana gone and..."

I slid my fingers from her ribcage up to her breasts and toyed with her nipples. "And?"

She tossed her head back and moaned. "Graham quit."

"He quit?" I removed my fingers from her nipples so she could pay attention. "Did he say why?"

She returned to shaving my face—the other half this time. "He said he had issues with the management, but he signed the non-disclosure agreement to get his severance package. I made sure of it."

Who would have thought?

Ariana De Luca putting out my fires.

She finished shaving my face and swiped the razor against the hand towel.

"I have a file on my desk." I gripped her ass cheeks and

pushed her toward me, grinding her pussy against my stomach as the razor clattered to the marble tiles and Ari's free hand gripped my shoulder. "It has an approved application for a bartender."

She placed her other hand on my chest. "My replacement?"

"You were a pain in my ass."

"And now?"

"You know I love you," I scolded as I gripped her hair in one fist and tugged a little, enjoying the way she moaned at the sting.

Running my tongue from her collarbone to her exposed neck, I let my teeth graze the sensitive skin. Her nails dug into my shoulder, no doubt leaving little crescent marks.

"Kiss me," she begged.

I feathered her lips with mine before pressing a bruising kiss to her lips. My tongue pushed past her lips, stroked the roof of her mouth, and clashed with hers. She sucked on the tip until my cock bobbed against her.

Using my shoulders to raise her body a little, she sank onto my cock. The water splashed at the movement before settling. She rocked her hips forward, a slow grind on my erection, drawing out my pleasure.

I let her set the speed, loving the way she took her time enjoying my body. The water moved around us in light waves, reacting to her unrushed movements. I steadied her with both of my palms on her back and leaned forward to capture her nipple in my mouth. It pebbled as I bit down on it.

Her pussy clamped harder around my cock, and she pleaded, "Again. I'm so close."

I released her nipple and kissed her lips instead. Reaching

around her body, I parted her ass and rubbed my finger against her hole. "Come on my cock, baby."

She came on me as I slid the finger in her backside. My other hand gripped her waist, and I took over, driving my cock into her pussy as it tightened around me. I came inside her, my cock as deep as her body would let me.

Water splashed over the edge of the tub. Her moans echoed across the room. Our lust and sex and the water's heat steamed the room. It was messy and foggy and loud, but she'd chased away my pain, and it was us.

ARIANA DE LUCA

Growing up, my aunt had always told me to be careful who you love. What happened to my mom had scarred her, and maybe she knew me too well, even when I didn't know myself, but she wanted me to find someone who treated me with caution and care. Someone who kept me whole.

That sounded boring as fuck, and after spending the past week without Bastian, I realized safe wasn't what I wanted.

I don't want to be loved like a shelved book, treated with painstaking, delicate care, kept pretty and pristine like a shiny trophy. I want to be used and devoured, kept near at all times, read over and over again until everything that's in me is memorized and consumed, the pages are bent and worn with memories, and the marks he left on me can't be erased.

Bastian could use me all he wanted and spit me back in mismatched pieces, because I'd do the same to him, and our broken pieces would learn to fit together. That is love. It isn't perfect. It's finding a way to be imperfect together.

The sheets laid tattered around the bed from our second round of sex. Bastian and I stared at the ceiling, our hands close together but not touching. I wore nothing but a sheen of post-sex sweat on my body as I waited for him to confide in me.

"Tell me you love me."

It came out of nowhere.

He sounded half-desperate, so unlike any version of him I'd ever seen. I didn't say anything. Just earlier, he'd told me not to. I didn't want this to be the circumstances in which I said those words for the first time, but there was no denying now how much I felt them.

I love you, Bastian. I love your wit. I love how unapologetic you are. I love that you build walls around yourself—not because you're cruel but because you love too hard. I love that you love me. I love that you're mine.

I kept the words trapped in my mind, where they'd stay until he healed. Grief is another name for love. It's all the love he wants to give but no longer can. For all the love trapped in his body, there's an emptiness in places once full and a fullness in places once empty. A lump in his throat. A hole in his soul.

I want his love. I want it so much my own throat feels that same lump, my own soul shares that same hole. But I don't want his love because he's looking for some place to house his grief, and I was the first to tell him, "I love you." When he hears the words from me, they will be untarnished by grief.

Bastian waited a few minutes for me to say the words. When I didn't, he replaced them. "Go to his funeral with me."

"Okay."

I knew the risks it'd bring. My half-brother would likely be there. Damiano De Luca scared me, but if Bastian was going to the funeral, there was nowhere I'd rather be. I turned to look at his face, wondering what ran through his mind.

I cupped his cheek. "Tell me what you're afraid of."

He didn't hesitate, and it struck me how fearless this man was. "Healing. Being okay and happy in a world without him."

I hadn't given him the three words he wanted to hear, but he gave me an answer to a question I wasn't sure my dishonesty deserved.

Jupiter and Ganymede, Vince's voice filled my head, and for once, I considered it.

Jupiter and Ganymede.

One spins. The other chases.

It was an odd time for hope to consume me, but maybe all these years, that thing inside me that told me to keep going, to look forward to the next day, wasn't duty. Maybe it was hope.

Love was broken, but maybe we were the type that could make broken love work.

38

The coward is the one who lets fear overcome his sense of duty.

—George S. Patton

ARIANA DE LUCA

Most people thought right and wrong was black and white.

I knew better.

While the guppies who sat behind a bureau desk all day insisted there was a clear line between right and wrong, I begged to differ. The line was jagged. Curved. It went left when you thought it'd go right, and right when you thought it'd go left. There was no keeping up with it, and the only thing you could do was hope you were doing the right thing.

Being with Bastian—choosing Bastian—felt like the truest decision I would ever make.

I doubted anyone in this office would see it this way. I'd been called in. Not a recall and extraction, but called to a covert meeting regardless. I didn't know for certain, but I suspected Jenn had told Wilks about our last meeting.

Wilks patted my shoulder as I passed him and took a seat. The warehouse we stood in was empty with just a table in the center and a lone bulb hanging overhead. I saw Jenn, Simmons, and two analysts at the table.

None of them looked pleased to see me.

The coffee Jenn handed me tasted bitter as I brought it to my lips for something to do, struggled with its heat, then set it down. "You all look happy."

Wilks took a seat at the head of the table. "We know Vincent Romano has died. We also know his body is being flown in to New York, accompanied by Andretti royalty to signify the end of their blood war.

I didn't know how he knew—probably a mole or another agent undercover—but he didn't single out a source of information, which meant he was covering me because this was information we both knew I should have passed along to him.

"The bureau has approved a limited release deal with a low-risk prisoner to, frankly, stir chaos and see what sticks."

Stir chaos.

On a family that had just lost one of their beloved.

I hated this job.

Simmons shut the file he'd had open. "Monica?"

Wilks nodded.

I shot forward, grasping for any excuse to stop this. "She's not mafia affiliated."

An unpredictable snake unworthy of two dimes to rub together would have been a more accurate description. Monica had betrayed Asher, helped a hit team break into his penthouse, and sabotaged Lucy and Asher's relationship from the start.

Wilks cocked his head and gave me one of his soul-searching stares. "She was Asher Black's assistant."

"Yeah. Assistant to the CEO. As in, a legal business we've never been able to connect to the mafia."

"Do you have a problem with this, De Luca?"

I held back a wince at the last name and shot up from my seat. "It's unethical."

"Which part? The number of lives that have been lost to the Romanos? The drugs they push into the streets? The number of lives that will be saved?"

They'd been shifting from the illegal businesses to the legal ones. The drugs had been reduced drastically in the past decade—not because we were good at our jobs but because *they* had changed. Of course, I couldn't say that. Siding with the Romano family was tantamount to admitting I'd gone too far undercover.

I gentled my voice and tried to keep it casual. "All of that, and the part where we stoop as low as them. That woman hurt an innocent kid."

"If you're talking about Lucy Black, she's hardly a kid, and she's not so innocent."

"Because she married Asher Black? She's just a college student."

And someone I'd met, knew was kind, and couldn't stomach hurting. Monica had physically endangered Lucy and Asher. It was why she was in jail. She'd let a hit squad into their building less than a year ago.

Wilks barked out a laugh. "You trying to tell me she didn't know what she married into? The girl's twenty not twelve, and she's pursuing an Ivy League degree. Don't bother, De Luca. This conversation is done."

I sighed, sitting down to ease my approach. "This is a woman who does not deserve to be free, and we don't know if she'll do anything to help us, but what we know is she has never had anything to do with the Romano family."

"We don't need any of her knowledge, kid. We just need the chaos her presence will bring to shake things up during a time where they're vulnerable, so they make mistakes. That's all."

That was all?

They hadn't seen Bastian last night.

Or the night before.

Or the night before that.

They hadn't seen Lucy, Asher, Niccolaio, Tessie, and Gio. Real people in real pain. Tessie had barely eaten since Gio and Asher broke the news to her, and it was a struggle to get her to keep anything down. She was eight years old. *Eight.* And that was part of the vulnerability Wilks wanted to exploit.

Bastian had invited me to the funeral. I planned on going, of course, but the bureau didn't know that. What Wilks knew was, I was an illegitimate De Luca princess, and my half-brother Damian would be there.

Damian didn't know I existed. Being at the funeral could change that. I'd already planned on going for Bastian, but I needed to know if the bureau would make me.

My eyes studied each and every one of them as I said, "I

was invited to the Romano funeral. It's dangerous. Every American and international Made Man with any lick of power will be there. I'm not going."

"You have to." The answer came from Jenn. No hesitation. No pause. Just an instant answer.

Simmons nodded. "A great opportunity you'd be stupid to pass up on."

The two analysts shook their heads in agreement.

Wilks ran a hand along his jaw, and I waited for his answer with bated breath. He was the one who knew how truly dangerous this would be. Jenn only knew I was a De Luca. She didn't know I was the daughter of their last boss.

Wilks nodded. "You need to go."

The coffin of my heart shut—sealed and padlocked—and I knew irrevocably that I would never return to the bureau. Never.

I nodded. "I'll go." Sliding back the chair, I slid my jacket on and addressed everyone. "I have to go. Funeral arrangements."

Halfway to the door, I heard footsteps chasing me and paused as they caught up. I turned to face Jenn. She looked so different in the dim light. Or maybe she'd changed so much these past few months, I hardly recognized her. She felt like a stranger.

Or maybe it's you who's changed.

When Jenn opened her mouth, I braced myself for her words. "I see that look in your eyes Ariana. You care about them. You're in too deep. You're questioning everything you've been taught and all your morals. You're going to spiral, Ari. I've seen it happen to dozens of agents before you. There's that look they all get in their eyes when they question the point of all this, and you have it." She placed a hand on my wrist. "You need to remember what side you're on. You need to remember the greater good."

I faked a smile and wrapped my arms around her in a hug. Probably the last hug I'd ever give her.

There was no greater good.

They worst part of lying to someone who is worth the truth isn't the guilt. It's the knowledge—the bone-deep premonition—the lies will cost me everything.

Before the funeral, I shared a car ride alone with Bastian. My last opportunity to come clean before I met my brother for the first time. I could tell him about my cover. I could tell him I was Angelo De Luca's secret daughter.

I didn't.

I had too much to lose.

Fear led my path to destruction.

We were here, we were in love, and it wasn't enough.

Bastian pressed a kiss to my temple after he helped me out

of the car. "I have to give a speech. Tessie will find you and sit next to you. Will you be okay?"

I nodded as we stepped inside the church together for the viewing. "I'll be fine. Don't even worry about me."

I watched as he made his way to the first pew, in front of Vince's open casket. He'd been killed by a single bullet to the heart. An instant, painless death. A mercy killing, Bastian had explained to me, like there was some mafia code of conduct.

My pulse sped up as he left, leaving me alone with the wolves. I'd never met my half-brother before, but I'd stared at his thin file more often than I should have. He'd dethroned Angelo De Luca, our father, and taken over the De Luca syndicate. From what I'd read, he'd done a good job. Which probably meant he was ruthless.

I had to force my shoulders back and my head high as I took a seat at a pew. Damiano De Luca took a seat beside me, leaving one seat between us. His posture was casual, but I knew he'd taken this seat on purpose. It just couldn't be a coincidence.

Counting down from ten to ease my nerves, I tried to stop my fidgeting. He stayed silent for a moment as my discomfort heightened by the millisecond. The wooden pillar dug into my thighs, and I forced myself into focusing on that irritant and not the one beside me.

"Am I bothering you?" he finally asked. He sounded polite and well-mannered. A wolf capable of disguising himself as a lamb.

Gio stood at the podium giving a eulogy for Vince, but I couldn't pay attention to it.

I tried to keep my voice calm and polite but closed off to more conversation as I murmured, "No."

From the corner of my eye, I saw his lips twitch. Like he

was working to suppress a smirk. At a funeral. I took in his features. They were more Italian than mine. Dark hair. Dark eyes. Tanned skin. Expensive haircut and the face structure of an aquiline Roman statue. A viper.

In this lighting, my hair looked dark today, too. No honey in it's brown at the moment. Maybe it was just how drab I felt. Tessie ran to our pew, scrambled over a few laps, and took the empty seat between us.

Damian, in a move that made him actually look human, sent Tessie a small smile. "*Ciao, piccola. Come ti senti?*"

Italian. I didn't speak it, and not knowing what he had said had my alarm bells ringing. He continued in Italian, each word spiking my pulse.

Tessie turned to him. "*Grazie, Damiano.*"

They knew each other. At least it sounded like they did. It also sounded like she was comfortable around him, so I tried to relax but couldn't. My spine remained stiff as a smile eclipsed Tessie's face, and she waved to a brunette as she walked past.

It was the first time I'd seen Tessie smile in a while. Go figure it'd be to someone who made Damian freeze like he'd seen a truck barreling his way and couldn't bring his legs to move. The brunette with the amber eyes and bare face looked comfortable here. In her element. A cascade of dark waves, lips a natural red, and a fitted black dress to compliment her curves.

She returned Tessie's smile. "Tessie, I've missed you." Her smile flattened as her eyes shifted to Damian. "D."

I'd never heard a nickname spoken with so much condescension. Shock ripped through me at her clear disrespect for a syndicate boss. I wondered what it felt like to have that much confidence. Or perhaps she was comfortable with Damian. It struck me as a little bit of both.

Her eyes narrowed as she watched Damian extricate himself from his seat and say goodbye to Tessie, completing forgetting me. When they both left through a side door, I relaxed in my seat, forgotten but safe.

"Who was that?" I whispered to Tessie as Bastian took his place at the podium, and my heart squeezed for him.

"Damiano De Luca. He's funny. I like him."

"And the woman?"

"Renata Vitali. She's so cool. I heard she has a real-life unicorn."

Renata Vitali. She probably didn't have a unicorn, but if anyone could find one, it'd be her, considering she was practically one herself. There'd been no pictures of her past the age of fifteen. It was like she'd disappeared from the planet.

She'd come from the Vitali family, mafia royalty that operated out of Italy, yet she had no Italian accent. She also looked as well-kept and flawless as I expected a mafia princess to look. No surprise there.

What did surprise me was Damian's reaction to her.

I hoped she kept him distracted all weekend because his interest in me reeked of danger.

39

Only when it is a duty to love,
only then is love eternally and happily
secured against despair.

—Soren Kierkegaard

ARIANA DE LUCA

After a slew of other funeral events—some several months long of traditional death rites activities, I'd been told—the highest level Made Men convened at L'Oscurità, which had shut down for the night.

The staff was still there, and I'd agreed to bartend for the night. I'd barely seen Bastian since this morning. I wanted to check up on him, but at least he looked better than he had last week.

Bastian sat in a corner booth with Niccolaio and Asher as I tried to keep up with the mountain of orders.

The woman who'd left with Damian earlier took a seat in front of me. Tessie had called her Renata.

She glanced at Frankie, Gio, and Eli Romano before returning her amber eyes to me. "I'll take a whiskey neat. Single malt Scotch." She slid her sweater down her arms, hooked it on the hook beneath the customer side of the bar top, and met my eyes with her eerie amber ones. "Macallan if you have it, please."

"I have a 35-year-old in the back..."

"That'll do."

I slipped into the cellar and leaned against the wall, giving myself time for a breather. Bastian met me within seconds, like he'd been watching me all night, waiting for a moment when I'd be alone.

"You okay?"

I glanced up at him. "I should be asking you that."

I felt like I had no place in the bureau's world. After being surrounded by Made Men all day, some who shared the same blood or last name as me, I was starting to realize I had no place in this world. I needed to find myself—to discover who I was without all these outside forces. I'd always been good at following my duties, but in all of that mess, I'd lost my sense of my duty to myself.

He took a step closer, his tailored suit making him appear lethal. "I'll be fine. We're supposed to be celebrating Vince's life tonight, so I'm trying to force out everything negative." He took the place next to me against the wall. "Fuck, it's hard."

"I don't think it'll ever be okay."

He shot me a look. "Thanks."

"I think you'll learn to live in a world without him, and it will be your new normal, but when you stop to think of everything you're missing without him, it'll never feel okay." I turned to him and stepped between his legs. "But that's okay. It's part of the grieving process."

He placed a hand on my lower back, just above my ass. "What about you? Have you grieved your mom?"

The answer came instantly. "No. It's why I want you to grieve Vince because torturing yourself like I do... it rips something from your soul." I didn't want the pain I felt for Bastian. I sighed when I remembered the drink I had to get Renata. "I'm supposed to be grabbing the Macallan."

Bastian pressed a kiss to my lips before releasing me. I dug through the bottles for the Macallan, and by the time I found it, he was gone. I took it up to the bar, poured Renata a glass, and slid it to her. She tipped me six one-hundred-dollar bills, then wandered down the bar as Damian walked in.

I forced my breaths to level as he approached me, settling in the gap between a bulky enforcer and an overly made up mafia wife.

"Ms. De Luca. Penny for your thoughts?"

Hearing him say our last name so casually had me coiled for a fight. Goosebumps dotted my skin. The hair on the back of my neck might have been raised. My limbs had tensed to the point where it was difficult to move.

I ran a rag across the bar top then poured him a beer on tap, though he hadn't ordered. I just needed something to do to expend my nerves. "I like to think they're worth more than that."

"A barter it is." His voice dipped lower. "I've had one hell of a month or two. Giovanni Romano has been asking about a girl poking around his territory. Imagine my surprise when my last name slipped past his lips."

Gio had been asking about me?

I dug my heels into the ground, doing my best to force my anxiety out of me. "It's just a last name."

"Cut the shit, De Luca." He had a hard glint to his eyes, one that didn't surprise me in a man who'd dethroned his own father. "You share my last name, yet I've never heard of you. Why is that?"

I worked my mind for a way to deflect. He'd basically just warned me Gio had asked around about me, so I latched onto it.

"Why would you give me a heads up about Giovanni?"

"Answer the question, or I'll answer it for you, and you won't like my answer."

The enforcer to Damian's left shifted, and Damian turned to glance at him. Renata and Damian made eye contact past the enforcer. I shifted my eyes between the two of them, knowing this was my opportunity to slip away to the other end of the bar.

My eyes caught Monica at the door as she waved at Dana's oblivious replacement. I couldn't catch a fucking break. Bastian stared at me from his booth, so I bit back my curse and smiled at him. He studied me for a moment longer before turning back to answer something Asher had said.

I racked my mind for a way to play damage control as Monica strode right to Lucy's table. She sat in the center with her best friend Aimee and Niccolaio's girlfriend Minka. I couldn't hear what she said from here, but Monica waved her hands in wild gestures, her angry eyes squinting and her blonde hair falling from her top bun.

This would escalate before anyone even noticed she was here. Instinct made the decision for me. I slid out from behind the bar and sped my way to them. Monica was raising her hand, and I caught it just before she slapped Lucy.

The silence descending on the bar unnerved me as I released Monica's wrist. We had everyone's attention. Every dangerous mafia *caporegime*. Every enforcer. Every wealthy businessman and politician. Everyone.

I tried to pass Monica off to security as quickly as I could while Bastian took long strides from the corner booth to meet me.

"You always surprise me, De Luca." His eyes skated over my body, cataloging it for damage. "Are you okay?"

"Yeah." I remembered I wasn't supposed to know who Monica was. "That chick is nuts."

Would I ever be able to tell the truth with him? I longed for the day it'd be just us. No lies, no pain, no guilt between us.

"That's an understatement."

He pinched the fabric of my dress at the hip and tugged me closer. I wasn't sure if it was intentional, but up until now, every intimate interaction we'd had had been done in secret. I felt the eyes on us as he pressed a kiss to my forehead, and the grime of the lies slid off me with just one kiss. He could bottle it up and cure death with his kisses.

I took a step back. "You should go back to your table."

"Why?"

"For one, everyone is staring, and this night isn't supposed to be about drama or me. It's about Vincent."

He stepped back and stared at me. "You're different."

"Than?"

"Than what I'd thought you'd be."

Than Elsa.

I saw the thought in his eyes. She'd damaged him, and I wanted to press my hands on him and put the pieces back together in a way that would fit mine.

"I'd hope so. You hated me when you met me."

In the corner of my eye, I caught the security guards talking to Monica at the door. She was three seconds from getting kicked out, so I urged Bastian back to his table. I needed to follow Monica. It blew my mind that no one else in the bureau thought releasing her was a huge risk. The woman was insane.

I skimmed my eyes across the bar, making sure no one noticed me before following Monica as she fled through the front door. My flat boots kept my footsteps silent, but I shook in the cold, my little black dress not covering enough skin.

These shoes were not made for following. I dodged a puddle, and my shoes made a small skid noise. Monica tensed and swerved into the nearest alleyway. Dumb move. She'd only blocked herself, and for the first time in a while, I was geared for a fight.

I followed her into the alleyway, picking up my speed because she knew I was behind her anyway. The moon barely lit us both as she swiveled around to face me.

"Stop following me!" She had wide, frantic eyes. Crazed.

I tried to call her down. "Monica—"

"How do you know my name?!" God, she sounded terrified. Recognition dawned on her face as I took another step closer, the moonlight hitting me from a different angle. "You're from the bar. You're one of them."

When I took another step closer, she yanked a gun from her waistband. A *gun.* I knew she was a risk to release. Her hands shook as she pointed it at me. She looked like she'd never held a weapon before.

The small gun wavered in her hand. "Don't move."

Less than a foot separated us. I considered the distance between us. I could latch onto the gun, twist it down and away from me until her finger broke in the trigger, and grab her gun. It would hurt her, but it'd likely save us both.

I did that, satisfied by my swift movements and training. Seconds later, I had the gun pointed to her face.

"Calm down, Monica. I'm with the FBI."

Someone broke past the shadows with a Smith & Wesson pointed at Monica just as the words slipped past my lips. I spun the weapon to him, freezing when I caught sight of Bastian's face.

He hid it well, but he was thunderstruck. Bastian had been burned before, but I had a feeling I'd just eviscerated him. I opened my mouth to explain, but there wasn't coming back from this. I'd always be the girl he let into his heart against his every instinct only to betray him on the day of his uncle's funeral.

We were destined to fail from the start, but it didn't hurt any less.

Damian chose that moment to stride into the light with his gun drawn on Bastian. I shifted my gun to him, trusting him less than I'd trust myself. Yet another weapon brushed the back of my head, and my pulse quickened as fear and borderline exasperation filled my throat.

I shifted a little, considering my options.

A light *tut* stopped me. "Don't bother." Renata Vitali. I recognized her voice. "Don't bother. I'll shoot you, then your boyfriend."

There are things you see when your life flashes before

your eyes. I saw the empty one-bedroom apartment that wasn't even mine. I saw my cleared-out cubicle at the local FBI field office. I saw my funeral, the five or so people who still knew I existed scattered around the graveyard grass, not a tear in sight.

What I didn't see was any of my family's faces. I saw Tessie's, tears streaming down her chubby cheeks, screaming my name. And I saw Bastian, his eyes thunderstruck and the breath stolen from his lungs, whether at my betrayal or the impending loss of my life, I didn't know.

And that struck me the most.

Why did that sting so bad?

Damian lowered his weapon, the trust in that movement shocking me. "Ren..."

Monica fled as soon as Damian's weapon lowered, and Bastian started after her, but I shook my head. "Don't. She has an ankle bracelet. What she knows, I can... I can figure out a way to explain to my boss."

Bastian stopped. He stayed. Which meant, to some degree, he still trusted me. It should have felt good, but it only hurt more.

Renata cocked her gun behind my head. "Your boss. And who would that be?"

Damian took a step forward. "Renata—" He sounded like he wanted to stop her. Like he wanted to protect me.

He wouldn't hurt you.

Gio's words from the night of Asher's wedding filtered into my head.

"Didn't you hear her? She's in the FBI." Renata's cold voice dripped disdain, and I considered, for the first time, that Damian wasn't the threat. She was. "This can be a Vitali matter if I make it one. Choose your words wisely."

Bastian dropped his gun to his side. I stared at him until he secured it in his holster, wondering why he was risking himself to save me.

"What do you want?" He cocked his head, then shook it. "What's the Vitali position here?"

The Vitali policed all mafia syndicates across the globe. I didn't know much about them. They kept themselves in the shadows, but that only made them more formidable.

I felt the gun lower behind me, and I was tempted to make my move, but Bastian shifted his head. A slight no. I listened to him.

"We'll be watching from afar, so long as you can deal with this internally."

Bastian took a step closer. "What's the catch?"

"There will be consequences should you mishandle this."

He nodded his head at her words and jerked his head toward the entrance of the alley. My eyes stayed on him, not even glancing at my half-brother as I brushed past him and followed Bastian.

The adrenaline had worn off. Exhausted weighed me down as Bastian led me to his car, and I was speechless as I took a seat in the passenger seat beside him.

"You're a liar."

"I am."

"Elsa's a liar."

"Please, don't compare me to her."

God, this hurt. I had no flesh left in me with the way the pain clawed beneath my skin, kicking, scratching, forcing its way through my body. He'd compared me to Elsa. He *hated* Elsa.

He hates you.

Bastian had been driving back to his place, but he swung

his sports car to the side of the road and stopped. I held my breath as he turned to face me.

"The truth. Now."

"I-I—"

"Faster. My patience is extremely thin right now, and I don't have the time to sit through your fumbling incompetence."

Jesus.

He hated me.

He has every reason to.

The words stumbled past my lips, as fast as I could speak them. "Damian is my half-brother. My mom had an affair with Angelo De Luca. She ran away before he found out. My aunt said it was to keep me away from this life. My mom died giving birth to me. My aunt raised me, and she died of cancer a few years back. I'm a... I'm a..."

"Spit it the fuck out."

"I'm an undercover FBI agent. My boss sent me to find intel on your family, and Vince—"

"You don't get to say his name."

I gathered the nerve to look at him. "He knew who I was and what I am, Bastian. I... I saw him before he went missing. He came to me and told me to open myself to you. He said I'm the Jupiter to your Ganymede."

Pain. Confusion. Anger.

They all flashed across his face. I'd hurt him. I'd hurt the only man I'd ever loved—the only person I'd ever truly loved in my life. I'd stabbed *him* in the back, but it felt like I was the one who'd gotten stabbed.

"You're not Jupiter. You are a snake." His eyes became slits, and when he spoke, his voice was cold. Detached. "I've learned my lesson in the past. Second chances are for fools. I'll take care of the Vitali and your brother because I clean up my messes, and you'd be an embarrassment for my family. Then I'll wipe my hands of you. I'll wipe you from my memory, and I'll wipe you from my future. I don't want to see you again." A sob tore through my throat as he pressed a button, and the butterfly door swung up. "Don't let the door hit you on your way out."

40

Think of giving not as a duty but as a privilege.

—John D. Rockefeller, Jr.

BASTIANO ROMANO

I hated liars.

I hated people who pretended to be something they weren't.

Like Elsa.

Like Graham.

Like Ariana.

I should have hated her.

I *wanted* to hate her.

But I didn't.

I *couldn't.*

I wasn't meeting with Damiano De Luca because I wanted to save my family from embarrassment. I was meeting with him because I wanted to save Ariana's life. A life I knew nothing about.

She'd betrayed me just like Elsa had. Only this time, I'd known not to fall for it, but I did anyway. I'd known Ariana's last name. I knew never to trust someone from her family. But I'd let her in, and she'd turned out to be a liar.

The worst part was, I knew, despite all the access she'd had since I'd hired her, she wouldn't use the information she'd acquired.

Not now.

Not after us.

Jupiter and Ganymede, she'd called us.

Reverently.

Like she truly believed that.

"We're here, sir." My driver kept his face ahead as he spoke.

The town car pulled up beside Damian's. The lot to the Wilton University campus brimmed with European cars. We nabbed two faculty spots in the front, not caring about rules.

My driver kept his eyes up front as I sat in the back seat, skimming the contract I'd drawn up earlier.

Damian opened the door and slid in beside me, his face carefully blank. I cleared mine, too, as I took a sip of the green smoothie Luna had made this morning on Tessie's behest.

"You hear from Renata Vitali?" I asked.

His throat bobbed, and I knew she was his weakness. "Yes."

We sat in silence.

The Vitali family could go after Ariana, and she'd be dead.

Done.

Just gone.

Like she'd never existed.

I shifted. "...And?"

"And she agreed to discretion, so long as the matter is sufficiently handled on your end."

I waited for the caveat, but when he didn't give one, I prodded, "What does discretion entail?"

"It means the encounter will be slipped into the Vitali archives, and so long as no attention is drawn to this weekend, there should be no reason for anyone to investigate."

Translation: keep my mouth shut and don't draw attention to this.

"What does she want in return?"

Renata was a hard woman to pin down. She'd disappeared from the mafia scene ages ago, and I couldn't figure her out. I disliked things I couldn't figure out.

"I've taken care of that."

"In exchange for what?"

He took his time answering, and his head hit the headrest as he relaxed into the leather. "One day, probably soon, you'll take over the Romano family. When you have the power, you'll use it to bring the De Luca family back into the syndicates' inner circle."

I had no plans to take over the Romano family. I was next in line, yes, but I didn't want the throne. It was the last thing I wanted, but I did want Ariana safe... and I realized that, even though she'd betrayed me, I'd make this sacrifice.

"And if I don't take over the Romano family?"

"You will." He turned to face me. "Your uncle is dead, and your dad and remaining uncles are approaching retirement ages. You're next in the bloodline. Or have you forgotten that?"

My face stayed blank, but my jaw shifted a tick. He'd riled me up.

"Your discretion and the Vitali discretion in exchange for a seat at the table?" I asked.

"Yes."

"Fine." I pulled out a pen and thick contract paper with the Romano letterhead and seal at the top. "If word gets out, this agreement will be nullified, and retribution will be sought."

"Understood." He watched as my pen moved across the page. "Have you heard of The Benefactor?"

"Why?" My pen stilled, and I didn't look up from the paper. I didn't like the idea of another party involved in this agreement. There was already a De Luca and a Vitali. "Are you amending the agreement?"

"No."

I continued writing. "Then, we have nothing to discuss, De Luca."

"Your family wanted me here." He kicked a foot up on the mini fridge, the arrogant little shit. "You may as well treat me like a guest."

My jaw ticked, irritation flooding my bloodstream. "I can assure you we couldn't give two shits whether you're here or not."

Damian eyed me before responding, "Oh, we have plenty to discuss, Romano. I received a handwritten invitation to Vincent's funeral, sent from your territory. Vincent is your *capo*."

He nodded to the paper I held and continued, "The letterhead and seal on the invitation was from your family." I finally looked up at him, and he pressed on, "Last I checked, the Hamptons is your territory. This involves you, and if it doesn't, your territory has more leaks than a used condom. Which is it, Romano? Are you involved or are you a used condom?"

"American politicians and foreign dignitaries vacation in the Hamptons. The Romano family stays out of the Hamptons as a courtesy for the work the politicians and dignitaries on our payroll do. In fact, the only mafioso in the Hamptons is..." My eye twitched, and I paused and looked down at the contract before handing it to him.

He waited for me to speak. I didn't, letting him simmer on that drawn out information, kicking down his arrogance. When he realized I wasn't going to continue, he skimmed the contract, took the proffered pen from me, and twisted the cap off the opposite end.

A small blade sat at the end of the pen. Pressing it to his thumb until crimson smeared across the surface, he stamped his thumbprint onto the contract.

More blood to bind us together.

ARIANA DE LUCA

I'd left my things at Bastian's, but I didn't bother retrieving them. For the first time in my life, I wanted the few belongings I owned. I wanted to hold onto them and treasure the memories. Of the shirt I wore while Tessie played silly, off-tune lullabies for me on the piano. The satin sleeping shorts Bastian tore off of me when he took me in the hallway of his penthouse. His Wharton shirt I loved to sleep in—the one that still smelled of him.

But I didn't deserve those memories.

I'd done this to us.

I'd let us come together, knowing the house that built us was made entirely of lies.

I'd expected Wilks to be surprised as I wandered into his office. Technically, I still had my cover to maintain. I shouldn't have even come close to the bureau's headquarters. But for weeks now, I'd been telling myself I needed to end this. Bastian and I were over, but it didn't change the fact that I couldn't work here anymore.

"I'm quitting," I told Wilks without taking a seat.

Again, he didn't look surprised. "Okay."

"Okay?"

"Yes. Okay."

I almost laughed at how little faith he had in me. "If you've always thought this day would come, why did you recruit me?"

"For one, a friend suggested you. And two, I've always believed in you."

"A friend suggested me?"

"Yes. A mutual friend."

We had no mutual friends.

"I don't understand. And..." I exhaled a breath, finally ready to lay out all my truths, including everything that frustrated me. "You never believed in me. I got the worst assignments, the worst caseloads. I was never given a chance to succeed here. And then you threw me into the deep end with this assignment."

"I knew you would be fine."

"How?!"

He slid a file to me. I couldn't wrap my mind around this conversation, and when I opened the file, the pieces fit together so clearly, I couldn't believe I hadn't seen it before. Wilks was the Romano's inside man. Vince was our mutual friend. That was how Vince had known about my cover. My last name. He'd given me to the bureau in the first place. He'd led me down this path.

And this folder... it was Vince's parting gift. His last request.

I shut it and drew it to my chest like a shield as Wilks spoke.

"I never gave you those assignments because I underestimated you. I gave them to you because I cared about you. I couldn't give two shits about Simmons. He could die, and I could move on unaffected, but the thought of you getting hurt..." He shook his head. "I don't hate you. I want what's best for you."

"I own nothing. I have no one. And now, I have no job. How is this what's best for me?"

"I've kept tabs on you during your cover. I didn't just hand you off to Dr. Clemson and wish for the best. Your belongings can be replaced. You're well-qualified. A legend who has learned to adapt under the worst circumstances. You can always find a job. As for not having anyone, it's not your time."

"What does that even mean?"

"It means you've spent twenty-nine years feeling guilty for something that's not your fault, and in the past months you've healed more than you've healed in your entire life."

I wanted to fight at his mention of my mom. Instead, I succumbed to the truth threaded within them. "Because of Bastian."

"Sure, but Bastian isn't enough. You need to find who you are. You need to discover yourself. Your identity. You can't give yourself to someone else before you know what you're giving away."

He was right, but I wished he wasn't.

"I'm tendering my resignation."

"You can't come back from that, and if the bureau decides, in the future, that you're with Bastian, they'll always be watching you two."

"I'm willing to take the risk."

If he'd take me back. It seemed improbable with each passing second.

"There's another way." He leaned forward, rested his

elbows on his desk, and pressed his fingers together in a steeple. "You could disavow. Keep your cover. There'd be no severance check. No bureau loyalty package. You were wiped clean from our agency databases when you started your cover, but since your cover is you..."

"I still have my Degory degree, my name, a social security number, and a fake job employment history that will pass off as the real thing. I can start over."

"You can build yourself a new identity."

An identity I wanted.

Someone I could be proud of.

Not Apate.

Not Ganymede.

Not a liar.

Not a con.

Me.

When love and duty are one
then grace is within your soul.

—Shannon L. Alder

Dear Ariana,

Nearly thirty years ago, I spent less than twenty-four hours in Devils Ridge, Texas. I had a contract that needed negotiating. I'd finished it as fast as I could, hoping to get out because everything about Angelo De Luca was toxic.

On the way to the airport, my tire blew. People passed me, ignoring my car on the side of the road, my waves and hollers.

But this woman, barely pregnant and scared for her life, didn't ignore me.

Maybe it was fate or maybe it was a leap of faith, but she stopped for me, knowing who I was and helping me anyway. I knew who she was. I knew her situation. She was the forced mistress of a man I wouldn't wish on any woman. She needed help. I could see it in her eyes, the tense lines of her shoulders, but she didn't ask. Instead, she helped me. A man I knew she suspected could be just like the one she ran from.

So, I offered to help.

It was her eyes.

Kind eyes, much like yours.

I took her to the airport, let her use my plane, and took her to her sister's. Something about her kindness was unshakeable. I can't explain it. I still think it was Fate. We'd listened to a s about Fate, and her name was the goddess of Fate's. Imagine every event in life that had to have lined up perfectly for us t meet exactly when we both needed to.

Fate.

I hired a private eye to keep an eye on her. When I got the ca seven months later that she was in labor, I hopped on the plane I barely made it in time before she was carted into her room for her delivery. She told me something felt off. That that da would be her last one on this Earth, but she also told me that she was happy it would be her baby girl's first day on Earth.

All she wanted in this world was for her daughter to be happy, too. She made me promise to protect her, and I agreed. For that woman who stopped on the side of the road for me. For that woman who took a leap of faith. For that chance that it wasn't faith but fate.

I took that chance on your mother, and now you've fallen in love with my nephew.

I told you about Jupiter and Ganymede, but I didn't tell you everything. The story of Jupiter and Ganymede isn't a nice one. Jupiter doesn't ask politely when he takes Ganymede and forces him into his life. Their burn is slow, and as time passes, Jupiter gives more and more to Ganymede.

Time is their savior.

Time will be yours and Bastian's, too.

I'm sorry. I made decisions about your life that weren't mine to make. I assumed things about you because I thought I understood you, but in reality, neither of us knew you. You hadn't found yourself because I'd never let you.

This letter is my apology.

To you.

To your mom.

I knew I was dying, and I wanted you near. I had no kids, and I found redemption for my failures with you through Asher. I was selfish in these past few months to force you near me. I knew I had so little time left, and I wanted to see Fate one last time.

But I've spent the past months silently watching you blossom with my nephew, and I saw what I saw thirty years ago again.

That glimpse of fate.

You and Bastian belong together. It is Fate not once but twice. You are Jupiter, he is Ganymede, and I was an obstacle when I should have been a solution. Time will be your savior. Not me. Take the time to find yourself, and I hope, when you realize the beauty in your soul, you'll find Bastian, too.

Yours,
Vincent Romano

P.S. If you love my nephew, get the contents of the folder to him. Help him find his happy ending and let him be yours.

A man truly loves you when missing you is his hobby and caring for you is his job and making you happy is his duty and loving you is his life.

—Unknown

BASTIANO ROMANO

The manila folder looked unassuming. I'd seen thousands of them in my lifetime. None had ever whipped a frenzy in my body like this one.

One of my building's guards approached me as I entered

the building to my penthouse. "Sir, I have a copy of the security film you requested."

I nodded my thanks and plucked the DVD from his outstretched hands. I knew what I'd find. A video of Ariana De Luca sliding the manila folder under my door. Didn't matter. I wanted to see for myself.

As soon as I reached my penthouse, I tossed my keys and phone onto the kitchen island, grabbed the manila folder and my laptop, and slid the DVD inside. I sped the tape and slowed it when a shot of Ariana filled the screen.

Zooming in, I paused on her face. She looked like she'd been crying. Her fingers clenched the file, a little too tight. I traced the grooves she'd left on the folder, wondering why it didn't smell like her.

She bent forward and slipped the folder under my front door. Instead of rising to her feet, her shoulders sagged and she took a seat on the floor in front of my door. Letting her head fall back against the wood, her eyes met mine through the camera, like she knew I'd be watching.

Two tears punished me as they hit her cheeks.

My only wish is you open your heart to the people who love you.

Vince's words chose the worst possible time to land in my head.

"She doesn't love me," I replied to his ghost, who had returned three days after Ariana had left and stayed the two days since popping up.

"You should eat. You look like shit."

"I'll eat when I fucking eat."

"Smart of you." Hallucination Vince crossed his arms and leaned a hip against the island. "You don't sound like a petulant child at all."

He had a point. When was the last time I'd eaten? I shut the laptop—I'd seen all I needed to see—and grabbed a granola bar from the pantry. It'd only been expired for two years. I could work with that.

Hallucination Vince followed me to the kitchen island stool. I took a seat and stared at the file as I inhaled the granola bar, hardly chewing between swallows.

He plopped onto the seat beside me. "Staring at it isn't going to magically make it open."

I spared him a quick glance. "I'd say you being here is pretty magical."

His fingers thumbed the edges of the file, but of course, it didn't move. "If hallucinations are magic, your Great Aunt Martina was a witch during her acid trips." When I didn't respond, he added, "You should open it."

I knew I needed to open it sooner rather than later. There could be anything in there. An apology letter. Surveillance photos of my family. Whatever she'd risked my wrath to deliver. I lifted the folder in my hand, judging its weight. Thick. Probably not an apology letter. Possibly surveillance photos.

"You won't know what's in it until you open it, Einstein." Hallucination Vince ambled to the piano and laid on top of it, sprawled on top like Roxie Hart in *Chicago*.

I flicked my gaze away from him and flipped open the folder. A note sat on top. The writing was messing. Like the note had been written in haste.

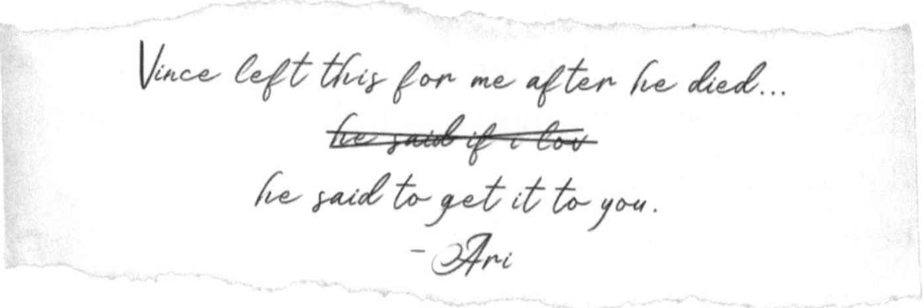

Setting aside her note, I sifted through the photos and documents in the file. Hundreds of them. Pictures of Everett. Of Elsa. Of a man whose face resembled Everett's. A copy of his Alabama driver's license told me his name was Waylon Smith.

The background check showed he'd lived in Alabama all his life. Born at his family home with a midwife. Home-schooled until fourteen. Local high school football hero until a knee injury stopped his career senior year. Not that he had a career. He'd been small-town Alabama good. Not national-level.

He worked at a factory just shy of the town's borders, and eight years ago, his high school sweetheart returned to town for a three-day affair spent entirely on a motel bed—as documented by high-quality surveillance photos Vince's private eye had taken.

That high school sweetheart? Elsa Johnson.

Buck-toothed and ass-faced, she stared at me from her high school year book photo, looking less like the future bane of my existence and more like a *High School Musical* extra.

"What did I leave you?" Hallucination Vince peeked over my shoulder, and I swore I could feel his breath on my cheek.

"You dug into Elsa for me." The words slipped past my lips in a whisper. Reverent. Disbelieving. Not because he'd done this for me—I'd never once questioned his love of me—but because he'd *succeeded* and done something about it. I couldn't stomach his sacrifice, so I swallowed the thought down until I finished looking through the file.

Three years of payments from Elsa to Waylon had been delivered through cash apps and untraceable cryptocurrency. These print outs had been dated just days before Vince had gone missing.

I scanned the list for the first payment. The month Everett had been born. Digging through the photos again, I checked all the dates and reeled at the timeline. Gio paid Elsa off. Elsa flew to Alabama and spent three days locked in a motel room with Waylon Smith.

Two weeks later, she returned to New York with a pregnancy test in hand. I welcomed her in, set up a bedroom for her, and built a nursery for Everett in a portion of my room because I'd thought he was mine.

Five years after Everett was born, she fled with him to Alabama, deep into Andretti territory, where I couldn't get him. She didn't know about the Andretti-Romano feud. She didn't know anything about my mafia ties. She thought I stayed away because I wouldn't kidnap my son—I'd do anything for him—and started extorting money from me with threats I'd never see him again.

I just wanted her to keep his identity a secret. She assumed I was ashamed of him, but in reality, the Andretti would have used Everett as a pawn in the war. So, I paid her off, and it turned out, she passed part of that money to Waylon.

The payments started when she left New York. I never figured out why she'd fled, but now I knew. Waylon was Everett's biological dad. When she left, she'd lied and said she'd paid for a sperm donor who looked like me. She'd been trying to keep Everett a secret from Waylon so she could keep Everett as a bargaining chip against me.

Truth was, Everett didn't need to be my biological son for me to love him. I'd raised him for five years, watched him take his first steps, taught him how to read, pushed him on the swings, fed him, bathed him, provided for him. We'd spent five years together, where I didn't just act like his parent.

I. Was. His. Dad.

And now I knew how to get him back.

I shot a text to Asher to fire up his company jet and meet me at the private landing strip. Then I called Niccolaio, who answered on the first ring.

"Bastian?"

"I need a favor."

I swallowed down the ball lodged in my throat. I'd thought Vince's sacrifice had been for Niccolaio—to fulfill the blood debt, end the Andretti-Romano war, and get the bounty off Niccolaio's head. But it had also been for me. Ending the Andretti-Romano war would let me enter Alabama.

It couldn't be a coincidence that Vince had chosen to turn himself over to the Andretti syndicate days after discovering what I needed to get Everett back.

Niccolaio didn't hesitate. "Sure. Anything."

"Asher already has a plane schedule, but I need to get to Alabama."

"I'll clear it with the Andrettis."

"*You* are an Andretti."

He paused a beat before answering, "I'll always be a Romano."

The silence stifled the air as we both let Vince's sacrifice sink in. He'd bound us together with his blood, forever family, forever brothers. I didn't take that lightly.

Niccolaio cleared his throat. "Good luck."

"Thank you." And I meant it.

After hanging up, I grabbed two-hundred and fifty-thousand dollars in cash from my safe room and tossed it all into an unmarked duffel bag. Hallucination Vince followed me back to my bedroom. I liked his company. I wanted him here, but I also needed to be on my A game. I couldn't risk anything happening with Everett, so I shot a text to Asher.

Tossing my clothes off, I hopped into the shower, reinvigorated for the first time since I'd learned of Ariana's betrayal. It wasn't lost on me that she'd given me this folder when she could have passed it along to her bosses at the bureau.

After she'd left, I had kept her things as they'd been—scattered around my penthouse like she still lived here. As soon as I'd dropped her ass off in the middle of the street, I returned home and sent the staff away.

I didn't have the energy to grab Ari's things and toss them out the front door. That was what I told myself as I stared at her toothbrush and shampoo sitting on the shelf in my shower. Fuck. She'd given me the file.

She probably made a copy for the FBI, too, I reminded myself.

Our man in the bureau, Uncle Vince's old friend Wilks would never let the bureau hurt us. But knowing Ariana had spent the past few months spying on me, lying her ass of like Elsa, pretending to fall in love—

"She wasn't pretending." Hallucination Vince cut me off, not giving me space even in the shower.

This was why I needed food and sleep on the plane. I couldn't remember the last time I'd slept for more than thirty minutes.

I squeezed shampoo onto my palm and ignored the fact that I had the hallucination of my dead uncle in the bathroom as I showered. "You don't know that."

"We both know she loves you."

"She's a liar."

Her lies had two parts—the lies she told me and the ones she told herself to justify it. A dual-edge sword filled with betrayals I wanted no part of.

"People lie. Actions do not." Hallucination Vincent pretended to fiddle with the shower head, standing half in my body. "With the access she gained inside your inner circle, she could have launched her career at the FBI and been their newest superstar. But she never reported anything useful or Wilks would have told us." He turned to face me and continued, "What she did do was teach you to bury Elsa in your past, help your sister feel less lonely, and support you as you grieved me. That doesn't sound like someone who doesn't love you."

"Stop."

I ignored him as I finished up my shower, but he kept going, "Whether I say something or not doesn't change the fact that she loves you."

"You're a hallucination. What do you know?"

"Exactly. Everything I'm saying are things you're thinking."

I shut off the shower and rushed to dry off and change. The sooner I got to the airport, the sooner I'd have food and sleep.

I couldn't listen to this.

I couldn't hear the truth.

For all he said about me looking like shit, Asher did, too. Bags had grown under his eyes, and I wondered when the last time he'd slept was. Probably why he'd brought along eight security guards rather than his usual four.

I ate my burger in silence—slowly, so my stomach wouldn't reject it—and slept for the remainder of the two and a half hour flight. When we landed, I woke up to an escort of twelve Andretti soldiers on the tarmac.

One of Asher's security guards grabbed the duffel of cash. I descended the plane with Asher and his guards trailing behind me. The nap hadn't been nearly as much sleep as I'd wanted, but it and the burger were enough to drive some semblance of sanity back into my head.

"Mr. Romano," one of the Andretti soldiers greeted with a dip of his head. Cordial, given the war that had only recently ended. "My name is Guilio."

I followed him as he led us to a black Escalade. "Will you be escorting us the entire trip?"

He nodded. "However long it lasts."

Asher and I slid into the back seat, followed by one of his guards. The rest split into the other Escalades as Guilio took the seat beside the driver. I shot him Waylan's address from one of the files.

Ten minutes later, we approached a ranch, well-kept and brimming with cows. It smelled like actual shit as we lowered the window and Waylan approached the SUV. In a weird way, he looked like me. His face held a more weathered tan and sunspots, and he had weight in his midsection and chin that I didn't, but he had the same general aesthetic—dark hair, dark eyes, and perhaps even a dark soul.

We'd see.

His curious eyes settled on me with eery precision.

He *knew*.

"What can I do y'all for?" he drawled.

Why did people say that? I'd never understand the appeal of improper English.

I spared him a disinterested glance. "Hop in."

"There are no empty seats."

The driver pressed a button, and the trunk popped up.

Waylan's eyes swung to the open trunk. "Y'all serious?" No one answered, so he continued, his head shaking, "No. I'm calling the cops." He dragged his eyes to the fleet of bulletproof Andretti SUVs approaching.

"That doesn't seem like a very smart thing to do, Waylan." I cocked a brow up as I pulled my phone out, amused by his flinch. Most times, fear trumped guns when it came to threats. "Are you not a smart man?"

"I—" The doors to the SUVs behind ours swung open, cutting Waylan off, and he scrambled around the car and into the trunk, using the inside lever to close it behind him.

I tossed a zip tie at him. "Tie yourself."

"But—"

"Now."

Asher had an amused grin on his face as he stared straight ahead. I'd given him the file when I entered the plane, so he'd been filled in. After I rattled Elsa's address to Guilio, the car started, and we headed to a nicer part of town.

"You're him, aren't ya?" Waylan's voice inched toward me in a whisper.

"Yes."

"I n-never meant to take the money. She stole my kid."

I turned to him. "He's not your son."

"I made him—"

"You donated sperm. Have you ever met him? Spoken to him? Read to him? Played with him? Fed him? Bathed him?" Silence. "That's what I thought."

We pulled up a long driveway lined with Southern magnolia trees I'd paid for. Opened the car doors and stepped onto cobblestone pavers I'd paid for. Walked up a set of stairs and past white, twenty-foot high pillars I'd paid for. And knocked on the purple-heart wooden double doors I'd paid for.

Asher had his fingers curled around Waylan's bicep, and the Andretti soldiers had the decency to stand in front of the SUVs with our Black Security guards, arms crossed and silent. The door swung open as the maid greeted me with shocked eyes. I'd never met her before, but it didn't surprise me that she knew who I was. Elsa probably warned the staff to never let me in.

"Bastian!" Elsa called out as she stepped down the last stair in the spiral staircase. She trotted to the door, her heels clacking on the bocote wood. Leave it to Elsa to ruin historic Antebellum architecture with imported wood floors. "I wasn't expecting you!" She tried to hide her irritation, but her eye twitched.

"Do you know the definition of the word extortion?" I didn't let her answer as I stepped past her and into the foyer I had paid for. The maid had the decency to speed walk away as I continued, "The practice of obtaining something, especially money, through force or threats."

"I don't know what you're talk—" Her high-pitched words died in her throat when Asher tugged Waylan past the doorway and shut the door behind them.

"I—" Elsa's eyes darted to me as she fumbled for something to say.

"Stuttering on women is only cute when you don't look like a five-dollar hooker." I dragged my eyes down her form. "No offense to hookers." I took a step toward her, enjoying the way her throat bobbed and her shoulders sagged. "You have ten minutes to leave this home."

"No, it's my home—"

I cut her off, "If you want to live some semblance of a happy life, get that mentality out of your head. You own nothing. You are penniless. You have no son. You have no money. You have no home. You have nothing. Your clothes belong to me. This house belongs to me. The cars belong to me. Everything you have spent the past five years building belongs to me." I reached into the duffel bag, pulled out the copy of Vince's folder I'd made before leaving New York, and tossed it at her face. The pictures and paper fell like a torrent of leaves onto the bocote wood. "You're done, Elsa. Stop embarrassing yourself."

She leaned down and picked up a sheet of paper with Waylan's driver's license photocopied on it. "I don't know what you think you have on me, but—"

"You've been extorting money out of me, and Waylan has been extorting money out of you. Last I checked, I live in New York, and you two live in Alabama. Interstate communication is FBI jurisdiction, and extortion is a federal crime. Federal extortion charges carry a sentence of up to twenty years in prison, and I have enough to put you away."

She took a step toward me and clenched her fists at her sides. "I'll fight this. I have lawyers."

"You don't have lawyers. Cryptocurrency may be difficult to trace, but once you have, stealing it doesn't take more than a talented hacker."

Niccolaio's hacker neighbor Dex had drained her account while I'd slept. Justice coursed through my veins as I watched the dread travel across her features.

"I—" She shook her head. "Everett will miss me. He won't let you send me away. He loves me."

The laughter I barked out was genuine. I *tsked.* "Oh, Elsa... Everett doesn't love you. Twenty years is a long time to spend in prison. If no one loves you now, no one is going to love you when your face is as pruned as a loofah."

Her chest practically caved in with the way her shoulders hunched forward. "What do you want?"

"I want you gone." I checked my watch. "I gave you ten minutes, but you spent nine of it talking. You have less than thirty seconds to get out."

"But—"

"Twenty-eight."

"I—"

"I think prison orange clashes with your fake tan."

"Please—"

"Eighteen."

She grabbed her phone and slid it into her bra. When she reached for her keys, I shook my head, and she screeched before huffing her way out of the door. It slammed on her way out.

"Daddy?" A drowsy Everett peeked his head over the balcony of the staircase. "Daddy!" His eyes widened as he woke in an instant and sprinted his way down the stairs. He flung his arms around my waist, then tipped his head and stared at me with his matching eyes. "Are you taking me home?! I don't want to live with Mommy!"

"Yes." I pressed a kiss to his forehead. "Go pack what you want now. I'll have the rest sent to New York later. Okay?"

He nodded his head and ran off. When I turned to Waylan, he looked stricken.

"That's my son?" His wide eyes followed Everett's disappearing body.

"No, that's *my* son." I stepped forward.

Asher let Waylan go, and he fell to his knees.

I dropped the duffel bag with the two-hundred and fifty thousand dollars on the floor beside him and said, "There is two-hundred and fifty large in this bag. Take it and get out of my life."

I supposed I could have sent an enforcer to take care of him, but at least he hadn't hurt Everett. Elsa had.

Waylan didn't stare at the bag, his eyes still trained on the spot where Everett had been as he spoke, "You're pretty rich, huh?"

"Yes."

"You can take care of him. Send him off to college?"

I nodded once. "If he wants to go."

"He'll be happy?"

"Yes."

"Okay."

Asher called Guilio to escort Waylan and his money home then ordered four of his guards to stay in Alabama to pack up the mansion. I'd sell it and the car and put the money into Everett's trust fund.

The Andretti soldiers escorted me, Everett, and Asher to the airport. Everett bounced with energy as he sat sandwiched between me and Asher, but by the time he stumbled onto the plane, he crashed out on the sofa.

"He'll be happy with you." Asher nodded to Everett.

Everett laid on the sofa bench on the opposite side of the plane while Asher and I sat facing one another in front of a chess match we were both too exhausted to play. This month had taken its toll on the both of us.

I moved a pawn on the chessboard. "Yes. Not just because anything beats being near his absent ovary donor, but also because he's always loved it in New York."

Asher slid his knight into E6. "Vincent gave you that folder?"

"Yes." I took his rook.

"How did he give it to you?"

"Ariana."

Asher paused, his fingers brushing his queen. "You've seen her?" He knew I'd broken up with her and why.

Lucy had pried it out of me and spilled the beans to him. Traitor.

I leaned back against the leather, the chessboard forgotten. "No. She slid it under the door."

"She could have used this information for her career."

"I know."

"She loves you."

"She also lied."

"It was her job," he pointed out. "When it came down to it, she chose you."

"Maybe, but it doesn't matter. I can't trust anything she says anymore."

"She loves you. You love her. You both make each other happy. Forgive her and move on."

"It's not that easy."

Asher shrugged. "Sometimes, you have to forgive people if you still want them in your life. Do you still want Ariana in your life?"

"No."

His lips drew up in a smirk. "Who's the liar now?"

43

The first duty of love is to listen,
while the last duty of love is to forgive.

—Unknown

BASTIANO ROMANO

Two Months Later

"Everett!" Tessie shrieked.

She'd flown in yesterday, and the two had been fighting since they'd met yesterday for the first time in over five years. I'd converted one of the larger rooms into a bedroom for Everett, and she was bitter that it was nearly triple the size of her room.

"What did I do now?" Everett threw his head back and groaned. His dark hair frayed in every direction from when Tessie had tossed a pillow at his head earlier.

I let them fight it out as I read a book on the living room couch, a little amused by their antics. I'd gotten so used to the quiet in this house over the past five years that just a little bickering between the two of them made the entire penthouse feel vibrant.

Still, something felt missing. Like a thousand-piece puzzle with a missing center piece. I could still make out the picture, but it wasn't right. I should have been happy. Elsa, as my private eye reported, worked the graveyard shift at a sanitary plant. Waylan, though I had no real grudge against him, had retreated to his ranch in silence. Ma let Tessie visit more often. Lucy and Asher finally had their honeymoon. Niccolaio and his girlfriend, Minka, had found happiness in each other, and Gio and I had been talking more often lately. Even Uncles Frankie and Eli seemed to be around more since Uncle Vince had passed away, and they realized how little time they'd been spending with the family. And Everett? He told me every day how happy he was.

And still, I missed Ariana.

I'd caved last month and looked up where she worked since she'd quit the FBI and had to force myself on a daily basis not to show up and take her away.

Tessie ran over to me from the piano. "Bastian, tell my nephew"—she'd never let Everett live down the fact that she was technically his aunt despite the small one-year age gap —"he's a big shit head."

I could tell her not to curse, but frankly, my brand of

parenting included not giving a damn about stupid things that were bound to develop while living under my household, and Tessie was my sister, not my kid, anyway.

I dog-eared my book like a heathen and snapped it shut. "I could tell him that, but then I'd have to tell you that those pink sheets you think I just bought you are actually old white ones Luna accidentally threw in the washer with a red t-shirt."

"You're mean!" Tessie crossed her arms. "I liked it better when Ariana did my laundry." She huffed out a breath. "There are too many boys here!"

Everett took a seat on the couch, using my side as a back rest. "When do I get to meet Ariana?"

I stared at the both of them, mulling over an answer.

Tessie answered for me, "When is she going to stop being mad at you?"

"*I* am mad at her," I corrected.

"Well, that's stupid." She pushed Everett aside and took the seat between us. "Doctor Phil says, 'There is no love without forgiveness, and there is no forgiveness without love.'"

Why was this my sister?

Just *why?*

Everett peeked around Tessie. "If there is no love without forgiveness, does that mean you can't love, Daddy?"

Tessie turned to him. "Yes, it means he doesn't love you."

They started yelling at each other again, and though my hallucinations of Vincent had long since fled with sleep and food, I could imagine what he would say to me right now, words he'd said to me when I was a preteen: *"If a mistake isn't forgivable, you wouldn't be mulling over it. Ever since you were little, you could always hold a grudge, but you know what I realized? You hold grudges because you care so much. It's because your love runs so deep, it takes longer for the pain in it to escape."*

I swallowed the nostalgia and watched Tessie and Everett fight, telling myself to be grateful for these moments instead of the ones I knew I was missing out on without Ari. A knock sounded on the door. I swung it open for one of the security guards.

He handed me an envelope as he spoke, "A courier dropped this off a few minutes ago. He said it had been preordered months ago and scheduled for delivery today."

I plucked it from his hands and unsealed it as he left. Vincent's familiar handwriting met my eyes as I slid the thick card stock out.

It's been months.

Well? What are you waiting for?

-Vince

ARIANA DE LUCA

Identity.

Four syllables.

A common word.

Easy enough to say.

But when it came to its definition, I spent most of my life unable to define it. I left the bureau knowing I needed to find myself if I ever wanted a life with Bastian. And I did. I'd spent the last two months working; browsing Netflix to figure out my likes and disliked; reading more genre fiction than I ever had before, fueling the loss of Bastian with mafia romance novels; and restaurant hopping all over the boroughs.

I had a better handle on myself. That didn't mean I didn't miss Bastian. It just meant that, when he was ready to forgive me, I'd understand myself better.

I huffed out a breath and squeezed the aches out of the back of my neck. Maybe fate was laughing at me because I'd struggled to find a job anywhere but here. The Dominic. The place I'd threatened to work for if Bastian refused to hire me all those months ago.

One of the servers, Carrie, raised her brows as she approached the bar. "Dominic is in a mood." She made Devil horns with both of her hands.

I bit back my laughter, feeling carefree. I missed Bastian and Tessie every day, but I'd also been taking the time to discover myself. To take life one day at a time as I found out who I was outside of the FBI, trusting fate to bring me and Bastian back together again.

But I missed him.

God, I missed him.

I'd given him the file, slipping it under his penthouse house door when I knew he wouldn't be home. It hadn't been a hard choice. I knew it would help him find his happy ending, and like Vince, I had faith that Fate would bring us back together again.

I wished Fate would hurry up, though, because it'd been two months, I was falling in love with who I was outside of the bureau more and more each day, but there was always the knowledge that I'd be happier with Bastian dangling above my head.

Jupiter.

Ganymede.

I didn't care which I was.

I just wanted to be Bastian and Ariana, two planets orbiting each other.

The Dominic's hostess, Anna, met us at the bar, her brows drawn together as she looked at me. "You have a visitor outside. A man. A *hot* man."

My heartbeat picked up, and I knew.

I just *knew*.

I glanced at the door but couldn't see anything through the downpour flooding the streets. "But it's raining."

"I know." She rolled her eyes and leaned her hip against an empty chair. "He's been out there for hours. Dominic won't let him in, and he finally let me come get you."

A frown drew my brows together, and I tossed the tiny server's notebook I'd been holding under the sink. I'd been working as a server instead of a bartender, but I didn't mind.

I turned to Carrie. "Can you cover my shift?"

"Yeah, go." She looked curious but held back from the questions I knew she wanted to ask as she waggled her brows. "A hot stranger. Please tell me the juicy story behind it. Later, though. I'll take your shift for the night if you tell me all about it tomorrow."

"Deal."

I wore a stupid grin as I slid my coat on and opened the door to the uncovered patio. He sat on one of the tables, ignoring the chairs some of the staff had chained together at the canopied side to protect them from the rain. I studied his dark hair. Just how I'd remembered it. The eyes. The nose. The lips. The body. Everything looked just how I'd remembered, but it still tore the breath from my lungs.

"Hi," I whispered.

Bastian crossed his arms, his lips curving into a smirk. "Is the service always this bad here?"

Always the asshole.

I couldn't hold back my smile. I knew he'd come to me.

Fate.

Jupiter and Ganymede.

I didn't know what we were, and I didn't care as long as we were together.

I took a step toward him. "Maybe just for you. I think my boss hates you."

His lips quirked up, even as water plastered his hair to his forehead. "I do own the restaurant that took all of his business."

"Own?"

"I bought it from Asher."

"Is that what you do now? Own a restaurant?"

It had been so hard for me to stay away from my phone and the internet, to not use my sleuthing skills to stalk him. I wanted to, but I also wanted to find myself, so when Bastian and I came together again, I'd be able to give him all of me.

"One of many things."

"And the rest?"

"Do you always accost customers with such personal questions?"

"Only the hot ones."

"In that case, hi. My name is Bastiano Romano, but you can call me Bastian."

"Hi." I wanted to grab his face and kiss him, but I refrained. Barely. "My name is Ariana De Luca. Are you mad at me?"

"I just met you. How can I be mad at you?" He continued as I rolled my eyes, but inside, everything tensed as I waited for his answer. "You gave me my son back. I could never be mad at you."

Vince had found the noose to hang around Elsa. She hadn't used a sperm donor. She'd slept with a man and had been paying him off to stay away from Everett since he'd been born.

"It wasn't me. Vince arranged for me to get that folder after he died."

"He was always three steps ahead, wasn't he?"

"Try twenty-nine years."

"One day, you'll tell me what that means."

I couldn't stop staring at him.

The man who loved harder than anyone I'd ever met.

The man who opened his heart to me even though it had been trampled before.

The man who'd fallen in love with a kid who wasn't his by blood and still sent a check every month to a woman he hated.

I took a step closer. "I'd like that."

His predatory eyes watched me approach him, hooded, calling to me. "I cut Elsa off."

"And Everett?"

"He's with me. Has been for about two months now."

"Are you happy?"

"Yes. Not as happy as I can be." He hooked his foot around my ankle and drew me closer.

I caught myself with two palms on his chest. "I missed you, Jupiter."

"What did you call me?"

"Jupiter."

"I'm not Jupiter." He shook his head. "Uncle Vince used to tell me the story of Jupiter and Ganymede. Ganymede revolves around Jupiter, hooked into its gravity, always near, always circling."

I fought the pain building in my chest. "You're not Jupiter?"

"No," he said, gutting me, but then he pieced me back together, "You are."

EPILOGUE

To be loved is a Success. To love is a Duty.
To be with someone you love is an Achievement.
To be with someone who loves you is Life.

—Nishan Panwar

ARIANA DE LUCA

One Year Later

"I feel like a virgin," I admit as we stand in line for popcorn.

Everett and Tessie are with us, fighting like they've been doing since the first time they re-met. I keep the grin off my face as they debate Power Rangers colors like it's a matter of national security.

Bastian groans and adjusts himself beneath his slacks. Who wears a suit to a movie theater? My man.

When he told me he was taking over the family business—a sacrifice he'd initially made for me, no less—I'd been worried. But he'd struck an agreement with his dad, taking full control of the legitimate side of things while his family began the shift from illegal to legal businesses.

"Don't tell me virgin fantasies get you hard." I keep my voice low so the kids don't hear. "You're popping my movie theater cherry not my actually cherry."

His pulls me into a hug, so he can whisper in my ear. "Keep talking, and I'll slide a cherry into your tight little ass and pop it with my cock piercing."

Like the deviant I am, I like that answer. "I dare you."

I can feel his erection between us, and I slide a hand between the nonexistent gap separating our bodies and stroke him. Then I step back and watch him button his suit jacket to cover his erection, but his suit is too tailored, and I can still see the massive outline.

He looks down, then slides me in front of him to cover it. I can feel his breath on my neck as I step up to order. The flustered teen behind the counter tries to keep her eyes on me, but they keep darting to Bastian. I don't blame her. I see him every day, and I still have trouble looking away.

"W-what can I get you?" Her voice cracks, and I can't help my grin.

In twenty years, I suspect Bastian will still get this reaction out of women. Possibly even some men. I've seen some do double takes as they walk past him, like they're checking if he's real.

"Gummy bears!" Tessie shouts, way louder than she needs to.

"No, sour gummy worms!" Everett's jabbing the clear display, right above a bag of gummy worms.

Tessie hip checks him out of the way. "No—"

"We'll take both," I interrupt with a polite smile. "And a large popcorn, a large Coke, and two small ICEEs.

I swear, I can't take these two anywhere, but I wouldn't have it any other way. After Vince's death, Tessie's parents agreed to split her time between them evenly. Now she's in New York every other month, which means she and Everett get to fight over literally *everything* every other month.

"Cherry!" Everett jumps up and down.

Tessie pushes him out of the way again. "Coke!"

"Nope." Bastian wraps an arm around my waist. "No caffeine. She'll take a blueberry and strawberry mixed." He arches a brow at Tessie. "Okay?"

"Fine."

I'm biting back another grin, always smiling at their antics. I can't believe this is my life, being hugged by the man in a bespoke suit who could model for *GQ*; wearing tattered sweats because it's what I like, and fuck everyone else; beside a kid who has become a son to me and the little sister I never knew I needed.

Bastian leans his chin on my shoulder as we wait for the awestruck teen to get us our junk food. "You look happy."

"I am."

The happiest.

I can't even quantify this feeling or describe it.

The kids grab their drinks and candy, I take the large Coke, and Bastian grabs the popcorn. When we get into the theater, it's completely empty. There are previews playing already, but no one is in here.

I look around. My hair flings into my eyes, and I brush the strands away. "Are we in the wrong theater?"

Bastian nudges me forward with a hand on the small of my back. "Nope."

"But it's crazy crowded out there. Are theaters normally empty?"

He takes the seat beside me, Tessie on his side and Everett on my side. "They are when you buy out the theater."

"What? No way."

"It's your first time," he says like it's the obvious thing to do.

Tessie shushes both of us. "You're not supposed to talk in the theater."

I roll my eyes, set the drink in the cupholder, and lean into the reclining chair. Everett grabs my hand on my left, and Bastian grabs my right hand. The last trailer ends, and the movie starts playing.

Long intro credits. Three guys fighting. A bunch of blood Everett and Tessie shouldn't see, but I'm sure they've seen worse. By the unfazed expression on Everett's face, I know it to be true.

And then the movie cuts off. Right out of nowhere. The screen flickers. I look back at the projector to make sure it's on before the screen lights up again. Two words consume it from wall to wall. Giant. In my face. All caps.

MARRY ME.

No question.

A demand.

Because that's the type of man my new fiancé is.

BASTIANO ROMANO

One Year Later

Dad half drags me out the door as I grab random things I think we'll need and throw them into the baby bag Ariana packed a few months ago.

His hand fists my collar, and then I'm unceremoniously shoved out the door. "Your kid is coming with or without you..."

I let him take the wheel as we leave my penthouse garage and head to the private hospital. I check the contents of the bag. Double check. Then triple check. Ariana is an absolute rage monster with her pregnancy hormones, so I tossed a vibrator and twelve-inch dildo in the center of the bag just to watch her reaction in the hospital.

"Have you named your girl?"

"Not yet."

I still can't believe he's beside me. Ten years ago, if you asked me what I thought about my dad, the words, "Dead to me" might have crossed my lips. Now he's driving me to the hospital to watch my first baby girl be born.

And I'm calling him Dad.

That happened after the first anniversary of Uncle Vince's death, and we admitted life is too short to hold grudges against the ones we love. We've been mending our relationship since. It hasn't been overnight, but it's happened.

The nurse rushes us to Ariana's room, remembering my face from the million trips we've taken here—and the large donation I made to make sure my girls get the best care. Everett is already here, sitting outside the room. He was with Ari when her water broke, picking him up from school.

He hugs my leg when I reach him then jumps onto Dad's back. "She's making weird noises."

I ruffle his hair, then enter the room. He's right. Ariana is moaning and groaning and making literally every noise in between. She sounds like she's speaking whale as the nurses tell her to breathe.

"I am breathing! How the fuck do you think I'm still alive?!"

See?

Rage monster.

She'll be appalled when the baby is born and she finds out she actually yelled that.

"Oh, thank fuck," she says when she sees me. Her hand reaches out for me.

I grab it and intertwine our fingers. "I think fucking is what got us here, Mrs. Romano. We could have stuck with anal."

The nurse's cheeks turn bright pink. I'm tempted to wink at her as Ariana clamps down on my hand with the force of a Sumo wrestler. At this rate, I'll be in the E.R. getting a hand transplant before the baby is born.

I let her hold down until my hand is numb, I don't think feeling will ever return to it, and I'm considering how I'll finger her without my fingers.

An hour passes.

Then another.

And another.

Ten hours later, I hear the first cry.

Our baby.

It's a blur as the nurses take her away, clean her, bring her back, and a million other things I can hardly process because another human has entered this world, and she's ours.

"What should we name her?" Ariana has a pen in one hand and a form in the other. She should be asleep, but for a former law enforcement officer, she never does anything she should.

I press a kiss to her temple. "Surprise me."

"My mother's name. It means fate." She writes something down, then hands it to me. "She's going to hate us for giving her a boy's middle name."

"It'll be fun. Think of all the teasing she'll get to blame on us."

Ari rolls her eyes as I take in the name and realize how blessed I am.

This wife.

This son.

This daughter.

This life.

It's all ours.

Everett trails behind when the nurse brings in our baby girl and hands her to me. I look down at her cherub cheeks until her blue-green eyes pop open.

Dalia Vincent Romano.

The End.

ACKNOWLEDGMENTS

Chloe, I love you. I miss you. I need you.

L, you are my family. Thank you for the hand massages when I've typed so long, my wrists and fingers feel a few seconds short of falling off. Thank you for caring for the fur babies when I'm cooped up writing. Thank you for tackling my problems as if they're your own because you know I'm trying to finish a manuscript and, contrary to popular belief, I almost never have my shit together.

Bau, you're my life. I love every inch of you—inside and out.

Rose, you have so much character, innocence, and heart. I love you so much. Even when you interfere with my writing. LOL.

Odette, you have been such a good friend to me since day one. I can't articulate how much that means to me.

Heidi, my butterflying-loving, word-slaying, fur baby-raising future wife. I love you so much. There is no way I can ever repay what you do for me. You get my words. You get me. Beyond that, you are such a phenomenal friend, I cannot wait to steal you away from your husband. (Brian, I'll send you a mixed tape with Trey Songz's "Mr. Steal Your Girl" as a consolation gift. Worry not.)

Heather, you make me laugh. You keep me sane. I feel so comfortable freaking out to you. You are a friend, a guru, and a therapist in one gorgeous package. Thank you. So, so much.

Ava, I cannot believe you deal with me. *Excuse me while I figure out how to put a Jeffrey the Facebook Alien sticker in here.* Real talk—I love your advice, our friendship, and you!

Amanda and Brittany—rather: loyal subjects of Parker's Dicktatorship—thank you so much for taking Bastian on last minute and tackling all these issues—including my mounting anxiety. You guys are seriously underpaid. By underpaid, I mean: I should probably start paying you. You guys make me laugh and smile when I am freaking the F out. (See a theme here? I freak out a lot.)

Tristan, thank you for being the smartest kid I've ever met. Thank you for being the inspiration for Tessie and every other smart kid I've ever written. Also, thank you for writing me an amazeballs Christmas story, then giving it to my sister for her Christmas gift. UGH. Not like I'm bitter or anything. (I am.)

D.C. and Lacy, thank you for breathing life into my manuscripts...especially when one is as late as this one. And it was embarrassingly late.

Gem, thank you for dealing with my super-late, unprofessional self. I mean, you're such a rockstar. I am amazed by you. In awe!!! You live up to your name.

Janice, thank you so much for all that you do. I can always count on you. That is something I treasure so much in life. Thank you.

I also have some amazing reader, reviewer, author, and blogger friends. The Parkerettes (best reader group ever), Carla, Amelia, Marla, Amara, Jocelyne, Krista, Brandie, the authors of Holiday Loves, and you. Yes, you.

(P.S. I know I'm missing people. I always do. Just know I'm grateful and have so much love for you.)

ABOUT PARKER

Parker S. Huntington hates talking about herself, so bear with her as she awkwardly toots her own horn for a few sentences and then bids her readers adieu.

Parker S. Huntington is from Orange County, California. She graduated pre-med with a Bachelor's of Arts in Creative Writing from the University of California, Riverside. As of January 29, the 23-years-old novelist is nearly done with her Master's in Liberal Arts (ALM) in Literature and Creative Writing from Harvard University. *Go Crimson!*

She was the proud mom of Chloe and will always look back on her moments with Chlo as the best moments of her life..

She has 2 puppies—a Carolina dog named Bauer and a Dutch Shepherd and lab mix named Rose. She also lives with her boyfriend of six years—a real life alpha male, book boyfriend worthy hunk of a man.

For more information:

www.parkershuntington.com
parkershuntington@gmail.com
facebook.com/ParkerSHuntington
twitter.com/authorPSH
instagram.com/ParkerSHuntington
amazon.com/ParkerSHuntington
facebook.com/groups/Parkerettes/
www.parkershuntington.com/newsletter

Made in United States
Troutdale, OR
06/29/2024

20908779R00279